In Search of Scandal

SUSANNE LORD

Published by Sourcebooks Casablanca, an imprint of Sourcebooks, Inc.
P.O. Box 4410, Naperville, Illinois 60567-4410
(630) 961-3900
Fax: (630) 961-2168
www.sourcebooks.com

Printed and bound in Canada.
MBP 10 9 8 7 6 5 4 3 2 1

One

London, March 1850

"FOR GOD'S SAKE, MAN. MAKE WAY."

The impatient command came from close behind, startling in its proximity. Will Repton clenched his teeth against a reply and edged to the right of the pavement, his limping gait either too slow or too unsightly for the haughty Londoners passing him.

Ignoring their frowns, he tucked his chin against the cold wind coursing down Oxford Street and trudged on. At the end of the block, he slowed. There was always a body rounding the corner, always a carriage approaching, always another woman averting her gaze from his twisted step.

So many bodies, so much bustle. He didn't remember London this way.

Could six years so alter a city?

Though it hurt like the devil, he straightened his stride entering Hanover Square. Here, at least, was unchanged. The same statue of Chancellor Pitt, the same handsome homes, the same center of wealth and pedigree.

This was Mayfair as it always was on a Sunday afternoon, and he was calling on Ben Paxton just as dozens might call upon their acquaintance.

If he didn't remember the London sky looking flat as paint in the space between buildings, he reasoned he'd not had the iridescent heavens of the Yangshuo Mountains to compare it with before. And if he couldn't shake the chill from his bones of late, he shouldn't be surprised. He was a good stone lighter and less insulated than when last he was here.

No, the city hadn't changed. He had.

Will had left London a hale and hearty envoy of the East India Company; he'd returned—after being twice-rumored dead—a famed explorer, celebrated plant hunter, and universally pitied cripple.

The wind threatened to dislodge his hat and the icy handle of his glass case bit through his glove, but it was the precious plants within that would suffer most from the cold. He hurried to gain the shelter of Paxton's door.

For a moment, a wry smile twisted his lips, standing at the affluent address. He'd not seen Paxton in years—long before his astonishing marriage to a countess—but the man was a friend of his father's.

And as wealthy and sympathetic investors went, he was an excellent prospect.

A quick turn of the bell key, the door opened wide, and Will froze in reaching for his card. The butler with the smiling face and crescent eyes so resembled a stevedore he'd met on a dock in Xiamen that Will nearly uttered *ni hao* in greeting.

No, London hadn't changed. But he could look

nowhere without the colors of the East seeping into its lines.

"Good afternoon," Will said. "I believe I'm expected."

He presented his card and followed the butler to the receiving room. In the quiet hall, the drag of his heel was conspicuous, but still he slowed to assess his surroundings.

Marble floors. Paintings crackled with age. Silk wall coverings.

Paxton had married *very* well.

A Chinese vase was displayed in an alcove. He was no expert, but centuries old to be sure. Yuan or Ming Dynasty—

A patter of footsteps slapped on the tiles behind him and he spun round, his muscles seizing in readiness. A boy—three or four or six, he could never discern the age of children—dashed past the stairs and vanished behind a door.

The sight came and went so swiftly, he clenched his eyes and grappled with the reality of the vision.

A disturbance of the air…a faint chortle from the room…

The boy was real.

Will dragged in a breath and willed his heart not to pound out of his chest. *Damn it.* His father had warned him Paxton had children.

"Don't mind our young master." The butler grinned from the end of the hall. "The boy has us all at his mercy. There's not a nursery in London that can hold him."

He nodded stiffly, unable to share the man's amusement. Ratcheting tight his nerves, he passed his coat and hat to the servant, who swiftly withdrew. Confused, he watched the butler disappear around a corner.

He'd always been announced before. At least at all the other fine houses where he'd solicited funds.

Will turned into the room and jolted to a stop. This was no reality he'd ever known—London, China, or otherwise. The parlor was screamingly female, stuffed with satin seats and tasseled pillows and a perverse number of breakable objects on every surface, but it was a gathering of men who swung their heads at his entrance.

Evidently not the desired addition to their party, the men ignored him to rearrange themselves in the parlor. One propped an elbow on the trinket-covered mantelpiece, another leaned suavely against the pianoforte, another feigned interest in a book. One young man, of a romantic bent, brooded out the window stroking the petals of a rose.

Eight—no, nine men. All posed in depictions of masculine leisure. Ridiculous, in light of all the doilies.

What business did they have here?

And where the devil was Ben Paxton?

He set down his small Wardian case, checking through the fogged glass that the plants hadn't been upset in their journey, and searched for a seat.

The only available chair held an ugly needlepoint pillow of a goat. Or perhaps a horse, though it appeared to have only three legs. Whatever the sorry creature was, it was named "Beatrice" according to the stitching beneath. A child's effort. Moving aside the pillow, Will sat—and slowly sank—into the overstuffed cushion.

"I say." A man in a red coat pointed to Will's case. "What is that? That little glasshouse?"

"I use it to transport plants."

"Indeed?" The man abandoned his pose by the fire to inspect the greenery. "And where are these transported from?"

"Pitigala."

"Piti—where?"

"Ceylon."

He peered inside. "Are there flowers? Shall we take them out?"

"No flowers. And I'd not open the case because of their scent."

The man's brows quirked with amusement. "Rotten luck there. Bit pungent are they?"

Will stared, trying to make sense of the man's words. "Putrid, actually. Much like a rotting carcass."

And he thought the room silent before…

Will scanned the bewildered faces; the man with the rose even suspended his brooding to squint at him. Could they somehow smell the carrion plants he carried?

Sighing quietly, he scrubbed a hand through his hair. It *was* too long. Just this morning, Mum had said it was time to see to it. Now that he was back in Civilized Society, as she put it, he couldn't lumber about like one of his beloved shaggy-haired yaks.

Given a choice, he'd prefer the company of his pack yaks any day. He fingered the frayed edge of his cuff. It might be time to get himself to a tailor as well.

A salver heaped with civilized calling cards sat on the table at his elbow. The uppermost name belonged to a viscount. Beside it, a bouquet of rosebuds. Around the room, more bouquets. Several, actually. The perfume of the flowers wasn't near as thick as all the colognes…and hair tonics…and shaving soaps—

They're here for a woman.

Will shot to his feet, flinching at the protesting pain in his leg. "I'm in the wrong room."

The man in the red coat laughed. "No, never tell me that! You must stay and present your offering to Miss Baker. The look on her face would be beyond price."

"Miss Baker? Who is—" *Right. Paxton's sister-in-law, Charlotte Baker. The countess's sister.*

His jaw tightened with embarrassment. The butler mistook him for a suitor of some Society miss. It was ludicrous.

Men like him did not marry.

"Excuse me," he grumbled. No doubt the girl possessed a colossal dowry to draw this gathering.

He turned and nearly plowed over a woman standing in his path. His heart jolted from the near collision—but there was little that didn't jolt him lately.

He stepped back. And stood corrected.

Charlotte Baker needed no dowry.

Past the spangles and beads sparking into his eyes, a porcelain doll had come to life. Glossy, dark curls framed the flawless oval of her face. A little nose tipped over lips so pink and pillowy, they shaped themselves into a smile even at rest. And as he stood staring, her cheeks blushed perfect, matching roses and the effect was complete. Another figurine as ornamental as the dainty teacups in the room.

But decorative as she was, her curves were more

than functional. Those would stir the primitive in any man. And after Tibet, the primitive in him was very close to the surface.

He wanted to drag her someplace private and…and…

Keep her.

Will grimaced at his lack of imagination. It was a mad thought.

Yet another mad thought.

"I beg your pardon," he muttered as he picked up his case and sidestepped past her. "I was directed to the wrong room."

"The wrong—? Oh, but…sir?" Her hands fluttered up but withdrew. The tentative gesture, to delay or help, he ignored. The little doll and—*Christ*—her *chaperone*, followed him into the hall.

"It must have been Mr. Penny, Ben's valet," she said, hurrying to keep pace at his elbow. "He is at the door today because Mr. Goodley, our butler, had eaten a little mutton that had gone off, I'm afraid, and he must have assumed…well, today is Sunday—"

Will stopped in the middle of the hall. Every door was closed.

And Miss Baker was still talking.

"—and as it is Sunday and you are…well, you are"—she shrugged and tilted her head—"well, not here for me, as I am now aware. I am very sorry."

Will tensed at her remorse. Stemming from pity, no doubt. With his drab suit and shaggy hair, he would not compare favorably to her suitors.

Or had he imagined the remorse? More likely she laughed at him.

Will eased his gaze onto hers, and his mind

stumbled to see eyes of such pure blue they appeared almost violet. No, not violets. Delphiniums.

He redirected his gaze and blew out a frustrated breath. Damn it all, he didn't think flowery thoughts. He was a botanical journeyman, paid to catalog and classify. *Blue* eyes. Merely blue.

Yes, she was a pretty girl.

Not that it mattered in the least.

He sought the butler or valet or whatever he was, but only the redheaded chaperone stood watching him with bald amusement. He tightened his grip on the handle of his case. "Miss Baker—"

"Yes, I am Charlotte Baker." Three skipping steps in jeweled slippers brought her to stand unnecessarily close. "But we have not met, I am sure of that."

He watched that smile suspiciously. Wouldn't his mum be heartbroken to see him now? Standing so near a beautiful, unmarried girl with only escape on his mind?

"Will Repton, miss." By the widening of her eyes, he surmised his name was known to her. It was all those damn newspaper stories. "I'm here to meet with Ben," he added to discourage questions. But there was no need. His name had effectively rendered her mute.

He cleared his throat. "Where should I—"

"*You* are William Repton?"

His frown deepened, concerned by the raw astonishment on her face. "I...well. Yes."

"No. William Repton, the *explorer*? Of China? *That* William Repton?"

He sidled away and pointed to the nearest door, careful to keep an eye on her. "Is this the room then?"

She launched forward, startling him backward and

nearly into upsetting the Yuan or Ming vase—he still didn't know, he was no expert—and *for God's sake, what did she want?*

Miss Baker hooked his elbow and his eyes careened from the small gloved hand to her widening smile to her big delphinium eyes. "Miss Baker—"

"Do please put that case down."

"But Ben—"

"Ben will not mind. He is well aware I have been desperate to meet you and has been positively maddening in not inviting you sooner. He would not begrudge me this chance—I pray you will not—and I simply must know you better. Please?"

She batted her lashes. *At him.* The sight both aroused and disturbed.

Taking his speechlessness for compliance, Miss Baker emitted a kittenlike squeal and pulled him back into the horrible parlor.

Christ, where the devil was Ben Paxton?

"Gentlemen!" she announced. "How fortunate we are. I must introduce William Repton. No doubt you are aware of the man and his achievements. He is here to meet with Ben, but I would not let him go."

The men stared, half-curious, half-dubious, as Miss Baker led him to a short settee. Commanded to sit beside her by a dainty hand, he folded his stiff leg, gritted his teeth, and lowered with control. The arrangement was too close; if he turned his head, they'd brush noses.

"I hope you will not find the flavor of our tea too pedestrian given your learned palate, Mr. Repton." Miss Baker poured him a cup of tea. "Our housekeeper prides herself on her blend. She has been induced to try a variety from Assam which I find a bit bracing but lovely with milk. How do you take your tea? Sugar? Lemon? Or perhaps with a sprinkling of tobacco?"

The last was said with a giggle to the man at the pianoforte before she directed her smile back at Will. "I am being silly, of course. That is a jest between the viscount and myself. Sugar?" She waited with sugar tongs poised over his cup.

He blinked. "No." Her smile dimpled. "No, thank you."

"Forgive me, Miss Baker," the red-coat man said. "But 'Repton' is not a name known to me."

The man, who was evidently a viscount, scoffed. "Come, Matteson! You cannot be in earnest. The man is written of ad nauseum in the periodicals."

"Indeed," another man put in. "You cannot tell me you have avoided the tale of 'Chinese Will'?"

Recognition struck the man like a board to the back of the head. "Oh, deuce take it! *You* are Chinese Will?"

Will turned to Miss Baker to beg his freedom, but she only beamed brighter.

"There are *two* Mr. Reptons of accomplishment, actually," she said, her gaze not unlatching even as she addressed the others. "*John* Repton is supervisor at Chiswick Gardens. But his son, my—*our* Mr. Repton, is England's most remarkable plant collector. His reports are sublime and archived at the Geographical Society. Mr. Helmsley, you are a member. Have you not read them?"

Mr. Helmsley aborted his sip of tea with a clumsy gulp at being blindly addressed. "Ah…regretfully, no, Miss Baker." He leaned forward in an attempt to catch her eye. "But I shall do so post haste now that I am aware of your interest and we may have a meaningful intercourse on the subject."

The other men committed to reading the reports themselves, but the pretty hostess seemed unaware of their attempts at ingratiation. Will glanced at her, feeling her rapt attention like a bonfire.

No sensible woman looked at him like that.

Perhaps there was something wrong with her.

"Favor us then, Mr. Repton, with tales of adventure." The viscount didn't mask the imperious edge of his voice. "My father will be mortally jealous when he learns I have met 'Chinese Will,' the man himself."

Will frowned into his teacup, plunked the dish on the table, and turned to summarize the last six years of his life in as few words as possible.

Charlotte was too overcome to listen. How was it possible?

But thank God. *Thank God! Here he was!* The man who could redeem the family name. The man she dreamed of. The man she was destined to marry—even if William Repton was not yet aware of the fact.

At last *here* and just as she had seen him a hundred times before. *More.* Never in London, never in any real place, but he was already so very dear and familiar.

And she didn't imagine him so from the countless accounts of the incredible Mr. Repton.

He was familiar because he looked just the way she imagined her beloved explorer would look if she could invent him. Hair that was many shades of blond, and never—no never—thinning. Easily, the thickest hair of all the men in the room—though it was a bit long for fashion. Her heart panged tenderly for the lock curling at his collar.

And those were just the right shoulders—slightly too broad and muscled for his frame—because she did so love a man's shoulders. And that face...

Well, she had never assembled his features so perfectly before. But for whatever *this* mood was, with its corresponding "just get on with it" expression, she would only choose this square chin, stern brow, and piercing blue eyes to form this handsome, heroic face.

A heroic and somewhat irritated face.

She dropped her gaze. Goodness, she must not stare moon-eyed at the man. What nonsense had she prattled on about before?

Why, *why*, had she mentioned the mutton?

"I wonder how you were able to read them, Miss Baker?"

Lord Spencer's voice recalled her to the present. "Do forgive me. What did you say?"

Lord Spencer—Hugh, as he had asked to be called—flicked an uneasy glance to Mr. Repton and reset his smile more tightly. "The reports, Miss Baker. The Geographical Society is exclusive to men. How did your little person conspire to read them?"

"Ben is a member and retrieved them for me." Charlotte beamed at Mr. Repton, willing him to look at her, but he seemed to prefer scowling at his boots. "Or most of them anyway. I have not read the final installment."

"Nor should you," Mr. Repton said.

"But I must."

"There is nothing in them of worth to a lady."

"Nothing of…?" But he appeared entirely in earnest. How could he not know what his writing meant to others? To *her*? "But you are too modest. The reports are full of sound and color and *feeling*! When I read them, it is just as Aristotle wrote—the soul never thinks without a picture—"

"Miss Baker—"

"It is not my mind that thrills at the adventure—"

"Miss Baker—"

"—but my very soul—"

His head reared, passion sparking in his eyes. "Then you see what you wish to see."

Her breath caught in her throat. Those intense eyes, the flushed cheekbones, the hot, panting breath laving her cheek. The man was magnificent!

His words were utter nonsense but he delivered them with such glorious conviction.

Another lady might have been chastened and turned shy in the face of this growling man. But she had always been a bit more…well, *buoyant* than most.

And his chest was heaving so attractively within that awful coat.

Unable to repress it, she smiled hugely and his glare faltered. "Now I am all the more curious why our perceptions should differ," she said softly.

His eyes widened and she remembered herself. "Would anyone care for more tea?" She reached for the pot. "Though perhaps it does not refresh. I cannot credit how warm the parlor is."

All the men were instantly solicitous of her comfort.

All except for Mr. Repton, who had taken a firm grip of his temples.

Doubt trickled over her. Had she said something to distress him? Were the memories of his travels painful?

Perhaps they were. It appeared he had been injured, though he limped only a very little. She had watched him walk a few paces, and his back was straight above his slim hips and hard, sculpted backside. The memory of which warmed her already-heated cheeks.

She could not recall ever noting the shape and muscularity of a man's bottom before, but there it was.

Quite a vivid picture, really.

She pressed a napkin between her damp palms. The parlor *was* too close, but then she had not expected most of these gentlemen, as they were not of a society she encouraged. Only Lord Spencer was Upper Class Proper; the rest only Upper Middle.

Only Lord Spencer. After three seasons...

How odd...how odd and remarkable and wonderful that none of these men mattered in the least now. Not now that she'd made a discovery all her own: William—no, *Will.* A fitting name for one who made his own place in the world, Society and lineage and rules be hanged.

Here was the husband she yearned for. Not a mere aristocrat but the Talk of London. And quite literally, the man of her dreams.

She angled a glance at his profile. Yes...the very picture.

If only these men would leave. If only he would look at her again. She leaned close. "Mr. Repton, I—"

"His Grace, the Duke of Iddlesleigh," Mr. Penny announced from the door.

The men swiveled their heads as Iddlesleigh entered and Charlotte stiffened with surprise. And shame.

Thank goodness he had not found her alone. But *honestly*! An unmarried duke ought to have a better use of his time than to always be hunting for his next mistress. Undoubtedly he would have requested her favors and she would have declined with all the humble gratitude a powerful man like him would expect. She may be common-born but she was no one's cocotte.

Not his, not Lord Welston's, nor Misters Ware's, Adkins's, or Playfair's. She almost suspected the men of wagering on who might win her virtue as often as the stupid offer was made.

"Dearest Charlotte." Iddlesleigh brushed his lips over her fingers. "I see from this entrenched party of admirers, I am shamefully tardy. Will you forgive me?"

She removed her hand, mindful not to yank it from his touch. "You are always forgiven, Your Grace."

The duke hoisted an imperious brow at Will, who stared out the window as if watching a tedious bit of theater. It was obvious that Iddlesleigh desired Will's seat and expected him to surrender it to his betters.

It was not obvious to Will.

The duke paused pointedly until Lord Spencer surrendered his seat and the duke sat. His Grace turned to Will. "I am not acquainted with you, sir."

Charlotte touched Will's sleeve and a hard muscle jumped under her fingers, thrilling her. "This is Mr. Repton, Your Grace. Do you not recall that we spoke of him at the musicale last week?"

The duke's eyes sharpened. "Indeed. The plant hunter."

"Your Grace," Will mumbled at Iddlesleigh and stood abruptly. "Miss Baker, thank you for the tea. If you'll excuse me."

No! No, no, no! He could not leave! "Yes, of course." She stood to offer her hand in farewell but Will was already at the door. Faced with the delicate challenge of chasing after a man with all correctness, she began with a bright smile for the benefit of the room and called after him. "Allow me to show you to his study."

Will stopped short at the sound of her voice and let her precede him with a huff of breath. She blinked at the sound. Did he truly not like her?

At the door, he lifted his plant case and walked to the center of the hall, his head swiveling from one closed door to the next. Slowly, he turned back with what was becoming a familiar frown. That could not be his usual countenance. It was horribly out of place on the Mr. Repton she knew.

"Will you direct me, Miss Baker?"

"I am sorry to have kept you—"

"Miss Baker—"

"—but you must know how ardently I—"

"Thank you." Will held up a staying hand, then—looking embarrassed at the uncivil gesture—dropped it. "I do thank you, but…"

His eyes caught on something behind her. Patty stood at the parlor door. Her maid really was a lax chaperone; she did not even bother to look up from her novel.

Will shook his head and whatever he muttered was too low to hear. Not that she could attend. His jawline was magnificent. Would it appear so even when he was not clenching it?

"Miss Baker, I'm sure you understand my eagerness in seeing your brother-in-law, having matters of actual importance to discuss."

Matters of *actual* importance. Oh dear. She really ought to take offense at that. Very likely she would, later.

"Yes, of course," she murmured.

Blast it! God—! Save him from virgins!

He'd hurt her feelings. Of course he had. He was a yak's ass. A steaming pile of horse apples. A maggot in the—

"Jamie?" Miss Baker turned to the footman. "Mr. Repton was shown to the wrong room. Would you see him to Ben's study?"

The footman's lips bunched with smothered laughter and Will stared over the boy's head. What matter if the lad was amused by the picture he made as one of her callers? God's sake, the woman attracted the likes of a duke.

He *had* changed. He'd always been patient before. And slow to anger. And kind to women.

But *damn it*, weren't servants supposed to be helpful?

"Yes, miss." The sniggering footman set off down the hall. "This way, sir, if you please."

Will inclined his head to Miss Baker, letting his eyes touch that beautiful face one last time. That beautiful, pouting—damn it—*sad* little face.

He bowed stiffly. "Thank you…for the tea, Miss Baker."

Her eyes shot to his and her brilliant smile was blinding him again. "You're welcome, Mr. Repton. And please do call anytime. Anytime at all."

He stared. Did she just invite him to call? On *her*?

Perplexed, he walked away but something made him stop and look again.

Still there. Still beaming.

There was *definitely* something wrong with her.

And yet…

"Why?" he heard himself ask, frowning at his own stupidity.

Her head tilted in question. A trait of hers, then. A bloody adorable one. "Why did you read my reports?" he asked brusquely.

"You are a hero."

"Right," he muttered. "Good-bye, Miss—"

"But then because—" She glanced back at the parlor of admirers and, for the first time, her face wore a look of uncertainty. "Because I felt you were writing to me. And to me alone, and if I did not read every report as soon as they arrived, then you would be all alone. And not just feel alone, but truly…*be* alone."

"I wasn't alone," he blurted.

But you were, a voice in his mind hissed. *You were alone at the end.*

"It is silly, I know." Her blush deepened, but still she smiled. "Everyone tells me I am prone to fanciful notions. I realize those who actually experience have no need for fantasy. I am endeavoring to be such a person."

She eyed him expectantly—*hopefully*—but he was at a complete loss. With a quick bow, he turned and left her in the hall.

Thank God the study was empty. He set down the plants and massaged the tension in his neck. At twenty-eight, he'd stared down the sheer wall of an eight-hundred-foot gorge but was shaken from a minute's proximity to one happy…*confusing* chatterbox of a woman.

There was much to get used to again. Crowds, comforts, *women*. He and the crew had subsisted on the crudest food and meanest shelter, growing tough as the weathered hides they wore on their backs.

Yet rugged as they all were, he'd been the only one to survive.

He breathed deep. The study was cool and dim, the table topped with horticultural books and a number of terrariums filled with exotic orchids. No doubt Ben Paxton had built those himself.

Good. Marriage to a countess hadn't stripped the man of his interests.

Steps approached from the hall and the towering Ben Paxton strode in. "Will! Damn good to see you. Welcome back."

"It's been a long time." Shaking his hand, Will was struck by the smile Ben wore. It was strange enough that a botanist had wed a countess, but the Ben Paxton he remembered working alongside his father was a man who spoke little and smiled even less. Marriage had granted Ben happiness at last.

Would he be unwilling to invest, then? An ambitious man would aid his return; a family man would not.

Ben gestured Will into a chair. "Sorry to keep the famous 'Chinese Will' waiting." He chuckled at Will's grimace. "Sorry. I confess. I read the series in the *Illustrated News* to my son. You're his hero."

"Best he not meet me in the flesh, then. Congratulations on your family."

A proud light lit Ben's eyes. "My son was the reason for my delay. I was looking for him."

Will tensed, fighting the urge to scan the room. "Did he find his way back to the nursery?"

"The nursery? Oh no, he's needed in the ladies' parlor with his Aunt Charlotte. It's Sunday, after all."

"Sunday?"

"Right, sorry. Charlotte's friends call every day, but *Sunday*, the bachelors visit." His voice lowered with good-natured weariness. "A receiving day for her suitors and she's using my son to help choose her husband. It's one of her tests. So tell me—"

"Tests? I don't understand."

"You know, *tests*. For a husband. Is he easy with children? Does he esteem his mother? Are his trousers too long or too short?"

Will checked the length of his own pants, then frowned at his own stupidity. "How is that a test?"

"Evidently the wrong inseam signals a defect in personality. And since she planted that seed in my head, ironically it's proving true more often than not. Charlotte has new tests every week." Ben seemed to consider what he'd said. "New tests and new suitors, actually. It makes me wonder if these men aren't testing her right back."

Will frowned in incomprehension.

"Because she was born common," Ben explained. "And uncommonly beautiful, like my wife, Lucy. Did your father not tell you of the Bakers?"

"I assumed the family was of some rank."

"Their father was a schoolmaster. My wife married the earl very young, but he died before Lucy was..."

well, *polished.* But Charlotte was of an age to be schooled. She's been bred for a coronet, but I'm not certain these worthies can overlook her blood."

"That's bollocks."

"Yes...well." Ben grinned without humor. "That's Society."

Will squared his shoulders. He had to stem the course of this discussion before it devolved further into aristocratic nonsense. And before he began imagining how many of Miss Baker's tests he could pass.

"Have you heard I'm to return?" Will asked.

The smile slid from Ben's face. "Return?"

"Another expedition into China."

Ben's reaction was the same as the others'—disbelief, followed by the same careful questions. "Your parents would rather you not go, I imagine?"

The question triggered an ill-timed frown. He'd give anything to spare his parents their fears, but he had no choice but to bluster this out. "You know my father, Ben. He's never wandered more than twenty miles from home. He doesn't comprehend how vast the world is.

"There are varieties of plants in Asia you and I have never seen or read of. Dozens, *hundreds.*" Will rose to retrieve the carrion plants. "I found these specimens near the Burma plantations. They're remarkable. The taxonomists at Kew are still struggling over them—"

Ben raised a staying hand. "It sounds extraordinary, Will. But you've spent a decade collecting. Why not let others go with your counsel?"

"I know the language, the people, the areas to avoid—"

"Most of China and the whole of Tibet is an area to avoid. You nearly died. Your entire crew was lost."

"That attack was an aberration. The massacre—" Will stopped, seeing Ben stiffen. He'd forgotten. Some couldn't bear to listen. His family, his friends, couldn't listen—not without bracing themselves as Ben was doing now.

Strange then how the rest of England thirsted for every bloody detail.

Will sat back in his chair. "The men and I trekked hundreds of miles, season after season, recording every discovery, and in the end..." *All dead.* "It's unfinished."

Ben nodded slowly. "And you believe you have luck enough for the return?"

Luck...no, not nearly enough. But if he couldn't persuade Ben, what hope did he have to raise the money? He'd been rejected by a dozen already.

"I've no use for luck." Will set his face in a careful mask before his next lie. "There's no plan to enter Tibet."

"And your injuries?"

Will didn't even blink. "Healed. And healing."

Ben's eyes returned to the case and the mysterious plants within, and Will leaned in. "Can I count on you for one hundred?"

"That doesn't seem enough."

"You're not the only one I'm asking."

He might have asked Ben for a thousand times that amount, but he was a friend of his father's and there were too many risks to guarantee any return on his investment.

But *Christ*, he needed a bit of luck soon. The winds

would change; he needed to be on a ship by the end of August, and with the money in hand to boot.

"I'm torn, Will. I'm meant to be loyal to your father. How can I lend aid that would enable his son to sail from England?"

Because they're waiting.

Will breathed, deep and steady, trying to hold the dark memories at bay.

He never could.

"I have to return, Ben. It's like the land takes a bite of your soul." *The ground was thirsty.* "There's nothing like the discovery of a hidden world—" *Where are the children?* "Hidden and waiting to be found. And you find yourself all alone in nature, in a world so vast—"

Dead. All dead.

Will clasped his hands to keep them from shaking. "A world so vast, even God can't find you."

Ben was silent, and Will lowered his gaze to hide the darkness the man would see there.

"I'll need a few days, Will. I'm sorry to say I'm undecided on the matter."

This is how the conversation would always play. A less tactful man would've said it aloud. Undecided because he nearly succumbed to fever. Undecided because of his injuries.

Undecided because miraculously, inexplicably, *suspiciously*, he was the lone survivor.

It had been a bitter day when he learned he could no longer count on the patronage of the East India Company after all he'd endured. His trauma made him an undesirable investment and they had no qualms over saying so.

Will would raise the two thousand and fund the expedition himself.

And there'd be no one to interfere with the true purpose of his return.

Will forced his lips into a relaxed smile. "Of course. I'm happy to share the proposal with you and your wife at any time. I look forward to meeting her." Will paused, careful to match a neutral tone to his next words. "I did meet your sister-in-law, briefly."

"Only briefly?" Ben returned his attention to the journal. "You mean to tell me Charlotte didn't shackle herself to you and heap a hundred questions on your head?"

He opened his mouth to reply but where there should have been words, there was only an image of—God almighty—Miss Baker, *shackled*.

"I'm glad of it anyway." Ben paged through his sketches, unaware of Will's distraction. "Charlotte's begged me daily to call on you so she could know you. She was already harassing me to collect the last installment of your reports from the Geographical Society."

Ben lifted his head to meet his gaze. "She knows nothing of the violence that occurred there. You understand I'd rather she not know. The newspapers haven't printed that story, thank God."

"Only because they don't have it. The broadsides got hold of the report, though. Printed some grisly drawings."

Ben frowned, shaking his head. "Charlotte doesn't read those—her brother and I don't allow it. She's lived gently. The incident would distress her."

The incident. Blessedly, a memory of delphinium eyes rose, rather than the usual visions.

"I only mention it because Charlotte wishes to read the final volume. I've managed to put her off, but I warn you—she's criminally charming and accustomed to getting what she wants. But I imagine you'll like her well enough."

"Like" wasn't quite the word that came to mind. "Lust" wasn't, either—though he was fairly certain that sentiment was in play.

There was something else about her. Something… *warming*. Like she'd disturbed some heavy curtain and let slip a ray of sun into a cold, dark room.

He shook his mind free of the thought. There could be nothing between him and the popular Miss Baker. But damned if he didn't wonder what she was doing right now in that back parlor. And if she'd spared him another thought.

It didn't matter. He'd vowed to his friends that he'd return. There might be one he may yet save.

And there wasn't a woman alive who would sway him from his course.

Two

"You would not marry a man who enjoyed a fox hunt, would you, Patty?"

Patty's attention was occupied with centering Charlotte's brooch, but her lips pursed in a considering moue—over the brooch or the fox hunt, Charlotte could not tell.

"If I ever saw my Emmet atop a horse, I'd like to keel over dead." Patty glanced at the clock atop the mantelpiece. "Lord, your gentlemen will be arriving any minute." She fussed at something on Charlotte's blouse. "This pleat's got the very devil in it. I crimped it myself for ten minutes."

The parlor had been laid ready for Charlotte's visitors, but as it was Sunday, her maid was taking extra care with her appearance.

"But hypothetically," Charlotte continued, "would you accept such a man?"

Patty wrinkled her freckled nose and stepped back to assess her handiwork. "Can't say I'd be all that inclined to."

"That is exactly my feeling. How men could

find sport in running a poor animal to ground is beyond understanding."

"Which gentleman is the hunter, love?"

"Oh, several of them hunt. Mr. Hatfield is most keen."

"Is he the one with the teeth?"

There was no misunderstanding. "That is Mr. Matteson."

Her maid paused. "Surely he's not still in contention? None of his teeth touch each other. It's like a tooth graveyard."

Charlotte frowned. She'd not get that picture out of her mind now. "He really is the sweetest man, but no. I have never encouraged him."

"What's all this, then? Are ye narrowin' the field a bit?"

Charlotte bit her lip against a giddy smile. For the hundredth time that week, an image of Will floated to mind and, for the hundredth time, she sighed. "It may be narrowed quite."

Patty bent to study her, her eyes growing round. "What's happened? Have you chosen?"

Charlotte pressed her hands together. She could not stop them fidgeting lately. "Well…it is not as decided as all that. He has not expressed an intention to court me."

"Well, that don't sound right at all," Patty muttered, indignant on Charlotte's behalf.

Charlotte squirmed, taking up the needlepoint pillow she had sewn of her childhood pony to hug. As usual, the maids had set it wrong side up. "But he might have called any day this week, Patty."

"He'll call, don't you fret."

She watched Patty's face for another glimmer of assurance. "He *is* aware I receive visitors on Sundays…?"

"There you are!"

Charlotte beamed. "I did think perhaps today, but if not, Ben could—" She squinted at the wall, confused. "My needlepoint sampler is gone."

Patty's eyes slid from hers. "Is it?"

"*Look*. It was there yesterday."

Patty didn't turn. "Oh, I remember. The frame cracked. One of the girls said. It cracked."

"Another one? And I was so pleased with how I had stitched the kitten's stripes."

Patty's smile tightened. "That was meant to be a kitten, was it?" she asked wanly.

"That is the third I've hung that has—"

"*So tell me* of this gentleman!" Patty grabbed her hands and squeezed. "*Ben could…?*"

Charlotte focused on the topic at hand. "Well, Ben could invite him to call, but he is being particularly obtuse to my suffering." She flung the pillow behind her—but gently, as Beatrice had always been her favorite pet. "A lady ought not press for information on any bachelor, but *honestly*, it cannot be borne."

Charlotte lifted her chin, a martyr to love. "I suppose I will have to ask Ben to invite the man to dinner."

Patty raised a brow. "You've never dangled after a man before."

"I know! This is what Ben has reduced me to. He is a most unfeeling brother."

"All right, all right." Patty sat beside her. "Which lad is it then, love?"

Charlotte hesitated. She'd not told anyone. And marrying for love—as much as she hoped she might—struck against every dictate of her education. Had she not witnessed a lady or two among her circle marry for love, and descend from a state of comfort and fortune to an inferior condition?

But Will was a hero. And she was wealthy in her own right. And Patty was nearly a sister to her. "Do you promise not to tell anyone?"

"I think I can manage to keep it out of the papers."

Casting a furtive glance into the hall, Charlotte clutched Patty's hand. "Oh, Patty, once you meet him, I will be forgiven my machinations. He is the perfect man."

"Then he'd be the first since Jesus."

"He is not a peer," she warned. "He holds no title at all."

"No title? He's not a soldier, is he? Or a clergyman?" Her hands flew to her cheek. "Oh, sweet Joseph, tell me he's not on the stage."

"No! *Honestly*, Patty." She pulled the woman's hands down. "An actor? I've not surrendered my wits. No, he is courageous and extraordinary and admired by everyone."

Patty's face was still pinched with worry. "Well, don't be a month about it. Who is it?"

Charlotte paused for effect, pride in her own brilliance swelling in her breast. "William Repton."

"The explorer? The cranky one what was here last week?"

Charlotte blinked at the description. "Well, I…I do not believe he is habitually cross. He was quite overwhelmed, I'm sure, by the company last week." Her maid looked unconvinced, sinking her pleasure a little. "Do you not think him admirable, Patty?"

"Ah, love. I'll give you he's impressive and right

handsome, but he's not like the gentlemen you keep company with."

"Exactly! And he's likely never held an oyster fork *in his whole life*. Do you see? I no longer have to accept any highborn man who would remind me of my lineage any time he was out of sorts with me—and that is just the sort of thing they would do, I can just see it." She raised her chin against Patty's sympathetic look. "I am not ashamed of my family. But we both know it to be the truth. I would have endured such an alliance for the family, but I do not have to. Not now."

"What are you—"

"Because *he came.*" She blinked against happy tears. "He actually came and he is perfect. A hero, and not only that—he is who I *want*. I can marry for love *and* elevate the family name."

"Charlotte—"

"There are other heroes, of course. I had entertained hopes for a young physician who had made great advancements in anesthesia—but he so rarely blinked, Patty, it was quite impossible." She lowered her voice to an appropriately discreet and compassionate tone. "I could not help but wonder if he breathed too much chloroform himself.

"But a *mariage d'amour* with London's most daring adventurer will make us the darlings of Society. Everyone wishes to know him and we will be welcomed everywhere, and that will extend to Lucy and Ben. No one would dare speak of their marriage. And the children—" She paused to collect herself, reaching to tuck one of Patty's rust-colored curls beneath her cap. "The most discriminating doors will open for *all* of us. Even Wally." At Patty's doubtful expression, her smile shrank. "Well. Likely they would. Later."

Patty sighed. "Ah, lass, why are you worryin' about all that?"

Charlotte paused, struck by the question. "I always knew I would marry for influence. But I had so hoped to marry for love, as well."

"A loveless union was never anyone's plan for you."

"No, I know," she said meekly.

"Besides, what of Lady Wynston? Look at what the old dragon's done for you these three seasons."

"And I am eternally grateful for her sponsorship. But her influence never swayed the *ton* to accept Lucy, Ben, or Wally. I want my family in Society with me."

"Ah, Charlotte." She cupped Charlotte's cheeks, staring grimly into her eyes. "Are you for certain this Mr. Repton will do?"

She bit her lip, trying to contain her widening smile. "I have never been more certain of anyone. And I do not know why, except…oh, I thought I had dreamed him, Patty, but that is wrong. I *recognized* him. Almost as if we had met before and loved each other from the first." She laughed, hugging Patty. "Yes, he will do very well." She sat back to grin at her maid. "But first, he must return to the house so he can recognize me, too."

At last, Patty smiled. "I suppose he must, then."

"You *do* think it possible, don't you? We may seem very different, but I will love him better than anyone."

"Heaven help the man who doesn't fall in line with your wishes."

Charlotte stood. "I ought to find Ben now."

"Later, Charlotte."

"But—"

"*Charlotte.*" Patty, suddenly all discipline and propriety, pointed her back to her seat.

She flopped down. "I really have no wish to receive visitors today."

"I know, love."

She sat up, straightening her skirts over her crinoline. "But I would not want to be accused of dallying with affections. Though I have been discouraging attention all week. At the charity concert for the Ruislip school, I collected my own lemonade."

"Is that why all the London gentlemen are falling into decline?"

She swatted her maid, smiling. "No gentleman will be pained by my distance. The duke had no serious intentions, and the others were not long invested in their pursuit."

"What of Viscount Spencer?"

What of Hugh…? She had no reason to doubt his intentions were anything but honorable, but how could she know?

She shook her head. "No earl-in-waiting will grieve any lady long."

Goodley appeared at the door. "Lord Spencer," the butler intoned. "And Mr. Matteson."

Patty went to her chair in the corner and Charlotte smiled at her visitors, remembering to temper its warmth.

Lord Spencer bowed deep, presenting his lavish bouquet. Always such lovely gifts from Hugh, always so proper and solicitous. He would have been a brilliant match, and perhaps a better-than-average husband. He had passed many of her tests.

But there would be no more tests. There was not a test she could devise that Will Repton could ever fail. He was the answer, every time.

She must find Ben and insist he invite Will to dinner *at once*. After her visitors took their leave, of course. A quarter hour more.

Surely they would not stay long.

"Mr. Paxton has asked that you wait in the study," the butler said.

Will nodded approvingly. A proper butler today. And good thing. He'd not forgotten today was Charlotte Baker's receiving day for hopeful bachelors. There would be no repeat of last week's nonsense. The door of the frilly back parlor was open but he couldn't see even a foot into the room.

Will absently checked the buttons of his new coat.

Good. That was…good. Better to not be seen by Miss Baker.

The butler cleared his throat. "Sir?"

Will wrenched his gaze to the butler waiting for him at the study door.

"Is there anything you require?" the butler asked.

"No. Thank you." His thigh protested his carefully disguised limp across the entry hall. One last glance at the back parlor—just in case—and he entered the study.

Right, then.

Right.

Better she not know he was here. Miss Baker might

corner him all over again, plying him with tea and her pretty smiles. He was here for one reason only: to secure Ben's agreement to be his cultivator here in England and the man's one hundred pounds.

So that was…that was *two* reasons then. "Enough," he grumbled under his breath. With no one to witness his gait, he limped toward the table to lay down his materials.

"I hurt my leg, too."

Will started at the small voice. At the end of the room, in a wingback chair almost comically large for its occupant, sat the young boy he'd seen dashing across the foyer a week ago. His pulse pounded in his neck but there was not the usual sickening plunge of his stomach.

Perhaps because the boy made such a benign picture sitting there.

Or perhaps because he had his father's familiar gray eyes.

"You must be a Paxton," Will said.

"I'm Jacob."

Will drew a blank. What did one say to a child dressed in a miniature admiral's uniform?

He made his way to the most attractive seat—the one farthest from the child he could manage. Minutes passed and the boy wasn't leaving.

Will cleared his throat. "I'm Will."

The words had an undesired effect. The boy slipped from his chair and climbed into the one next to his.

"Are you Chinese Will?" the boy asked.

"Maybe. Yes. I think so."

"Papa said you sailed in a ship to China. Did you

see a shark or octopus?" His eyes grew huge. "Or a pirate? Did you fight him and hurt your leg?"

Will stared. The child appeared to be in earnest. "A pirate?"

The boy nodded.

"No." He grimaced at the sentence he was about to utter. "I fought no pirates."

"Did you see any pirates?"

"No."

"Not even one?"

"No."

The boy slumped in his chair, his small face collapsing in a remarkable expression of world-shattering disappointment.

His thoughts flew back to Tibet. To the children. The baby had been weeks old and the boy…Emile was six.

"What are you? A boy your size?" Will asked. The boy didn't seem to discern his meaning. "How *old* are you?"

"I'm almost five."

"So you're four."

The boy nodded. "Almost five." He pulled up the leg of his short pants to reveal a bandage on his knee. "I hurt my leg, too."

Where the devil was Ben Paxton?

"Yes. Well." Will glanced at the boy and his unwavering stare. "As men, we must bear the pain stoically."

The child twisted his little body on the chair, dangling till his small, booted feet met the floor, and then he was bounding to the door. "I'll tell Aunt Charlotte to kiss your leg and make it better. Just like mine."

"What? Wait, uh—!" *What was the boy's name? "Jacob!"*

But it was too late. Will made it to the door in seconds but the child had disappeared.

Surely her visitors would not…stay…LONG.

The thought repeated at the quarter hour, and the half, and every interminable passing minute until it was a shrill mantra in Charlotte's mind.

If only these men had come at a common hour. But as one stood, another arrived, and rather than take his leave, as well-mannered ladies knew to do, the departing gentleman would be persuaded to stay a minute or two or ten longer.

And Will had not come…

"Capital, sir! Do you approve, Miss Baker?"

Hugh's voice pulled her from her thoughts. She smiled, not knowing how to answer. Fortunately, Lucy took that moment to appear at the door.

Unfortunately, she was carrying a fully laden tea tray.

Oh no. No, no, no. An unnecessary husband test was about to commence—and she had spoken of this test in jest—

"Good afternoon, gentlemen." Lucy was with child and, at seven months, her condition was apparent on her slight frame. Carrying a tray was rarely undertaken by the lady of the house, and certainly not by a countess under normal circumstances.

But the Baker circumstances had never been normal.

With her sweet smile, Lucy posed with her tray above her rounded belly. "I thought I might refresh the tea."

To a man they stood, but not one went to her aid. Lucy set the tray upon the table herself. The men resumed their chatter and Lucy sat with a secret, speaking glance at their shocking lack of chivalry.

But Charlotte understood all too clearly what Lucy did not. This was no simple failure of manners. The men withheld their aid because Lucy had married Ben, a man far below her in point of rank.

"Good afternoon," a male voice sounded from the door.

Charlotte's heart sank further as her brother strode into the room. Wally was a secret husband test all her own. And the most important.

"Might I join your party?" Wally stood behind the divan, turned out impeccably, as always, in a beautiful coat of superfine wool, embroidered waistcoat, and silk tie.

Oh, dash it! This was all her fault. Why did she not tell Lucy and Wally to stay away?

"Yes, of course." She forced a smile.

As usual, the men were wary and silent, so Wally spoke first. "I was just discussing this queer weather with my valet. I wager we will have hail tomorrow and spring breezes the next, as changeable as the year has been."

Hugh shifted on the chaise longue, Mr. Hatfield checked his timepiece, and Mr. Matteson picked at the crumbs on his plate. This cool treatment was hardly unusual. Wally was inured to the unease of men and their insults.

But she was not. In the silence, her heart hardened in an all too familiar way. No gentlemen passed this test.

Pressing on—perversely, it seemed to her—Wally stepped from around the divan and set his arms wide to present his coat. "Tell me, gentlemen, do you approve of this new collar? My tailor tells me it is quite the thing on the Continent, but I am undecided."

But the men said nothing. Worse, they eyed Wally's collar as if bats had converged within and would swarm the room any moment.

She couldn't bear it. All said Charlotte Baker rarely took offense, and that was true enough.

Unless it was an offense against her family.

She surged to her feet, hot with fury at these…*guests* who insulted her brother and sister without compunction.

The men were startled into a flurry of movement as they stood. Lucy gaped at her from the settee, oblivious of any insult. The innocent question in her eyes wrenched Charlotte's heart.

"Miss Baker?" Hugh reached toward her. "Are you unwell?"

How could he pretend innocence? She should let him see the betrayal in her eyes, the anger. But she lowered her lids instead.

She would not cause a scene.

She never caused a scene.

She drew herself tall and repinned her smile. "I fear I am overwarm. Would you pardon me?"

She swept into the empty hall, relaxing her fists and breathing deep. How could she have thought to marry any of them? It was impossible. They would never respect her family. Or her.

Quieting her thoughts, she conjured Will as she had last seen him, just *there*. Where he looked at her one last time before entering Ben's study. And the way he looked at her…as if he'd never seen a woman like her. As if he did not entirely approve.

Perhaps she had been a trifle enthusiastic.

Please come back. Please, just one more chance.

Jacob's running footsteps sounded from the hall and he careened around the corner, flinging himself against her skirts. "Aunt Charlotte, do you remember how you kissed my knee and made it better?"

"I do." She crouched to speak with him, the last vestige of her upset crumbling with the sight of his pink cheeks, tousled hair, and military skeleton suit, complete with gold braiding.

"Chinese Will hurt his leg."

She blinked at his prescient choice of topic. "Why, yes he did. How did you know?"

"Will you kiss it and make it better?"

Her heart answered enthusiastically at the idea, but Charlotte kept her countenance. "Sometimes you cannot kiss a hurt away if the injury is too big. Do you understand?"

"Come with me to Papa's study."

"I have guests, love."

Jacob swung a baleful glance at the back parlor. "Please. It's important."

It was not like Jacob to plead, and his little face was so anxious. "All right." She stood and let him tug her into Ben's study.

Charlotte bent to search his face. "Is something the matter, sweetest? Do you need Nurse?"

Jacob beamed a smile and dashed out.

Confused, she straightened to follow. Until a soft clearing of the throat stopped her.

In the back by the window, bathed in a shaft of sunlight, was a golden man. He pivoted and took an uneven step.

Will!

The lurch of her heart was staggering, and she braced herself with the table. The blue of his eyes could be seen from across the room, and she was riveted. "You came," she managed to say.

He bowed, and the bow was fast and jerky and utterly thrilling. Could she dare hope she made him a little nervous?

Her heart slowed and strengthened, and all at once she was calm.

Here he was. Here was the same joy as before, the same recognition. Familiar as...*family*. Though she had never dreamed Will standing in sunlight before. Not with his hair glittering such a glorious gold and that bronze flush deepening the high planes of his cheekbones.

She wet her lips and his eyes settled there. Heartened by the focus, she smiled. "I hope I am not disturbing you."

He looked at the book he'd been reading as if wondering how it had come to be in his hands. He returned it to the bookcase. "I was waiting for Ben."

"Oh."

Oh dear. This blush had no business on a woman of her breeding, maturity, and happy temperament. But there was nothing to be done—the man had the most blush-inducing shoulders.

She approached his sunlit corner but stopped several feet away. Oddly, Will was looking rather cornered.

Would he smile or speak or, at the very least, look at her?

Or was this how he ensnared her heart? Denying

her any satisfaction in knowing him until all that was left was to replay the moment they met over and over? To fall asleep to the memory of him, wake with fantasies of him beside her, and conjure his face all the hours in between?

But knowing what she knew of him—of his bravery and spirit and compassion—she was convinced there was no more romantic man in the entire world.

Had she truly found him? Was he the man she'd been waiting for?

Would his next words seal their destiny?

"I suppose you're here to kiss me but I warn you, there were multiple breaks and none conveniently placed."

Her smile slipped. "I beg your pardon?"

"Did your nephew not solicit you on my behalf?" His eyes flickered to her mouth. "A healing kiss for my leg?"

Comprehension dawned, and with more relief than humor, she smiled. "Oh, that. Yes. Well, he's four."

"He has your talent for fanciful notions."

"Oh yes. He believes all horses understand French."

Will blinked. "I meant your kiss."

"Well, Jacob's scrapes have all healed, so you should not discount their potency just yet."

At that, Will actually winced.

Her smile didn't falter, even though that particular overture usually had a different effect—*oh!* She had seen this before. In more than one man, actually.

He was shy of women.

Well, of course he would be. The man was not out and about in Society.

No matter. She was practiced enough in

conversation for the both of them, and she liked shy men very well.

And if Will were shy, she would like him best of all.

Blithely, she ignored his deepening scowl and ventured closer, feigning interest in his books and maps on the table. She looked up, confused that they were the same distance apart.

Until she took a step…and he retreated.

No. That could not be right.

She took an experimental step forward and he mirrored the movement in reverse. Step. Retreat. Step. Retreat. Oh, *honestly*.

She stood still. "You and Ben must have much to speak of."

He tipped his head, which she took to be an affirmative.

"I cannot begin to imagine the adventures you have had. You must have felt as if you were dreaming all the while."

At last he looked at her. A slow inspection that nearly set her back a step. "It feels London is where I'm dreaming." He lowered his gaze. "Maybe I'll wake when I return."

Her heart stopped. "Return?"

"Yes."

No! "Return to…" *Please, please no.* "You are going back?"

He looked sharply at her, their eyes tangling before he raised his gaze over her head. Was that a rhetorical question, then?

"I see," she whispered. She gripped the back of a chair, alarmed by threatening tears. The pricking sensation novel and horrible. *I don't cry… I never cry.*

Will cleared his throat roughly and the sound freed a word from her lips. "Where?"

He hesitated, but then edged close to open a book atop the table. A map of Asia.

"There's a province here I aim to return to." He leaned on the table beside her, pointing to a city on the map. His hard, muscled arm brushed against her.

And stayed there.

She stood perfectly still, not wanting the contact to end, and locked her eyes to the map. But from the corner of her watery vision she could see the strong edge of his jaw and the crisp clips of hair at his neck.

His hair had been trimmed since last week. And the shirt and coat he wore were new. The work of a second-rate tailor. The strangest pain knifed through her. She would never let him wear such unworthy clothes. And who had cut his hair? A barber? Or did he see a woman—?

Warm breath brushed her ear, scattering her stupid, miserable jealousy.

She blinked the wetness from her eyes and faced him. His gaze was lidded but his lips were so close, she couldn't look away when they moved to speak…

"Here." His voice was low and rasping. And commanded her attention back to the map. "By Chengdu."

She dragged her gaze to where he pointed. "That's… it's so far west. You will not go into Tibet, will you?"

He stiffened and stepped back, the warm press of his arm gone. "No." He swung the cover shut, making her jump. "Those regions are unstable." He turned and put half the room between them.

What happened? He was back at the bookcase,

retrieving what appeared to be the same book he'd been perusing before.

Her eyes stung and suddenly she wanted to throw his stupid map at his stupid, handsome head.

But of course she would not. She may have been born common, but she had been given the finest education a lady could wish for. She would not be ridiculous in her disappointment. And that was all this was. A disappointment. Her first, and therefore keenly felt.

Very keenly felt indeed.

Her friends would say it was for the best. That as notable a man as he was, he could not raise her rank. That love was a fine notion, but a frivolous one for a well-dowered, well-bred lady with everything to recommend her. Except a name.

It *was* for the best. Her options may have been dwindling, but in her circumstances, all men fell into two camps: those who would marry her, and those who never would.

Mr. Repton was not so perfect after all.

She drew in a breath. "And how long will you be away, Mr. Repton?"

He didn't look up from his book. "Five years."

The same breath rushed from her body. *Five*. She could not wait and yet…no one had ever unearthed her heart as he had done. Could she at least have his friendship?

"I see…I would—" She lifted her chin so she would be heard across their distance. "I would so like to hear more of your expedition. My ladies' group meets at Lady Abernathy's salon to discuss current events. Your expedition was our topic this month."

His brows lowered and she rushed on. "And I

have read all your reports except the last, though I am hopeful Ben will retrieve it for me soon." *Oh, bother it!* Could she sound more like a child? "But you know that already."

"And you know I recommend against reading them."

His words were so low, Charlotte barely heard him. And then she hardly knew what to say to his disapproval.

"I do not see why not," she said, her misery making reckless her words. "I find it disgraceful that the Geographical Society bans entry to women. It is not feasible for many people—and not just women, Mr. Repton—to travel, so if I had one adventure worth reciting—"

She cut herself off, aware her voice had risen. "Many will look to you as a messenger and teacher. A source of wisdom and inspiration and a common humanity."

He lifted his head, and something clawed beneath that blue stare. "There's good reason for my caution, Miss Baker. Some things aren't fit to be read, as they're not wise or inspiring." His jaw tightened. "Or even human. As to the rest, I doubt there'd be much to interest the ladies of Miss Abernathy's salon. I wasn't collecting flowers over there."

She stared in shock. No one had ever spoken to her with so little regard for her good opinion. Or her feelings.

"I see," she said numbly. It was not shyness at all.

"I see," she said more firmly. "Good-bye, Mr. Repton."

His lips parted to speak, but a sort of blank resignation settled upon his features instead.

She spun on her heel and fled.

But not before hearing what could only be the slam of a book rammed back onto the shelf.

Three

Will tried to ignore the boy, but he wasn't moving from the door. He was deep in conversation with Ben in the man's study when he sighted Jacob's face peeking at them from behind the door. Weeks of observation now had proven the boy's nursemaid as relaxed a servant as the others.

Five minutes later, the boy hadn't quit his position and the child's stare was like a magnet, drawing his eyes again and again.

"Where is the schedule of deliveries?" Ben asked.

Will started, returning his attention to the matters at hand, and flipped through his papers. "The schedule, right… I have it." He produced the pages, frowning at his own distraction. He'd secured the best cultivator in England in the form of Ben Paxton, but apparently the man's participation was conditional upon the presence of his four-year-old spawn.

Ignore him. Don't look at the boy, don't look, don't—blast it! Beaten, Will tilted his head and looked pointedly back at Jacob.

With that, Ben turned in his seat. "What are you doing there, Son? Is this important?"

The boy's eyes widened and he nodded.

Ben turned back to Will. "Sorry about this." He swiveled in his seat. "Come here, then. Hurry now."

Jacob, wearing a sailor suit, dashed to his father's side.

Will pressed his lips against laughing. Little induced him to laugh of late. Only Jacob could startle the humor out of him. And it almost always felt a little like pain.

But he was grateful for the boy. After what had happened, the sight of children was awful to him. Their cries excruciating, screams unbearable. But Jacob was so happy and alive.

And in possession of the most eccentric wardrobe he'd ever seen.

"You know Mr. Repton?" Ben prompted.

"Hello, Mr. Repton." The little boy cupped his small hands to his father's ear and shared his secret words.

"I think Mr. Repton will be fine," Ben whispered back.

"I don't think he will, Papa."

"Shall we ask him?"

Jacob nodded, twisting his small hands.

Ben crossed his arms and looked at Will gravely. "Will, my son is concerned that if you don't bring a box of sweets for Charlotte soon"—Ben's lips quivered with amusement—"you won't have a hope of marrying her."

Will scowled at the once-sensible Ben Paxton.

Ben grinned. "She likes Turkish delights."

Jacob tugged on his arm, shaking his head. "Caramels," the boy whispered.

"Sorry, Will. Caramels are better. Charlotte

shares her sweets with"—his eyes pointed to Jacob—"the household."

Ignoring Ben's amusement, Will shifted his gaze to the boy. Jacob never failed to remind Miss Baker to him as a potential wife each and every time he visited. As if he'd somehow forgotten the woman who plagued his every stray thought.

And all his carnal ones.

Jacob bounced closer and Will leaned back. The child had the presence of mind not to clamber atop his lap, but there was no telling where he might stop.

"If you married Aunt Charlotte, you could live here and we could play every day."

He nodded slowly—miserably—at the boy's reasoning. "That sounds very pleasant."

"Aunt Charlotte knows a lot about China, and when your leg gets better, you can dance with her. And she's almost as pretty as Mama. And she's nice and tells stories. And even if her drawings are really bad, Mama says she tries and that's what's important."

Will looked to Ben to help him.

"It's true, Will," Ben said soberly. "Trying *is* what's important."

Never any help at all.

A grinning Ben stood, swept Jacob under his arm, and carried him to the hall. "All right, Son. Aunt Charlotte must choose her husband without our help, and we'll not bother Mr. Repton with any of this again, will we?" Ben set him down—mercifully on the other side of the door.

"Sorry, Will," Ben said. "Jacob's heart is set on you for Charlotte. It's amazing how astute he is."

Will's head reared back. "I swear I've made no advances."

Ben laughed. "*Of course not!*"

The hell? The idea wasn't that ludicrous.

"I mean Jacob has noticed Charlotte's suitors have been...well, *culled.*"

Will's heartbeat slowed in his chest. "What do you mean?"

"We think she's chosen the viscount."

Will looked at his hands. The palms rubbed absently together and he stilled them. "The viscount? I don't—which one is he?"

"Viscount Spencer, Hugh Swift."

Spencer. Pale. Dark hair. Mustache framing square teeth. His father, the Earl of Harlowe, was on the board at Kew. A prize prospect, actually.

The door cracked open and Ben's wife peeked in. "Darling? May we have a word?"

We? Will leaned to see into the hall.

Ben shot to his feet as he always did when summoned by Lucy. He took her hand, dipping his head to listen to her, and the pink of his wife's cheeks deepened.

The strange vise on Will's ribs tightened. The widowed countess had damned the *ton* to marry Ben, but she didn't seem to regret the choice. Happiness seemed to make her sparkle up at him. No wonder Ben was so good-humored.

The countess had chosen love.

Charlotte had chosen a viscount.

She was there, hidden behind the door. He didn't know why or how, but there were times he felt Charlotte move down the hall to her parlor. Just as at other times he felt her climb the stairs, or walk past the door of the study, or felt the house cold, empty, only to learn later she was not in.

It was a waste of time knowing such things.

His preoccupation with her was merely an escape from his work, his memories, the fear he would be too late. God knew his brain wasn't the most reliable organ of late.

And at night...what matter if he conjured her? She was a convenient face to recall in his insomnia, a curious puzzle of womanhood, a beautiful trigger for his lust with an erotic body that guaranteed his release.

She didn't matter. She couldn't. Wives were for other men.

Ben swung the door wide, revealing Charlotte and another richly dressed lady behind the door. "Will, our friend, the Marchioness Wynston, desires to be introduced."

Will moved to the door, all the while recording the dark silk of Charlotte's hair and her green striped dress. One of his favorites. She always wore a jade bracelet with it almost exactly like the one he'd bought for his mum in China.

"You are quite the object of interest about Town," Lady Wynston said.

He bowed. "Lady Wynston—"

"If you will excuse me," Charlotte murmured before walking away.

Will's head swiveled to watch Charlotte leave. She hadn't bothered to say hello. She always had before. Is this what their acquaintance had evolved to? His presence so commonplace he shouldn't even expect her paltry greeting any longer?

Will cleared his throat and returned his attention to Lady Wynston. And blanked. What had the woman said?

Lady Wynston hadn't watched Charlotte's departure. Faded blue eyes inspected him beneath a miniature bonnet exploding with purple feathers. What had his father said of her? She was rich, eccentric, and fond of younger men, which, Will estimated, would include anyone shy of their eightieth year.

"Milady, I'm pleased to meet you," he said.

"I imagine you are." Her voice was threaded with amusement. "Ben, allow the ladies a moment with Mr. Repton."

Ben left him alone with the women. Will waited for the ladies to settle and was delayed again by a footman carrying in a small dog that was placed reverently on Lady Wynston's silk lap. The dog's stare instantly latched onto Will. The social order of the house was clear enough—ladies first, Pomeranians, then miscellaneous males.

Lady Wynston's perfect posture mirrored the walking stick balanced on the floor beneath her beringed hand. "All of London is fascinated with your travels. Our Charlotte especially."

"Yes, she…uh." Will frowned at his own incoherence. "Perhaps less so now. She left."

"Indeed she did." Lady Wynston's gaze sharpened, scanning him from tip to toe. "With surprising haste."

Mrs. Paxton sprang to the door. "Ah, here we are. Thank you, Mrs. Allen. I will take it from here."

Ben's wife turned from the door carrying a heavy tea tray.

Ben's *pregnant* wife.

With no thought of concealing his limp, he hurried to relieve the woman of the burden. "Allow me, Mrs. Paxton." *God's sake*, did this house not have any proper servants?

"Oh!" She laughed, her eyes wide. "You passed, Mr. Repton. *Bravo*."

He placed the tray on the table, puzzled by her words.

"I do not know what Charlotte is about these days," Lady Wynston said, the name like a swift mule kick to his stomach. "Dashing to and fro, her pretty head everywhere but atop her shoulders. In my time, a lady was careful not to exert herself lest she excite herself to a swoon."

"Charlotte would never swoon," Mrs. Paxton assured him with a smile, pouring their tea. "She thinks it extravagant."

Lady Wynston nodded approvingly. "Excellent girl. Very modern." Her ladyship rapped her cane on the floor and he straightened to attention. "You young men may find the notion of a beautiful girl fainting dead away into your arms a pleasant sort of pastime, but do not hope for it, Mr. Repton. In truth, swoons and their recovery are perfectly tedious." She patted her hat. "Though I daresay Charlotte would swoon very prettily. Accomplished creature...she could not help but make charming work of it." Lady Wynston shook her finger at Will. "But do not hope for it."

"No, I...hope for what, exactly?"

"Perfectly tedious," Lady Wynston murmured, accepting a plate of cake from Mrs. Paxton. "Thank you, my dear. Though I cannot say I approve of Charlotte's excessive interest in your adventures, Mr.

Repton. Still"—she tilted her head to study him—"I am not so ancient as to deny the appeal of the rugged adventurer, hurtling bravely into the undiscovered country. His virile body sculpted to brawn and sinew by the very forces of nature he seeks to tame. His taut, bronzed skin glistening—"

Mrs. Paxton coughed.

"—with the dew of toil beneath the relentless sun. And Charlotte, beautiful innocent of the world, her insatiable curiosity a tender bud blossoming beneath the experienced ministrations of the bold explorer—"

"Biscuit, Mr. Repton?" Mrs. Paxton shoved a plate of sweets beneath his nose, her cheeks red.

Will held up a defensive hand. "Thank you, no."

Lady Wynston sniffed. "But I suppose it is a harmless sort of diversion. If one is intrigued by the Orient. I, myself, have a most charming chinoiserie wallpaper in my morning room, but that is neither here nor there."

The Pomeranian gave a jaw-splitting yawn and resumed his unblinking stare.

"Yes...well." Mrs. Paxton stood, propelling Will to his feet. "If you will excuse me. There is a household matter I must attend to."

The click of Lady Wynston's cup in her saucer reclaimed his attention and he sat quickly. He doubted anyone kept the marchioness waiting long.

"I asked the dear girl to allow us a moment alone," Lady Wynston said. "I understand you plan to return."

"Yes, in August."

Lady Wynston put down her cup with a hand tremulous with age. "My late sister was related to the missionary you knew in Tibet. Marcel Bourianne, and his wife." Her creased lids lowered. "And their children."

Will's jaw tightened. "Yes, I knew them. I'm sorry."

The lady's eyes shaded with sadness. "I know you must be. Very sorry, indeed. I tell myself they received some sort of Christian burial…?"

She paused in way of a question, but he said nothing.

There was nothing he could say. The Tibetans did not bury their dead. Not in that frozen tundra. He and his men had ridden past a *jhator*—a sky burial, they called it. Complete with the wake of vultures. That was a sight none of them wished to see again.

And yet it had become their fate.

Will blinded himself to the lady's compassionate stare, not wanting to remember. Or see. *The ground was*—"The Bouriannes were kind to my crew. We were delayed at their mission on our route to Bhutan. Our French was poor, as was their English, so we spoke a little of each to one another. The youngest boy, even. Emile."

"God's plans are mysterious, are they not? To send a family around the world to do His good work and yet not deliver them home."

"A great mystery." Will met her eyes and knew the woman could be trusted. "But perhaps one may yet return."

Surprise flickered in her eyes.

"I never…*saw* the infant. I couldn't confirm her death. Before I was forced to leave Tibet, I wrote a letter and begged it be delivered to the Apostolic Vicariate in Hong Kong, asking they search for the child. They have missions throughout Asia, contact with foreign scientists, physicians, other explorers. I don't know if it was delivered. I was delirious with fever. And here in England, I've mailed inquiries, begged for help, for anyone to search, to *try*, and there's been no response."

"It does seem a difficult undertaking."

"But not impossible."

The formidable lady studied him. "That is the reason you return."

He gave a short nod.

"Yet you claim a botanical expedition when soliciting investors."

"It will be. *After*. A great deal of money is needed. Not for the passage on an Indiaman, but the bribes—for passports, papers, information." He paused. "You understand this is not information I'm sharing widely. Or at all."

"I am the soul of discretion, Mr. Repton."

A silence settled between them until he had to ask. "Did you ever meet them?"

"Only Marcel, long ago. He was a child then and terrified of me." Her brow quirked. "An astute boy, I think." She diverted her attention to stroke her dog's head. "I never met him again."

"His son, Emile, wouldn't have feared you."

"Brave, was he?"

"Yes."

"Then we will hope the infant is brave as well."

Slowly, he raised his head and met her eyes. "Do you hope?" he asked, his voice hollow. "Is it possible the babe was spared, do you think?"

Her eyes crinkled with a small smile. "Yes, Mr.

Repton, I hope. Live as long as I and you will see a miracle or two."

He steeled against threatening tears, fighting an urge to hug the old woman. It felt good. To share this hope with another person. He raked a hand through his hair, embarrassed to look at her in his state.

Perhaps he was not so mad after all.

Lady Wynston retrieved her tea. "And her name?"

"Aimee."

She lifted her regal chin. "You will call upon me tomorrow, young man, and we shall further discuss the needs of your *expedition.*"

"Yes, milady. And thank you."

She was quiet and Will caught her studying him. "How long are you to be away?"

"Five years. I'll need to be there several growing cycles."

She pursed her lips, looking displeased. "A pity. No doubt your travels leave you little time for other pursuits. Young ladies, for example. Even the modern ones who dislike to swoon."

His eyes shot to hers, then to the door, afraid someone might overhear. He turned back with what had to be a damn sheepish look on his face.

"Do not concern yourself, Mr. Repton. As I said, I am the soul of discretion."

"It doesn't matter. Long before I met Miss Baker, I vowed to return." He shrugged tightly. "She will likely be married within a year."

"Very likely. She is of an age. As are you. No one would blame you if your conviction wavered. I imagine it has, a time or two."

He nearly laughed. Within sight of Charlotte, his conviction wavered again and again. “A time or two, your ladyship.”

We think she’s chosen the viscount…

He leveled his gaze. “But I’ll not allow it to happen again.”

Four

DAMN HIS TIMING.

Will's hackney drew alongside the glossy phaeton parked in front of Paxton's townhouse. There was no question whom the carriage belonged to. He'd seen that blasted crest on the side often enough. Viscount Spencer—Charlotte's beau—had come to take her for a ride. *Again.*

And the man himself was walking to the door.

Lord Spencer heard Will's steps and turned, revealing a bouquet of colorful tulips. "Mr. Repton. How is the plan progressing for your expedition?"

"It's progressing," Will grumbled.

His eyes narrowed to examine him. "You are here often."

"Ben's agreed to be my receiving man here in England. This location is more central than my home in Richmond."

"Yes, capital, capital. That would certainly explain your frequent presence."

Will stilled, suspicious of the man's intent. It was irrational, but the man raised his hackles.

Spencer lowered his voice. "Perhaps I ought to enlist you to spy upon my competition. You might tell me if you observe other gentlemen call for Miss Baker?"

"You think she entertains other bachelors?"

Spencer held his eye, an undeniable challenge. "Charlotte has quite the cadre of admirers. I shouldn't like to think there was another vying for her after all my efforts."

Damn your hide. If only Spencer's father wasn't one of his most promising prospects.

But looking at the man, Will was damn sure he could take him in any contest of strength. The viscount was trim enough, but his pallor was odd. Even for a hothouse aristocrat, the man looked bloodless.

Will glanced at the floral offering. "I believed Miss Baker partial to white flowers."

Lord Spencer turned the doorbell, not taking his eyes off him. "I instruct my man to bring what is best from the market. We are not all *florists*, Mr. Repton."

Before he could reply, Goodley opened the door. His presence routine, Will made his way unescorted to Ben's study. But not before sliding the usual box of caramels onto the front table for Charlotte.

Or rather, Jacob.

Ben sat at the table, engrossed in his reading. "Morning, Will. Have you read this Richard Burton's account of Goa?"

Will grumbled some noncommittal sound, set his parcel on the table, and sat in a chair with a view of Spencer's phaeton.

"You seem distracted," Ben said.

"Hm? No."

Ben followed his stare out the window. "That's a smart little carriage, isn't it?"

Will shrugged out of his coat, yanking at his sleeves. "Appears he's taking her into the country."

"Yes." Ben resumed his reading.

Will frowned at Ben. And his damn book. And then the damn carriage. "Where will her maid sit, I wonder?"

Ben looked, his eyes sharpening on the carriage, and harrumphed. "Well, he'll make room for Patty or he'll not be driving Charlotte anywhere."

Good man. Somewhat appeased, Will sat back. "You think he suits her?"

"He's in line for an earldom, which suits Charlotte, I suppose. And yet..."

"And yet?"

"I'm not convinced she has any great feeling for him."

The idea shouldn't please him. He had no claim to the woman. Why begrudge her some rich gallant who brought her flowers every time he called?

Maybe it was those flowers. Attention to detail was Will's hallmark, and *this one*—Charlotte's most ardent suitor—couldn't be taught that she liked white flowers.

"Why say that?" Will hoped his nonchalance convincing. "That she has no feeling for him?"

"Lucy says she doesn't," Ben said, speaking like a man utterly domesticated.

"Yes. Well. Do you think Spencer will offer soon?"

"I wouldn't be surprised. Lucy's planning her first house party at Windmere later this month to know him better. A week in the country will force him to cut line or propose, don't you think?" Ben's smile flashed as an idea dawned. "You must come."

Will stared back, speechless at the idea.

"And your parents. I've never been able to persuade them," Ben added, growing excited by the idea.

The last place Will wanted to be was trapped in the country when Charlotte announced their engagement. "No, we shouldn't intrude on Miss Baker's party."

Ben waved that off. "That's nothing, and I'd like the company. And Spencer's parents have accepted. An excellent time to pitch the expedition to Lord Harlowe."

Will sank in his seat. He *had* planned to make an ask of Spencer's father. It would be idiotic to refuse.

"My parents have always wanted to see Windmere," Will admitted. "But the Reptons might make for poor company. We aren't accustomed to socializing in Miss Baker's circles."

Ben sighed. "Neither are we. It could be a complete disaster. Think on it. It'll be refreshing to have men there who do not desire to marry my sister."

Charlotte sat at her dressing table and jiggled her head, once…twice…three times. She searched her reflection in the looking glass for sagging pins, but her coiffure was intact. Her sapphire earbobs were secure, her boots laced. There was nothing remaining on her person to be trussed, buttoned, or bowed, but…where was everyone?

Patty had not returned to inspect her ensemble. Lucy claimed to detect Cook's lemon tarts baking in the oven and hurried belowstairs. Odd that Jacob was not buzzing about her. He was likely in the kitchen, too.

"Patty?" she called. "Lucy?"

Silence.

Did no one care? She had been left alone in her preparations and Hugh was waiting downstairs. And she…well, she…

She swiveled back to her mirror. Her ears were red. A rash? Her cheek was a bit feverish, wasn't it? Lethargy. Most definitely. Perhaps she ought not expose the good viscount to this mysterious female malaise.

"*Wally?*"

Nothing.

Oh, *honestly*! She could not cry off. She was two-and-twenty and many considered her a failure already not to be married. And there was the very real danger of being relegated to the realm of the unmarriageable. Six men now had strongly suggested they would "enjoy the pleasure of her company."

She shook the vile thought aside. Her family must never know she had been treated so. They were proud of how she equipped herself in the First Circles, and she would give them no cause for worry. The time to settle the business of marriage had come. Accepting a man of rank was the correct course for the family. It must be.

If only Mr. Repton were not here every day.

No. *No.* If only his attractions had not attacked her like a fever. From the first sight, she was afflicted by his beauty. And every day, the sight of him allowed no recovery.

It was the worst possible malady—to be in lust with the unfeeling man.

With a mildly depressed sigh, she pushed to her feet and proceeded downstairs to meet the viscount.

"Hello, Hugh." His tulips were lovely, even if they

weren't white, and she warmed at the sight of the caramels on the table. That really was Hugh's loveliest gesture. Jacob adored his sweets.

Deep male voices rumbled in the study and she closed her ears to comprehension. She smiled at her guest. "Hugh, you needn't always bring me such lovely gifts."

"You cannot deny me the pleasure of choosing the lucky blooms that will bask in the sun of your smile."

She laughed as Hugh made an extravagant bow. But when he straightened, his eyes caught on something behind her. Puzzled, she turned her head.

Through the open door of the study, Mr. Repton stood leaning against the desk, watching them. His gaze raked her before he turned his attention back to Ben.

Why must he always look so disapproving of her diversions? And worse, of her dress? If she tried, she might find fault with all manner of his appearance, too.

Well…not today perhaps, as he looked rather handsome in those buff trousers. But a gentleman might have kept his coat on instead of displaying his… admittedly wonderful shoulders in that navy waistcoat.

He dressed rather well of late, not that there was any mystery in that. Wally had shared his tailors with the man. Odd how friendly they were for men with so little common ground.

Hugh raised a wry brow. "I should pay my respects to your brother."

"Oh, that is not necessary."

But Hugh was already entering the study. "How are you, Mr. Paxton? I have come to take this delightful girl on a ride to the Heath. The weather being fine, I could not resist the journey with such a charming companion."

"Yes, you'll not get finer weather," Ben said.

Mr. Repton harrumphed, the small sound infused with disagreement and surprise.

Which was no surprise at all to her.

"What's that, Will?" Ben asked.

"Oh, nothing." But then he shrugged those muscled shoulders. "Just that I saw clouds to the north. I would cover yourself, Miss Baker."

Charlotte looked out the window to a blindingly sunny day.

Mr. Repton frowned at her chest. "A cloak would serve best, actually."

She looked down at her dress. A cloak would utterly ruin the effect.

"Will's right, Charlotte," Ben said. "Tell Patty to bring one for herself, too."

Patty? "But Ben—" He raised a quelling brow. "Yes, of course," she mumbled, feeling like a child.

Was it too much to hope to go out without a chaperone? She *was* two-and-twenty. And many ladies went out driving with their beaux. And their destination was Hampstead Heath, not Gin Lane.

Abashed, she angled a glance at Mr. Repton, who was reading the newspaper as if she were no longer in the room.

She turned to the footman. "Please ask Patty to prepare herself for an outing."

"With cloaks," Ben added.

Will coughed, but when she shot him a suspicious glance, he was nose-deep in his paper.

She mustn't pay any mind to Mr. Repton. The man only spoke to warn her and Hugh against showers and the cold on impossibly beautiful days such as this. *I should wear a hood, Miss Baker. Do you not possess an overcoat, Miss Baker? Do you think it wise to wear that dress, Miss Baker?*

"I do have a gingham in the coach, of course," Hugh said.

Mr. Repton frowned at his reading, lowered his paper, and rubbed his eyes.

They were deeply shadowed today and rimmed red with sleeplessness, so evident in contrast with his blue eyes. How often had she peeked into the study to see him bent low over his papers, as if the weight of his head couldn't be borne by his neck? The man must not sleep well—

He angled from her study and raised his paper higher.

Stuffing her sympathy, she started for the door but something upon Ben's table caught her eye. A small brass statuette of a man and woman, closely facing each other, stood dead center. It appeared Asian.

Oh! Another artifact!

Mr. Repton had brought many to share with the family since his return, and those were her favorite moments because he shared them with her, too.

Or, at least, he did not object when she listened.

But he would have already explained the statue to Ben. He would not like to repeat himself.

Disappointed, she still sidled to the table for a closer look.

The statuette was unlike anything she had ever seen. The male figure had three faces and many outstretched arms, but they embraced a female figure whose leg wrapped around him. The expressions they wore were serene and smiling, as if they were in love.

Every one of the statue's hands held something different—not that she understood what they were. And they stood on some sort of animal. And there were flames radiating from their heads.

She clasped her hands before she touched.

She would not ask. She wouldn't.

Turning from the table, she caught Mr. Repton watching her over the top of his newspaper and she looked away quickly.

"Is this some sort of idol from China, Mr. Repton?" Hugh asked, her delay drawing him to the table.

Her head shot up. *Oh!* Oh good! She flashed a grateful smile at Hugh.

"It's Tibetan." Mr. Repton set the paper down and, to her surprise, moved to stand beside her.

Whenever he presented his treasures, she liked to pretend Mr. Repton spoke to her alone. And positioned as he was, her fantasy was nearly complete. With his back to Hugh, he pulled the statue close so she might better see.

"The crate arrived only yesterday," he murmured. "I'd almost forgotten what I'd shipped."

Because no one asked in the space of a second, she blurted, "Who are they, Mr. Repton?"

"They're Buddhist gods named Hevajra and Nairatmya." He lowered his voice and the timbre sent little prickles to her toes. "They are Tantric deities. In Tibetan Buddhism, this union of male and female symbolizes the union of wisdom and compassion, so they are often shown in this sort of sexual embrace."

Was he serious? She swung about to check his intelligence, but he was looking somewhere in the vicinity of her dropped jaw. She bent to examine the statue closer. A sexual embrace…?

Hugh scoffed. "Are you saying they're engaged in—?"

"But I can't see!" She squinted to see between the two brass-clad bodies. "And which is 'wisdom' and which 'compassion,' Mr. Repton?"

She caught a smile flickering on his lips. Amazed at the sight, she could only murmur, "They're lovely—"

"They're obscene." Hugh laughed loudly.

Her mind blanked at the discourtesy. She looked to Mr. Repton, wanting to apologize for Hugh's behavior if only with her gaze, and he must have felt her focus, for his eyes shifted to hers.

And what she saw burning in their depths made everyone and everything else fade into thin air.

"Here is your girl, Charlotte." Hugh made for the door.

Patty emerged from belowstairs, an eager smile on her lips, so Charlotte smoothed her expression, serene as Hevajra. "Yes…thank you, Patty. We are driving to the Heath." She drew on her gloves.

"Capital." Hugh drew up. "Ah, I nearly forgot my father's missive." He retrieved an envelope from his pocket and handed it to Mr. Repton. "The earl has invited you to a dinner and dance Friday next, Mr. Repton. You will be among friends, as the Paxtons have accepted."

Mr. Repton accepted the invitation as if it were

covered in horse leavings, but, true to form, denied them the satisfaction of an instant reply.

"You must accept, of course." Hugh's voice was tinged with impatience. "Father desires to know you. I should not bring that heathen idol, though." He chuckled. "And there'll be diversions besides dancing. Cards and such. But if that does not tempt you, at the least, you will see what a fine dancer Miss Baker is."

Charlotte colored, piqued at Hugh's continuing obtuseness. "I am sure that is little incentive to anyone." *Come, Mr. Repton. Refuse and we will be on our way.*

"I'd be happy to attend." Mr. Repton returned her astonished stare with a trace of challenge in his own.

Flustered, Charlotte groped blindly for Hugh's arm. "Shall we, Hugh?" He didn't move, but stared rather intently at Mr. Repton. "Hugh?"

"Hm? Oh yes, capital." Hugh bowed his farewell. "Good day, gentlemen."

She made for the door.

"Miss Baker."

Charlotte swung around. Mr. Repton had never called to her before. Yet now he looked as baffled as she that he had.

"Another caution, Mr. Repton?" Hugh asked. "You needn't worry. I'll keep Miss Baker warm."

Mr. Repton's eyes flickered over hers in the instant before his face turned to stone.

It was too fast an exchange for her to understand, but then…that is how Mr. Repton always looked at her. The instant their eyes met, he would look away.

And she was left feeling as if something had been torn from her.

"It's nothing." Mr. Repton turned his back on them.

Her heart sank. What did he mean to say?

"Come, Charlotte," Hugh said.

Ignoring Hugh, she hurried after Mr. Repton and touched his elbow. He turned, his eyes wide with surprise.

"Tell me," she whispered. "The statues. Which is 'wisdom' and which 'compassion,' Mr. Repton?"

His eyes warmed, and he dipped his head to speak low in her ear. "The female is wisdom," he murmured, adding a small grin. "I thought you might have guessed."

Their eyes locked and held. And she wanted to weep from the sweetness of the moment. She nodded, smiling.

She turned and swept out of the room without another word.

But not before collecting her cloak from the foyer table.

Five

Will folded his new coat and set it over a chair in Ben's study. The black fabric, a merino wool-silk blend, was light and soft and the finest garment he owned. The finest he'd *ever* own, likely. And hadn't the tailoring cost him?

But that's what Wallace recommended, so that's what Will bought. He wasn't about to appear at Spencer's ball, in front of Charlotte, in the same suit he wore nearly every day.

He crossed to the window, wanting distance from the coat, from the whole night to come. Evenings like this weren't natural. Dress balls and long dinners and conversations with men who could buy and sell him ten times over weren't natural.

But that was later. More pressing matters were at hand.

Outside, the pavement was empty. Will checked his timepiece. Seth Mayhew was late. Not very, but left alone as he was, Will noticed. The household was upstairs preparing for the ball. Even Jacob had abandoned him, and tonight Will had an errand for him—one he was eager to dispatch before the ladies came down.

Charlotte in a ball gown…he'd never seen that.

He pivoted on his heel and made for the whiskey Wallace had poured him earlier, taking a long, reckless swallow.

Six minutes past.

Would Mayhew help him? They'd never met, but as a fellow plant hunter, might he agree?

The butler appeared at the door. "Mr. Mayhew has arrived, sir."

"Thank you." Will shook out his clenched fists and followed the butler, not wanting to appear as if the servant were his. Mayhew knew Ben had volunteered his conveniently located home for their meeting, but Will felt presumptuous enough without appropriating the servants.

The man in the hall crowded the entry. Seth Mayhew—South American explorer. Or conqueror. Anyone might assume the latter. The man was colossal, broad and imposing as a three-masted Blackwall frigate.

Expeditions *weakened* most men.

"Mr. Mayhew, I'm Will." Will's hand was gripped and pumped hard.

"Call me Seth." The voice boomed in the hall, seeming to sail with the force of a westerly wind. His eyes were sea green and the skin at the corners creased from squinting in the sun. Even his hair was tied back in a queue.

Here was Jacob's pirate.

Will corralled his thoughts and gestured Seth into the study. "Thank you for coming. Ben Paxton is dressing for a dinner."

"Life of the gentry, eh?" Seth grinned, his eyes

sweeping Will's evening kit. "You look a fair bit like Quality yourself."

"I'm only invited because I'm a friend of the family. How was your sail?"

"Stupendous. We didn't shipwreck and we didn't sink."

Will nodded. That really was the only answer to that question. "You were seeking medicinal plants, I understand."

"Among other things." Seth pointed at Will's waistcoat. "Where'd you have that done up?"

Will looked down at his chest. "What?"

Seth's gaze swept the room until his eyes landed on the coat. The burly explorer sprang to his feet and took up Will's pricey garment, holding it at arm's length to inspect it.

"Damn, look at that." Seth's mighty voice was subdued with admiration. "Can't even see the stitches." Seth held the coat toward him. "Would you put it on?"

Will blinked, but pushed to his feet. He wasn't about to deny the man anything. "Certainly."

"I know it ain't fitting to ask, but you're like me in the shoulders and—*see*! That looks fine, *damn* fine. My tailor said I'm not built to wear a suit like that." Seth slapped at his own frock coat with a sneer of disgust. "Said this is the best he could do."

"I'd say that's a sorry excuse. You look well-proportioned to me." Will shook his head. Why the hell were they talking tailors? "I'll, uh…I'll give you the shop's direction." Will cut off a strip of foolscap and wrote down the information.

"Obliged." Seth took a seat, his grin back in place. A question flickered over his face. "Ay? What was you asking before?"

For your help. "Brazil," he said smoothly. "You were hunting medicinal plants, among other things."

"Right. Hardwoods, too. But any ornamentals I found were mine."

"That black orchid with the coral lip you discovered…that's a stunner."

Seth's grin widened. "They named her *Catasetum phantasma.* It means 'ghost orchid.'" He leaned forward. "I'm up to my waist in the Rio Gurupi, water like liquid copper so you can't see to know what's swimming between your legs—*and there she was.* Like a fairy peeking from the moss of a tree. On the ship, I damn near slept with that Wardian case in my arms."

The man was a true plant hunter. It wouldn't occur to him to mention the bit about the orchid selling at auction for a thousand pounds. The money would always be incidental to the prize.

Will had been like that once. Cressey, too.

But it would never be that way again.

Will started cautiously. "Much as I'm curious about your work, I had a purpose in asking to meet today." He paused. "You know what happened in Tibet?"

"I do. Bloody horrible business."

"A relation is offering twenty thousand pounds for the return of the infant."

Seth's eyes widened. "I thought—"

"There's a chance she survived." Will leveled his gaze. "I want you to send word to George."

"Send word to George?" Like a sea change, Seth's

eyes darkened. But that same slow grin stretched across his lips. "George ain't crossing into Tibet."

"Christ, no. I'm not asking—" Will held up a staying hand, a tremor in his fingers. He wanted Seth's help. Desperately, he realized now. But the man wasn't all easy affability, as he seemed. At least not where his family was concerned.

"I need George to spread the news," Will said. "And send word back. I've sent letters throughout Asia. No one's replied."

Seth's glare eased. "No one, eh?"

Will shook his head.

Seth crossed his arms. "Not sure I can reach George anymore. My last letter was addressed poste restante to the Canton post office and never collected. They were supposed to hold it two months..." He cleared his throat. "They held it four. George said Canton, but you know...expeditions don't hold to no schedules. But I'm sending a letter on the next mail steamer. One to Hong Kong, too." He hesitated. "I suppose I can add your news."

"Thank you. Believe me, I'd never encourage George to—"

"Encourage or not, George won't be told anything."

Seth's eyes clouded with regret. No matter the man's grinning mask, he and Seth were the same. Men who left home and didn't marry and told themselves the months, the *years*, spent searching for what didn't exist yet mattered.

Men who weren't afraid of the usual things. Even the right things.

Maybe they just feared different things.

The door cracked open and Jacob, dressed in his sailor suit, peeked in.

"Jacob, come here," Will called.

The boy stopped in his tracks at the sight of Seth, who crossed his arms across his massive chest and winked. "Ahoy there, lad."

"Jacob, this is Mr. Mayhew." Will moved to where he'd set his parcels. "Can you help me with a task?"

Jacob hurried to follow him. "I can do it, Mr. Repton."

After giving Jacob his instructions and setting him off, Will turned back to a grinning Seth.

"So you're courting Paxton's sister-in-law?" Seth asked.

"No!" Will frowned at the brew of emotions the question stirred. "Why?"

Seth hiked a thumb at the door. "You sending the lad upstairs with those."

"I'm a friend of the family."

"Mind your step there, or you'll be a friend *in* the family." Seth chuckled. But interest lit in his eye. "Is she pretty?"

"Uh…is she…?" Will studied the man. Charlotte would like this Seth Mayhew. The man wasn't ugly. And he was well-traveled and friendly and, unlike Will, his only ghosts flowered in the Amazon. "A bit, yes," he mumbled.

Seth sighed, linking his fingers atop his head. "Has no one claimed her yet?"

"Uh—"

"Is she dark or fair? Or redheaded? Is she clever? Quiet women, or ones too severe, don't like me much. When might she be coming down? I can see her myself."

The hell! "She's a lady," he bit out, before remembering he needed the man's help.

Seth barked a laugh. "Then she'll have no truck with the likes of me! The women in Brazil didn't, either. Said I was too damn big for 'em, and I suppose they was right." He winked. "Not that it stopped me from trying."

Will stared. Perhaps he and Seth weren't *exactly* the same.

Seth rubbed his hands together, the mirth in his eyes giving way to a bit of gravity. "Write up your letter to George, but don't count on a reply." He grinned. "But hell, we're plant hunters. We're accustomed to disappointment, aren't we?"

Will stopped his gaze from angling to the ceiling separating him from Charlotte. "Yes. I'd say we are."

The debate over Charlotte's coiffure was two hours old and passions were escalating now that the carriage was being prepared to convey her to the Harlowes' dinner. Charlotte already struggled to feign an iota of pleasure over the evening. She hardly required her maid battling her now.

"Patty, surely you are not serious. Pearls will quite overwhelm the arrangement." Seated at her dressing table, she argued with Patty's reflection in the mirror.

"And you think plumes better?"

"Well, something must be done with these sausages you curled into my hair."

Her maid crossed her arms. "With all respect, Charlotte..."

And at that point, Charlotte ceased to listen. Once Patty uttered "with all respect," the woman's position was intractable and the argument was over.

Pearls it would be.

And they would be appalling.

The evening should have been the highlight of the season. Hugh's family home boasted a magnificent ballroom and all her acquaintance would be there, and best of all, Ben and Lucy, who were never invited to assemblies. And even though it was not quite proper for Lucy to be attending so close to her lying-in, Hugh had insisted.

If only Mr. Repton were not attending…

Wally's frowning head appeared from around the door. "Charlotte, why are you not ready? Will is downstairs."

"I know!" Charlotte snatched her gloves off the table to twist them in her hands. "Why did Ben offer him a seat in our carriage, anyway?"

Wally leaned against the door jamb, raised a brow, and she was ten years old again. "*As you are aware*, Will doesn't even keep a horse."

"He will not enjoy the company. We are far too silly for him," Charlotte said balefully, hoping to be contradicted.

But Wally only squinted at her head. "Pearls?"

She slumped in her chair. "Is he…did Mr. Repton dress properly?"

At this, Wally's eyes brightened. "Actually, Will did not own an evening kit. But he does now and looks very smart, if I say so myself."

"And why would you say so yourself?"

Wally stroked his impeccably cut coat. "I sent him

to my own man, Zegnorelli. The Italians know how to suit a man."

A bouquet of miniature white trumpet-shaped blossoms was thrust beneath her nose and she startled upright. "Oh…how pretty!"

Jacob hopped in excitement beside her, the flowers in his tiny grip. "Mr. Repton brought them for you."

The words were an arrow to her heart. That wasn't true. He would have brought them as a gift to the house. "Are you sure they aren't meant for your mother?" She raised her brows in gentle question.

Jacob shook his head, the joy leeching from his face at her doubt. "Mr. Repton told me to bring them to you. And he brought sweets, but he said those were mine."

"All right, sweetest." She'd not interrogate her nephew further. She kissed his cheek. "Thank you."

Patty took a closer look. "Goodness, aren't those fine?" She turned to her with a grin. "I have an idea."

Moments later, her hair was divested of pearls and dressed with a few sprigs of the white blossoms, and both maid and fastidious brother agreed Mr. Repton's flowers were the perfect complement to her ivory ball gown.

She really was the most fortunate of ladies. Her family was so generous in her clothing allowance that she was always *la mode.* The silk was light as air, and delicate seed pearls sewn along the edge of her bodice glinted at her bosom. And even if the neckline was low and the waist tightly cinched, she had no doubt of its propriety.

She looked rather well this evening and pulled a face at the irony of it all. Mr. Repton did not notice any dress she wore. Ever. Unless it was to judge them entirely unsuitable against London's many monsoons and gale-force winds.

She straightened a pearl on her beautiful gown. And it *was* a terribly beautiful gown.

Perhaps he will notice tonight…

Frowning at her own foolishness, she pulled on her gloves, and walked down the stairs with Wally and Jacob.

Mr. Repton would not speak to her. She must not hope or allow him to depress her. Arranging her face into a mask of placidity, she entered the front parlor. Mr. Repton faced the door and she couldn't avoid his eye upon entering. She looked away quickly.

Or as quickly as she could.

Goodness but the man was fine in black. So this is how the man of her dreams appeared by lamplight. His hair gleamed low and rich as antique gold, and the suit clung to his powerful shoulders and hugged his lean hips.

She'd never seen a man so blatantly handsome. And so…*disconcerting*. Transformed into the sort of seductive rake ruinous to a woman's heart—yet not at all suited to the role, serious as death as he always was.

But tonight he was different. Very different. He'd never kept his gaze on her this long before.

Or her bosom.

Carefully keeping her chin level rather than check her décolletage for what else might be drawing Mr. Repton's focus, she sat on the divan.

Men could not help but assuage their curiosity, she supposed. Day dresses covered a lady with all modesty, but evening gowns were another matter. She did credit him for his discretion; his eyes bounced right back up and away. And he was a man, after all, and a man might *look*.

She just had not expected—well, *male* attention from Mr. Repton.

Oh dear. He was looking at them again.

"Another?" Wally asked, indicating Will's glass of whiskey.

"Uh, yes. Thank you," he said.

"I see Mr. Mayhew is gone," Wally said.

Will replied that, yes, this mysterious Mr. Mayhew had come and gone and nothing more. Surely it was not polite to reply in so abbreviated a manner? Not while she sat stewing in curiosity.

Reminded she had not yet greeted him, she waited for Wally to see to Mr. Repton's drink. Always, *always*, she was the first to speak. They might not speak at all if not for her overtures. "Good evening, Mr. Repton."

He bowed, his eyes catching on the jasmine in her hair.

"Thank you for our bouquet." She checked one of the delicate flowers in her hair, and aware the gesture might appear coquettish, dropped her hand. "I have never seen such flowers, and was so charmed, I wore them in my hair."

He looked into his whiskey. "I'm sure I've never seen jasmine in a lovelier setting."

She laughed with surprise, the sound harder than she intended. "Pretty words, Mr. Repton."

His eyes swung to hers.

"Charlotte." Wally lowered his brows in censure. "You are usually much more accepting of compliments. Mr. Repton will be shy of you in future."

Shy, indeed. But her heart was already sinking. Mr. Repton would welcome any excuse to avoid her tonight. And she had given him one.

She could not help that she did not possess the gravitas he preferred. And she would not be made to feel gauche, or silly, or—*bother it all*—lower than she already felt.

She flashed what she hoped was an unconcerned smile. "I am sorry, Mr. Repton, but you must be cautious with such a declaration. If you recall, you wrote of your encounters with night-blooming jasmine in the valley of the Li River. How that was the most magnificent landscape of your life. That there was not a sight on earth to rival it."

Mr. Repton held her gaze silently and she returned it with studied naiveté.

"That passage was among the volumes *forbidden* for my reading, of course. But you will pardon my transgression, won't you?"

Mr. Repton's hand flexed on his glass but he said nothing.

Of course he didn't.

With his near-daily presence in Ben's study, she had approached him a dozen times—out of the demands of politeness, out of sincere curiosity, out of a pathetic need just to be near him.

And each time he begged her pardon and sent her off. He shared nothing of himself.

Even when he shared his artifacts, it was not as if he invited her to listen.

"Do I not have it right, Mr. Repton?" she pressed, a strange desperation rising in her. "A few blossoms wilting in a woman's coiffure would hardly compare to such a view. And while the ladies' magazines like to assure us a man in love may hold the sight of his beloved above any of God's creations, that is hardly the case between us. Not that I am at all convinced that sort of emotion is even possible among the English. The *Italians*, yes, but—"

"I don't know this style of fashionable conversation, Miss Baker." Mr. Repton looked away, a muscle clenching in his jaw. "You'll forgive me."

The mild rebuke sent heat rushing to her cheeks.

What was the matter with her? She, who had always been so adept at conversation, at pretty behavior, could not put a step right with him. Even Jacob pouted reproachfully at her.

"In any case, the flowers are lovely," she said quietly. "And Hugh has never done half so well."

"Why hasn't he?" Mr. Repton set his glass down hard on the mantel.

"I beg your pardon?"

"Spencer. Why hasn't he learned your favorite flowers?"

"Well..."

"He brings you tulips and roses and carnations. Never snowdrops or narcissus or lily of the valley, not that those are your favorites. Neither is jasmine, but I thought you'd like how the perfume changes at night. Never once have I seen him bring you peonies."

She could only stare back.

"White peonies, right?" He considered her, his voice gentling. "No—*cream*. With a pink blush at its heart, marked by stripes of raspberry and a tangle of gold stamens within, revealed only in bloom." He blinked and diverted his stare. "That is your favorite, I think."

"Yes. How did—?"

"Mr. Repton, how dashing you look!" Lucy exclaimed as she entered with Ben.

To her relief, Mr. Repton moved to greet them. Already feeling bruised, a flare of jealousy stabbed her as he sketched a bow to Lucy and rose with a smile.

Mr. Repton took Lucy's hand. "Mrs. Paxton, you're looking extremely well this evening."

"Are you going to give Mama her flowers?" Jacob piped from his chair.

"We received the flowers, Jacob," Wally said. "The jasmine, remember?"

But Mr. Repton moved toward the window seat and produced a bouquet of long-stemmed roses that had been hidden from view. "My apologies. I should have sent these up earlier. They're from my father's garden."

Lucy clasped her hands in delight. Ben must have told him yellow roses were her favorite.

So he had intended the jasmine for her alone…

The first time Mr. Repton offered her a kindness and she'd dashed his efforts to the ground and stomped on it like a child. No lady of sense or breeding would act as she had done.

Tonight was going to be interminable.

Lucy smiled at her. "Charlotte, what beautiful flowers in your hair."

Miserable, she pasted on her smile. "Yes, Mr. Repton brought them."

Ben stepped closer. "Madagascar jasmine? How

in the world did you manage these, Will? They're rare flowers."

Mr. Repton crossed his arms and his eyes skimmed hers before traveling to the drapes, the ceiling, the mantel where his whiskey waited. He made for the drink. "The, uh…Chiswick cultivates several varieties and Cavendish allowed me—"

"The Duke of Devonshire?" Ben asked.

"Right." Will picked up his glass and held it.

The room fell silent, contemplating this rather impressive connection to one of England's most powerful men. Until the contemplation pivoted to her head—and undoubtedly the presumption of beheading a duke's prized flowers to ornament one's hair.

A clearing of the throat sounded from the door, and Mr. Goodley announced the carriage was ready.

Ben helped Lucy into her mantle and Wally hoisted Jacob into his arms to walk them to the door. Charlotte followed, and stood on tiptoe to kiss her brother good night. "I wish you were coming with us," she whispered.

And Wally answered as he always did. "Next time, dear heart."

"Miss Baker?" Mr. Repton signaled her to precede him from the room. Of course the man would not offer his arm.

Ben and Lucy settled in the carriage and, as always, Ben leaned across the carriage to speak close with his wife.

"Ben, do please sit beside Lucy," Charlotte said. "It will pain me to watch you bent at that angle for our entire journey."

Ben grinned his thanks and complied, and Charlotte slid over as far as she could on the bench as Mr. Repton took his seat beside her.

"You must see the Harlowes' hothouse this evening, Mr. Repton," Lucy said as the carriage rolled into motion. "It is one of Ben's designs and perfectly exquisite."

"I wouldn't miss it," Mr. Repton said.

"Let's see it together," Lucy added. "Charlotte, leave the second waltz open to join us."

Will sensed Charlotte's body stiffen. She would resent not dancing with her beau to entertain him.

It was his aim, wasn't it? And the task was accomplished. Charlotte Baker was thoroughly disenchanted with Chinese Will.

And she'd laughed at his compliment.

Across the carriage, Mrs. Paxton put a hand to her back. She was increasing, and no matter how luxurious and well-sprung the vehicle, it was obvious she was uncomfortable. Ben was immediately solicitous, murmuring into her ear and rubbing her back. And preoccupied as they were, the silence between Charlotte and himself grew heavy.

Will crossed his arms and flicked a surreptitious glance at her. The discretion wasn't necessary. She was looking out her window.

There *was* a sight to rival the Li River Valley, and that was Charlotte in her angel's gown, with jasmine in her hair. If he somehow lived to be old and past dreaming, he'd always have that to remember.

God, she was a beauty. Why was it the sight of her

unleashed some new temptation? He was not a man who indulged in anything, yet at this moment, he was tempted to pluck a blossom from her hair to crush against his lips, to release those silken curls from their pins and watch them pool on her shoulders, to touch her…

All of her was temptation. He stole another look at her breasts. He'd always known they were ample—any man would guess that from the shape of her in her day dresses—but he wasn't prepared to be rendered speechless by the flesh. The creamy perfection of that skin. The proud, magnificent shape of them.

How had he missed those before? He'd seen her leave for balls. Countless times. But then, there'd only been the sound of slippers from the hall to alert him. And by the time he raised his head, she would sweep by in a blur, a fluttering hem the only clue of what she wore.

It was better he hadn't seen.

So damn beautiful. And yet she wasn't self-admiring. Or maybe she just wasn't coy with him. At least not since the day in the study. He grimaced at the memory. Hadn't he buggered that one good? They might have been friendly. Even friends.

Now all he had were the moments he dangled some trinket from his travels to lure her close. The jade amulets, the prayer wheel, the rosary of amber beads—he must have brought two dozen artifacts by now. Those exchanges were safe. An acceptable level of involvement.

And completely pathetic.

He took a deep breath. Somehow he would make peace with Charlotte Baker. He needed more peace in his life. It was bad enough to wake each day to a nightmare, to the knowledge he still had hundreds of pounds to raise, to the reality his letters hadn't persuaded one soul to search for Aimee Bourianne.

His thoughts were turning down a dark path. He looked out the window. At nothing. Ben and his wife were speaking low, and Charlotte hadn't stopped staring out her window.

He might try to speak with her to…well, because… *Hell*, just because.

"Forgive me if I don't ask you to dance this evening," Will said to draw Charlotte's attention.

She blinked with what appeared to be surprise. "Of course, Mr. Repton. You are under no obligation."

"That's not—I won't be dancing with anyone."

She was wearing the same thin smile she always wore with him these days. "I see." She turned away.

A pain cramped his heart. He stiffened his jaw and stared at the back of her head. At the row of pearl buttons down her back. Out his bloody window again. That went as well as he expected—

"Did you…did you dance before?" Charlotte asked.

Jesus, thank you. He swiveled his head back. "Before?"

"Before your injury?"

"Yes. But never at a ball. Public dances only."

"And you enjoyed dancing?"

He shrugged. "I suppose, but I wasn't skilled. Even my mum, who indulges me in everything, begged me not to dance and shame the family name. And this from a woman whose husband scolds the aphids on rose bushes."

She searched his eyes a quiet moment, then, to his

astonishment, a *real* smile softened her lips. Cresting Mount Everest couldn't have been more satisfying.

"I suppose I will forgive you so long as I do not see you dancing the Portland Polka with all the other ladies in the room."

Will lifted his gaze from her smiling lips and nodded mutely. How quickly would he muck this up?

"Though you may change your mind once you see Lady Sybil." Her cheek dimpled. "You will fall hopelessly in love with her. Everyone does."

God, he'd missed that dimple. "I wonder," he murmured. "Will she have jasmine in her hair, too?"

That chased her smile away.

Ah, hell. Stupid, *stupid* thing to say.

She checked the jasmine in her hair, and if she were anyone but the incomparable Charlotte Baker, he might have thought her shy.

"I—well…these are rare, aren't they?" she said.

"Extremely," he said huskily.

And the way she dropped her eyes, she must have guessed he wasn't speaking of the flowers.

She folded her hands in her lap. "Have you tried to dance? I see you walk gracefully when you are not used up by the day. Your leg seems to pain you more in the evening."

So she'd taken a study of him? But then, he never limped as bad as he might when she was near. "I've not tried, no. You'll be committed for every dance, I imagine. Lord Spencer might claim them all."

"Oh, no. It is not good *ton* to reveal partiality to any one lady."

"Right…good *ton*." He flexed his fingers inside his

new kidskin gloves. Damn things barely kept his hands warm on a May night. “I don’t know Lord Spencer. Is he deserving of you, then?”

“Deserving of me?” Charlotte leaned on her arm to speak close, granting him a breathtaking view of her breasts. “He is far above me in rank and consequence. You mustn’t say such things aloud this evening, Mr. Repton, and presume upon the good graces of our betters.”

God, her smile was adorable. If she were his, she’d not get away with that. Not without a kiss.

A kiss flat on her back.

“But I suppose you will be forgiven a great deal,” she said. “After all, you are the intrepid explorer, leaving sighing females and applauding aristocrats in your wake.”

He raised a brow. “That’s one of the more ridiculous things I’ve ever heard.”

Her eyes, at last unguarded and curious, roamed his face. She’d not looked at him like that for weeks, for an eternity.

“We shall see, Mr. Repton. Would you care to wager upon the level of excitement your presence will inspire?”

“That sounds a humiliating wager. Would you require ladies faint straight away upon meeting me? Or the men hoist me atop their shoulders and march me around the ballroom?”

She laughed, and his stomach—and parts lower—tightened pleasurably in response.

“You will be the most sought-after man this evening, I’m afraid. Trust a veteran of three seasons and three hundred soirees, fetes, and flower shows.” She fixed her big blue eyes on him, and by the dim light of the carriage lamps, he could have sworn they looked sad. "There is no one like you. You are a hero."

Before he could puzzle out her quiet words, she continued more brightly. "You cannot hope to avoid attention tonight. But if you do not wish to wager..." She shrugged, a small smile on her lips.

He leaned toward that smile. "I'll take your wager, Miss Baker, because I'm sure to be ignored."

"You cannot really think so?"

"I can and I really do," he murmured. "I only hope I can keep from slurping my soup at dinner. And speaking endlessly of the challenge of cleaning my linens at camp. And I pray I don't find Lord Spencer's mum irresistible and try to steal a kiss in a darkened alcove."

Her eyes widened in amused horror. "That is not fair. You cannot pretend to be dull or boorish or... just odd."

"Now you're confusing me. You know I won't have to pretend. And I've always been drawn to matronly women."

Laughter burst from her, before her gloved hands stifled that pleasing sound.

Will couldn't stop looking at her happy face. He'd never made her laugh before. And he liked it far more than he should. "What do you forfeit when I win, Miss Baker?"

"I do not wish to wager anymore," she said, her eyes bright with mirth.

Here was the genuine Charlotte Baker—unguarded, full of joy, irresistible. He'd recognized that in the first seconds of meeting her.

And he'd fled her ever since.

He sat back. "No wager…you concede I am dull then?"

"I concede no such thing, but you are contrary enough to spoil this challenge for me. So no wager and no excuse not to charm the *beau monde* with tales of adventure."

Charlotte leaned close to whisper a great secret, which amused him, as there was only the two of them on that carriage bench. "And I daresay, Mr. Repton, you may make several conquests this evening."

"Conquests?"

"Of investors in your next expedition."

"Ah, right, investors. When would you suggest I rattle the tin cup?"

"Mock me if you wish, but many gentlemen are keen to speak with you. Marquis Palmerton and Lord Russell have already asked my account of you and—"

"And what was your account of me?"

Her beautiful eyes shied from his, but he angled his head to look into her face. Because he desperately needed to know.

"The house looks lovely, Charlotte."

Will started at Lucy's voice. He'd forgotten the Paxtons were there. Just like his father—too engrossed in his wife to pay attention to the world around him.

Just like his besotted father…the idea rendered him speechless.

The carriage slowed. Through the window, the earl's house loomed. Flickering torchlight dramatized the stone facade, and the white-frocked ladies twirling beyond the glazed windows reminded him of bubbling champagne.

A sparkling home.

It suited Charlotte.

The footman opened the carriage door and Will stepped out, turning to help Charlotte alight. But before he could hand her down, Spencer appeared and claimed the right.

The magic carriage ride was over.

The entry hall was ablaze with candlelight. The sparkling crystal drops from the chandelier above reflected rainbow shards of light onto Charlotte's gown, and her skin shimmered like a pearl as she moved into the crowded ballroom.

The ceiling soared and massive canvasses of pastoral landscapes covered the walls. Candlesticks circled the ballroom and bouquets of lilies and hydrangeas perfumed the air.

It was all so…exuberant. Like Charlotte herself.

Yes, it suited her.

They'd laughed and spoken easily in the carriage. They might have even flirted, but he was no fool. Even if he were free to court her, she'd not belong in his world.

She belonged in this one.

Good. He tried to force some conviction behind the thought. It was good. A married woman was not a distraction and the sooner Charlotte was married, the better.

Now where was this Earl of Harlowe and his deep pockets?

Six

The Earl of Harlowe's dining room wasn't so much a room as a hall, and not so much a hall as an arena. An army of footmen lined the walls to begin the dinner service, and instead of one long banqueting table, there were two dozen tables arranged about the room.

All very impressive. All excessively grand. But the splendor of the room was nothing compared to the carriage ride.

Mr. Repton had spoken to her! Of his own volition. Without frowning much at all. She must do nothing to derail this fragile friendship.

She took her seat, but how would she sit still?

Her family and Mr. Repton were seated with Hugh, his parents, and twin sisters, Helen and Hester.

Oh dear. The table was set for dinner served *à la russe*, with nine utensils and five glasses at the ready. He had joked, but what if Mr. Repton *did* slurp his soup? Would he know which glass to use for the champagne, the sherry, and the hock? She'd only ever seen him drink tea and gobble a few biscuits at the house. After all, what use would a plantsman have for table etiquette?

A little faith, Charlotte. Mr. Repton would not flounder. Besides, in this intimate seating arrangement, he need only acquaint himself with Hugh's parents and the golden-haired twins who flanked him.

And it appeared Mr. Repton had made fast work of acquainting himself with the twins.

"How ever did you bear those long months at sea, Mr. Repton?" Hester asked.

"You are terribly brave," Helen cried, "to travel to such an uncivilized land."

The twins were posed on either side of Mr. Repton, their hands clutched to their bosoms, pushing their breasts into a decidedly vulgar display. Charlotte thinned her lips in disapproval at the spectacle. Not that the man didn't appear entirely pleased with the novelty of two matched females.

She was tempted to throw her finger bowl straight at their pointy little heads, but she was a lady. And it was certainly no concern of hers if Mr. Repton's gaze was more occupied with cleavage than consommé.

Which was cold and far too salty.

"Yes, enlighten us of the Orientals, Mr. Repton." Hugh's father, Lord Harlowe, was a red-faced, blustery walrus of a man who saved his conversation exclusively for men. His heavily bagged eyes would linger indecently on female flesh—the younger the better—but evidently he found them useless for intellectual stimulation. "Were the coolies difficult to manage?"

"Not at all. The native people purchased our supplies and procured our shelter—things Englishmen could not do outside the port cities. And they were immune to many fevers plaguing the Englishmen. They were strong and hardy, though they did not stand even as tall as Miss Baker."

Lord Harlowe laughed his wheezing laugh. "As small as a woman? They must have been useless carrying supplies."

Mr. Repton paused in lifting his spoon from his soup at the words. He met her gaze and looked pointedly at his spoon with a quirk of his brow before lifting it to his lips and drinking. Without a slurp.

Cheeky. She hid her smile behind her napkin.

In that second, in the lock of their eyes, a shared laugh passed between them. And it unnerved her how wonderful that felt.

"On the contrary, my lord," Mr. Repton continued placidly, "when I fell ill with fever in the jungle, the men fashioned a sort of palanquin out of bamboo and canvas and carried me for hours to make our camp."

The twins gasped in horror and pity, breasts squeezed into sympathetic service again.

"They saved my life on more than one occasion," Mr. Repton said. "Though when they carried me uphill in that palanquin like a baby in a sling, their revenge was not allowing me the comfort of riding backward, so my feet were always higher than my head."

The table burst into laughter and when Mr. Repton's eyes sought hers, she was spun with a giddy, whirling delight.

The next course came, and the next, and Mr. Repton was a great success. Lord and Lady Harlowe appeared delighted with his fascinating stories and were not once diverted by his table manners, which were perfectly correct. The twins were breathlessly in love, and there were a number of women who were casting far too deliberate glances his way—the cattle.

And with each passing course, she grew more depressed. Mr. Repton had not let her know anything of him for weeks now. She knew his face and fame would awe. She knew, had he loved her, they would have Society at their feet and her family would have friends in their future. But she had not known how clever and charming and humble he was. Until tonight.

The truth barreled over her, crushing her and her precious jasmine blossoms into the Chippendale chair—he shared nothing because he had no real wish to know her. Tonight, he had no choice but to be amiable to all her wealthy acquaintance. Tomorrow, all would be as before.

Why else would his eyes linger as they did on the silver ice baths chilling their champagne glasses? Or flicker over the diamond bracelets on Hester's wrists? Or rest on her with that strange distance? It was as though he were witnessing the evening as a spectator.

Or, as he would take their money, a speculator.

"Hugh, why did you not tell us of Mr. Repton's travels?" Hester scolded her brother.

"Yes, I want to go to Asia now," Helen said. "Would that not be romantic, Charlotte?"

She startled at having a question from either twin directed at her. The sisters tended to ignore other females if there was a bachelor within ten paces. "Yes, Asia would be the adventure of a lifetime, would it not?"

Lord Harlowe barked a rude laugh. Goodness, how the man could be Hugh's father…

"But there are adventures to be had right here in England. In Snowdonia. Or Cumbria." She smiled at Hugh. "I hope to explore myself someday."

Hugh laughed. "Oh, my dear. I am imagining the number of porters required to carry your hatboxes."

"Are you imagining an escort for her as well?" Lord Harlowe sneered. "Everyone knows you are no adventurer, boy."

Charlotte tensed and the table fell silent. Hugh's fingers curled around his knife. Oh dear…

She touched Hugh's arm and smiled. "I think I could limit my wardrobe, my lord. There are just so many wonderful reports published by the Geographical Society—"

"But women are still banned from the club," Lord Harlowe hastily assured the table.

She looked at Harlowe while he looked at her bosom.

"The north of England is hardly exotic, Charlotte," Hester said.

"Quiet, girl," Lord Harlowe said. "The north can test a man. When I was your age, I summited Cross Fell in the Pennines. But I possess a constitution like Repton here. Vigorous, keen for a challenge. Some *men* wallow in their infirmities"—he eyed Hugh—"others rise to every hardship they accept."

The knife in Hugh's fist quaked.

"I would agree with Lady Hester, I fear." She hurried to speak in the silence. "Cumbria is not exotic in comparison to Mr. Repton's travels."

She knew her eyes lingered too often on Mr.

Repton, so she started with guilt when Hugh touched her hand beneath the table. He was always attentive, always a gentleman. And so clearly of late *her* gentleman. But tonight there was an anger coursing through him that she could only attribute to his boor of a father.

"It will pain me to dance with anyone but you," Hugh whispered. "Do not forget to save me the first two waltzes."

"Oh, but I am committed for the second," she said. "We are to show Mr. Repton your mother's conservatory."

"Indeed?"

"I would much rather dance."

"Well...we mustn't be uncharitable, my dear. The man is lame. A stroll in the garden may be the highlight of Mr. Repton's evening."

Charlotte stiffened but could not search Hugh's eyes for cruelty, as his lips were at her ear. Across the table, Mr. Repton watched her with a hooded stare. As if he had heard.

Helen lured his attention back with a touch of his arm and he smiled at her.

Honestly. She could not be jealous, she *would* not be.

All this time, Mr. Repton had painted himself the most aloof man in London to her alone. She could not let one night—one uncharacteristic night—lower the wall she'd erected around her heart. No one made a fool of Charlotte Baker twice.

Well...she was far beyond twice at this point, but never again.

For one evening, Mr. Repton had extended an olive branch and she would not let this rare opportunity pass.

How ridiculous she was. But she could not deny how much she wanted to know him a little.

Let's just see Mr. Repton avoid her friendship tonight.

Charlotte Baker never sat down.

Of course the evening would play like this. Will had prepared for it. He was just surprised at how little he liked watching her dance.

Spencer had waltzed nicely with her—and that was fine, he supposed. But she'd never dance again with that bastard she had to wrestle to keep at a proper distance. And the short one with the fading hairline peered too often down her dress.

Off the floor, the men were no better. They touched her too freely—her arm, her shoulder, the small of her back. They bent too close. They *leaned*. And the bloody Earl of Harlowe—he wanted to smash in the man's face at the way he leered. Much more of this and he'd—

He ground his teeth. He'd not do a damn thing. He had no claim on her. And Harlowe had all but promised three hundred pounds—double the ask he'd intended to make.

Did these bastards know nothing? She was a lady—anyone could see that. The best in the room. Damn them all, the Quality *did* treat her different, just as Ben said. She was popular but she wasn't one of them. Not yet. But once she married Spencer—

He snorted. *Spencer*. Who never brought her white flowers. Whose father was an upright ape.

He shook the thought aside. Where was Ben, anyway? She was *his* sister-in-law. He ought to be in the card room, pitching his expedition into every open ear. Instead he was playing chaperone so some gent wouldn't drag Charlotte down a darkened hall.

The dance ended and Charlotte gestured for her partner to deliver her to him. What was this? He looked left and right to see if she'd intended someone else.

She curtsied to her dance partner. "Thank you, my lord. You are the loveliest dancer."

The man pitched forward in his haste to bow. Will didn't even try to muster a nod for the beaming, red-faced man even though *this one* had behaved. Dazzled as the gent was, he staggered a half-dozen steps and predictably plowed into a passing couple.

Will turned back to a glowing Charlotte. Her smile faded and only then did he realize he was still wearing the narrow-eyed glare he'd trained on the lummox with her.

"No need to look so set upon, Mr. Repton," she teased, but her voice sounded strained for the effect. "I have not come to wrestle you onto the floor. This is the second waltz, and we are to gaze rapturously at Lady Harlowe's glasshouse."

The second waltz already? Should he have known that? Was there an order to these things?

Charlotte looked about. "Where are Ben and Lucy?"

"I've not seen them since supper."

Will didn't miss the droop of her shoulders, the small pout of her lips. He crossed his arms and refused to look at her disappointed face. She could sit out one bloody dance, especially if it only offered another manhandling by some fresh lecher.

"I suppose it would be improper for us to go alone," she said.

Damn it all, the second waltz. *Where the devil was Ben Paxton?*

"It's warm," he muttered, his vision full of all the men who'd touched her this evening. His complaint hung in the air but damned if he knew how to break the silence. The fact that she'd be dancing with nearly every man but him stung deeper than he cared to admit.

She started as if remembering something. "Oh! We might take some air on the terrace."

The terrace? Charlotte's hand slid around his elbow and her upturned face wore a look of expectation.

Right. Charlotte Baker wouldn't stand about like a wallflower. It was humbling enough for a lady like her to be paired with him. He led her toward the doors before her embarrassment grew any more acute.

The terrace was cool and dark after the heated ballroom and its blazing chandeliers. From their vantage point, the milky glasshouse rose behind the black form of a hedge. Stone steps led to the garden below, replete with twinkling fireflies and glowing lanterns strung in the trees. Ironically, peonies with their petals blown wide perfumed the air.

A jealous man might mention how easily Spencer could deliver her a bouquet. But the fact wouldn't be lost on clever Charlotte anyway. Besides, he needed to keep his mouth shut or she'd ask—

"How did you know peonies were my favorite?"

Damn.

"I have never told anyone."

He brushed an invisible leaf off the stone railing. "I don't know. They match you."

"Match me?" She frowned, appearing to consider

this. "They are stupidly provoking flowers. They drop their petals if you so much as look at them, and their blooms are too big for their own stems."

"Yet they're adored. And flamboyant and messy, but so charming no one minds." He looked at her, his gaze roaming her exquisite face. "A stunning beauty. So voluptuous and impossibly pretty, all others pale beside her."

She stared and, hearing his own words, he cringed. Hell, it was nearly a declaration.

He looked out over the lawn. The conservatory stood far from the house. "I, uh…I suppose we shouldn't venture down there without a chaperone."

"I suppose not," she whispered.

He slumped on the stone railing and prepared for the next silence. She'd leave him soon enough. She'd pretend fatigue or thirst or a loose bit or bob from her dress—

"Perhaps Ben and Lucy are at the glasshouse."

He kicked the balustrade, not caring if he scuffed the new leather. "Perhaps."

She looked at the ballroom, then the lawn, then at him. "Well then. Shall we?"

He blinked. "Shall we what?"

"Join them, of course." She slipped her hand round his arm and pulled him off the railing. She cast a furtive glance over her shoulder and started down the stairs with his carcass in tow. "For all we know, they are waiting for us, Mr. Repton. Now that I think on it, it is just the sort of thing they might do, do you not agree?"

He didn't at all but his heart rallied, some mad

excitement fluttering there. "Are you sure this is proper, Miss Baker? Your leading me down a moonlit garden?"

"Hush, I most certainly am not." Her lips pressed against a smile. "Quickly, please."

They hurried down the steps, and so she wouldn't feel his limp, he bore the pain of bending his knee deep. Reaching the lawn, Will's ache eased quickly. It was getting stronger every day. Surely by August—

Charlotte tugged him forward. An arched gate was carved into an ancient yew hedge and the glasshouse was framed within its entrance. Their approach should have been dignified and reverent, but Charlotte dropped his hand and ran ahead, stretching her neck a time or two to check no one saw from the house.

No, this wasn't proper at all.

Chuckling, he jogged after her, admiring the grace of her slender back and flouncing skirts. It was nonsense. It was, without a doubt, a horrible idea.

And it was damn fun.

God, what a strange night this was. He'd not felt this in years. In forever. Right now, and across the dinner table, and in the carriage, she pulled back the curtain and flooded his cold world with sun.

She made him happy, she made him want.

God help him, she made him forget.

Charlotte slowed to a stop before the conservatory, panting lightly from the run. "Beautiful, isn't it?"

He'd rather study the way the moonlight glossed the ringlets of her hair and transformed the blue of her eyes into something electric, but he obligingly took in the large conservatory.

Paxton's design was a miracle of curved glass

encased within a delicate filigree of scrolled ironwork. With the perfumed garden and Charlotte beside him, a fairy-tale landscape if ever there was one. "Very, but Ben's stoves are foremost functional. See the plants flourishing within?"

She groaned, but it was a very ladylike groan. "What an obscenely practical thing to say."

He bit back a smile. "It's why I chose Ben. A plant finder is only as good as his cultivator back home."

She frowned a little as she studied him—perhaps she wondered at this new thaw between them, as he did.

To his surprise, she reached for the door. Automatically, he stretched an arm across the threshold to block her entry. The move brought him close and the scent of jasmine heated him in the cool night air.

Did she think him too large for her?

It was a stupid, errant thought...but he was as muscled as he'd ever been, and the top of her head only reached his chin. That made her taller than most ladies, yet everything about Charlotte was delicate as a flower.

And the difference in their sizes was stirring something dangerous in him.

She tilted her head and her eyes were questioning. It took him a moment to speak. "I can't let you enter in that white frock. You'll brush against a muddy pot."

She smiled and released the door. "This gown will never do for exploring."

Granted permission of a sort, he studied the body and to hell with the dress. This close, he could almost feel that satiny skin and the pressure of her corset on her round breasts, forming that glorious valley between. The perfection of her shoulders. The delicate line of her collarbone. The impossibly small waist and glorious curves of her hips. *Good God, Charlotte.*

He swallowed, his mouth dry as the Tibetan high plain. "You're very beautiful in it."

A blush rose on her cheeks. And even in the dark, he could see the blue of her eyes.

"Did Wallace send you to his dressmaker, too?" he joked weakly.

Her eyes sharpened, searching and strangely indignant. He was rubbish at compliments—but still surprised when she started down the long avenue of lawn. He hurried to walk abreast of her. "It's a pretty dress is what I mean to say."

Her steps slowed. "You speak with my brother often."

Confused, he nodded.

"What do you two speak of?"

"Many things. Books, industry—and tailors. He recommended the man who made this suit."

"You look very fine in it," she said softly.

He barely kept the stupid grin off his face. He'd taken pains with his clothes since meeting her, and never more so than tonight. It was sheer vanity, but he wanted her to see him in something as smart as what her viscount might don.

Idiot. What was the point of new clothes? The bouquet of rare jasmine? The rush for roses for Lucy to distract from the gesture? He might have used those funds in Tibet to loosen a tongue or open a door.

"I am glad you are friends. Wally cannot—he attends few assemblies." She paused. "Did you know of his trial?"

Everyone knew of the trial, of the accusation that Wallace and the late earl were lovers. What made the moment awkward was that he knew the charge to be true.

His father had learned the truth from Ben. Wallace's inclinations were to men and while he lived a chaste life to avoid drawing further scandal to the family, the gossip never died. The sodomy trial had ensured that.

"I knew," he said.

"You do not seem disturbed by it. Everyone else is."

Her voice was sad, and though this was the incomparable Charlotte Baker, he nearly buckled from the tenderness flooding him. That hurt her. Of course that hurt her. She loved her family, she was full of love for—

Stop it.

The voice was familiar. The same voice every time he thought too long on Charlotte. *Enough*, it said when his eyes lingered. *Focus*, when her steps passed in the hall. *Faster, harder*, when he slowed his hand to imagine making love to her rather than jerking to reach a swift release.

He tried to shrug off the tenderness. "Those men are only disgruntled their bespoke suits aren't half as elegant as his."

She stared straight ahead. "We should return."

Damn. "No, I…I'm not disturbed by it." Christ, she looked so sad. "When I was a lad, my father impressed upon me that there's almost infinite diversity in nature. In flora and fauna. My cousin raises sheep, and every odd season there's one ram that refuses to breed with the females and mates only with males. In Asia, I saw snow monkeys do the same."

She stood still—to better hear how he would bungle this, no doubt. "I don't mean to speak of sheep...but there is *purpose* in nature. And if something exists in nature, I think we must at least try to understand any animal acting upon his nature, including man, cannot be seen as unnatural. My father believed as much and so do I."

She looked at him steadily and he prepared to be chastised for his philosophizing. Or worse.

But then her face transformed with happiness and... something *more*. Something—

Stop it, STOP IT—

Something so vulnerable that he ignored that stupid, hated voice. Because all he wanted, in all the world, was just to hold her and tell her everything would be all right.

"I think I will like your father very much," she said quietly.

He breathed a quiet sigh of relief and nearly chuckled, imagining his father meeting Charlotte. He'd have to warn Mum to lay out his clothes or he'd be meeting her in a clashing suit.

They walked deeper into the garden.

"Ben says your father is a brilliant botanist," she said.

"He's certainly that. And distractible and utterly dependent on my mother. And she on him, I suppose."

"They're friends?"

"The best of friends."

"That's lovely. Lucy and Ben are like that. I think we are fortunate, Mr. Repton, to know what to aspire to in marriage."

"Is that what you aspire to?"

"Of course."

How sure she was. And yet Spencer, bloody *Spencer*, with his smirk and tulips…

"So you know it's not just friendship. It's passion, connection, wanting to do anything for the other's happiness. Like my parents do for each other. Like—" This was none of his business.

None at all.

He shrugged. "As you're of a mind to marry, it's good you don't find the prospect of finding such a companion as daunting as I."

Now Mr. Repton thought her naive as well as silly. Well. She should have known better than to speak of such things. The man did not strike her as romantic.

And when had she suggested that she and Hugh shared such a love? There were other matters to consider in choosing a marriage partner, and love could grow. *Now* who was the naive one?

But she and Mr. Repton were endeavoring toward something like friendship, so she kept her ruminations to herself.

The faint strains of waltz music floated from the house and Mr. Repton closed his eyes to listen.

Charlotte stilled at the sight. The blue light of the moon bleached his golden hair of color, and he looked flawless as the alabaster statues of gods that lined the avenue at Windmere.

Did he wish to dance? With his injury, was he embarrassed to? So often, she had dreamed of dancing with him and yet...dream men were altogether more complicated in real life.

But she would never have another chance.

"Have you ever waltzed, Mr. Repton?"

He didn't move except to open his eyes. "I've learned, yes."

She frowned slightly at the reemergence of the man's most annoying trait of silence. "I see."

Should she ask? Would he frown at her?

He raked a hand through his hair. And then she saw it—a small twist of his lips that could only be disappointment. Excitement fluttered in her chest. He *did* wish to dance! He just needed a partner. A *friend*.

What a strange, wonderful night this was!

"We might dance here," she said as lightly as she could. "If you wish."

She could not discern if he was intrigued by the idea or found it absurd. He scanned the square of lawn surrounded by dense yews, the lanterns illuminating their grassy dance floor. The night air was still and the music carried easily to them. The jasmine perfumed the air and the peonies...

Pained by the romance of it all, she hurried on. "Or perhaps you are fatigued? I would not wish to tax you, though the waltz does not have to be strenuous. I have danced even with Jacob."

His brow quirked. "You must think me a complete invalid."

"Oh, I would never—" At the teasing light in his eyes, she blushed hotly. It was the nearest thing to a smile he had ever given her.

He stepped closer and his breath stirred the hair at the

crown of her head. A warm hand molded to the small of her back and she could no longer draw air into her body.

"Am I standing too close?" His low voice sent a shiver to her toes.

Indecently so. "Not—not at all." She closed her eyes. *This is Will Repton and he is an accomplished, world-traveling hero, who is entirely unimpressed with you and must be a little disguised to even allow you this close.*

She really ought to walk away and she would. She absolutely would.

Later.

Eyes trained on the folds of his necktie, she placed her hand on the broad shoulder she loved and relaxed the other in his light clasp. And they were dancing. And rather well. Mr. Repton moved with only the smallest hitch to his leg, and she felt his intended direction with the slightest pressure of his hands.

And he was not cold alabaster at all, but warm and strong.

The hand on her back made no demands, but she had to hold herself away. His shoulder would be heaven to rest her head upon. Just as she had dreamed so often.

It was traitorous to Hugh and hopeless to think... but how perfect Mr. Repton would have been, if only he'd been someone quite different. Someone who would stay, who wished to marry, who did not think her all things silly and frivolous and unworthy of the attention he granted everyone else.

She quieted her mind. This was their first dance—their only dance. In the dark, she could read no expression in the shadows of his eyes so she imagined them warm and gentle and brimming with affection. A sweet fantasy…

At least she would always have the power to imagine that.

Too soon, the music came to an end. Mr. Repton stopped short and she bumped against the hard wall of his body. The flex of his hand on her waist distracted her a moment, but then she realized parts of her were pressing more brazenly against him than the rest of her. Blushing, she stepped back, but he held her close. She relented instantly, enjoying the iron brace of his arm against her back. Enjoying the look in his eyes—still shadowed—but in her imagination, still warm and gentle and brimming with affection.

The excitement and rapture and hope of the dance bubbled through her. "I think that was the nicest dance of my life."

The thump of his heart against her breast was the only response he gave. And then a breeze stirred the treetops, a lantern swayed to throw its light, and his face was revealed.

And his eyes were nothing like she imagined.

"I would think it was merely the nicest dance of the last half hour," he said.

Her joy withered, the cool words recalling her to the distance early in the evening, to the distance of their entire acquaintance. Whatever reprieve the night had granted was at an end.

And above that, above shattering her hope *again*, shame threaded its heated fingers over her scalp. He had seen how the men of the *ton* treated her—gripping her too tight, ogling her, smiling in ways that suggested she might do anything to secure her place in Society. *Anything.*

Her right hand was still captured in his and his hand hadn't dropped from her waist. But he didn't speak.

Of course he didn't.

A rare anger boiled through her body. What matter if Mr. Repton was the very picture of her perfect man? Appearances deceived. And she would not credit him for tonight's agreeableness as it was likely some strategy to pry open the purse strings of her acquaintance.

And the lovely things he'd said of Wally…

"I do not understand why you dislike me, Mr. Repton."

"You think I dislike you?"

She scoffed at his bewildered tone. "Of course you dislike me. You never speak unless I speak first, and then you never say more than is necessary. You share nothing at all, which is even more infuriating after tonight, as you have revealed you have many stories to tell.

"You seem even to dislike my friends. You eye Hugh with disapproval each time he calls at the house, and perhaps he is not so worldly as you, but he is usually kind—"

"Usually?"

"—and gentlemanlike and yet you delight in playing the harbinger of foul weather any time I venture outdoors with him."

"What do you mean, 'usually'?"

"I am two and twenty and I know when to carry an umbrella and wear my shawl, so your cautions cast a pall on my outings, which I enjoyed greatly until you became the resident Cassandra. And I know why you are here and why you think all of us live lives of meaningless dissipation, but *you do not know all.*"

She caught her breath and unclenched the grip she had taken upon his hand. "You cannot pretend to like me. I just wonder—I have always wondered what I have done to offend you."

His arm tightened and his lips were right back to hovering over her ear. "Wait…"

More silence. *Honestly!* She would not stand here and let him trample her heart.

She ripped herself from his arms. "It is fine. I hardly require every man to like me, Mr. Repton. Be assured I am aware of your feelings and you will not have to suffer my attentions anymore."

She whirled to leave but a steel hand gripped her arm.

"*God! Blast it!* Now what have I done?" he growled, his blue eyes wintry in the moonlight. "I thought we were getting on. I wouldn't mind being your friend, as long as you understand that's where it ends."

"*Wouldn't mind*? I have more friends than I can count, I hardly need—"

He yanked her hard against him. "Then what do you want?"

"I…I will not argue—"

His hands gripped her waist. "What do you want, Charlotte?" He growled. "*What do you want me to do?*"

Her words died in the face of his rising frustration. What did she want? What had she ever wanted but him? She wanted him still. From the first sight, the first instant. Every day, every hour, she wanted him. In a deep, tender, precious place she could not touch with reason. And all he did was sneer and push her way.

"Why didn't you ignore me as you normally do?" she asked hollowly. "Why did you talk to me at all tonight?"

He said nothing. He didn't move. Something furious and wild thundered through her breast. "You don't belong here!" Her fist clenched, wanting to slap that frozen look off his face. "Say something!" She launched against him, gripping him about his hard neck. "Say *anything*!"

But his stubborn lips were sealed, and before she could stop herself, she mashed her mouth against them.

Instantly, she regretted it. Their chins knocked, their teeth scraped, and a grunt of surprise sounded from his throat.

Oh God, what was she doing? She didn't know how to give a kiss and he certainly didn't want hers. His hands dropped off her and she sobbed sharply against his mouth. Mortified, she crumpled against his neck.

Oh God, oh God, how will I face him?

A hard hand seized her neck and forced her head up. Blue eyes blazed into hers. *"Damn it all!"*

Warm lips clamped to hers expertly. Shocked, she sank to her heels but his arm tightened and locked her against the hard wall of his body. His deep groan shook her—but it was a sound of surrender.

Like a lull in a storm, his lips softened and molded to hers, and he was kissing her slowly, thoroughly, as if memorizing the terrain of her mouth. Dazzled, she clung to him, her feet unsteady on the ground but trusting he would not drop her.

My first kiss…this is important…I must remember…

Beneath her hands, his hard shoulders bunched and flexed. His tongue parted her lips and sank deeper, all of him sank deeper, and she expected to feel the cool grass beneath her with her weight set so far back, but the pull of the earth was denied by his arms. A rough, strong tongue dragged across the roof of her mouth, sending shuddering vibrations of pleasure between her legs.

Dear God…him. Please, he's the one.

Every nerve in her body sang. She hooked her arms around his neck and kissed him back with all the yearning and hope her lips could convey. She couldn't feel him enough, couldn't get close enough.

This, *this*, was passion. This was love.

This was the only test that mattered.

"Will," she breathed.

He growled in answer. His teeth raked her neck, a hot tongue licked her and left her wet where her pulse drummed.

Please stay. It's you.

He couldn't have heard her plea, but in an instant his mouth lifted and she was hauled upright, her feet planted rudely on the ground.

"No," she gasped. She moved to bring him back but her lips slid over the rough grain of whiskers on his cheek. He put her firmly away and she swayed on the tilting earth.

"*Damn it.*" A handkerchief was fumbled from his pocket and dragged over his mouth—a flash of snowy white in the dark.

Hope and fear and desire were suspended in a cold cloud about her.

He lifted his head and his eyes were blacker than the night could ever paint them. "I can't pass your bloody…*tests*."

Her heart cramped in her chest, her mind reeling—

"You want me to talk and entertain and be a *messenger*?" The handkerchief shook in his fist. He stalked her, loomed over her, taller and broader than she had ever thought him to be. "I don't want to talk. I don't want your smiles and your questions and your…your kiss— *Christ*, I don't care what you do, they're waiting so *leave me alone!*"

His growled words were a heated stream on her face and she couldn't move, paralyzed by this anger. No one had ever—no, they had yelled and cursed her after Wally's trial. But those people…those people hated her. She blinked. Hot tears traveled down her cheeks.

Why…? She never cried, she was happy—

His handkerchief was pressed to her cheek so fast, she jumped.

"I'm sorry." His voice was tight. "You can't— Christ, I'm sorry." His face was hard as stone, intent on drying her eyes, and she realized he used his fingers rather than the handkerchief now. "It's my fault. It was a mistake."

"A mistake," she whispered, searching his face, but he turned sharply and stuffed the linen back in his pocket.

He raked a hand through his hair. "We should return."

She nodded, but he was not looking at her. He walked away, the sight of his back heartbreaking. And utterly familiar.

All was exactly as before. No hope. No words. No friendship.

No. Not like before. *Worse.*

The man had kept his distance from the first moment. And with every silence, every slight, he'd shown her he wanted no part of her life.

It was time she believed him.

Seven

On the third Wednesday of the month, Lady Henrietta Abernathy invited a select group of two dozen like-minded ladies to her parlor to discuss the serious topics of the day. As the ladies were all of the upper circles, the serious topics of the day necessarily encompassed fashion, home management, and the myriad issues wrought by ill-trained servants.

While Wally jokingly referred to Charlotte's monthly foray to Lady Abernathy's salon as her "bluestocking" night, the ladies of the club balked at the moniker. Well-bred ladies rejected such narrow classifications and, as many of them were yet unmarried, rumors of intellectualism could be socially disastrous.

Still, Charlotte never missed a gathering, though the topics weren't always to her taste. Tonight's program was the medicinal use of herbs in tinctures and poultices by the Apothecaries Society. A not unpromising topic of discussion, she supposed, as she wended her way to a seat.

Nothing revived like education. And she was sure to learn *something*, as heretofore she had been largely ignorant, or rather, uninterested in such things. Yes. Tinctures and poultices were sure to be fascinating. This was her life, her *real* life, as it was before Will Repton.

She was happy then, and would be happy again. Once she no longer felt that peculiar pain in her chest whenever she remembered how he'd pushed her away after kissing her. Or when he told her he did not want her questions, or to leave him alone—

Yes. She was sure the pain was a little less acute than it had been yesterday.

And life was not so bleak as all that. She and Hugh had made great strides the last few days, and she no longer resisted the idea of knowing him better at the house party. There were fewer obstacles between them now that she fully accepted the reality of her circumstances.

And now that she acknowledged Mr. Repton could never love a woman like her.

Charlotte was settling her skirts on one of the few empty seats in Henrietta's grand salon when Henrietta herself came bustling over to her.

"Charlotte, I do so adore you." The auburn-haired lady was beaming and holding out her beringed hands as she navigated the seated ladies about her.

Charlotte stood to receive a kiss upon her cheek from her hostess. "Well, I adore you, too, Henrietta. What have I done to deserve this special welcome?"

"Do not be coy, dear. You know very well what you have done." Henrietta leaned conspiratorially toward her. "Let us keep it dark. We'll surprise them all. Ah, but once the ladies see how handsome your dashing friend is, I pray they do not all swoon from their seats."

Henrietta threw her hands up about her ears as if to make herself slimmer, and tottled carefully back to the front of the room between the chairs.

My dashing friend? Charlotte lowered slowly back to her seat.

At the front of the room, Henrietta clapped her hands for attention. "Ladies, ladies! There has been a change in program. I am delighted to tell you we have a special guest presenter."

A happy buzz of curiosity swept the room and Henrietta signaled for quiet. "Our guest has traveled thousands of miles by land, sea, and water buffalo to the deepest realms of Asia. And if you were in attendance at our March meeting, we spoke of this man's great adventure featured in the *Westminster Review*."

Oh no.

The room erupted with an excited chorus of gasps.

No, please. She looked through the open door leading to the hall and her heart lurched. Mr. Repton stood in the foyer, watching her. She jerked her head back around.

"He is here to speak of his expedition into that exotic frontier," Henrietta said. "Please welcome Mr. William Repton."

The ladies clapped and he entered, carrying a number of small boards with maps and illustrations. As he faced the audience, the ladies sat up straight.

What was he doing here? They'd not spoken since the night they kissed, nearly two weeks ago. She had not even *seen* him since Ben, Lucy, and the children had traveled to Windmere for Lucy's confinement.

She had been preparing to see him only sparingly

at Windmere at the end of the month, and never again after. Ben was not to return to London for months after the baby arrived, and by then, Will would have sailed.

And she would forget him. She had to.

"Thank you, Lady Abernathy." Mr. Repton bowed to the room. "Ladies."

Charlotte slumped in her seat as far as her tight corselet allowed. Even in the back of the room, his blue eyes could pierce her heart.

"Thank you for allowing me to speak this evening. I was made aware of your monthly meeting through your friend, Miss Charlotte Baker."

Oh good God.

Several ladies cast speculative glances her way, and she lowered her lids when his eyes sought hers across the room.

Receiving no encouragement, he cleared his throat and continued. "As she proves, a curiosity of the world is not the exclusive domain of men. I hope you will find my experiences with the Chinese enlightening and enjoyable."

He placed his display on the easel, flashed a nervous smile, and clasped his hands together. "Well. Let's begin..."

Against her better judgment, she tilted her head to see the map he'd placed on the easel, and for the next hour, Mr. Repton kept her friends riveted and laughing as he spoke of his journey through Asia. He spoke of the colorful people and the hardships on the ship and on the trail in search of plants.

He did not speak of his injury. Nor did he speak

of what drove him to spend every day preparing for his return, or why he was always so tired. And he certainly did not explain why he was here unless…

Was this an apology? If it was, did he not understand this was no way to make amends?

At the end, after all the questions, the ladies surged forward to meet him. Charlotte remained in her seat to chat with friends. She must appear undisturbed by the course of the evening. All knew she'd been encouraging Viscount Spencer for weeks now. Did they suspect a transfer of affection to Mr. Repton?

Oh no…that would not do. She still needed to secure a nobleman's affection, and ultimately, his proposal.

She was well-liked. Would anyone dare to accuse her of caprice? Surely not without confirmation.

She would give them none.

Kissing her friends farewell, she made her way to the hall and requested her carriage. She would not acknowledge Mr. Repton's participation in tonight's assembly beyond her polite applause, and there would not be a whiff of impropriety surrounding them.

Quickly, she drew her shawl about her shoulders. How odd would it appear to wait outside on the pavement?

"Miss Baker?" Mr. Repton's voice sounded from behind her.

Oh, bother it! She turned but did not look at him. "Good evening, Mr. Repton."

"You're leaving?"

"Yes, my carriage has been called. Good night." The footman opened the door and she swept out, cringing at the dual disasters of her carriage being nowhere in sight and the sound of Mr. Repton following her out.

"May I wait with you?" He stepped close and she shied from that familiar scent of bay rum and clove. Her quick retreat seemed to embarrass him. "I thought…I've not seen you. I hoped we might speak. I could see you home."

See me home? "That is kind but unnecessary."

He frowned at her refusal but didn't press.

She should not be rude, though her heart was cramping. And *drat him*, she had missed him so. "I…I enjoyed your presentation."

His eyes shot to hers. "Was there anything you wished to know? I thought you'd have questions."

Tell me why you are returning. Why you do not sleep. Tell me what hurt you.

Tell me why you couldn't love me.

She shook her head and stared at the street corner, wishing the carriage might materialize.

He cleared his throat and looked down the street as well. "All right. More importantly, how do you like my ensemble?" Mr. Repton straightened his jacket with a quick tug and stood with his hands upon his hips to be inspected.

She ran a cursory glance over him, afraid he would see the longing in her eyes. "I like it very well."

"I asked Wallace what I should wear before such discerning ladies." He stroked his waistcoat distractedly. "Jacob had recommended a sailor suit, but I didn't have the right shoes."

She could not even feign a smile. "There really is no need to wait—"

"I just…when we kissed—"

"I kissed *you*, Mr. Repton. And only caused greater discord between us—"

"No, I was—"

"Please, let's not speak of it." She took a deep breath. "That night was just another of my fanciful notions."

He looked at her, confusion on his face. "Won't you let me make amends? I thought coming here…" He bent his head to speak closer. "Tell me what I might do."

Alarmed by his nearness, she stepped backward and he frowned. "You're angry."

"No."

"You're avoiding me."

"No, I…I suppose you do not understand what your presence suggests to my friends, Mr. Repton?"

He looked blankly at her.

"I am in no position for others to think I am encouraging you."

Comprehension dawned, but a rather mulish look came over his face. "I see. I didn't think—"

"Your presentation was remarkable—but please do not extend yourself any further on my behalf."

He frowned, then pulled out a small wrapped package from his pocket and thrust it at her. "I brought you this."

Stupefied, she stared at his neck. "Oh…I—" Emotion stole her words and she pressed her hand against her heart. The paper was not elegant at all but she adored his gift already.

"Your birthday is Saturday."

She nodded, too moved to speak. Oh no…there was no falling out of love with Will Repton.

"It's nothing all that dear. But you have that green dress…" He trailed off at her confused look and frowned, rubbing his jaw. "The striped one? You wear that jade bracelet with it." He pressed the gift at her. "I thought—"

"I cannot accept," she blurted. "I'm sorry. It would not be proper."

He leveled his chin, gazing over her head, and slid the package back into his pocket. "I didn't…sorry."

Mr. Repton looked embarrassed and she…well, *dash it all*, she wanted his present.

"It is because we are not related," she said. "Not that…well, surely no one could find fault with your *showing* me the gift."

His eyes met hers. "No?"

"That is, if you cared to show me. But as we are both here…and you went to the kind effort of delivering it this evening…?"

"Right, I could show you."

Her heart began to thrum, and she couldn't stop the excited smile from stretching her lips as he stepped close to unwrap the gift between them at waist level.

This felt like their first secret. Like the most wonderful gift of her life.

Like friendship.

He crammed the paper into his coat pocket and handed her a leather jeweler's box.

It was a jade necklace, far finer than her bracelet, with beads of many colors. White jade tinged with russet. Translucent celadon. Deepest jasper. She lifted the necklace higher to borrow light from the streetlamp. Each bead had been carved with astonishing detail and multiple layers, revealing a hidden world within. Gnarled pine boughs framed rushing waterfalls. Cranes winged over jagged mountain landscapes. A dragon and phoenix tumbled round each other on their small sphere for all eternity.

"Oh my," she whispered. "It's beautiful."

"I found this in the markets in Canton."

"I remember—that is, I remember your writing of them."

"I know I've not behaved as I should," he said. "I hope we can proceed on friendlier terms."

Friendlier terms. It was too late. It had always been too late. "If that is your wish."

Her polite words appeared to annoy him. He scrubbed a hand through his hair, upsetting the perfect knot of his tie. "I just thought, since I am friends with your family…and I wouldn't want any trouble with Spencer at your house party."

"No one knows that I kissed you. I believe," she added uncertainly.

"I've not told anyone. I never will." His gaze settled on her mouth. "And I kissed you back, if you recall."

With regret, she returned the beautiful necklace and he took it without a word.

Her carriage rounded the corner. A trio of ladies exited the house and cast curious glances at them.

She held out her hand. "Will you shake my hand, Mr. Repton?"

He complied instantly, looking bewildered.

"For our audience," she explained. "Good evening." She turned, signaling he must leave, and pretended to button her glove.

"He's a fortunate man. If Lord Spencer is your choice," he said behind her. "I wish you happiness."

Happiness… "Yes, I…thank you." Her stays had been drawn too tight. They'd been oppressing her all evening.

"If there's anything I might—"

"Thank you." She couldn't breathe. Why couldn't she breathe? "Here is my carriage."

The coachman moved to hand her in, but she nearly leapt inside to gain privacy. Safe within, she rested her head against the squabs.

She would be happy again, *she would*. She would have purpose. She would know where she belonged. Perhaps as soon as she wed.

Perhaps as soon as she was Viscountess Spencer.

Eight

"I WONDER IF I SHOULD HAVE PACKED MY FISHING ROD."

Will's mother didn't even look up from her novel at her husband's comment. "I wonder at your wondering, because you do not care for fishing, John."

"I don't?" his father asked.

"The last time you fished, you fell asleep in the sun and came home with a painful burn," his mother said.

"Ah yes, yes. So I did."

Will vowed to never, ever ride in a closed carriage with his parents again. Their conversations were pointless. Being strapped up top with the trunks might've been a preferable mode of travel.

His mother, long familiar with his father's rambling mind and mad enough to still love him despite it, laid a hand of comfort upon her husband's neck. "There will be much to divert you. Don't be uneasy. You were eager to learn how that *Desprez* China rose would fare in the midlands. It's nearly June, it should be in bloom. The Saint-Priest—"

"The *St. Prist de Breuze*?"

"Right, that one."

His father's eyes gleamed with a new excitement, and he patted his mother's lap and kept his hand there. He leaned against his wife. "Did you pack your new bonnet, Lizzie?"

Will had no idea if this was some sort of lover's code, but his mother swatted his father playfully with her book. He'd long ago abandoned trying to decipher their secret language. His father was understandably besotted. Elizabeth Repton was still a handsome woman.

As for his father, his brilliance in matrimony and botany didn't extend to sartorial concerns. The man didn't give a whit if his trousers matched his coat. Only his wife kept him looking presentable. Still, at the end of the day, his father's hair would be tugged and mussed into impressive dishevelment for a man merely working with flowers.

"William." His mother's stare pinned him from over her book. "You must not allow your father to disappear on his daily rambles. I've told him he will be expected to be social."

"You will have to meet Charlotte Baker, Father," Will reminded him.

He sighed. "I wonder if we will have a chance to know her at all. If Charlotte is half as comely as Lucy, every young man there will be soliciting her attention."

"She's already got a beau."

Will caught his mother casting a regretful eye over him, her bachelor son. The lamentable state of Mrs. Elizabeth Repton, long denied a grandchild from her only offspring, would not be rectified soon.

"What do you make of her, William?" she asked. "Will she be able to countenance our country ways?"

"Don't worry, Mum. She's an elegant lady but doesn't put on airs."

"And is she a pretty girl?"

Will wiped his face. "Very." He looked out the carriage window, the bucolic scenes of Derbyshire only sinking him further. "More beautiful than her sister."

His parents' brows rose and they both aimed calculating looks at him.

"And she's likely accepting Viscount Spencer's marriage offer at this party. You two must be addled if you think a woman like her would accept a man like me."

At his parents' dashed expressions, he regretted speaking.

Mum sniffed delicately. "I suppose it is addled to want grandchildren before I'm too old to lift them?"

He leaned forward to kiss her cheek. "Just a few years, Mum, and I promise to wed the first lady I see as I walk down the gangplank on my return. Provided she's plump, pretty, and fertile."

Mum pushed him back to his seat, her humor somewhat restored.

"Look at that stand of elms, William." His father was peering out the carriage window.

What appeared to be a stand began to form two long rows of trees as the carriage turned. "We may be nearing Windmere. Ben mentioned an alley of elms along the drive to the house."

The carriage crested the hill and began a long descent, and the majesty of Windmere, with its honey-gold stone and three stories of tall, sparkling windows, appeared, its green hills rolling from it in all directions. Yellow dahlias sprouted cheerily from planters surrounding the circular drive, and soon the carriage wheels rolled onto crushed gravel and a wave of servants descended the front steps. And there was Jacob, bouncing with excitement.

"Oh my. My, my, my," his father whispered. "I'd no idea Windmere was a palace. Lizzie, to think we'll be sleeping beneath a roof as fine as that."

But Will didn't hear the rest of his parents' conversation, or pay any heed to the grandeur of the house. Charlotte was near. She was home.

Damn me…I can feel her.

Charlotte steadied herself against the window of the blue parlor. The Reptons alit from their hired carriage, but she was still not prepared to greet them as Ben, Lucy, and Jacob were doing.

Here he was.

The thought rose unbidden as it always did with every fresh sight of Will Repton. Here he was in her favorite place on earth. Familiar…adored…impossible.

The party moved into the house, and with a steadying breath, she walked into the library where she had last heard voices. It appeared everyone was descending from the library's terrace to the gardens. The senior Mr. Repton must be eager to see Lucy's rose garden, having procured most of the bushes himself.

Ben and his mentor, John Repton, were bent in study over a rose bush, while Lucy and Wally followed Abby as she stumbled happily between the flowers. Will Repton and his mother stood with their back to her as she entered the garden.

Jacob saw her first. “Aunt Charlotte! Mr. Repton is here!”

Mr. Repton’s gaze met hers briefly before he bowed.

“Welcome to Windmere, Mr. Repton.” She had only a second to admire his hair glittering in the sun before she turned to meet his mother.

Mr. Repton presented his mother. “Mother, this is Charlotte Baker. Miss Baker, my mother, Elizabeth.”

Charlotte smiled at the woman, whose eyes were the same glorious blue as her son’s.

Mrs. Repton’s eyes crinkled with her smile. “My word, there is great beauty in the Baker women. William told me as much and still I am all amazement.”

Charlotte flushed at the compliment. “Oh, how kind of—”

“Come, dear,” Mrs. Repton said. “John has been eager to meet you. Let’s see if we can lure him from the love of his life.”

There was no sight in the world more delightful than the silver-haired man buried deep in Lucy’s roses congratulating Ben—no, the roses themselves—on their excellent appearance.

“Father?” Mr. Repton’s deep voice close behind her made her start. His expression was pained looking at him. “Miss Baker is here.”

Charlotte beamed at the darling man straightening to greet her. A father and son could not be more different. Will Repton was serious, detailed, economical in mind and body. And John Repton had misbuttoned his waistcoat.

“Oh my, Miss Baker!” John Repton regarded her with a smile. “My, my, my. Yes, charming. We are long overdue in meeting Lucy's little sister. I've brought you a *Blanche de Belgique* rose and was telling Ben to plant it nearer the Flemish varietals." He grew a little serious at this point. "Now, I almost brought you the *Madame Carolina* rose for obvious reasons, but Will tells me you're partial to white."

"Indeed I am." Charlotte hastened to reassure him. "Thank you. I will always treasure it. Will it bloom this late in the season?"

"Yes, I daresay it will." John gave her a pat on the hand and studied her a moment longer. "Yes. The *Blanche* rose is exactly right, I think."

His eyes sought his wife's and the warm smile he gave Elizabeth made Charlotte's heart ache with yearning. Elizabeth Repton, like Charlotte's sister, was loved.

"Liz, who's that you're speaking to?" John Repton ambled toward his wife. "That strapping young man cannot be Jacob Paxton. Master Jacob was just a wee babe yesterday when we plucked him from under that cabbage leaf." With a cheerful wink at her, John Repton stooped to speak with Jacob, leaving Charlotte with his son.

"Don't trouble yourself if you don't know the reason for not bringing a Carolina rose my father was speaking of." Mr. Repton stacked his arms over his chest, taunting her with the glorious breadth of his shoulders. "Most people don't understand his mind. Even I can't tell you what he intended."

"But I do understand. A Carolina rose might seem obvious because Charlotte is the French version of the name Caroline, and Carolina is the Italian."

Surprise flickered across his face, chased by something

like bemusement. A small sadness panged within her. How many times had he misunderstood his father? It was as if the men spoke different languages.

She tried not to stare and failed. In the sun, the late-day growth of his beard was golden, darkening to amber on the underside of his hard jaw.

Mr. Repton caught her study of him and sobered his countenance. Walking to the end of the rose garden, he looked out over the lawn.

In the distance, the water spray from the powerful gravity-fed fountain misted and shred like a horse's tail streaming in the air—only one of Windmere's many treasures. The gardens were immense and surrounded on all sides by Ben's design, but nearly every visitor to Windmere asked to see Ben's masterpiece first…

"Where is the Palm House?" Mr. Repton asked.

"It is on the south, behind the kitchen gardens."

Mr. Repton looked at Ben and his father, engrossed in conversation.

"Would you like me to show you?" Seeing his jaw tighten, she regretted the offer. "But then, anyone would prefer Ben to guide them."

"No." He looked at the vast lawn, not at her. Never at her. "I'd be pleased if you would. Thank you."

She led him onto the lawn to the back of the house. Evidently, his curiosity had overcome any discomfort he might have felt being alone with her. Unless over the course of two weeks, he'd forgotten everything they'd ever said and done to each other.

There was no reason not to walk with him. He was a guest at her home and the grounds were filled with garden staff.

Though she would not like to run into Hugh. The viscount's attentions these past weeks left her in no doubt of his intentions. And she told herself daily the progress was welcome. She just needed a bit more time before she was prepared to keep company with both Hugh and the man she'd kissed like a wanton in his garden.

"Windmere is wonderful," he said. "When did you come here? How old were you when your sister married the earl?"

"I was eight."

"You must have loved living here," Mr. Repton said.

"Oh, I did. I had a pony."

His eyes softened. "Well, I should think so. Did you braid flowers in her mane?"

She smiled, flushing a little. "Beatrice never seemed to mind."

"Beatrice…?" His eyes widened, as if he had just realized something. "That was a pony."

"What was?"

"The pillow, in your parlor in London. I decided it was a goat. How old were you when you made it? Eight? Nine?"

She looked at him. "Twenty."

The smile wobbled on his lips. "Oh."

A goat?

"Right. Well." Mr. Repton plucked a blade of grass to fidget with. "Has Viscount Spencer arrived?"

"Yes. He and his sisters rode into Highthorpe, with a few other guests. Helen and Hester are anxious to renew your acquaintance. In truth, there are many ladies who wish to meet you."

"I'm not here to meet other women."

"Oh?" She hoped her tone was convincingly teasing. "Are your affections engaged elsewhere?"

He looked confused.

"You said 'other' women."

"No. No women, Miss Baker," he said, definitely not looking at her now. He squinted. "I see the top of the Palm House. I can find my way now. Thank you for directing me."

And without a backward glance, Mr. Repton left her standing alone on the lawn staring like a stupid cow.

Drat the man! She wiped her eyes. One minute he thrilled her with a teasing smile, and the next, he stripped her of all composure.

This was unnatural, this melancholy. She cradled the nape of her neck and squeeze at the tightness there.

"Charlotte?"

Her eyes flew open at Hugh's voice. He was approaching from the direction of the front drive. "You've returned," she said, stating the obvious.

"Highthorpe is a charming village. I bought a pair of gardener's gloves for myself, inspired by Windmere's many glories."

Charlotte had to smile at that. Pottering about in a garden was the least likely locale for Viscount Spencer. "An excellent notion, Hugh, and eventually those gloves will be a thoughtful gift for your gardener."

"You wound me, Charlotte. I only wish to cultivate interests we might share." He smiled and pulled playfully at a ribbon on her sleeve. "My estate in Hertford is in a woeful state. I daresay, in time, the grounds might be as pleasing as Windmere. It wants a woman's hand, I think." The last was said with a meaningful look into her eyes.

Can we be happy, Hugh? She stared into his eyes, seeking an answer there.

He lifted her chin and kissed her.

She had vowed—no more tests. But perhaps this one last time…

She pressed her lips more firmly against his. Apparently encouraged by her response, his hands came atop her shoulders and his lips parted hers slightly.

Something akin to panic welled within her. She felt…nothing. She opened her eyes and waited for Hugh to stop the kiss a second later.

His pleased smile broke her heart. Nothing at all. Only fondness.

Was that enough?

Nine

The hunting tower stood majestically apart from Windmere's house and gardens, atop a steep rise of earth with an endless panorama about it. Yesterday, Will had found the tower on his morning walk. Perhaps for that reason, the leash of deer grazing along the slope paid no heed to his climbing the hill a second time.

The muscles in his calves burned from the exertion, but as running was yet difficult, he climbed as steeply as he could, as fast as he could. And he relished the exercise. He needed to be strong. Four months on a boat could wreak havoc on a man's body if it wasn't strong to begin with. While on land, he preferred to climb.

He could forget the nightmares he'd woken to when he climbed.

As for the pain, he stomped that down. He had another mile or two before the leg collapsed on him entirely.

The wind fought him as he ascended, roaring in his ears and stealing his breath. He was gaining the top when a flutter of blue flashed behind the tower. Two more strides, and he knew it was a skirt. Four more, and Charlotte appeared, leaning against the stone tower.

His pounding legs slowed to a stop before he crested the hill, but it was too late to turn back. Charlotte, appearing startled, straightened to face him.

"Sorry, I'll leave you be," he said between panting breaths. He bent at the waist, bracing his arms on his knees. "I didn't mean to interrupt your walk."

"I rode my horse. I was—"

"Expecting Spencer?"

"Not at all."

She looked affronted and he swiped his words away, too breathless to explain his weak jest.

"Goodness, Mr. Repton. Did you walk all this way?"

He tilted his head up to squint at her. "I require exercise in the morning."

"Would not a more moderate pace be safer?"

She was clearly disturbed by his hard breathing, so he straightened to appear more at ease. "I'm in no danger. And I've not had air this fresh to breathe in months."

Her nose was still crinkled with worry.

"Well. Good morning to you."

"Wait, Mr. Repton."

He looked back at her in question and, appearing surprised by his compliance, she frowned. "Rest a moment, at the least. That is...please. If you would indulge me."

Such a lady. Even when she was scolding him. A minute wouldn't harm. Besides, they couldn't avoid each other the entire week.

"I even left my horse at the bottom to rest," she said. "But I love the view from here. I feel as if I might actually go somewhere. Though I would still be on the estate if I ventured only as far as my eye reaches. Miles and miles, but that is the purpose of the tower, I suppose. Not that anyone in the family enjoys to hunt, thank goodness. Do you hunt, Mr. Repton?"

"No."

"Oh." She nodded. "Good. I find nothing sporting in a hunt, do you?"

He nearly smiled. Was it just his silence she disliked or everyone's?

He surveyed the rolling hills, the clusters of woods, a sparkling ribbon of river cutting the velvet green with its crooked path. Then his gaze stole back to Charlotte, the view he always sought.

Her bonnet dangled from her fingers and the wind pulled strands of her hair across her cheek and set them flagging in the air before her. He'd never known how long her hair was. It would reach the curve of her back. And that dress was the plainest he'd ever seen on her, the hem muddied.

With her wild tresses and pink cheeks, she might have been a farmer's daughter. A farmer's daughter just ravished in a barn or against a tree or over a bale of—

Damn it. The blood plummeted from his head to lower regions, and he bent to brace his hands on his knees.

"I come here when I wish to be alone." She plucked at the ribbons of her hat and flicked an expectant glance at him.

Clearly she was done being alone. Charlotte didn't seem the solitary type, anyway.

A gentleman would utter some encouraging reply.

Her vexed sigh carried on the wind and he scrambled to think of an appropriate encouragement.

"If you were wondering, Mr. Repton, I was contemplating marriage."

She sounded almost embarrassed, so he put away the snarl twisting his lips. But not without difficulty. "I imagine that topic isn't far from your thoughts these days."

"I find it daunting." She winced. "No, 'daunting' sounds terrible. *Confusing.*"

When he looked at her, the woman's gaze lifted from his mouth and darted away. "What's confusing you?" he asked without enthusiasm but with at least a modicum of patience.

"I have been told certain things about…well, love and so forth, that are at odds with my experience and—not that I would ever want to distress you as I did before, but perhaps if you were granted the benefit of foreknowledge—"

"Miss Baker?"

"Well." Her cheeks darkened. "You will think me mad, but there is little time left." She turned back as if preparing to pounce on him. "Would you grant me the favor of kissing me and not asking me why?"

He was glad he was already braced or he might have dropped on his arse. "Yes—*no*, I mean no. Absolutely not."

She scanned his face uncertainly. "Not kiss me or not ask me why?"

"Both—*neither*. I'm a grown man. I'll take no part in your parlor games."

Her jaw dropped. "I've come to you with a sincere request for help."

Tormenting woman! He shut his eyes, struggling for the patience he *used* to have.

And failed.

"And do ladies beg kisses from any available man?"

Her cheeks were flaming red, and for the first time, it appeared she would leave him with the last word. Mumbling beneath her breath, she crammed her bonnet atop her head and stomped away.

"Wait," he called, but Charlotte continued her angry plod down the hill. He followed at her heels, like a damn dog. "Tell me why and I'll consider it."

"No." She flung the word over her shoulder. "I don't want you to consider it."

His patience exhausted, he caught a swinging arm and forced her to a stop. Again her eyes dipped to his mouth and away. He was trained to notice details and *bloody hell*—"You want to compare us," he grumbled.

"No." Her chin dipped a fraction. "Not exactly. I only wish to convince myself I do not enjoy your kiss more than Hugh's."

"And why do you need convincing? He's kissed you, hasn't he?"

She nodded, looking miserable.

"Is he so terrible?"

Her eyes rolled. "This is impossible."

Baffled, he watched her leaving again. "What?"

He started after her and nearly knocked her down when she came to a sudden stop. "Hugh professes to love me but there is something wanting in the physical expression of our affection. And you do not even like me—"

"I like you fine."

"—but your kiss was…it was not unwelcome."

He was beginning to understand the provoking woman. Too slow to avoid angering her, but understanding her nonetheless. Charlotte was conflicted over enjoying his kiss more than Spencer's.

Well. The fact wasn't unpleasant to hear. But it probably wasn't kind to dwell on it with her suffering and all.

He frowned over a new thought. "I shouldn't trouble yourself. It was one kiss under moonlight. Your romantic heart throbbed for the poor cripple dancing with you in the dark. It was pity working on your heartstrings."

"And why should I pity a…a dog-hearted knot-head who lacks the feeling granted even a dog or a…a stupid—" She stopped, apparently at a loss for a sufficiently dim-witted animal. "You're like a goat! But not…as clever or…"

Despite himself, he grinned. "Am I being insulted?"

But he doubted she heard him as she was already stomping down the hill.

"And I will remind you, Mr. Repton," she tossed over her shoulder, "you *yelled* at me afterward. Quite ferociously. I am *three* and twenty now, and not swayed by stuff and nonsense such as moonlight. Hugh has kissed me in the willow garden, the Temple of the Muses, *and* on the nature walk—and that is a romantic setting that cannot be rivaled. He has kissed me in many romantic places."

That erased the grin from his face.

The woman's skirts billowed behind her, her small fists at her side.

Just let the mad woman go. Don't torture yourself, don't be an idiot.

The wind blew her bonnet off her head and she scrambled to retrieve it. A loud "bother it all!" floated back to him.

But it sounded all weepy.

Damn it. "Come back, Miss Baker."

"No!"

"Please?"

She stopped and tilted her head in question. Even with her chin jutting out angrily, that was still bloody adorable.

"I'll not tease you," he grumbled.

"You will kiss me?"

"Evidently." *The nature walk…bloody hell.*

She looked unconvinced, so he softened his countenance. She took a step toward him, stopped to smooth her hair, and was at last near enough for him to put his arms about her. But when he did, she tensed.

Protectiveness surged over him. "Is Spencer gentle with you?"

She nodded absently to the question and he released the breath he held. He drew her close. His shirt was damp with sweat and a momentary qualm rose over holding her in his state. But the feel of her body against his was too large an enticement to let go.

Why was she still tense? "Does your beau hold you at all? " he barked, then breathed to start again. "Or does he just arrow in on your lips?"

"He holds my hand." Her eyes met his. "Do you think that is the trouble?"

He shrugged, the movement jerky, arrested as he was by the blue of her eyes.

"An embrace *would* foster intimacy." She slid her hands to his shoulders and he damn near swooned.

God, what was he doing? But Charlotte wanted her answer. She lifted her chin, shut her eyes, and pursed her lips. He had to press his own shut against laughter, but the impulse stemmed more from frayed nerves than amusement. "Shall I proceed, then?"

At her nod, he lowered his head but she dropped her chin, shying from him. His lips followed to slant across her mouth. With only the slightest pressure, she opened for him.

God bless her, it was like before. His body jolted with pleasure, and there was the added bliss of the wind teasing the perfume from her hair and tickling his cheek with those silken strands. But he wouldn't lose control. Simply kiss her and let her go.

But there was nothing simple about this. Charlotte Baker was the sweetest woman he'd ever held, and she molded against him as if they'd been halved by some divine hand.

She was a paradise to kiss…the softness of her mouth astonishing. He tightened the space between them. He couldn't give her an inch—and she didn't wish it. Even in his delirium, he knew she didn't wish it.

The proof of his desire would be evident through the thin cotton of his trousers, but he was powerless to step back. And he should. He lusted for her and she was not his.

She was Spencer's.

The thought was a plunge into icy water. He held

her hips and put her firmly from him. But she didn't open her eyes.

"Miss Baker?" His voice was clogged and resisted working. He squeezed her gently. "Miss Baker?"

Her eyes fluttered open. He couldn't see where they focused, if at all.

Had he held too tight? Bending low, he scanned her face. Her cheeks were still pink, and her lips silken from their kiss.

She blinked and moved a step back, covering her lips with her fingers. "All right," she whispered. "That was…"

"What?"

"Not the same." She assessed their positions, his embrace. "Your arms are around me and Hugh—"

"—hasn't held you?"

She shook her head. "If you do not object, perhaps you might kiss me without—"

Without holding you. He swooped to capture her mouth again. *No hands. Fine. Simple enough direction.*

Her lips were warm and pliant, and he kissed her as gently as he could manage. Still, he didn't restrain his tongue and it twined lovingly with hers. The pulse in his neck throbbed thickly and his head whirled tasting her like this, suspended on her lips, floating with only her body to tether him to the earth.

Frustration flared when she retreated from him. He followed, not letting her mouth leave his. When she understood to stand still, triumph surged through him. She would never feel this with Spencer. It was impossible. She wasn't meant to be touched by anyone else.

Forgetting her rule, he seized her about the waist.

It was a mistake. Instantly, she tore free and turned her back.

A fierce wind buffeted him—nature scolding him for his passion.

He waited, but there was only the low roar of the wind. Her hand lifted quickly to her face and he couldn't see to know if she wiped her eyes or her lips.

And Charlotte wasn't talking.

"That was not like Spencer?" he asked gruffly.

"No."

Her voice was small, and instinctively he moved to comfort her.

But comfort wasn't allowed. Comfort would lead to expectations and hope—hers, his. Neither could be offered.

He struggled for an air of indifference. "Now you've kissed two men. You'll need at least a dozen for scientific study."

"No. You are enough."

Her lifeless tone unnerved him. But damn it, she'd *asked* him to kiss her. "Will you return with me?" *Turn around, Charlotte. Let me see you.*

"Please go ahead. I have kept you from your exercise." She paused. "And…thank you. You have helped me to know my mind."

So. She could accept Spencer's lackluster kisses after all. If passion wasn't in line with a gently bred lady's expectations.

"At your service." He cursed himself for the bitterness leeching into his words.

She was not to blame. And he should know better.

"Marry Spencer, Miss Baker," he said. "Teach him

what pleases you and passion will grow. Spencer has passed most of your tests. In time, he will pass this one as well."

Before a vision of Spencer making love to Charlotte could take root, he turned, and for the first time in months, pushed his crippled leg into a punishing race back to the house.

❧

She could not bear this for a week. Not a week or a day or an hour. She must accept Hugh immediately. She would be mad to refuse a viscount.

Why did she kiss Mr. Repton? Why did she test him? How could she lay open her heart and nearly ruin everything?

She barely remembered her ride from the hunting tower in her haste to find Wally. He would know what to do. He would remind her of her resolve and rein in her stupid, romantic schemes.

Voices spilled from the open door of the library, and she darted behind the stairwell. She must not be seen in her current dishabille. Wally's voice wasn't among the laughing group.

She spun around, moving to the next likely locale. The blue parlor. She pushed open the door and found him alone, reading in his chair. Without a word, Wally stood and closed the door. His arms were around her the next minute. "What is it, dear heart?"

Safe in his arms, tears streamed unchecked down her cheeks and there was no end to them. "I'm sorry, I'm so sorry."

"What has happened?"

She shook her head, her throat too tight to speak.

"All right, dear heart. It's all right."

"I…Lord Spencer—"

"Ah." Wally sighed. "You have decided against him."

"No!" She pulled back. "I—why would—I will accept him when he offers and"—a short sob burst from her—"and I will be a true wife and…"

He raised a brow, waiting for her to continue.

"…and a devoted companion and"—she wiped her eyes, but the tears were streaming—"and do you have a handkerchief?"

Wally walked her to the divan and sat beside her. "Charlotte, *breathe*." As he did when she was a child, he put his arm about her and pressed her head to his shoulder. "I think I must refuse my consent should Lord Spencer apply to me. I would oppose any marriage plan that appears fatal to your happiness."

"No, when I am the viscountess, you and Lucy and Ben will enter Society again, and the children—"

"The children are fine. And you are not to worry about us. We are content in the company we keep."

"But—"

"Do you love Spencer?"

She started to speak, but a hiccup cut off her word. Miserable, she shook her head.

"Then you do not marry him."

Her vision blurred under new tears. And yet she could breathe again. And she was so tired. "Wally, do you ever wonder…?"

"What, dear heart?"

"If you had never met the earl? What our lives would be? If you had never loved him and he never gave us all we have? Our lives would be so…so ordinary. I think I may have liked that life."

Wally was quiet.

"I'm sorry—I did not mean…I am glad you loved him," she said.

"I wonder that all the time, dear heart." He smiled. "But I see the woman you have become and feel only pride."

"I never want to disappoint you."

"How would you ever?" He hugged an arm about her. "I confess, I am not surprised about Spencer. Of late, I began to doubt his character."

"How do you mean?"

"In that it never deepened upon familiarity. Shall I acquaint him with your feelings?"

Wally had discouraged several men on her behalf. Many who had abused him with insults during those exchanges, she learned later. And those men had extended little time or expense on her. But Hugh…

"I must tell him," she said. "But I hardly know what to say after all this time."

"You simply tell him marriage isn't in accordance with your feelings."

She closed her eyes, soothed by Wally's hand stroking her head. "He does not love me. If he did, I would have known it. There would be such a depth of feeling, there could be no disguising it in his kiss or his arms, and no withholding it. And he would be mindful only of what brings me happiness, even if that brought him only suffering." She looked at Wally. "I think love is like a madness. Is that how it was with the earl?"

Wally looked inward, perhaps remembering those

too-short years with his love. Charlotte had been a child when Jacob Adamson, the Earl of Lynham, had come into their lives. She had not understood until years later that the man who had married her sister, and took her and Wally from their cottage into the grand rooms at Windmere, was not Lucy's lover, but her brother's.

"I suppose it was a sort of madness," Wally said. "Why else would we have done what we did to be together?"

Her eyes stung with fresh tears. For the first time, she truly understood Wally's loss. "How did you survive it?"

"He loved me as I loved him, and there was not a day we let pass without telling each other that. It was in every embrace, every look. It was in every good morning and every good night." His voice softened. "It was in his final words to me."

Wally looked into her eyes. "When you find a love like that, dear heart, *then* is when you marry."

Charlotte hugged him. "Yes…in every good morning and every good night."

Buffered by a warm kiss on her brow, she returned to her room to repair her appearance. No matter the cataclysm wrought in her heart, a lady dressed in a manner reflecting the utmost courtesy to the gentleman—no, the future earl—she was to disappoint.

And yet…she had the strangest feeling Hugh would not be disappointed at all.

She feared he would not even be discouraged.

"Fresh air and a full stomach. I will sleep well tonight." John Repton leaned back in his chair and stretched, the remains of their supper before him.

Will looked at his own plate without interest. Thank God most of Windmere's guests had gone into the village for dinner. He was of no mind to be social. Those that remained, including the Reptons, were served meals in their rooms.

"We must have walked five miles today," his mother said. "Isn't that right, John?"

"Oh, miles and miles. Tomorrow we must tackle the labyrinth, Lizzie."

Will considered the sense of setting his father loose in a hedge maze but said nothing. This was their holiday, after all.

His mum eyed him. "Are you unwell? You've not eaten."

"I…uh, I ate earlier." A harmless lie. He had no appetite. "Did I mention the Earl of Harlowe committed three hundred pounds to the return?"

"That's wonderful, Son." His parents replied with the measured happiness he'd come to expect when the topic was his expedition.

Not that he found pleasure in the earl's investment himself. And his bloody leg was throbbing from the run earlier. And nothing on the table tempted him. And he'd got no work done all day. And there seemed no end in sight to his brooding.

Likely because there'd been no sight of Charlotte since the morning.

"I've not seen the family since this morning, have you?" Will asked.

His parents looked at one another, silently consulting as was their habit. "Neither have we," his father said.

His mother's eyes widened. "Do you think

Charlotte has accepted that viscount? Would they be celebrating?"

His gut twisted. *Marry Spencer, Miss Baker—*

"I don't know." He pushed to his feet, the chair tipping on two legs in his haste. "I'm to bed."

"Good night, Son."

But his feet carried him downstairs to the deserted hall. He could inquire of the family; the servants would think nothing of that. A few would be belowstairs, if he could find the stairwell. A footman glided silently around him and he followed.

The kitchen held a small gathering of what he discerned were the upper servants, clustered in fervent conversation. "Excuse me."

The servants turned with varying degrees of contrition or surprise upon their faces. The valet assigned to him was first to stand. "Your pardon, Mr. Repton, sir. Is there something you require?"

"I wished to inquire of the family. They are missed upstairs."

The valet looked uncertainly at Goodley, the butler. His name was easy to remember, being the brother of the butler at Ben's London house. They even looked alike, but tonight Windmere's butler wore an expression heavy with concern.

"Mrs. Paxton did not feel…well, if I may speak freely, we are anticipating the arrival of her babe this evening—a tad early, but well within the parameters of a safe delivery, we are told, and with all expectation of one. Mr. Paxton is seeing to her comfort, and Mr. Baker insisted on going to town to collect the doctor."

"I see." That explained the family's absence; Charlotte would be at her sister's side.

Goodley's expression of concern crumpled unashamedly to one of appeal. "This is not my place to say, but you seem a bosom friend of the master's." He lowered his voice, but this was only a play at discretion, as the servants could hear every word.

"What is it?"

"We've not told the master, considering Mrs. Paxton's delicate condition, and Wallace Baker is likewise unaware. But…our Miss Charlotte has not been seen for hours."

His heart stilled. "Why not? Is she in the gardens?"

"We've searched the gardens, the house, the outbuildings. And all the horses and carriages are accounted for." He paused. "No one has seen Lord Spencer, either," Goodley added with a harder edge to his tone.

The arrow in his chest pierced deeper. He scanned the faces around the prep table. "Where is her maid?"

"Patty and her husband are searching the grounds," Goodley said. "Her concern was most acute after learning Miss Charlotte was to tell His Lordship she could not reciprocate his affections. I'm afraid he is a disappointed man this evening, Mr. Repton. And I don't think a man like that cares to be thwarted in his aims."

Will held tightly to his control. Hugh Spencer wouldn't react badly—he was a viscount.

But Will had witnessed horrors rise in an instant and men become beasts without provocation.

"When was she last seen?" Will asked tightly.

"A little before the dinner hour," Goodley said.

Beyond the window, the moon was rising. Not in the gardens or in the house…

There might be one place they'd not looked.

Will turned to the valet. "Bring me a lantern."

Ten

"Repton has stolen your affections from me."

Hugh's words were quiet, but the cold light in his stare chilled her.

Had she made a mistake? The nature walk seemed the kindest path to take—one mile to gently explain her feelings; the other to salvage their friendship. But the man's steps were maddeningly slow, and the light in the wood had faded. No matter how she answered his questions, no answer satisfied.

"Please, Hugh, we mustn't delay. We'll not see the trail soon."

"You were enamored with him from the first. I was there, remember? I saw how you behaved, as everyone behaves. Fawning over him, flattering him."

What could she say that he would believe? They were far from the house. The white birches stood like specters, their rustling leaves menacing whispers.

"Hugh." She dared to circle his cold wrist, his fist clenched solid as a cudgel beneath it. "There is nothing between Mr. Repton and I, truly. But I cannot offer you the devotion you deserve."

The light in the wood receded quickly, as if a cloud had passed overhead and settled. She blinked and widened her eyes in an attempt to see more clearly.

"This is enough." Her voice was shrill to her own ears. "I will answer any question at the house."

She tugged his wrist and was yanked back.

"I do not care to hear your lies. Think a moment, if you can squeeze a thought in that feathery head of yours. You cannot marry better. If you fancy Repton will raise you, you're mistaken."

"That is not—"

"This conceit of yours requires an adjustment. Our marriage is all but decided." He paused, and his eyes seemed to deaden. "Is this my father's work?"

"Your father?"

"He thinks I am his to command. But *I* choose." He stepped closer, his breath stale with tobacco on her cheek. "And I chose you. Do you know what that costs me? The next Earl of Harlowe, aligned with your diseased brother and a fake countess for a sister? A whore some call—"

"No!" Fury roared to life in her. "Release my arm!"

"What do you require? Jewels? A grand house like your beloved Windmere?"

She pulled at his grip. "Hugh—stop!"

"Passion? Have I been too reserved?" His eyes hardened. "Do women of low birth require a ready cock to persuade?"

Speechless, she stared.

"Did Repton persuade you?"

"How dare you—"

Hugh's face contorted with a snarl, and she was

thrown and falling. An animal cry of fear escaped her throat. The trees blurred. The forest floor slammed the back of her head and branches cracked beneath her.

A bolt of panic surged through her. *No, please God!* She scrambled to rise but he tackled her back to the ground.

"*No!*" Her arms swung, her legs kicked, desperate to upset his arms and knees pinning her to the earth.

"Calm yourself!"

"*NO!*" She bucked in terror. Hard hands patted her, seeking to calm her, but the attempt was insane. He was crushing her, his knees boring into her stomach. Wrenching a burning wrist from his grip, her elbow cracked his nose and he fell off with a curse.

Scrambling to pull herself forward, she was flattened as his weight landed hard on her. "Charlotte! I won't hurt you!"

"No!"

"*Goddammit*, just—" The rest was a cry of surprise.

His weight was lifted. She could breathe—she was *free*! She pushed to her feet and ran.

Vertigo spun her; her feet met the ground blind. Branches snagged her skirt, her hair. *He would catch her. He was behind her!*

"Charlotte, stop!"

He's coming!

"Charlotte!"

Will?

She turned. The amber glow of a lantern illuminated Will standing over Hugh's body—hunched and broken-looking against the trunk of a tree, his neck bent oddly. *He was dead!*

Oh no, no…he was dead…

Hugh lurched upright to sitting and she tripped over her feet.

In a flash of movement, Will's greatcoat swung in a billowing arc. He gripped Hugh's hair and yanked, forcing the man to look him full in the face. "You don't touch her," he growled. "You never touch her."

Hugh's body whipsawed into a tortured arch, his tears silver in the lamplight. "I won't! Stop—I can't breathe, my heart—"

"Quiet!"

Hugh writhed under the grip on his scalp, his lips pressed thin against sound.

In the stark quiet, her ragged breathing was unrecognizable as her own.

"Charlotte," Will said quietly, as if waking from a dream. He sprang his fingers free of Hugh as if it burned to touch him, and Hugh crumpled like a puppet with his strings cut. Will's eyes locked on her and he plunged up the incline, his running gait hobbled with what must be agony.

Her heart tore at the sight. "Don't run." She tried to call but only a thin whisper eked through. "Don't run."

In an instant, he loomed over her, reaching, and she shied violently. Her feet tangled in the dense brush and she fell, landing hard on a ragged stump. But her body was so insensible, she did not cry out.

He cringed. "No, Charlotte."

It was not her mind recoiling but her skin, her nerves, her blood—excited to a frenzy and unable to return to normalcy. He lifted her, her feet meeting ground, but it was Will who held her weight, rooted and stronger than even the trees around them.

"He won't touch you," Will said, his voice edged with fury. Smothered against his chest, the words rumbled through her. One strong hand braced her; the other traveled over her head, her arms, her back, searching for injury.

To her shame, her breath hitched raggedly in her throat and the more she attempted to contain the tremors shaking her body, the worse they became.

Will's hand stilled, cupping her head. "Where are you hurt?"

She shook her head, and he seemed to understand she was uninjured.

"I didn't know…Hugh never—" She broke off at the feel of his lips on her temple, his large hand holding her head still against his mouth.

"It's over," Will whispered. "It's over." He looked back at Hugh.

Or where Hugh should have been.

"Spencer!"

Will's roar was so startling, she flinched. Released abruptly, she swayed but stayed upright. Will crashed down the brush to the trail. Hugh was gone. And so was the lantern.

"Spencer!"

No lamp glow could be seen; she could barely see Will. Only his white shirt resisted the absolute dark enveloping them.

"Damn it." Will's low curse floated to her.

"Come back." But she was already stumbling toward him. She did not see him return as much as feel him, hearing branches snap underfoot. The blackness of the wood was complete, impenetrable to her eye.

"I'm sorry, Charlotte." His voice was a trace of heat in the cool, damp air, his body more of the same, so she held his sleeve, tethering him close. "We're here until sunrise. The trail's gone."

Hugh had trapped them here, vulnerable in a terrain that was treacherous come nightfall.

Will's arm circled her shoulders and she wondered if he did so to comfort her or keep her in place. "We'll be fine."

But her flesh prickled, sensing the invisible presence of snagging thorns and prodding branches, the centipedes and vermin scuttling near. It was only nature. No different in the dark as in the day.

No different…

"The hermitage," she whispered, remembering Lucy's folly. She peered into the dark as if she might see it, but only darkness crowded back. "It is not far. We were close to coming upon it."

"A hermitage?"

"Ben restored it for Lucy. It's her favorite retreat. There may be a lantern or candle."

She inched to the path but Will held her still. "Trust me," she said.

He diverted his hold to her elbow.

"The ravine was to our right." In the dark, she swept the path before placing her full weight upon the ground. Will's arm was hooked around her waist and the other stretched before them.

Was this the way? The incline was too steep. She stopped to regain her bearings, but how could she know? It was impossible to see; what if she was leading them away, what if—

"It's all right, Charlotte. We can stop."

"I was sure it was near."

His arm gave a comforting squeeze. "Then let's go a ways more."

His voice held no blame or frustration, so she took a deep breath. An owl screeched overhead and she jumped. "I'm so glad you're here."

"But you wish I'd kept hold of that lantern, don't you?"

In the dark, she smiled and pressed the hand he kept about her waist firmly against her.

After what might have been two or ten or twenty minutes in the dark, and a dozen, startling pricks from unseen branches, they slowed to a standstill. She was glad he couldn't see the misery surely on her face. "I'm sorry—"

"*There*, Charlotte." His voice was threaded with pride. Slowly, the ancient, rounded structure revealed itself, a bone-white glow in the blackness. "Is that it?"

"Thank God," she gasped.

The way was steep, but Will's footing was sure. Even in pain, and with her cumbersome form clinging to him, his strength was remarkable. A skill no doubt gained in his work.

Will fumbled for the latch, and the door groaned open. Will held her back from entering into the blackness, but the hermitage held no fear for her. The seventeenth-century hovel was as familiar to her as any room in Windmere, and she made her way unerringly to the hearthstone and lit a Lucifer match. The sudden flare of light threw the room's dimensions into sharp relief. The flames caught in the fireplace and bathed the room with a golden glow. There were no candles or lanterns, no table or chair, only a narrow rope bed along the curved wall and a rag rug on the stone floor.

Will stood at the door, his gaze locked on the bed.

"I'm afraid this is it," she said.

He started at her words and diverted his attention to the ceiling and walls. The corner of his mouth curled with a half smile. "Good work, Charlotte."

Despite everything, her cheeks burned with pleasure. *Honestly*, this constant blushing was utterly ridiculous. She cleared her throat, but she couldn't bluster her pride away. "Well. It is a roof."

He closed the door and limped to the center of the room, appearing confused as to what to do next.

She hugged her arms about herself, wanting more to hug him. He favored his right leg and the pained stance wrung her heart. "We may as well sit. Surely someone will come. Once Hugh gains his reason."

"If the bastard has any decency."

She let the curse pass in silent agreement. "My brother will come, he will find us."

"Wallace wasn't aware you were missing. It was the servants who told me."

"Oh no." She frowned with regret. "Everyone will be in such a state."

"They'll not worry long. If Spencer returns to the house, he'll be forced to tell our whereabouts."

That did seem the likeliest scenario. And the most favorable to her reputation, so she staked her faith upon it.

The fire dipped and sputtered and they both stared. "I am useless at starting fires," she said.

"I'll see to it." Will quickly knelt at the fire, seeming relieved to have a task.

She rather wished she had one, too.

Charlotte sat on the corner of the narrow bed and watched Will work. The door wasn't latched and she stood to fix the lock. At the sound, Will turned, but just as quickly turned back.

She cringed, realizing how unnecessary the act was. There were no roaming bandits or poachers to fear. She latched the door from habit, but at present, locking herself in with Will only heightened the awkward intimacy of their situation.

She perched on the bed, careful not to make noise. Will straightened and took off his coat, holding it open before the fire, and the breath left her lungs.

The firelight revealed a thoroughly male silhouette through the thin linen. Almost as if he stood naked before her—a broad, powerful back tapering dramatically to a lean waist and the muscled ridge of his hips. Arms that bulged with muscle flexed and rotated the coat before the flames. She dropped her eyes, but in the next second, as Will was unaware, she looked again. *Oh my…*

She really ought to look away. Likely she would, later.

He turned and she started guiltily.

"Here." He held out the coat. "Put this on."

"I cannot—"

He draped the coat over her shoulders. The toasty wool melted the tension from her shoulders. She *had* been cold.

"Better?" Light blue eyes searched hers with concern as he crouched and drew the ends of the coat tight about her. Her heart gave a helpless thump.

Dear God, he was the most beautiful man. Mesmerized, she nodded.

He straightened and limped back toward the wall, as far from her as he could possibly manage.

She slid to the edge of the bed. "Please sit down."

"I'll sit here. In China, I sat on the ground more often than a chair."

"That does not account. There is room on the… here." She had not intended to sound cross, but there was no missing how his face had shuttered at her suggestion. "Please, Mr. Repton—"

"I'm back to 'Mr. Repton,' then?"

"Well…I will call you Will. If you prefer."

"I do prefer." He grinned. "That makes us very nearly friends. That must be quite a prize for you."

She smiled, relieved by his show of humor, dry as it was. "It is far worse for you. Now that you've been cried upon twice, and endured my kisses, and rescued me from—" She would not say the words aloud. "You have been far more friendlike to me than I have to you."

"I wasn't minding the balance. And if I'm to be honest, I enjoyed the kisses."

His eyes warmed with humor and the look was devastating, melting all those things vital to her resolve and strength.

"Did I thank you, Will? Thank you."

He smoothed the floor with the toe of his boot in an oddly boyish fidget. "You don't need to thank me."

Before she could protest, he scrubbed a hand through his hair and the collar of his shirt gaped open, revealing the start of a muscular chest and a dusting of light brown hair—effectively wiping every other thought from her head.

"If no one comes, we'll leave the wood as soon as the sun rises," he said. "Perhaps we can avoid the houseguests knowing. I imagine you know a secret way into Windmere?"

"Do you suggest I am experienced in sneaking in and out of the house?"

He studied her seriously. "I think you might be, actually. Is there some lucky stable hand from your youth who dreams of your kisses?"

She laughed. "You know very well I have no skill in kissing."

He looked at her until her cheeks flamed red and, for the first time, she was the first to drop her eyes.

He cleared his throat. "We ought to separate as we near the house. You can claim an early morning walk, and let me in through an unused door."

Finding a deserted path into Windmere would be difficult as early as the servants rose, but let him make his plans. The man seemed the type who would not rest without one.

"I do not care if the entire house sees us." She lifted her chin. "We have done nothing wrong—*you saved me* from Hugh's assault. If anyone dares whisper of impropriety, I will denounce them roundly and never speak to them again. *Ever.* And I will not allow anyone to speak against you."

He gave a nod as if the matter were easy and settled

and fell squarely within the bounds of common sense. But her words were pure bravado. How scandalous the situation would appear if seen. Impending ruin was no light thing, so she was grateful of Mr. Repton's inexperience in the ways of Society. Besides, what could be done?

And at the moment, Mr. Repton—*Will*—was rubbing his thigh. "Your leg...?"

"It's fine, but"—he could not hide a wince as he stretched his leg experimentally—"I might need to rest it."

He started to sit on the ground and she leapt up, his coat tangling in her ankles. "Yes, indeed." She tugged him toward the bed. "Lie down. This instant."

He tried to resist, but after looking into her determined face, he limped toward the bed. "Normally it's fine." He lay down, expelling a sigh of relief.

"Is there something I can do? Shall I massage it?"

"God no!" He chuckled, but she didn't see what was funny about the suggestion.

He slid nearer the wall. "You can...I'll lie on this side."

He faced the wall. Would they not speak a moment or two longer?

She had never lain beside anyone before. And of all the anyones in the world, it would be him. Gingerly, she sat and lifted her legs onto the wool blanket stretched over the straw mattress.

Facing the fire with her back to Will, she arranged his coat atop her and shifted to get comfortable. Why had she not worn a weightier dress? The silk of her gown held the cold within its folds.

And Will had given her his coat…

Careful not to disturb him, she rolled to face his back, inching as close as she dared. Will's breathing was even, he must be asleep. Was he cold? His linen shirt appeared fine and he had no waistcoat. Surely his coat would cover them both—

"You do crowd me, Charlotte. The bed is little enough as it is." Will's voice was deep and loud in the tiny hovel.

"Sorry," she whispered. "Are you not cold?"

"I'm fine."

"The first of June should not be this cold. You are cold, are you not?"

"I'm fine."

"I cannot take your coat," she said, her voice muffled beneath the wool.

He turned his head and lifted an amused brow at the sight of her, all but buried beneath the garment. "All right, then. Give it back."

She gasped, burrowing deeper under the coat. "I… well, I thought we might share?"

In answer, he chuckled and presented his back to her again. "I'm not cold."

"Honestly, Will. You must be."

His shoulders hunched, as if that silent signal of irritation would dissuade her.

"Will? We are sharing your coat or I'll not use it at all. We are adults and nearly friends. Will?" She waited. "Will?"

He sighed and mumbled something about relentless women.

"Did you…did you agree? I think I heard you agree."

"*All right,* Charlotte. I'll share the coat." But he made no move to take his half.

Satisfied, she inched closer until her nose poked his back and she could arrange the coat over his shoulder and herself. It slipped off him, then her, until she had it placed just so. She was stiff and uncomfortable balancing on her side, but at least they were covered. Somewhat. In places.

"Don't move or—" The coat slipped off him. "You moved."

He grunted and flopped over, threading a strong arm under her neck to hug her and arrange the coat over them both. "There," he breathed. "This works, doesn't it?"

She lay very still, assessing this new, exquisite embrace she found herself in. There was no seduction in his touch. No arms or fingers molding against her. Yet his body warmed her instantly and she dissolved against him like snowflakes on a hearth. A contented sigh escaped, and she peeked to see a muscle jerk in his cheek.

"Comfortable?" Will murmured.

"Yes." Whatever emotion she heard in Will's growl, she ignored. His strong arm was around her and despite his grudging tones, she felt safe. And strangely cherished by this man she loved.

For one night, she would pretend he loved her, too.

"Are you comfortable?" she whispered.

He moved a curl of her hair an inch to the right. "Now I'm comfortable."

She smiled at this rare silliness. She was completely boneless, savoring the warmth of his body and the security of his arms. The sensation all the more acute after Hugh's cold, grasping attack.

Lying with Will was as natural as her next breath. It was an accomplishment, of a sort. For once, her heart didn't race at his nearness. There was only the simple acceptance in what he must be to her—no longer her hero or her conquest. He was just a man. More special than most, but just a man. And despite their troubled start, he might even be her friend. If she could stop desiring to crawl inside his skin, she might be his friend in earnest.

But for tonight, she ignored the hard, muscled length of him and sought only to give and receive comfort. The man was so wonderfully heated. "How did you stay warm in China?"

"I didn't snuggle with my crewmates if that's what you're asking."

"You wore animal skins, didn't you?"

"On the coldest days." He paused. "My, uh… my mate, Cressey, had this fox-fur coat with the most godforsaken stench. He had no choice but to wear it, but he was always trying to negotiate a trade for anyone else's." He chuckled. "There were never any takers, but he never stopped trying. We made him walk in the rear when he had that mangy thing on."

"The poor man."

"He used to try to wager it in card games. He said he'd give his sister's hand in marriage to any man who'd trade with him. Jack told him Helen of Troy couldn't induce a man to wear it."

"Who are they? Cressey and Jack?"

"Cressey was...Owen Cressman. A collector with East India, too. And Jack...the places we went because of him."

"Because of him?"

"He was responsible for our passports."

She smoothed her hand up his back, wanting to comfort. "I suspect you had many happy moments amidst all that swashbuckling."

He drew in a deep breath. "We did. Many moments."

His breath grew shallow and uneven, his body tightening. "If I'd been wrong, Charlotte. If I'd not found you—"

"But you weren't wrong."

His arms relaxed, but something told her not to question Will about his friends. Not now. "How did you know where to find me?"

A moment passed before he spoke. "The house and outbuildings were already being searched and I felt... you said you kissed Spencer on the nature walk." He paused. "You refused him. Why?"

Because I love you. "We were not connected."

"He never brought you peonies."

All the wasted time with Hugh...all the false laughter and conversation and excusing his arrogance. "No. He never did, did he?"

He snorted. "The simplest task."

"And there was the other *incompatibility*."

He tilted his head, his chin scraping her forehead, and she could almost feel the question rising in his throat.

"Desire," she blurted. "The lack of, that is."

He cleared his throat but said nothing.

"Lucy and Ben are passionate. She has told me from the first they felt an overwhelming attraction to each other."

"Odd that, when they're both so unfortunate-looking."

She laughed and Will's chest quaked against her with his chuckle.

"My mother and father"—a pained half-smile flit across his lips—"still feel passion. They feel it almost every night and every morning and, once that I'm aware of, they felt it in the conservatory behind the house. Thank God it was winter and the glass was frosted. Hearing them in the throes is difficult enough."

She hurriedly ushered the image from her mind, but a choked laugh escaped her. "That is rather wonderful, though."

Will shrugged, but his smile tickled her brow.

"Spencer inspired no passion at all?"

"Never. Which I cannot account as he is handsome and trim and manly—"

"Yes, all right," he muttered, idly twisting the buttons on the back of her gown. "You'll begin again. Win back any of those besotted suitors. Hatfield seems agreeable, and he'd support you well. Matteson is a wealthy prospect. His teeth are unfortunate, but your children aren't doomed to the same fate. Maybe—"

"Thank you, but I would rather you not trot out the most eligible bachelors for my consideration. I would rather not think on it at all. All new suitors... all new tests." She yawned.

"No need to worry," Will whispered as his arms snuggled her closer. "The perfect man is preparing as we speak. He's just been busy. What with overseeing his kingdom and counting all his big bags of money. And I wonder how he'll ever manage to leave the castle with all the ladies swooning in his path."

Breathing in the cloud of warm male skin and sun-dried linen, she smiled at the silly picture. "He will never make it to London. Too busy saving orphans and cast-off puppies."

"No, after the sculptors are done chiseling his likeness in marble, he'll be free to find you."

"Well, they had better be quick about it." She smiled. "Will...?"

"Hmm?"

"Thank you for finding me."

His chin settled atop her head. "You're welcome."

And in the second before Charlotte succumbed to sleep, she wondered at how Will Repton had come to feel exactly like a friend.

Eleven

*T*HE GORGEOUS GIRL WAS UNDER HIM. *C*HARLOTTE'S *soft, writhing body, undulating in rhythm to his thrusting hips, her legs parting for him to sink deep, deeper. A round swell of breasts overspilling his hands. Keep her…*

Dark hair caught and lifted in a warm wind at the hunting tower. A kiss in a midnight garden. Jasmine in her hair. So near.

"Charlotte…" *He heard a voice,* his *voice, grinding out her name.* "Mine…so sweet…"

Her perfume, her soft skin, so real. She sighed and he shuddered. Another kiss, another stroke…her breasts…her warm breath…hair through his fingers, slipping like silk… so real…

All so real. Not like a dream.

Not like—oh God! Not a dream! He was on top of her, his cock rock hard against the V of her legs, gripping her hips low against his. And she was awake.

He pushed off her, his sluggish limbs clumsy. "What the—?" The back of his head cracked against a wall. Pain slammed and reverberated through his skull and he clutched his head.

"Will, be careful!"

Why was she in his bed? Where—?

Charlotte was glued against him, thigh to thigh, stomach to stomach, and he shoved back against an unyielding wall. Her fingers spread over his scalp, soothing his head. He twisted away from the caress to see where he was, what he'd done, the revulsion in her eyes.

Memory flooded back. The little hermitage. Still dark. Only the dying red embers from the fireplace gave the faintest glow.

Charlotte, looking at him in the spellbound way she first looked at him, as if entranced by every movement of his face, every word from his lips. Her cheeks were flushed from sleep and her hair had come unpinned and lay in long, curling tresses over her breasts. He'd never seen her look so young and innocent.

Innocent. And here he was wielding a cockstand. And she, fresh from an attack by that bastard Spencer. "God," he groaned, clutching his head in his hands. No, God would not spare him this humiliation. "I'm sorry, I was..."

"Dreaming."

She urged his hands down and he let her pull them away. The pupils of her eyes were wide in the faint light, leaving a narrow ring of blue. "Your poor head. Does it hurt?"

Before he could answer, she kissed the crown of his head and her breasts pressed into his face, inflicting another sort of pain. "My head is fine," he said into her warm bosom.

"What were you dreaming?"

"I..." *Don't answer that.* "I don't know."

"You said my name."

Those eyes were unrelenting.

"Do you remember?" she asked.

Yes, sweetheart. "It was a dream."

Did she just press her body against his? She had to feel his heart trying to pound through his chest and, *Christ*, the other thing. Her lids lowered and he could not see where she focused—his heart, or his cock jutting into her stomach.

He squirmed back but there was no room to retreat, and his body wasn't ignoring the lush bounty of her breasts pressed against his chest or the long, slender strength of her legs tangled in his.

"I need to stand, Charlotte." His voice was hoarse, but that was the least of his concerns. "Will you move back?"

"It's still dark."

He swallowed, desperate to hide his humiliating lust, but his flesh only jerked more urgently. God, she would feel that, too. "Just a little ways, so I can—"

"I don't want you to." Her fingers were still entwined in his hair and she hitched higher so their mouths were level.

This was mad. Charlotte didn't really want him. She'd kissed two men in her life and he was the less objectionable of the two. He caught her hands, but her lips kept advancing. And God...her eyes...

"Before I met you, I dreamed you. Dreamed you dancing with me, kissing me, loving me. Then I met you and started to dream other things."

"Pushing me down a ravine? Holding me under the Serpentine?"

She ignored his desperate attempt at humor and pressed her sweet mouth against his.

Paralyzed with pleasure, he let her. Let her kiss him, let her explore him with her shy tongue.

Damn me…damn me…she was perfect…

With his mouth engaged, his attention arrowed to her breasts. His favorite breasts, hitching and heaving against him. Mindlessly, he matched the rhythm of her breathing. As if making love.

Her hands traveled low on his back and he jerked as if singed with fire. His head reared back, desperate for air, for reason. "Don't, Charlotte."

She slid her leg over his hip, hooking him close, teasing his cock with the release it sought. He clamped down on the craven urge to grind against her softness but—*ah…dammit*—she discovered the sensation herself. Her eyes widened as she rubbed lightly against him, and her soft gasp made his body tighten all over. Christ, she felt so—

Enough!

He hurtled over her, falling to the ground stupidly and scrambling to stand. "That's enough." He kept his back to her, and his erection out of sight.

"Will?"

He staggered to the wall and leaned his dizzy head against the cool stone. The soft rustle of her skirt told him she was approaching and he braced. "I'm sorry, Charlotte—"

Hands smoothed over his back and circled him, caressing the painfully rigid planes of his torso. Firm breasts pressed against his back, her body melding to his, and a groan rose in his throat.

She pressed soft lips to his neck and wiped clean every thought in his brain.

Charlotte was talking. Of course she was. But his blood raced in his veins, drowning all sound from his ears. There was only her lips, hot and wet on his skin. And deep, deeper than reason, his own primal voice grinding out…

Keep her.

Mindless, wild, he rounded on her and swung her onto the bed, her weight like nothing at all. Oblivious of his own brawn, he landed atop her. He chased the gasp from her mouth with a hard kiss, his body seizing with bliss at the feel of her beneath him.

He bit, then soothed her lips with his tongue—he couldn't stop. Some thread of sanity impelled him to check that she wasn't afraid, but her glittering blue eyes darkened, misted, under her sleepy lids.

Her tongue slicked a seductive arc over her upper lip, leaving it to glisten. "Will."

Tamed, mesmerized by the erotic sight, he didn't resist when she pulled him down and melted his brain with her soft, wet kiss.

He'd been warned. Charlotte charmed what she wanted from those she met and he had no defense against her. Deep down, he'd known that the second he'd set eyes on her. And what the dangerous woman wanted now was him.

And not just his kiss.

The thought jarred him. They had to stop. Addled and weak with lust, he grasped for control, for sanity. But she denied him both.

She lured his tongue into her mouth and she was sucking on him, shredding his reason apart.

Keep her…keep her, she's yours…

Charlotte…sweet, curious, Charlotte…let her know the weight of him. He settled full on her, reveling in the feel of her body, accepting him, cradling him. She gasped and spread her thighs, tilting to meet him. As if by instinct.

"God," he groaned.

She pressed more urgently, her legs climbing his hips to wrap around him.

Innocent…she was innocent. Passionate like he'd never experienced, but innocent. She had to remain—

"*Please.*" She sealed her lips to his throat, suckling tight on his flesh.

God in heaven, he'd leave her *mostly* innocent. He unwrapped her legs and lifted off her, trying to soothe her, to slow her.

An ugly awareness surfaced that he was debauching her in the woods, in a shelter they'd come to out of desperate straits, but it hadn't a prayer of persuading him to stop—only to gentle his hands. He slid his mouth over hers, wanting her to remember, forever, that he was the first.

No matter he couldn't stay—he *couldn't* keep her—he'd be the first to make her come. He'd watch her come.

Her hands clutched handfuls of his hair in a grip that should have hurt, but he reveled in her possession. Her eyes met his, telling him without words of her need.

And beneath the need, something else. Something so endlessly, blazingly tender, he had to shut his eyes against the sight.

He stilled his lips, letting her kiss him as she desired.

Show me what you want. In answer, her mouth slowed, then retreated.

He laughed, faint and near breathless. "God, you're a puzzle." He captured her chin in his hand, the softness of her skin thrilling him. "Are you shy with me now, sweet Charlotte?"

"You stopped kissing me."

"I didn't want *you* to stop." Emboldened, he slipped his hand under her skirt and her eyes fluttered open. "It's all right," he murmured.

Steadying the slender thigh beneath the soft cotton pantalets, he lowered his mouth to hers. He massaged her higher and slid his hand inside the opening of her drawers. Her gasp broke open on his lips when he stroked the soft, slick folds at the core of her.

"God, you're so soft, so ready," he whispered. He parted her, slowly, gently, because he'd never done this before. Her breath hitched and struggled past her lips. Her eyes glazed, so he stilled his fingers. "Look at me."

His demand surprised even him. Those eyes could undo him but he needed to see into her when she came.

She focused again on him, her beautiful face softening with a wondering smile. His cock surged, twitching against the confines of his trousers, and he gritted his teeth for control. Obediently, kindly, she watched him, her fingers flexing on his shirt.

He smiled. "Tell me if you like this."

"I do."

"I've not done it yet."

"I liked what you were doing. What do you call—"

He eased his finger into her narrow sheath and—

"*Oh! My—!*" She drove her head back into the mattress, her neck exposed to his lips.

He kissed her on that creamy throat, returning the torture she'd inflicted upon him, and teased the most sensitive corner of her with his thumb, sliding his finger gently in and out.

Never had he touched a woman like this—never more intent on drawing out her pleasure or remembering every moan, every clench, every silken stroke. "I'm inside you," he said huskily. "Do you feel me inside you?"

"Yes…I feel…"

The way she held him, hugging him tight around the neck to hold him close, flooded the hollow in his chest with tenderness, with gratitude. No woman had ever held him like this, wanted him like this. And after what he'd done…

"Will…don't stop. Please."

She was so small, he could weep at how fragile her body was. She squeezed on his fingers and—"Ah God!"—his body seized with violence, his back arched, and he spilled his seed into his trousers with a hoarse cry.

Christ. He'd never gone off without a stroke before. Never lost control. Not even when he was a lad.

Spent, panting, he concentrated again on her. "Come for me," he rasped. "I've got you, let it come."

She tightened and pulsed around his finger and he coaxed her closer, faster, and deeper, until she was bearing down and her heated channel was quivering with miraculous spasms radiating to the ends of her. With a final cry, she shuddered and went limp under him.

Triumph blasted through him. He laughed, sinking on her shivering body, joining her in the ecstasy.

Damn if he wasn't primitive. He wanted to shout, to pound his chest and glory in the spasms he'd caused. Capturing the tender earlobe with his teeth and traveling to her panting mouth, he claimed her there. Slowly, reluctantly, he removed his hand from her clinging softness.

"Only you," she whispered, burrowing closer. "Only you…"

And then her eyes opened.

There.

There it was again. That tenderness, that trust. And something else. Something he hadn't seen before. And it made him feel…

Christ, it made him feel he was crossing the Leaping Tiger Gorge in Yunnan. The swaying rope bridge. The six-hundred-foot drop. The wind howling in his ears, mocking his balance. A vertigo like he'd never known…

He clutched the wool blanket on either side of her and dragged his gaze away. He arranged her skirts with a hand that seemed hacked from stone.

God, what had he done? Look where they were. He'd tarnished the dazzling Charlotte Baker in a hovel in the wood. The incomparable of London Society, subjected to his emptiness, his darkness. Beautiful, innocent Charlotte.

Christ, why hadn't he thought…?

He dropped on his back and stared at the ceiling, praying he might have rendered her speechless for once. Just once. Just until he could gather his wits.

But he knew better.

Charlotte was never speechless.

"That was the most astonishing thing I have ever felt," she whispered. "How did I not know my body could do that? You were incredible." She pressed his hand to her breast. "Feel my heart. Do you feel it?"

He couldn't feel his hand. Why couldn't he feel—?

"I have never felt so wild, so removed from reason." Her hands slid down her body to twist in her skirt. She kicked her feet on the bed and laughed. "That was—is it always like that? No, I would only feel this with you. No man could touch me like you. No wonder men and women seek love, if this is their reward. *Quelle joie, quel bonheur!*"

"Love? I—is that French? I don't speak—"

"I know you are not in love," she said quietly. "But this was the most extraordinary experience in my life. And I do not expect anything from you, I vow, but my life has altered course. The world is spinning on a new axis." Her eyes widened with her gasp. "This is an historic day in my life. I have to tell Lucy—no, I cannot but—" she pushed up onto her elbow. "*Honestly*, Will! I just told you this is historic. Put your arms around me."

The scolding worked; his body unlocked. "I don't know what to do, Charlotte!" He flung clumsy arms around her, far from the tender embrace he ought to give, *wanted* to give, but she nestled willingly enough against him. "Are you…are you all right? I just…I hadn't prepared for this."

"I know," she said softly. "But in that little space between plans, you must leave room for the unexpected.

You must leave room for *life*. The loveliest things can happen when you do not expect them." She grew quiet. "When you do not even hope for them."

"That's not my experience."

She stroked his cheek and his heart buckled. "I am sorry for that. But this has been wonderful for me, if not for you, so you may count this in your experience."

Quiet minutes passed. His heartbeat slowed. Charlotte seemed happy, at least.

Damn me. She deserved more than this. He hadn't loved her the way a man should. Not properly, by joining his flesh with hers.

But he'd never have that right.

She fidgeted with the collar of his shirt. "I know this does not compare with all the experiences you have had, or the other women—"

"No—"

"I know they pleased you far more, but you mustn't worry. I would never ask you to—"

She raised her head to look into his eyes, and he was terrified of her next words. If she asked him to stay, to love her, to marry her—he would refuse her nothing. Not when she looked at him like that.

Her eyes shied from his and she rested her cheek on his chest.

"I will never ask," she said quietly. "How strange. I thought I would have to sail over an ocean to feel this alive. There are so many rules and constraints and yet…when I'm with you, the way you make me feel and what I know and all I experience when you're with me…my life here suddenly seems so limitless."

She kissed him above his heart and, like her slave,

its answer knocked against his ribs. "You understand, don't you?"

Understand? He barely knew his name. If he hadn't been lying down, he would have dropped.

She was an avalanche, a tempest at sea, a six-hundred-foot drop. He prided himself on being prepared for every contingency but how did a man prepare for her? She never behaved like he thought she would. No vista he'd seen or terrain he'd crossed had ever frightened, and exhilarated, as much as her.

Didn't he avoid what he couldn't control?

Aimee was waiting, and he was losing his way. He would stay here forever if he looked too long. He would abandon the return, abandon the only chance to find the child, *he couldn't.* He couldn't stay, she was waiting— "I wish I hadn't met you."

Charlotte inhaled sharply.

"No"—*Christ, what had he said?*—"no, I didn't mean to—"

She pulled from his clutching arms and stood, but not before she could hide the tears in her eyes.

He reached for her, but she slipped away.

She opened the door. In the faint light of dawn, the black woods had turned blue. "The sun is rising."

"I didn't—" But he *did* mean it. He wished he hadn't met her, not now. Not when the memory of her would lengthen every minute away from her. "Charlotte?"

"It's time to go."

"You don't understand—"

She shook her head, her eyes sending a warning not to speak. The foreboding look so unlike her, so unbalancing that he staggered, and she swept by him out the door.

"I'm leaving." *And I would have pursued you, made love to you, done anything to keep you.*

Even if I didn't deserve you.

But she didn't hear his last words, as she'd already started down to the path.

❧

The end of the wood was steps away and Charlotte paced steadily toward it. Behind her, Will followed without sound. The great lawn stretched to the house, bathed in the cold, gray light of dawn. The birds had not yet risen to crack the stillness and no wind disturbed the trees. She might have been all alone in the world.

And what peace there would be in that.

Will took her arm, startling her. "Charlotte?"

His eyes, usually so evasive, were beseeching. And sobering in their remorse.

All was clear again. She wanted Will—and he wanted to leave. To sail and roam and battle the darkness that clung to him. How could any woman compete with that? With a whole, vast, dangerous world?

"Will you be all right?" he asked.

I wish I'd never met you…

"Of course," she said softly. She was Charlotte Baker, after all. And she was buoyant and did not take offense and was prone to all sorts of fanciful notions. She added a false smile—which he did not return. "Wait ten minutes and go in through the library terrace. I'll unlatch the door. No servants should see us."

"Charlotte—"

She pulled out of his hold and ran. The air was mercifully cool on her hot, itching eyes and the grass wet at her ankles. The house loomed mammoth and serene. Windmere…when she was a child, it had been a castle and she a princess on her pony.

But this was her home, her family, and she would always have them, no matter what she daydreamed.

She could explain to her family, Hugh would leave, nothing would change. Nothing *had* changed. Not really.

Not on the outside.

Will was never going to stay. He had fascinated her. He had ignited her passion, and for that alone, she must be grateful. She *would* be grateful, *she would.*

Even if this was all the love she would ever have.

The door for deliveries was open as she expected, and she waited with cocked ear until she was assured no one was about before climbing the back stairs to the hall. The house was quiet. Thank goodness all were still asleep.

The library door opened soundlessly and she slipped inside—and her heart stopped in her chest. Everyone—Hugh, the earl and countess, Ladies Helen and Hester, Lady Wynston, *everyone* appeared to have gathered here, and their heads turned at her entrance.

Hugh stood in the corner of the immense room, his face like stone, and a tide of revulsion nearly buckled her knees. He had not changed his clothes.

"There you are, child," Lady Wynston said dryly, her eyes sharpening on Charlotte's unbound hair, the open buttons at her neck, the darkened hem from running across the dewy grass. "Already taken your exercise? Just as Lord Spencer returns from his ride. And here I thought I kept country hours."

"I...you're awake." The startled faces crinkled with confusion at her words.

Bounding steps sounded on the terrace outside, and all heads swiveled to watch the famed explorer, Will Repton, race up the steps and slide to a stop, shirttails flapping and coat unbuttoned.

Oh no.

As if they heard her silent groan, all heads swiveled back. It was done. In the quiet, in the hastily lowered lids, in the shared, shocked glances, Charlotte Baker had been accused, tried, and judged.

Yes, she had been compromised. And rather well, actually.

All it had cost was her entire heart.

Twelve

Will hesitated only a second on the other side of the glass. The surprise on his face hardened to stone, and his eyes latched onto hers with solemn apology. With unshaven chin held high, he marched to the glass doors leading into the library and its gaping audience. Kenneth, the footman, hurried to let him in, but fumbled under Will's stare.

Reluctantly, she slid her attention to Hugh, asking her a silent question. The almost imperceptible turn of his head told her he'd not spoken of what had happened.

"Charlotte," Hugh began slowly, staring his warning. "Surely you can appreciate we would all be excited over the birth of your nephew last evening. Many of us woke early expressly for that reason. Especially as the servants were up and down the stairs all evening."

"My nephew?" *Lucy had her baby!* "My...my nephew, yes."

The terrace door clicked open and her shock and joy was interrupted by the sight of Will stalking toward Hugh, a murderous look on his face.

"Oh! Mr. Repton!" A half dozen quick steps put

her in Will's path. The man didn't cease till his hard body knocked into hers.

Behind her, Hugh stumbled back from Will's approach, into a chair…the table…another chair. What did Will think he was doing? "Might I have a word?"

"I have business with Spencer." Will moved her aside.

"If you would oblige me?" She gave her sweetest smile but gripped his arm, unbending as steel.

Will swiveled his glare, like a lion spying more attractive prey.

"I will not delay you long." Their eyes locked in battle but Will hadn't a hope of winning. Despite the intimacy they had shared, the man still could not hold her stare.

"Please," she whispered.

Will grumbled something unintelligible but trudged behind her. The fascinated onlookers stared until she closed the library doors from the hall. Swinging around, she dashed to the stairs, taking the steps two at a time.

"Where are you going?" Will bellowed, his patience apparently at an end. "You said you needed to speak to me."

She stopped short and leaned toward him to hiss, "*Come here.*"

With stomping steps, he joined her on the stairs.

She reined in her patience. "I do not want to *speak* to you. I *want* you away from Hugh."

"Why do you care what happens to—"

"Oh, honestly! Lucy had her baby last night and I need to go to her *right now* but I cannot trust you not to harm Hugh, so go to your room."

"Go to my room?"

"Yes. What do you imagine you might do? Start chewing on the man's head in front of everyone? He is a viscount, for heaven's sake, and his father an earl. Go to your room or have a bit of breakfast or see to your parents. They must be concerned over your whereabouts."

His crossed his arms over his chest, looking undecided as to what to do next—even though she had provided three perfectly acceptable alternatives.

"Everyone saw us, Charlotte," he said grimly.

They had. They *had* seen. She was ruined. It was over.

Why, then, was she smiling? "I don't care." She shook her head, amazed. "I must be mad, but I don't—I have a nephew! I mean, another nephew—a *new* nephew!"

Will was looking back at the library doors as if nothing would please him better than to rip them from their hinges.

"Will, please. Promise me you will not go in there. I want to see Lucy."

He gripped his temples. "Go to your sister," he muttered.

It sounded near enough to a promise for her. With an unladylike squeal, she bounded up the stairs.

Lucy and Ben's door was shut and her knock was admirably restrained, when she wanted to shout out loud, laugh, cry. A baby boy! Dear God, let them all be well…

The door opened and she hurried to kneel at the side of Lucy's bed. Lucy looked tired, but beautiful and happy. Ben was beside her still dressed in last night's shirt and trousers. A day's growth of beard darkened his weary face, but his expression was one of pride. Jacob was sprawled at the foot of the bed, softly snoring, and the baby was in Lucy's arms.

"Dearest, are you unwell?" Lucy asked. "They told me you could not be roused from sleep."

Charlotte hugged Lucy around her precious bundle. "Oh, Lucy, I'm so sorry, I am well. Are you all right?"

"Yes, love, everyone's ecstatic. Meet Edward. Isn't he perfect?"

Charlotte eased back the swaddling. The baby's fathomless gaze blinked at her gasp and her heart flooded with love. "He's the reddest thing I've ever seen." She laughed through her tears.

Another baby...Lucy's baby.

Another nephew.

She slumped on her knees beside the bed, her head dropping onto the mattress, and she began to laugh. And then cry.

"What is it, dearest?" Lucy asked, stroking her head.

"Charlotte?" Wally's voice came from behind her.

She wiped her cheeks and rose on unsteady legs, prepared for a scolding. Instead, her brother gathered her into his arms and pulled her from the bedside so they'd not be heard. "I was so worried, dear heart. Do not ever frighten me again. Where were you? Are you hurt?"

"I am not hurt—not at all. I will explain everything." She left his arms to kiss Lucy's brow, then followed him to his sitting room.

To her dismay, Will was waiting within.

"Are Lucy and the baby well?" Will asked.

She nodded. Oh dear. Will had not changed his clothes. That fact would not go unnoticed by—

"Why are you not dressed?" Wally scanned him, his face turning grim. Slowly, he faced her. "Tell me what happened last night, Charlotte."

"Will you not sit?"

"*One* of you tell me right now."

Her brother's cheeks darkened, a telltale purple she did not dare to disobey. She took a breath. "Hugh and I were on the nature walk and it grew dark. Mr. Repton came along with a lantern and Hugh took it. We could not see the path to come home."

"Tell him everything, Charlotte," Will said.

She looked at him, silently pleading to spare Wally those details.

"Tell him or I will," he said.

Her brother stood straight-backed, appearing braced for a blow. "Hugh did not accept my decision to end our courtship. I could not make him understand we had to leave the wood before dark. He grabbed me and pulled me to the ground—"

"He dared touch you?"

"No, Wally! Will found us then. I wasn't hurt."

Wally searched her eyes. Then turned to Will, who nodded grimly in confirmation.

Wally pivoted to pull the bell for a servant. When he spoke, his voice was hoarse with rage. "I want that man out of our home. If he ever comes near you again, I will kill him—his money and title will not protect him."

Wally began to pace, and she sank onto the settee. A minute passed before her brother regained enough of his composure to speak. "And what transpired in the wood after Spencer left?"

"We were able to make our way to the hermitage and slept until daybreak," she said.

"Slept? You both have love bites on your neck."

Mortified, she pulled the ends of her collar together. "Will saved me."

"Saved you? Charlotte, he has ruined you."

Will jerked his head up. "She isn't ruined, Wallace, I swear it."

The men locked stares, until Wally wiped a weary hand down his face. "*Christ God*." He sighed. "I believe you, Will. I do. But a dozen members of the *ton* downstairs know you two were together. All will believe you seduced her away from Spencer."

"So she will not marry Spencer," Will muttered. "I don't see that as much of a loss."

Charlotte closed her eyes. Will did not understand. But it appeared her brother was about to enlighten him.

"True," Wally said. "She will not marry Spencer. She will likely not marry any Englishman of breeding, education, and respectability."

"Of course she will. And why the hell did she have to reject Spencer alone? Why did you let Spencer near her? You should have protected her. Surely you know men better than him!"

"You think I—"

"Hell! I could've done better for her, Wallace! Matteson's a decent man and rich enough, and what about—"

"*You* could do better?" Wally's face was nearly blue now.

"Wally…please," she said.

"*You* could do *better*, Will? Here is what I propose so this idiocy does not ruin my sister. *You* marry her."

She gaped, speechless, but Will surged to his feet. "The hell I will! I sail in three months."

Oh no…no, no, no— "Wally, what are you doing?"

But Wally stood and stalked Will. "If you wed, her reputation will be tarnished, but she will not be labeled a trollop."

She blinked. "A trollop? I am not even allowed to wear rouge."

"You found her where no one else thought to look," Wally said. "You rescued her. It is easy enough to proclaim you her lover already."

Will looked at her and her undoubtedly pale, rouge-free face. "No. No, there must be another way."

"There is no other way!" Wally said.

"*Enough*." Charlotte stood and dragged Wally to the end of the room, whispering so Will could not hear. "That is enough. Please, you cannot punish him."

"But if he married you—"

"I love him."

Wally stared, his eyes huge with surprise. "Charlotte…what did he do?"

"*Nothing*." With her eyes, she pleaded with him not to reveal her secret. "He does not know. I loved him the moment I saw him but I cannot *marry him*. He is leaving—he will break my heart."

Wally's eyes, so like her own, blazed with frustration. "Oh, Charlotte…"

She attempted a smile but it would not come. "It is our family's fatal flaw: to follow our hearts no matter where it may take us. I am sorry I disappointed you."

"No, dear heart. I am the one who is sorry." He stroked her hair gently. With a tired sigh, he faced Will. "Forgive me. I was not thinking clearly. I thank God you found my sister in time. I do not know what Spencer would have done to my dear girl."

Will looked confused by the sudden reversal. "That bastard deserves—"

"Yes." Wally held up a staying hand. "Yes. He thought he could have my sister any way he chose." He sank into his chair. "And that is my fault. No doubt you know of my past?"

"The trial? Yes—"

"And the truth."

She grabbed her brother's hand. "No."

Wally looked straight at Will. "I am called diseased and insane and possessed by evil because I loved a man, and I have marked Charlotte and Lucy with my own defect from birth. Blood will out, they say. And when this news gets out, that is what they will say again." Wally turned to her, his voice breaking. "I wanted everything for you—"

"I have everything." She turned her back on Will, the better to ignore his presence in the face of their shame. "I have you, and the children, and Lucy and Ben."

Wally rocked her in his arms. "Oh, my dear heart. I am so sorry."

Will was quiet behind her and Charlotte moved from Wally's embrace to face him. He stood silent and grim, but his eyes never wavered, a flame of something like determination blazing there. Determination to run, no doubt. The man would be so relieved to be away from Windmere.

"Will, we will not discuss last night with anyone downstairs, odd as that might feel. Hugh and his family will be gone and people will inquire as to why. Let me speak to them. I am sorry for any discomfort you and your parents will feel—"

"That's not good enough."

"You must trust me in this."

"Wallace is right. You can't throw away your life, your finishing schools, your friends. You belong with those people."

"No—"

He turned to her brother. "Will this work? If she marries me? She'll not be climbing the social ladder."

Wally sighed. "Forget all that, Will."

Will looked at her. She had misunderstood the determined look in his eye. He didn't want to flee.

He wanted to save her.

She shook her head, but he came to her as if beckoned. "What if we say we're in love? And you can file for abandonment when I leave or…we can say consummation was impossible due to my injuries." He dropped his voice to a whisper. "Not that it's true. I'm perfectly sound in that regard."

Charlotte gaped at him. What was happening? "This is ridiculous." But Wally and Will were silent, assessing the idea. "Wally? Tell Will this is ridiculous."

"Charlotte, I know this isn't your plan." Will's voice was gentle and placating and so unlike his usual tone, it stretched her nerves all the more. "It's certainly not mine, but you said yourself to leave room for the unplanned."

"I said to leave room for whimsy and serendipity, not for thoroughly deranged notions such as yours."

"Will this salvage your reputation?"

"What of your reputation?"

He appeared bemused by the question, sharing a look with Wally. Which she did not appreciate. Not at all.

"I'm a plant hunter, Charlotte. No one would fault me for falling in love with the most beautiful woman in London. And only my doctor knows of my injuries. A strategic whisper I'd been left unmanned—*not that I have*—and in time, you can marry again."

Wally spoke in her horrified silence. "Sit down, dear heart, you look pale. Will, if we do this—"

"If?" she cried.

"—it ought to happen quickly. In the next fortnight or so."

"I agree," Will said.

"And you must sleep in separate chambers," Wally added.

"Absolutely," Will said quickly.

Rather too quickly, in her opinion. *Enough!* She rounded on Will and lowered her voice to a whisper. "You do not want to do this. You said you wish we had never met."

"I didn't mean that exactly."

"You did." Her words broke and she steadied her chin against emotion. "I know you did. Besides"—she affected a cool expression—"I do not wish to marry. I do not need you to save me. This is absurd."

Will aimed his stare over her head.

She drew to her full height. "I said I do not need to be saved."

"I say you do and so does your brother. You might listen to us for your own good."

Her jaw dropped. "I won't listen." She made for the door. "*My own good*—honestly! If you men wish to pretend you will decide everything, *fine*. I will not play the role of spectator to my own life."

"For God's—listen to me." He caught her elbow and steered her into the hall. "Why not marry? I'm leaving in August, I'll take nothing from you." He probed her eyes, something weakening his stare. "Is it so impossible to pretend to love me?"

She flinched at the well-aimed words. "It is *you* who would never be believed in love with me, as dismissive and unnoticing as you are. See! You cannot look at me for longer than a blink. No one will believe you love me or even like me with any consistency."

He stepped closer, his eyes steady and blazing into hers. "I can make them believe. If I let myself, I could make even you believe. You already know I desire you."

Desire. Her eyes dropped to his neck. The deep red mark her lips had left on the tendon looked so vulgar. Yet at the time, she wanted to weep from the glory of tasting his skin.

Desire…that was all. And desire wasn't love.

"It's the best solution," Will said.

"To marry you?"

"Yes."

"And sleep apart?"

"Yes."

"Will we even share the same roof?"

He frowned. "We wouldn't have to. You might stay here. No one would know we were apart."

She crossed her arms over her chest, needing

someone's arms about her. Of course Will would leave her. Nothing would keep him next to her, not even marriage.

"Charlotte? Please. I can't be responsible for this."

"You are not responsible."

"Please. Marry me."

His soft coaxing banded her heart and tugged. If only he were truly asking. She closed her eyes. "How long?"

"How—? Uh…July? Or August? In time to annul before I sail."

August. Nearly three months with Will beside her. Could three months last her a lifetime?

"Charlotte?" Will's hand settled on her shoulder.

Could she bear it? Could she marry him and watch him leave her?

She looked into the face of the man of her dreams and there was the answer. "Yes." The word was out of her mouth before she could stop it.

His hand dropped from her. "I…good." His tone was relieved, but his manner was suspicious.

"I will marry you, and I will thank you for it."

He swept her face cautiously. "All right."

She would have her husband, her love… "But I have requirements."

He stood very still. Then with a quick nod of his head, he widened his stance and crossed his arms. "Yes, of course. Name them."

Stay with me. "Yes…I, uh…" Was she really doing this? "They are conditions, actually, which are perhaps more forceful than requirements. And they are not negotiable, but before you become too alarmed, there is only one—no, *three*—that I demand.

I suppose 'demands' would be the more appropriate term if we are to—"

"Charlotte. The conditions?"

"Yes, right." She clasped her hands to keep from fidgeting. "First, you must agree to talk to me."

"Talk?"

"Conversation, I mean. A half hour each day and not warnings about the weather. And I should like it to be uninterrupted, and you should initiate the topic from time to time."

"Because?"

She raised her brows, hoping to disguise her nervousness with annoyance. "Because that is what a wife would naturally require, and *this* particular conversation will grow tedious if you question every condition I set forth."

He pursed his lips, studying her face as if he might discover her reasoning there. Seeing nothing in her careful expression, he frowned. "Fine."

"Second…"

"Second?"

She heard Wally's words again. She'd not forgotten a one: *He loved me as I loved him, and there was not a day we let pass without telling each other that. It was in every embrace…in every good morning and good night…*

"Charlotte?"

"I require you bid me good morning and good night. Every day. With a kiss."

Will blinked. "What do you mean?"

"Exactly that."

He rubbed a hand over his face, mulling her demand for a thoroughly insulting amount of time.

"Oh, honestly! It is not as if I have asked you to wear a pink pinafore and skip through Hyde Park with a hoop and stick."

He sighed. "All right, agreed. And third?"

She began to speak, then had to start again. "We will sleep in the same bed."

"Absolutely not. What happened this morning would only happen again."

"And?" she asked, heartsore at his reaction.

His mouth dropped open to speak, but no sound came out.

Gathering the remnants of her shredded pride, she straightened. "Did you not notice I enjoyed myself? And you seemed to somewhat enjoy...*that*, too." What word might she use? She really ought to consult a dictionary. Very likely she would. Later, of course.

Will closed his eyes and expelled a harsh breath. "Of course I enjoyed that. I enjoyed it too well and I may not be able to stop myself from taking you next time."

Her breath caught. What a marvelous thing to say! "Are you suggesting you would force me?" she asked breathlessly.

"No! I—no!"

She smiled at the resurgence of his spirit. Here was the Will Repton she admired and loved. Everything was going to be all right. "Then there is no danger, is there? I promise to never allow you to *take me*, as you say. I will simply say no. So if we marry, you will not object to our sharing a bed?"

"*If* we marry? We *will* marry and I still object. We cannot—it is—I am not an easy sleeper. I have dreams and thrash about."

"I know. I enjoyed the thrashing about."

The man actually blushed. "I dream of other things. Of…nightmares, Charlotte. I've flung myself from my own bed trying to escape them. I might hurt you."

"You will not hurt me." Will looked so miserable, she almost surrendered. "How often do you have these dreams?"

"Almost every night."

Pain crimped her heart. "Not last night." Her voice was small with hope.

"No, not last night." He held her stare, and an awareness of their passionate morning seemed to flow between them.

"I will wake you." She straightened her shoulders. "As soon as you start dreaming. That will be better than suffering that unpleasantness. I come awake when Jacob and Abby cry all the time."

"Charlotte—"

"If we are to marry—"

"We will marry—"

"—then I want the experience of marriage. If you insist"—she grimaced and rushed through the rest of her words—"I will remain a virgin, but I have no use for an arrangement where we are apart. You do not seem to dislike me in that way, and though I realize this is inconvenient, you say you wish to help me. I wish to be of help to you."

From the stubborn set of his jaw, he was obviously not yet persuaded to share her bed. "I promise to never utter romantic nonsense or say I love you if that is your fear."

He looked straight at her, his eyes softening with

amusement. "You promise, do you? So I must promise as well?"

She kept her chin up. Even managed a smile. "It would only be practical. And I shall endeavor to be unlovable once or twice a day so you will not be deluded into believing yourself in love."

He grinned, but she sensed his reluctance to do so. It did not matter. Her heart was already fluttering, celebrating. This wonderful, ungovernable man would surrender to her. She felt it. And thank God, because there was nothing she wanted more, in all the world, than to marry Will Repton.

"And how will you make yourself unlovable to me?" Will asked.

"You hate to be distracted from work—I will practice the piano at inopportune moments. I shall learn your favorite foods and never have them prepared. Your neckties will be starchy."

"So you plan to torture me?"

"Mildly, yes."

Their eyes locked for one warm, divine moment, then he turned to return to Wally. He stopped at the threshold as if remembering something, walked back to take her hand, and pulled her back into the room. She sighed from the sensation. A lovely gesture. The man had never taken her hand before.

Oh no. There was no falling out of love with Will Repton.

Her brother rose from his chair as they entered, his eyes wide with anticipation.

"Wallace, your solicitor can prepare the marriage contract," Will said.

"All is settled, then?" Wally asked uncertainly, catching her eye.

"Evidently," Will mumbled. "I'll not be able to arrange a special license. Can we have the banns read in the parish church?"

A sudden bubble of joy rose in her chest. "The banns." Charlotte interrupted the men's negotiations. "Oh, please. I should like the banns to be called. Tomorrow is Sunday." Her name read aloud in Highthorpe, linked with William Repton, the man nearest to perfection, assembled in her daydreams.

Her husband, if only for a short time. But what was life without living?

The men nodded, evidently caring little for the romantic frivolities, and she just managed to keep from bouncing on her toes.

"And Wallace." Will plowed his free hand through his disheveled hair. "Charlotte and I will not sleep apart. I will respect the terms of this temporary union to the letter, we'll not consummate this marriage, but it is our wish—mine and Charlotte's—not to be separated."

At Will's proclamation, she bit her lip against a squeal. It was his promise, his vow. For three months, he was hers.

Wally's eyes arrowed to hers. "I think that a mistake."

"Yes," Will said grimly.

She would not dwell on the fact that Will was, in fact, agreeing.

"I ought to return to London tomorrow…settle some matters," Will said.

Her happiness dipped a fraction. "Tomorrow?"

He released her hand. "I should inform my parents."

Will started for the door, then paused. “I hope they might stay and enjoy Windmere a time longer?”

Charlotte clutched her hands together at her bosom. “Oh! Might they stay through the wedding? It is only three weeks more.”

“Don’t you wish to be married in London?” Will asked.

She held her breath. “If you do not object, I have always dreamed of marrying in the chapel here at Windmere.”

“But not to me. You might save the chapel for—”

Will must have seen the disappointment in her face, for he stopped and frowned. In another lovely, heart-wrenching gesture, he hurried to her and squeezed her hand.

“Whatever you want, Charlotte. It is our only wedding day, after all.”

Thirteen

"Now that we've launched our London gossipmongers, there will be no stopping the rumors," Wally said as the last coach rolled from Windmere onto the drive.

Charlotte exhaled a sigh of relief she did not know she had held. The last of the guests—gone. All finally gone, except for John and Liz, who waited with a sort of bemused anticipation of their son's upcoming nuptials.

"People will be kind, I think," she said. "And why would they not? They left content and with stories to tell—and not only of me. They witnessed nothing of you, Lucy, and Ben that was not good and respectable."

"The party was a success, but there is no telling if the reports will be met by friendly ears."

She said nothing. After the trial, her brother had been hurt terribly by the rejection of the *ton*, as had Ben and Lucy. Their bitterness ran far deeper than hers—but her hope that Society would embrace her family was undiminished.

After all, the years spent in London's finest private

seminaries, cloistered with the daughters of Britain's loftiest aristocrats, had taught her the workings of the *ton,* for good or ill.

She would marry the beautiful, heroic Will Repton. And he would leave her.

And she knew exactly what her acquaintance would do then.

They would sigh publicly, and plot ways to cheer her, and send invitations to prove their compassion. And the former Mrs. William Repton would attend every assembly with Lucy and Ben and even Wally until, like a war of attrition, their presence was tolerated. And hopefully welcomed.

That was the only way forward now.

She would wear her broken heart like a crown.

Rather than continue into the house, Wally sat upon the sun-warmed stone rail. "With the wedding a week away, we'll be far too busy to attend to the tittle-tattle spreading through London anyway."

The look of sad concern in his eyes was hard to ignore. She must not allow her family to worry over her. "The worst they will call me is capricious. And most will sympathize knowing the heart cannot be controlled." She smiled. "Especially those who have seen my fiancé in the flesh."

Before Wally could dwell, she jumped to her feet. "Let us call the carriage. I would like to search for new gloves for my gown, and later you will help me write the invitations for the wedding breakfast."

There were errands to run and letters to compose and visits to the parson, and she was grateful for every one of those distractions.

She shared with no one how she truly missed Will. Each day stretched long and colorless without the hope of seeing him bent over his papers or rubbing his temple the way he did when he was concentrating, or standing against the wall to read because he could never sit still for long. Tomorrow, *finally*, he had promised to return.

But the day came and went without him. And then the next. And only on the next was a letter delivered to her—a brief, horrid little note from Will saying he had been delayed and not to expect him until the day before the wedding. The innocent sheet of paper had been tossed into the fireplace a second later.

It was foolish to get upset over his cavalier attitude. He was not in love—he was not an eager groom, she was not his beloved bride.

But she had reached the limits of her tolerance by eight o'clock the night before the ceremony when there was still no sign of Will.

"He knows better than to upset his mother like this," Liz Repton muttered to her husband in the drawing room after dinner. "Fourteen hours before the wedding...I might expect this sort of thing from you, John, but not Will."

No one contradicted the irate mother.

"Excuse me." Charlotte stood and wrapped her shawl about her shoulders. "I think I'll take a bit of air. Will should arrive any moment."

No one contradicted her, either.

She descended the terrace stairs and commenced pacing amid the fireflies on the south lawn of Windmere.

Should they send riders out to search for him? Was he possibly hurt? Or ill? Or—

A movement from the corner of her eye made her turn.

Will! Thank God.

He lumbered toward her over the grass, his limp deep and lurching. His coat was creased and his necktie slack. The fatigue etched on his face warred with the keen light in his eyes that never once slipped from hers.

"You're here." Her voice broke.

"I was delayed." His gaze was unreadable in the dark.

Will studied her, waiting for her to speak, and she stared back, both annoyed and relieved at the sight of him. *I was delayed*, indeed! No explanation. No apology.

"Well!" she cried. "Are you well?"

He blinked. "Yes," he murmured. "Are you?"

"Perfectly well." She tried to calm the blood from climbing her neck and cheeks, but failed. To distract from the sight, she turned brusquely back toward the house. "Well. Shall we go in? We must get you settled and fed and warm in your room."

Charlotte ignored Will's sleepy grin and started her march to the house. His treatment of her was abominable. One slim letter in three weeks and he arrives hours before the wedding.

And he'd deprived her of his company all this time.

"It is late. I might have been asleep and not seen you," Charlotte said as lightly as she could manage.

"The roads were wet. It slowed the horses."

Tears slipped down her throat and her aching heart complained at his nearness. They walked without a word until Will caught her wrist, his fingers right on the telltale pulse. Annoying man.

"Could we speak a moment before you have me tucked in bed with a glass of warm milk?"

She stopped and pulled her wrist out of his hold in a play of adjusting her skirts.

"I…well, we're marrying tomorrow."

"I had not forgotten." Her tone was churlish but she couldn't help it. "Did you accomplish much? Your associates must have been all astonishment at your wedding announcement."

"Yes, but they know better than to delve into my affairs, especially when they have no bearing on the expedition."

She nearly gasped aloud. *No bearing*…she glared at an innocent hedge. Let the man speak if he wished to talk so much.

"We've both been busy, I think," Will began cautiously.

A noncommittal sound was her answer.

He rubbed his jaw. "I did wish to return days ago but, um…" He broke off at her lowered lids, her lack of response, and cleared his throat. "There was one errand in preparation for tomorrow I managed."

"Did you?" Another word and she would hit the stupid man. She had entertained a houseful of guests, modified her gown, written countless letters, and was expecting the entire village at a celebratory breakfast she'd planned, all in a house with a newborn that cried on the hour—and he'd managed one errand.

"Perhaps you're as tired as I feel, so I won't…I've something for you. I confess, I didn't think of it on my own. I was meeting with a supplier and his wife heard of our marriage and she mentioned it. A detail I'd overlooked completely and I don't overlook details, but you ought to have it, despite the nature of our arrangement. Perhaps you'll think it unnecessary—"

"The hour is rather late."

"Right." Will hesitated, then fumbled in his trousers pocket and came out with a small velvet pouch that he pressed into her hand. "Right." He cleared his throat. "That's yours." He pointed needlessly at the bag and kept his eyes upon it rather than on her.

She loosened the drawstring and retrieved a ring, a flawless pearl encircled with fiery diamonds. What was—? She gasped. A betrothal ring! For *her. From him!*

"You prefer a center diamond? Or a gemstone?"

"No." Her fingers tightened possessively on the ring. "No, it is extraordinary."

He looked at her, his eyes hopeful. "You like it?"

She bit her lip, trying not to smile too hugely or weep too shamelessly. "I love it. Oh, Will!" She hugged him tight, aiming her kisses at his lips—and one or two may have landed—but she was too excited to bother with accuracy. "I do, I love it."

She had never seen Will blush before, or that adorably crooked grin on his lips.

"I, uh…I bought several pearls in Shanghai and I thought this was the finest. The jeweler agreed with me." He paused. "Do you want to see if it fits?"

She nodded, too overcome to speak. She held out the ring and he clumsily slid it onto her finger. How beautifully it caught the moonlight. And how perfectly the ring fit. As if made for her…

But…had it been?

The smile slid from her lips.

"It suits you," Will said.

Her heart twisted in her breast. "It's lovely." The ring blurred behind tears that she quickly blinked away. "I will take good care of it until—" Her throat choked off the words.

Will looked at her. "Until?"

"The annulment. You will want it back, surely. For your next—your real wife." She flashed a false smile. "I must not get too attached or my heart will break when I say good-bye."

Will was quiet and staring, but she could not bring herself to look at him.

"It's yours, Charlotte," he said quietly.

"But—"

"I'll never have it back, so fall in love with it all you wish."

He stepped close and took up her hand, flattening it against the hard plane of his chest. "I was thinking only of you when I made this ring and the one you'll receive tomorrow. Never speak again of returning either to me."

Speechless, she could only stare at him. And past the fatigue in his eyes, and the bruises shadowing his lids, there was the look she had dreamed of. Warm and gentle and brimming with affection.

Her dream man…

He released her and, with a duck of his head, turned and left.

Fourteen

Will had mistaken the private chapel at Windmere as another decorative folly on the grounds. The miniature church was positioned at the end of a long, sunlit lane of lush green grass, hemmed in by a double row of ash trees and set before a massive planting of blooming fuchsia. No wonder Charlotte wished to be married here. Even he was struck by the overwhelming romance of the place.

He and his parents were greeted by a giddy, cherub-faced pastor and told Charlotte and her family were to follow. He'd not had a chance to see her since his presentation of her ring.

He smiled at the memory. She'd kissed his face, unleashed tears of happiness, squealed with delight over a gift. A *gift* intended for her alone. And then said she'd return it.

No, the woman never behaved as he expected.

At first, he'd thought a gemstone to match her eyes, but nothing had come close. Sapphires were too dark, aquamarine too light, diamonds too cold. Nothing could rival those eyes.

But the pearl reminded him of her skin. It even fit her perfectly, looking more magnificent on her finger than he could have imagined.

Thank God she liked it. She'd been so vexed with him for arriving late.

Well, a couple days were all she'd have to endure with him before he returned to London. Alone.

It was for the best. He'd say something to upset her, snap at her, have one of his nightmares and frighten her. Like Ben said, she'd lived gently. Best she stay here and never truly know him.

"Go take your place, Son," his father said.

His place? The pastor was waiting at the altar. Will passed the three empty pews on each side of the aisle. His mother beamed from her seat in the first row and he raised an ironic brow back at her.

Excited voices approached from beyond the open doors and a laughing Jacob ran in to climb onto a seat, followed by Ben holding Abby, and Lucy with baby Edward. Patty and her husband followed and sat in the back pew.

From the cool, dark interior, his eyes watered and burned with fatigue looking out at the brilliant colors coming from beyond the door. He wouldn't look his best for his own wedding. The nightmares had woken him at two and he'd sat the rest of the night in a chair. They'd not spare him even one night, it seemed.

But in the hermitage with Charlotte, he'd slept through the night. His only dream had been of her.

"She's here, Mr. Repton." Jacob had not yet mastered the whisper, and Will jerked his head up in attention.

There she was. Charlotte. Framed in the door. Glowing in her white gown.

Come closer.

He couldn't see beneath the gauzy veil.

Come closer, Charlotte.

And then she did. The magic blue of her eyes emerged, the pink of her lips, her little uptilted nose. The swish of her gown and, finally, the scent of...jasmine?

Wallace said something but he didn't hear, barely registering the man had entered beside her. A moment later, Charlotte was beside him and a guiding hand was turning him to the pastor—but his head swiveled back to the bride.

How was he marrying Charlotte Baker? How was anyone allowing this happy woman to join her life to his?

Beneath the veil, she returned his study, a small smile on her lips he was too dazed to return. He could never hold her stare—she was overwhelming to look at—and looked instead at her dress. It was familiar. Her angel dress. The dress she'd worn when they'd danced.

"William? Do you—"

Another coaxing prod to his back.

"I do," Will blurted. Good—the pastor smiled. He'd answered correctly.

Charlotte's eyes were wet with tears under the veil. She hadn't wanted this, not like this. Not with him.

God, had he done this to her? Had he made this happen?

"I do," Charlotte said.

"...presenting of the ring..." the pastor was saying.

Charlotte removed her glove and at the sight of the pearl ring, he retrieved the wedding band from his pocket. He slid the simple band onto her finger and kept hold of her. One of them was trembling.

"…pronounce you husband and wife." The pastor beamed. "On this happy day, with family and God as witness, I do not believe anyone would object to you kissing your bride."

He stared dumbly at the cheeky pastor. Kiss her? In front of everyone?

But Charlotte waited, still as a statue. A small sound, a sigh or a giggle, rose from under her veil and he jolted to action. He gathered the veil over her head, the fabric feeling as if it would disintegrate between his fingers.

There was jasmine in her hair and her eyes were bright, but not with tears. Not now. He turned his back to their audience. This moment was theirs alone. He cupped her soft cheek and bent to press his lips to hers.

Married…he had a wife…a curious, heartbreaking, brain-scrambling wife.

The most beautiful wife in the world…

He deepened the kiss, and it wasn't an apology. Not now.

Time slowed. There was only the sound of their lips clinging, only their breath stirred the air, only her in his arms. God, the way she fit him. The way she kissed with her whole heart—

Stop…they'll see. He lifted his mouth from hers and Charlotte blinked her eyes open and smiled. The sight stabbed him. She'd dreamed of a wedding here, in her little chapel, with a man who could pass all her tests.

And she'd married him instead.

He didn't care that this was just a formality. He

wrapped his arms around her, crushing her veil in his hug. "You wore jasmine in your hair," he whispered.

Her fingers tightened on the back of his coat. "You noticed."

"On you, I notice."

She stepped out of his embrace, smiling one of her brilliant, dimpled smiles even as she wiped a tear from her cheek. The woman never behaved the way he thought she would.

"Are you ready to celebrate our marriage?" she asked.

Bemused, he turned to the grinning faces all around them. "I'd not object to a small gathering, no."

A twinkle lit her eye. "And would you be terribly disappointed if it were a slightly larger party?"

Each inhabitant of the village of Highthorpe made every effort to attend the wedding breakfast of Mr. and Mrs. William Repton and wish the couple joy. This preponderance of goodwill and gaiety extended through luncheon, and then dinner, and was interspersed with bouts of impromptu dancing, music, and a race about the empire fountain in the gardens for the children and more than a few inebriated adults.

Charlotte was fawned over and squeezed affectionately by every reveler and effectively removed from the orbit of her husband for the better part of the day.

Going on eight hours and forty-three minutes now, according to Will's timepiece.

"How is my son, the neglected groom?" His father's cheeks glowed from too much punch, so it must have been a mighty twinge of pity to draw him from his merry table.

Will shrugged. "Wasn't the purpose of this party to convince everyone of my impetuous, irrepressible love? I've not been able to get near her all day."

His father beamed proudly at Charlotte across the crush of well-wishers that circled her. "You knew she was popular."

Charlotte smiled at him from across the room and he stifled the grin threatening to stretch over his face. Those little smiles were the only balm to his resentment of, apparently, the entire village of Highthorpe.

Feeling more charitable, he grinned at his father. "She's not popular. She's loved." His jealousy was ridiculous. To imagine he had any sort of claim. Especially when everyone had a claim on Charlotte, it seemed. So much rendered her irresistible—her curiosity, her vivacity, her beauty.

Charlotte smiled at him again.

He couldn't quite make those out. Was she afraid he'd inadvertently expose their marriage as a charade? True, he was dead on his feet, but his fatigue only left him wandering from room to crowded room in a sort of stupor.

"She has no fear of talking to anyone, does she?" his father said. "No one's afraid to speak to her, either. That is the greater talent."

"She's not spoken much to me today."

His father ignored his petulant tone. "Absolutely charming. You'll not find another like her."

Not exactly subtle. "Nonetheless, I must release Miss Baker at the end of August."

"She's Mrs. Repton now, Son."

"How much of that punch have you had?"

"Not as much as you think. You've never needed any advice I had to give—you knew your mind long before your mother or I could guide you—but if you let her go, you'll regret it the rest of your life."

He scrubbed his hand over his face. "What would you have me do? Pack her in my trunk and take her with me?"

"In all your plotting and calculating, had you not allowed a contingency for a wife?"

"Charlotte, on a ship with two dozen men? The journey to Africa alone is dangerous. And in Asia, I couldn't make any camp secure enough. I'd never leave her in any of the port cities. Shameen Island and Ningbo are out of the question. In Fuzhou, the locals are protesting the Protestants. Xiamen has an outbreak of typhoid every season. The wives seem miserable there. Even if I could find French-speaking servants in Shanghai, I don't have the money to—" He couldn't go over this again. Not again. "It's impossible."

His father was suddenly sober. "I see. I'm sorry, Son."

Christ, he was tired. He rubbed his eyes. "Where's Mum?" His ploy of distraction worked. His father was uneasy in any party without his wife to decipher all the social nuances.

"I thought she was after those little sandwiches she likes so well," his father said, his eyes scanning the crowded room.

"I see her at the refreshment table. Shall we?"

But his father was already on his way.

Will could isolate Charlotte's laugh over the din. She

was still surrounded, but she caught his eye as he followed his father, and his heart tripped like a schoolboy.

He left his parents on a settee with a fresh plate of cake and sandwiches and turned to find Charlotte's Irish maid, Patty, with a narrow-eyed stare screwed on him.

"Congratulations, Mr. Repton," she said dryly.

Despite the woman's tone, he nodded his thanks. "Enjoying yourself?"

"Passably."

"Good." He started to cross his arms and shoved them in his pockets instead. "Good. Charlotte looks beautiful. Her hair is, uh—not that she doesn't look beautiful every day."

"Humph."

He cleared his throat. "She seems happy."

"Never been natural to see her *unhappy*."

He couldn't tell if her words felt accusatory or if that was his guilt, but he stiffened at them. More neutral territory was needed. "How long have you been with the family?"

"Fifteen years." Patty planted her hands on her hips. "Charlotte seems happy, Mr. Repton, because she usually *is* happy. But that don't mean she can't be made unhappy. Don't think you know her in all her silk and satin. Family's what she treasures. And you're family now, no matter how little you like the circumstances. She's been excited for today, even if this isn't exactly the wedding of your dreams."

"I can't say I've ever had a notion of a dream wedding."

"You made that clear enough by arriving near midnight yesterday."

He dropped his gaze. "Right, I suppose I did."

The woman was protective of Charlotte. Loyal. Unafraid of giving her lady's husband a dressing-down if she deemed it necessary.

He decided he liked Patty after all.

Their attention was drawn by Charlotte being led to a corner by a gaggle of giggling women who kept casting sly glances at him. God only knew what they were saying. Charlotte's cheeks were pink and growing pinker.

Patty sighed and gave him a somewhat friendlier shove on his arm. "You might go on and get her then. Before they commence undressing you with their eyes."

Will frowned uncertainly at the mob of women. Charlotte squealed at something one woman said, nearly falling from her chair in her laughter.

"Perhaps you might retrieve her for me, Patty?"

She snorted and grinned. "If you want her away from their corrupting influence, you collect her yourself."

"Yes. Well." He checked his buttons. All appeared in order. With a hasty smoothing of his hair, he marched toward the women.

Charlotte sighted him drawing near and bit her lip to stifle her laughter. All the ladies turned toward him in unison, and he stalled in his approach. Feigning a desire for a drink, he angled from them, but Charlotte rose and glided to him in her impossibly graceful way.

"I promise we were not laughing at you," Charlotte said.

"I was after a glass of water."

She pressed her lips against a smile and tucked her

hand into the bend of his elbow. "You looked rather alarmed at my laughter."

"I assumed you were in your cups."

"The ladies think you a fine-looking gentleman."

"So they're in their cups, too?"

Charlotte's eyes roamed over his face. "You did not sleep last night. Did you have a nightmare, or were you tormented by the thought of marrying me?"

He quirked a brow at her and lifted her hand a bit to look at her wedding rings. "Are you all right? A little depressed, maybe?"

"Not at all." She smiled. "My reputation is saved and Jacob has a new uncle."

He scanned her face for the truth but she was the picture of a blooming bride, the apples of her cheeks glowing pink and her eyes sparkling.

Charlotte hugged his arm against her. "Thank you for marrying me."

He straightened one of the jasmine blossoms in her hair, too tired to puzzle out her joyful mood. "You're welcome." Then he remembered.

He pulled out the leather box he'd been carrying all day in his pocket and handed it to her.

Her eyes widened. "Is this—?"

"Your jade necklace."

He didn't think it possible, but her smile grew brighter. And those delphinium eyes were suspiciously shiny.

"It's proper now, isn't it?" he murmured. "And you have that green dress."

She nodded, and gave him the kiss he'd been hoping for. Even if it was only on the cheek.

Her eyes roamed his face with concern. "Would you like to lie down?"

"I won't take you from your party." His words were meant to be selfless, but selfishly he wished she would insist they leave.

"Everyone is too merry to notice our absence. Besides, we have not been alone all day."

"No, we haven't," he murmured. With Charlotte near, his body sank deeper into relaxation, edged with a pleasant awareness of their new bond. He didn't even feel the least bit shy.

Until she spoke her next words.

"Let's go upstairs, Will. It is time I put you to bed."

Lucy had assured her Michael was an efficient valet, but Charlotte hadn't thought to press her sister for other assurances, such as whether a half hour was a proper amount of time to allow a man to prepare for bed. Or if a gentleman's evening ablution would include a shave. Or if a wife might wander freely into her husband's chamber while he was being attended to, rather than wait an interminable amount of time in her bedroom as she was doing now.

Honestly, her sister really should have foreseen her need for several assurances.

What would a husband don as sleeping attire? A banyan, certainly. Would he wear a nightcap? She'd never pictured Will in a nightcap. Not in all the sleeping ensembles in all the imaginary wardrobes she had daydreamed through the years. She tried now to place a sleeping cap on his head—one with a tassel or a knit stripe, a biggin that tied under his chin, a satin turban or—*oh heavens*, surely not a fez?

No, she would not like him in a sleeping cap.

Perched on the edge of her bed, she tapped her feet on the carpet and smoothed the fine lawn of her nightrail over her lap. A few minutes more. She must not rush him. A premature arrival into her bedroom would only heighten the awkwardness of the situation. But then, a certain amount of shyness would only be natural and appropriate in this case, wouldn't it?

She must try to remember to be moderately shy then, and not unnaturally, immodestly excited as she actually was.

Please, please, do not wear a sleeping cap.

Will's deep voice emerged from the bedroom and she hurried to the connecting door to listen.

Only his thanking Michael and then the sound of the door to the outer hall opening and closing. Would he come now? Or another minute more?

Michael's service was done. Surely Will would be presentable. Again she inspected her nightrail, satisfied it was both pretty and sufficiently modest. Tying her peignoir tightly about her, she bent her ear to the keyhole. Nothing. With a deep breath—*moderately shy, Charlotte*—she knocked on the door.

"Yes?" Will's voice sounded from behind the door.

She opened the door and found Will by the fireplace, occupied with the belt of his banyan. No sleeping cap on his perfectly handsome head—excellent. A husband. Her husband. How wonderful to have him here, in such an intimate, matrimonial setting. She could remember him there, forever, looking masculine and unshaven. And tangling his belt into a knot.

The click of the door closing reclaimed his attention and he flicked a glance over her. "You're dressed for bed."

"Yes." Unaccustomed to cursory glances, she looked down at her dressing gown.

"It's early yet," he murmured. "Don't let me upset your routine."

"I retire early in the country."

Will was grumbling under his breath, his attention on the knot at his waist.

Oh, but this was fun! So fun and so wonderful and her heart would leap from her body any moment. "Is there something wrong?"

"The valet tied this oddly. I'm not used to them as it is."

"Valets?"

"Robes. And yes, valets, too."

"Oh."

"I don't usually wear them, but considering our arrangement..."

"Oh. Just a nightshirt, then?"

His fingers stilled. "Not exactly."

Her tongue felt glued to the top of her mouth. "Oh."

Intent on his belt, he worked the tangle apart and let the ends dangle, crossing his arms to hold his banyan closed. The breadth of his shoulders stretched the fabric taut over the cording of muscle beneath. "Michael seems a nice lad, but I don't need help undressing."

She wrenched her gaze off his shoulders. "You

mustn't think you will offend if you forego his service. You might choose your own valet."

"Hm."

Will's noncommittal answer was oddly sinking. But then, the poor man was exhausted—she must not read into his answers.

He walked toward her and she tensed with anticipation, but with a polite duck of his head, he reached behind her to open the door to her bedroom and continued in. She followed, until he stopped to stare at the bed. He raked a hand through his hair, causing his dressing gown to gape open. The start of a smooth, strong shoulder gleamed in the wide V of his nightshirt.

"A large bed," he said.

Stop ogling the man! "Yes."

His jaw tensed, but he kept his eyes locked on the coverlet. "You might want to reconsider, Charlotte. Sharing the bed. I don't want to frighten you. When I dream, sometimes I cry out. My parents tell me it can be alarming."

"You will not frighten me."

"And I thrash about. My blankets are usually on the rug by morning."

"All right."

"Likely I snore."

"I don't believe you do, actually."

"And I'm hot. My temperature. That can't be pleasant."

She waited, fidgeting with the cuffs of her nightrail. It was not as if the man could dissuade her from sharing the bed.

At last he looked full at her, from tip to toe, and

his lips quirked in a small, almost reluctant smile. But he appeared rather more amused than enticed. Her toes curled in her slippers. There was nothing wrong with her gown. It was modest, buttoned at her chin and hanging to her ankles. And as usual, her hair was braided to keep the strands from her face. Did he not like her hair this way? Did he expect her to wear it loose? Did married women not braid their hair? Surely they must. Sleeping with her hair unbound would strangle them both.

With an abrupt clearing of his throat that made her jump, Will made for the bed. "Well, good night."

"Oh. Did…did you wish for anything before you retire? Are you hungry or thirsty? There is water but if you wanted—"

"I only want for sleep. Which side of the bed is yours?"

"I sleep on the side nearest the fire."

He ignored her smile and sat on the bed, as if this were an everyday occurrence. She took a hesitant step toward him. Nothing was to happen, as tired as he was, but she so hoped for her kiss good night, even on the cheek. One loving gesture. Just so she might feel a little more of a bride's happiness.

And he had promised. But it seemed rather unkind to remind him of the prenuptial requirement when his lids were sinking.

"Remember, Charlotte, if you feel me thrash about, take yourself away."

"I will."

He hesitated a moment more, then shrugged out of his dressing gown. The nightshirt only reached his knees. She caught a glimpse of muscled calves before he slid his legs under the covers.

It was not kind to bother the man. Not only had he been forced to marry a completely superfluous woman, he was utterly exhausted. But could she—*should* she ask him for her good-night kiss? Would she ever be able to ask him again? "Will?"

"Good night," he mumbled from his pillow.

"I—good night."

Will answered with a grunt that was either agreement or a snore. She turned down the lamps around the room until only the faint light from the fire remained.

What now? It was early yet. She might read. Or write in her journal. Today was historic, after all—

She flinched at a stab of pain behind her eye and rubbed her temple. Her eyes were wet.

She might knit. Edward's blanket was not yet done. She might read. She might…

In her indecision, she stood still and waited for an answer to reveal itself. Will's even breathing told her he was asleep. Tenderness flooded her at seeing his taut features relax, the whiskered edge of his jaw, the fine blue veins on his eyelids, dark with exhaustion.

Her husband…her wedding night.

He had not kissed her good night.

She twisted the rings on her finger, then quickly removed them to her jewelry case. She would not think on it tonight. Very likely she would, later. Later there would be hours to understand. She would not think on it and allow herself to become depressed. This was what she had wanted, after all. Will as her husband. For a time.

She hurried to her side of the bed and slid under the covers. Had she stretched her arm, she still would not have been able to touch him. He was nearly on the edge of the mattress.

The fire crackled, the party continued downstairs, and Charlotte waited for the practicality of sleep to erase her foolish hope.

Fifteen

WILL WOKE AS NATURE INTENDED, WITHOUT A TRACE of fatigue. How long had it been since his eyes opened this easily? He couldn't remember a morning when he'd woken with a mind this clear. His surroundings were almost crystalline in their clarity: a shaft of sunlight streamed across the counterpane; outside the window, the clarion trill of birdsong; in his arms, clinging warmly, her cheek on his chest, Charlotte.

Damn me. Charlotte. His wife for the next three months by law. In practice, only for the next twenty-four hours or so. He'd tell her of his departure at luncheon, with her brother and Ben in attendance. Something told him to wait until he had reinforcements in place.

They would help Charlotte see the sense of his speedy removal to London. If she behaved as expected.

But when had she ever?

Her breathing was even. Still asleep. Carefully, he moved his hand to touch the silk of her hair. So incredibly soft. His body was coming to an awareness of all the other bits of her. In particular, her round breasts pressed against his stomach. He'd always been especially partial to those.

His wife. His gorgeous wife with a body designed for a man's pleasure, separated from him by a thin layer of fabric. And he wasn't allowed to make love to her.

The smile on his face must be a horrible sight.

Carefully, so as not to wake her, he rested his cheek on her head, closed his eyes, and reveled in the warm, womanly body, the light perfume of her hair. This was nice, he had to admit. Nicer than he ever imagined—or hoped.

Yes, he could have done very well without a morning like this to remember.

His cock twitched, lascivious and uncaring of her innocent sleep. A few minutes more and he'd have to release her or his erection would prod her awake.

She stirred and, feigning sleep, he let her wake in his arms to see what she'd do. Her supple muscles flexed as she stretched in his arms, her yawn was a warm puff of air, the tilt of her head disturbed his resting cheek from her hair.

"Good morning," she whispered.

And then her mouth puckered against his, soft and wet. The kiss startled his eyes open and he was staring into the smiling, delphinium blue of hers. Again the blood rushed to his cock. Again he was first to look away.

"You're on my side of the bed." The scold might be more convincing if he could take his hands off her.

"Isn't this cozy?" She nestled closer. "I cannot recall when I have ever slept this soundly. Did you sleep well?" She pushed up on his chest, her eyes widening.

"You did not have a nightmare, did you? Marriage may cure you of them. Or perhaps having a bed partner. Have you slept with many women since your return? What was the state of your sleep on those nights?"

He'd not been awake two minutes and already the woman was confusing him. "No. No dream." He unwrapped his arms from around her and rolled onto his back.

"But that's wonderful. Twice you have slept with me and twice, no dreams. What about the other times?"

"Other times?" He was careful not to look in the region of her breasts. Or her face. Or any other part of her.

"The other times you shared a bed with women."

"I've not slept with other women."

"You cannot expect me to believe that."

He dared a glance and regretted it, assailed by the pink of her cheeks, the satiny look of her lips, the tendrils of hair escaping so fetchingly from the braid and gilded by the sunlight. How could a woman be so adorable and seductive at once?

Beaten, he closed his eyes, pretending tiredness but still seeing her face. "Do you imagine me some sort of Casanova?"

Charlotte was plucking idly at the neck of his nightshirt and he stiffened with each brush of her fingers against his skin. "You are charming when of a mind to be."

"I strike you as charming?"

"Are you avoiding my question?"

"Which one?"

"The women you have slept with. There must

have been a number because in the hermitage you displayed skills—"

A breathy sigh interrupted Charlotte's words, and his eyes flew open to look at her. The sound hadn't come from her. Disappointingly.

A more forceful grunt. Another moan. It seemed to come from the other side of the wall. "What is that?"

"Nothing." Charlotte buried her face into her pillow, her ears bright pink. "You mustn't listen."

Another sigh. An answering gasp. A muffled giggle mingling with a low, pleading rumble of—

"Is that Ben? And—" *your sister?* "Oh."

Charlotte launched atop him and cupped her hands over his ears, her face blushing furiously. "You must not listen."

She looked so pained, he couldn't help teasing her. Just a little. Stifling his smile, he pulled her hands from his head to his chest and angled his ear to the wall.

"Will!" she squeaked.

"Hush."

"You look like a ridiculous schoolboy."

"Quiet, Charlotte, I can't—" A thump of the headboard against the wall and he goggled his eyes at her. "Didn't the woman just give birth? Not that...I suppose she could do things to him—"

She tilted her head in question.

"Never mind."

"That is my sister." A series of moans floated through the wall and Charlotte's mouth turned down in a pout. "And you'll get used to it."

He roared with laughter.

"*Stop laughing.*"

"What? I'm impressed."

"They love each other very much."

Oh Jesus. He laughed harder.

"Oh, honestly, their passion is hardly surprising." She covered his mouth with her hands, her generous breasts pooling on his chest, and his amusement was giving way to a passion of his own.

His shoulders trembled with his effort not to laugh. "How do you sit across from them at the breakfast table?"

Charlotte frowned uncertainly. "They take breakfast in their rooms."

Will guffawed, unable to restrain himself. He hadn't laughed this well in years.

Charlotte pushed a pillow into his face. "You are a child."

Will removed the pillow to see her pad across the bedroom into her sitting room.

But he didn't miss the smile on her face.

After an invigorating climb to the hunting tower, Will returned to find Charlotte had ordered a hot bath and shave for him—though he sent the valet right off—plus a plate of rolls, cheese, and fruit to tide him over to noonday.

So this was what was meant by wifely comforts. He devoured a slice of cheddar. Best he not get used to them.

Still...he'd never slept so well as he had last night.

No. One more night and he was to London. Two hundred miles should be ample distance between them. Charlotte could get back to her life, and as for him, there was no more time for distractions. Five hundred was still needed for his expedition and he'd not find those funds in Derbyshire.

Not sure where he might work and keep out of the family's way, he brought his ledgers and maps to a small parlor near the kitchen. It was there Ben found him.

"Morning, Will."

"Good morning." Will struggled to conceal the smile that quirked his lips remembering the entertainment the man's intimate sounds had provided him and Charlotte. Those were sounds he needed to forget. And fast.

Ben eyed him, his tone suspicious. "How did you sleep?"

"Best sleep I've had in months."

"And uh…Charlotte slept well?"

Will narrowed his eyes in question. "I believe so."

"So…you both slept well?"

He sighed, but refrained from rolling his eyes. "Yes, we both slept well. I was too tired to chase Charlotte around the bed and she was spared the exertion of fending off my lecherous advances."

Ben had the grace to frown. "Sorry, Will. I know this isn't easy."

"I return to London in the morning anyway. I would have left today but the horses needed a day's rest."

"Tomorrow?"

"I've much to do in the City. Harlowe's investment is gone now that I've stolen his daughter-in-law. And you'll not credit how long it took Buss-Sykes to deliver my new hydrometer—"

"Will…to leave tomorrow, Charlotte won't like it. She planned to stay a fortnight, at least."

Will looked at his ledger to hide his guilt. "Yes. Well. She's not coming with me."

"You expect to leave her here?"

"It's for the best."

Ben's normally genial face hardened. "The *ton* will think her abandoned."

"There are two million people in the city. I doubt my return will be noticed."

"You don't understand. There are no secrets in Society. Someone will see you and all will know by nightfall. You can't go back without her."

Damn right, a primal voice in his head growled. *Keep her.*

He sank in his seat, shutting his ears to that selfish, baiting voice. He hadn't considered…would he be more newsworthy now that he'd married? But then… he'd married the most beautiful woman in London. *Ah…hell.*

"I'll stay out of sight in Richmond," Will said, thinking aloud. "Conduct my business by messenger."

"Many of Charlotte's circle have homes in Richmond."

Damn. He scrubbed his jaw and began to pace. *Damn, damn, damn.* "What am I to do with her?" he muttered, more to himself than Ben.

"What do you mean?"

"A room in my parents' house won't do for Charlotte. I suppose I could lease a house. Hire servants. Not the full staff she's used to, but I might manage a maid and cook."

Ben waved that off. "Everyone assumed you would stay at our house in Mayfair."

"Goodness, there you are. I have upset the house

looking for you." Charlotte entered the parlor, coming to stand beside him as if that's where she belonged.

God help him. He was really going to live with her.

"Why were you speaking of the London house?"

"I'll let Will explain." With a pointed stare of warning, Ben left the room.

She glided to her seat, her eyes huge with curiosity. With her skirts pooled around her, she was an angel atop her cloud of violet silk.

What a bastard he was.

Charlotte grew uneasy at Will's grave countenance. She had hoped his happy mood would continue after their morning.

Will had laughed and that was a sight never seen. *Ever.* He had been laughing *at* her, of course, but she could bear it for his amusement.

Now, though, he would not look at her. "I am interrupting your work."

"No, I was—" He shook his head, and consulted the ceiling.

She had been giddy all day, thinking how wonderful it would be to wake each morning and laugh with him. To stroke his jaw, rough with whiskers. To see to his comfort. Her good-morning kiss still left her tingling, even if she had sneaked it upon a defenseless, sleeping man. But she would not dwell on the impropriety of that behavior.

"I return to London tomorrow," he said.

"Tomorrow?"

"There are matters I must attend to and to take you from your family, with the new baby..."

The realization of what he was saying slammed into her stomach. "You mean to leave me here."

"I thought—"

"I thought your planning was done?"

"Yes, somewhat, but—"

"We are married a matter of hours and you would abandon me?"

"I'm not abandoning you. It's not as if we're truly married."

She gasped. "Not—" Well, she could not argue with that. She stood, but the way she wished to march was blocked by Will. He eyed her warily, as if she were some hissing goose that might fly at his head. "Why leave?"

He dropped his gaze and a horrible thought occurred to her. "Do you plan to see a…a *fille de joie*?" Her voice sank to a whisper on the last, vile words.

"A what?"

"You heard me—a courtesan. I know there are places men go and I forbid it. You may not touch another woman. That is my fourth demand. You are my husband and—"

"Charlotte—"

"You are my husband." A strange panic was tightening her chest and she rushed on. "And I will not allow you to treat me with so little respect. It is true we had not discussed my rights—my *proprietary* rights—to your male parts—"

"My what?"

"—but it should have been understood your attentions be exclusive to me as mine are to you. If you require…*that*, I will see to your needs."

He gaped at her, blinking with confusion. "My male parts?"

Her cheeks must be aflame but she held his dumbfounded stare.

"No, Charlotte…why would—? I don't have all the money I need to return to Asia. It will be easier in the City to meet with prospects."

Relief pierced her, followed by shame. "Oh."

Why, *why*, did she mention a courtesan?

She walked with as much dignity as she could muster to the door. "Then I will see to our bags." She smoothed the waist of her skirt, her stomach roiling beneath her hands. "Are we…are we to go by carriage or rail?"

At his lost expression, she regretted everything she had said, everything she had done to keep him next to her. It was humiliating. Is this what love would subject her to? Was she to be such a burden?

"Will?"

"Yes, right. I'd arranged a carriage."

He wouldn't meet her eye. He had meant to leave her. That was why he was so lighthearted this morning, imagining he would be unburdened of her.

She lowered her eyes to hide her sadness. This was the choice she had made. A one-sided love. What had she expected? That Will would set aside his maps and pencils and plans to indulge her stupid fantasies and play the husband?

The only husband she would ever have…

She drew a steadying breath. "You ought not treat me with so little courtesy. I am your wife until the annulment and you should not forget it."

Without a backward glance, she swept out of the room.

She would pretend.

Let him try to stop her.

Sixteen

The two-day ride to London should have afforded Will ample hours to devise a contingency plan for the unexpected development of a wife returning with him to London, but the journey was too full of Charlotte. Too full of her conversation, her perfume, her smile. Too full of her absorbing the scenery out the window while he absorbed the sight of her.

But he was out of time. They'd entered the city and in the shadowy interior of the carriage, he studied his bride. At present, she was slumbering with her head upon his lap. He had to give her credit—she was an excellent sleeper, with an unerring instinct for surfaces affording optimal comfort in less-than-ideal environments. She'd closed her eyes leaning against the wall of the carriage but once asleep, she had, immediately and unconsciously, commandeered his lap as her personal pillow.

Not that he minded. If she had commanded him to trot alongside the carriage, he would have. Thankfully, Charlotte seemed to have forgiven him for planning to return without her. He had expected her to sulk or ignore him for most of the journey, but instead she'd sat beside him, sometimes quiet, sometimes sharing her stories, even drawing out his stories—the stories he *could* tell. Always with a smile on her lips and a glow in her eye, as if a carriage ride was a great adventure.

She had traveled this way before, of course. Numberless times, most likely. How could this tedious ride with him be an adventure?

But it had been nice. Even fun.

He smoothed a tendril of hair off her cheek. Her skin glowed, flawless as a pearl. He'd thought her a living doll…

No doll—a soft, warm, bloody complicated woman. And a passionate one.

One point of contention in this marriage was clear. He could not share her bed. Not when he strongly suspected Charlotte—curious as she was—desired to make love purely for the experience. *Male parts*, for God's sake.

He had no choice but to renege on their agreement. Not that he would tell her outright. He'd resort to subterfuge, keeping such irregular sleeping hours that Charlotte would not look for him to join her in bed. Once she'd gone to bed, he could steal away to a guest chamber. Not the surest plan, but the best he could manage.

Avoidance did strike him as the coward's way, but there was only so much temptation a man could take. This morning at the inn in Daventry, he'd almost had an apoplexy restraining himself. He'd woken, clinging tight to his slumbering wife, his cock fully at attention and aching for release. He nearly fell from the bed in his haste to escape the heated sheets.

She'd offered to see to "his needs." Chuckling humorlessly, he butted his head against the squabs—but lightly, so as not to disturb her.

Six years without the comfort of a woman. *Six years, Charlotte!*

He felt a powerful urge to push her off his lap.

The woman had no idea the extent of his needs where she was concerned. To bring her pleasure, though. To see her writhing with passion again. Would that be wrong? As long as he was careful, her virginity would stay intact.

He smoothed a tendril of hair off her cheek. She was so soft. Even inside…

He clenched his body against the memory.

The carriage wheels rolled differently. Cobbled streets. They'd entered the better end of the city. Soon enough, Charlotte could sleep in her bed and he could put this long day behind him.

The carriage slowed and he nudged her awake. "We're here, Charlotte."

"Good…so tired."

He lifted her to sit upright, only to have her flop bonelessly against him. He dipped his head to look into her sleeping face. The woman did not come awake easily.

A lantern approached and the carriage door opened. Jamie peered in, curious as to why the passengers hadn't disembarked.

"Miss Baker is just now rousing," Will said. "We'll need a moment."

"Yes, sir."

"Repton," mumbled Charlotte.

"What's that?" He tugged her cloak under her chin.

"Mrs. Repton."

"Right. Thanks for the correction. Jamie was looking scandalized."

The footman grinned. "I'll go on ahead, sir, and light the lamps. No one expected your return. I'll get the fire lit in Miss—your rooms, sir."

"Thank you. Just her room."

"Shall I wake the staff to attend to you?"

He'd not thought of that. It seemed unkind to wake the servants to undress them. "No. No need. I can, uh…attend to her." Probably.

He'd shrugged into his coat and stuffed his gloves into his pockets, and found Charlotte facedown and asleep again on the seat. He hadn't the heart to wake her. Besides, she looked light enough to carry.

She *was* an excellent sleeper, not stirring even when he hoisted her into his arms. The careful descent from the carriage and up the stairs shot little darts of pain from his knee to hip. Sitting motionless for so long had caused his leg to stiffen, so he hobbled gracelessly up the steps.

Halfway up, the lumbering motion roused Charlotte and she peeked her eyes open. "Does your leg hurt?"

"I'm fine."

"Put me down."

"Almost there." He tightened his hold. The only time he could touch her was when she slept.

The footman had left a door open to a room aglow from a crackling fire. The furnishings were feminine and their trunks were on the rug. This must be it.

He laid Charlotte on her bed. He closed the door

for privacy and returned to study the traveling costume she wore. The long cape was easy enough to remove, but there was a perplexing amount of buttons all over her body: on her gloves, at her sleeves, from neck to waist, and along her hip.

Charlotte would be of no help. Her breathing was deep and steady and she'd curled onto her side.

Start from outer to inner. Steeling himself, he disassembled and removed her cloak, gown, and petticoat, then began unthreading her corselet. Why the woman wore the device was a mystery. Her thin chemise bore the indelible impressions of the eyelets and seams of the stays. Would her skin be marked the same in such tight constraints?

He rubbed the fine linen along a deep wrinkle, hoping the skin beneath hadn't been pinched all day. Remembering his purpose, he stopped his hand. The chemise was loose and looked comfortable enough, and there was no need to remove the pantalets beneath. Her stockings, though…

How were they held up? Why did he not know these things? A twenty-eight-year-old man ought to have undressed a woman before, oughtn't he?

He probed gently along her knee until he reached the garter. Remove the stockings, then he'd leave. Careful not to touch her skin with any meaning, he untied the garter and rolled down the stocking. Down the silken skin turned golden by the firelight, down the slender, erotic curve of her calf, the taper of her ankle, the delicate, arched foot…

There. The deed was done. And with a minimum of discomfort, really. He wasn't some rutting animal, lusting for a sleeping woman, so vulnerable and warm and smelling of white peonies in summer. He palmed his brow, his hand coming back damp with sweat.

He pulled the blankets over her and she tucked in.

Before he looked too long, he left the room. There was a chair in Ben's study he could use. And he could fall asleep anywhere.

It was staying asleep that was the trouble.

He'd not dreamed of Tibet the last three nights with Charlotte beside him; he was overdue for his nightmare. The thought delivered a grim smile to his lips. At least if he cried out, Charlotte wouldn't hear.

He lit a lamp and the familiar study was illuminated. A stack of letters, white on the dark wood table, could not be overlooked. He'd asked his parents to forward his mail here, but—as usual—there was no communication from Asia. Never any letters.

In the careless sweep of his eye, a name stopped him: Viscount Spencer.

The bastard had written to Charlotte. He lifted the letter and glared at the name, trying to glean the contents by the slant of the writing. What could he mean by writing to her? After what he'd done?

"Goddammit." Kicking off his boots, he flung himself into Ben's deep wingback chair and propped his feet on a low stool. Sleep would elude him now. Setting his jaw, he glared at the letter, seeing Spencer again in the wood, holding Charlotte down, hurting her.

What the hell did the bastard think he was doing by contacting her?

But he would not keep it dark, either. Let her read

the damn thing. He flung the letter on the table before he could be tempted to burn it.

It may not be a true marriage, but Charlotte was his responsibility and he'd not allow Spencer, or any man, to hurt her.

But what would become of her after he'd gone?

Seventeen

THERE WERE CERTAIN FRUSTRATIONS AND MISUNDERstandings to be borne in marriage—Charlotte understood this from the ladies of Henrietta Abernathy's salon—but waking without her temporary husband was an event she would not suffer to be repeated. If Will thought he could abandon her in the country, ignore the terms of their agreement and sleep apart from her, then…

Well, she had no actual recourse in the matter but the man would soon learn she did not like it. Not at all.

And she would have her morning greeting at the first opportunity. And her kiss. Privacy permitting, she supposed. She could hardly fall upon her husband before the staff.

She descended the stairs. Jamie was crossing the hall with a tray of china. "Good morning, Jamie. Have you seen Mr. Repton?"

"He's had his breakfast, miss, and is at work in the study." Jamie ducked his head and went on his way.

The door was closed. Perhaps she should not

intrude. Should she go in to breakfast? Perhaps he would come to talk with her…?

This was intolerable. The man would just have to bear a short interruption. She made for the study before she might change her mind.

A stranger's deep voice carried through the door. "You'll want for a solicitor. One of them ones on Fleet Street to name your kin. Beneficiaries, they's called."

"Yes, that's been done," Will answered. "Not that there's much of an estate to speak of."

Charlotte's steps slowed, uncertain over what she was hearing.

"Enough to see to your parents?" the stranger asked.

"Yes, thank God. Enough to see them through their lives, at least. Even for my wife in humbler circumstances." Will's voice was dry and amused. "She'll not have much use for anything I can leave her, but I did what I could."

Her breath hitched in her throat. He was speaking of his will. Why would Will bequeath anything to her? The marriage contract required no jointure on his part and—not to put too fine a point on it—her dowry was eighty times the man's estate anyway.

It was rather vulgar to put the point on it, but there it was.

The gesture was really rather sweet—*oh, honestly*, she would not stand here and listen to Will speak of death as calmly as the weather.

Drawing a breath, she knocked and peeked into the study. Will sat across from a large, muscled man draped wholly at his ease in Ben's wingback chair. "Good morning," she said. "Please forgive my interruption."

The men stood. "Come in, Charlotte," Will said. "This is Seth Mayhew. Mr. Mayhew has just returned from an expedition in the Americas. Seth, may I introduce Charlotte Ba—uh…my wife."

Mr. Mayhew's eyes widened and he let loose a booming laugh. "Your wife now, is she?" He gave Will a friendly shove. "A *bit* pretty, you said." He shook her hand and made her bracelets bounce. "Well then. Missus Repton, very pleased to meet you."

"How do you do, Mr. Mayhew?" Mr. Mayhew's hands were rough with calluses, and his skin dark from sun and wind. The Americas must be wild, indeed. But he was a fine-looking man.

Oh dear, did she have a penchant for explorers?

"I didn't know plant collectors married ladies like you," Mr. Mayhew said.

"Fortunately, they do," she said. "Though I had the devil of a time persuading him."

He let loose another booming laugh and squeezed her hand. It was that unashamed handshake and the steadiness of Mr. Mayhew's clear-eyed gaze that convinced her of his worthiness. This man's counsel may help keep Will safe, and that made him most attractive in her estimation. "May I offer you some tea, Mr. Mayhew? Or perhaps you would prefer coffee?"

The creases at the corners of his eyes deepened with his smile. "I would at that, Mrs. Repton. Thank you."

"I thought you might. Will, may I have a word please?"

The small smile on Will's lips faded. He followed her into the hall. "Charlotte, about last night—"

"Not here, please." She instructed a maid to bring in a tray to the study, along with sandwiches as Mr. Mayhew was too robust a man for petits fours, then moved to the back parlor and shut the door behind them. Sitting on the settee, she smiled and patted the seat beside her. "Will you sit?"

He eyed the seat suspiciously for such an oddly long duration she was compelled to look at the cushion herself.

"I suppose you aim to scold me." He crossed his arms.

"Scold you?"

"About last night."

"Scold you?" she repeated, confused. She was hardly some fishwife out of Billingsgate.

"You *were* asleep and I didn't want to disturb you."

Scold him. It was really rather an insulting notion.

"And I was comfortable in the study."

There was not even a chaise longue in the study. Was he so intent on avoiding her he'd sleep with less comfort than a hall boy? Her jaw plopped open to admonish him—but she would not like to be thought a shrew. In fact, she would not succumb to his stupid silence at all. They had an agreement, after all, and the marriage was not her idea in the first place. He was entirely in the wrong, and the man could not be so obtuse as to not comprehend that.

Scold him, indeed.

At her continued silence, Will's eyes slipped uncertainly to the door and back. "I know we discussed sleeping as husband and wife but upon further thought, that is not sustainable. You have to admit, the arrangement isn't comfortable—well, it *is* comfortable, we sleep well together." He widened his stance. "But I'm a man—"

Her brows quirked at the proclamation.

"—and as a man, I have needs…you know we can't commit to any sort of carnal, uh…and you are really…so that's why." Will glared at the needlework pillow of her beloved pony, God rest her sweet soul. "I insist, in fact."

Will set his jaw in a stubborn line and, before she might respond, plodded on with other reasons why they ought not share a bed. All blather and nonsense about late hours and her maidenly innocence and his manly urges, so she closed her ears and indulged in examining him.

He did look fine in his light gray waistcoat, the blue of his eyes so striking in contrast. That was the same one he wore the night before the wedding. And she rather liked his hair like that, even as careless as he was with styling it. Rumpled from sleep was best, of course, but that sight was hers alone. Perhaps she might persuade him to try some of Wally's pomade. Peter could purchase a jar when he ran his errands this afternoon. Where would he purchase it? Surely Michael would know, wouldn't he? If the shop was in Piccadilly, he might collect her new book at Hatchard's.

Sighing, she rose and gently shook her skirts to order. Instantly, he stopped talking. As usual, he delved into her eyes before diverting them across the room over her head.

"You have not wished me good morning," she said.

His jaw tightened. "Good morning."

She stepped closer until she brushed his crossed arms. "That was not very husbandly."

He shut his eyes and exhaled. Angling his head, Will hovered his lips an inch over hers. He knew what she expected, so she smiled and pursed her lips. Tentatively, he touched a small kiss onto her mouth.

Satisfied, she beamed, happy he was so biddable in the matter. But he didn't back away. Hard arms cinched tighter than her corset, bending her backward as his mouth descended.

Her heart leapt. Goodness, the man knew how to kiss!

He pressed more firmly until, with a growl of frustration, he lifted his lips. "Open your mouth," he commanded, his voice hoarse and deep. At her compliance, he groaned and invaded her with his tongue. Her legs went to jelly beneath her and she held tightly to his neck, letting her head loll back on her neck under his skillful attention.

Oh yes, this was definitely the man she loved! No one else would ever do.

Thirteen more weeks of Will's kisses. What a bargain she had made.

Too soon, he broke their kiss and rested his forehead against hers, his panting breath steamy and thrillingly intimate. "Good morning."

"Good morning," she whispered.

While he mastered his breath, his hands smoothed the fabric at her waist. "I wrinkled you."

"I don't mind."

"This braid thing is loose."

"I'll fix it."

His fingers came to a rest, gently spanning her waist. The sweet man. Why did he resist ravishing her? They might do all manner of pleasurable activities short of breaching her burdensome maidenhead.

He cleared his throat roughly. "I should get back to the study."

Back to the study. Back to work. Back to China. She corrected the childish pout on her face with effort. "Your coffee will be cold."

His lips pressed together and she suspected he was trying not to smile. He straightened, setting her from him. "Are you done scolding me?"

"Yes, I think so. That was a lovely 'good morning.' I will expect a 'good night' as well."

He blinked. "Yes, well." He raked a distracted hand through his hair, tousling it more.

Charlotte smoothed his hair—Peter really must get that pomade this morning—and swept toward the door.

"And we are agreed on separate rooms?" he called.

Her stride did not waver. "Absolutely not."

"But—"

"You must not keep Mr. Mayhew waiting." She smiled at him from the door. "I'll have Michael unpack your things."

That night, and for many nights to come, Will discovered depths of willpower and restraint he never knew he possessed. There were moments, of course, when his lust overrode his reason. Times when his good-morning and good-night kisses quickly overheated. Times when his cock swelled at the seductive sight of Charlotte straightening her stocking or tightening her stays. Or sorting her mail...stirring her tea...threading her embroidery needle.

Of course he had tried, once more, to avoid her bed by feigning work until two a.m. But the scheme had been found out and the look of hurt on her face was one he vowed never to be repeated.

So each night, as he did tonight, he hurried under the blankets and hid his erection as best he could beneath the ridiculous, blowsy nightshirt he wore for modesty's sake. And each night, Charlotte talked.

He, of course, did too. As decreed by her second marriage requirement.

"You enjoyed Cook's menu tonight." She flipped over to face him. "You had two servings."

He grinned and rolled to face her, propped on his elbow and resting his head on his hand. "I did." He pulled the blanket to beneath her chin. The less he saw of her body, the better. "I like toad in the hole."

Her nose crinkled, but she laughed. "Toad? In the what?"

"The sausages. Baked in the batter? Mum makes it for me all the time. It's one of my favorites."

"That was *cake salé à la saucisse de morteau.*"

"Is that French for 'toad in the hole'?"

"No, there is no— It is French for 'savory cake with sausage.'"

"Right." He flipped onto his back. "Toad in the hole. I'll have Mum make you some."

Charlotte nestled deeper under her blanket and when he glanced at her, she giggled. "Toad in the hole?"

He shook his head, the smile on his face growing. "Good night, Charlotte." He pushed up to plant his good-night kiss on her lips. Always the most treacherous maneuver of his day—Charlotte on her back, her lips so soft and warm, near enough for him to smell the perfume of her skin.

Her hands cupped his neck, lengthening their kiss. He didn't object. He never objected.

Steeling himself, he raised his head.

"Good night," she breathed. Her fingers slid slowly off him and the sensation tingled low in his back.

It was gratifying, at least, to know his attraction was not completely one-sided. Time and again, he caught Charlotte studying him, lingering on different parts of his body with a soft, curious light in her eye.

And he was never the first to initiate their closeness in bed. Always she was the first to spoon against him and snuggle close.

But then, he might be imagining her attraction. As she was an expert sleeper, he did make for a generously sized pillow.

The days were easier. Being out of bed was easier. And strangely, they lived in harmony, all to Charlotte's credit. He had no idea what to do with a female like her—never had done—so he watched her happy comings and goings, a bundle of petticoats and feathered hats trailed by a maid, and remained confounded.

Her schedule of house calls, philanthropies, and shopping kept her dashing in and out of the house most of the day in a different dress than she wore at breakfast. Though he was learning white cotton or muslin meant she would be staying in, donning a coat she called a *paletot* meant she would go out walking or shopping, and a silk or satin dress without a hat meant she was receiving visitors.

At night, after changing into another dress for dinner,

she wrote letters, read a few pages from one among the many books she was currently reading but never finishing, and drew little sketches she laughingly stuffed into her book whenever he drew too close to see.

That hurt his feelings a little. Not that he had any right to see.

The only thing that concerned him was that Charlotte remain her happy self, and he would do his best to keep her that way. He would be an obliging husband—and with her, it was easy. There were no tormenting dreams to disturb his sleep, the preparations for the journey were progressing smoothly, and at some point, he could not be sure precisely when, his nerves had no longer tightened at every sound. His rested body and mind were, at times, so light he found himself laughing aloud at Charlotte's anecdotes.

She was a puzzle he enjoyed solving every day despite his efforts at polite distance. He was learning all her subtle expressions and what they meant. Luckily, as a collector, he'd developed an eye for detail and a keen memory. A small quirk of her left eyebrow meant curiosity. That one was always at play on her face. When her lips pursed into a small moue, she was deciding on something. A certain tilt of her head to the left meant she was receptive; to the right meant her mind was decided.

There were multitudes of expressions that were never lasting. The longer he spent with her, the more he understood her mind was more agile than his, capable of overlapping one topic to the next the way water flows into a vacuum.

It was no surprise he liked being near her—his body damn near tingled at the sight of her. What surprised him was that he counted the best part of his day at the dinner table when he could finally sit with her and hear her news.

He didn't share his news often—there were too many dark secrets tied up in them—but today, he had good news to share. He waited for her wine to be poured so he might have her full attention.

"I secured a promise of the last two hundred pounds, Charlotte." His fingers tapped eagerly on his thighs beneath the table. "I wonder if you'll guess who the investor is?"

She kept her eyes on the tablecloth. "Do I know the person?"

"He's a member of the Geographical Society."

"Is it Mr. Helmsley?"

Will blinked. The woman was preternatural. "Well…yes."

"I thought him most likely. He was here the day we met."

"I remember."

She pushed the broccoli about her plate. "You must write to Ben with your good news. Lucy wrote that Jacob has taken to telling the baby tales of your expeditions, embellishing a little, of course."

"Am I wrestling sea monsters and playing cricket with Poseidon?"

"Well, you must or else your nephews—" Her face crumpled and she pushed from the table. "Excuse me."

Before he could lower his fork, Charlotte had swept out of the dining room. *Damn it*, what stupid thing had he said now? He shared a perplexed look with the footman and shoved back from the table to follow.

In the hall, a maid pointed mutely to the back parlor, correctly ascertaining he sought his wife. Charlotte stood by the window holding a handkerchief. "What's wrong? Are you unwell?"

"There is no need for concern. I am well." But her blue eyes shimmered with tears.

He didn't like this. This damn impotent panic. "What is it?"

"Nothing. Truly." She tried to smile but didn't succeed, dabbing at her eyes. "I am overtired."

This wasn't a side of Charlotte he was at all comfortable with. Generally, there wasn't a side of the woman he *was* comfortable with, but he counted on her buoyancy of spirit more than he should. It was a gift to the floundering husband he was.

She straightened her shoulders and smiled a watery smile, which made him feel worse. "I think...you're tired of my company in the evenings—"

Her eyes grew huge. "No! I love our evenings together."

The denial soothed him, but there was something else bothering him. "I see you get so many letters. Are they invitations to parties or...things?"

She blinked her eyes and looked quizzically at him. "We are invited everywhere, but I did not think you would like me to accept, busy as you are."

"Oh." He hadn't considered she'd actually want, or need, him to attend with her. "Well, I'll accompany you, if you wish. Just tell me what night and where."

"Truly?"

He crossed his arms and ducked his head to hold her hopeful gaze. Thank God she was no longer crying. "Yes, truly. Were you not expecting my acquiescence? How will you manage to avoid my company in public now, Mrs. Repton?"

Lowering her chin, she smiled at him through her lashes and he swayed a little on his feet. That was one of her expressions he was powerless against.

She stepped closer and smoothed the lapels of his coat. "There is a danger that accompanying the most fascinating man in London might grow tiresome, with everyone volleying for your attention."

"It is my cross to bear."

The laughter in her eyes dimmed. "You dislike crowds though, I think."

What a bloody horrible husband he was. She was accustomed to nights of music and dancing and dinners—not quiet evenings with a man who scribbled in journals and squinted at maps. And wasn't he supposed to escort her about town to maintain the fiction of their marriage? Sweetheart that she was, she never complained. "I shouldn't mind them if you're there."

She clasped her hands with pleasure but uncertainty lurked in her eyes. "Truly?"

He was bloody, bloody horrible. "It's been too long since I presumed upon the good graces of my betters."

She smiled. "Well, if you are in earnest, there *is* one party I thought we might attend."

Eighteen

The summer charity ball for the London Municipal Garden Society wasn't exactly the glittering soiree he'd envisioned Charlotte asking him to attend. The guests were staunchly middle class and wouldn't know French couture if it walked up and squealed *bonjour* at them. Nevertheless, Charlotte donned one of her finest gowns: a Parisian masterpiece of black tulle and lace, draped over silk taffeta and trimmed with jet beads and satin ball fringe.

Will hadn't lived with the woman this long without learning something of fashion.

With her hair styled in long, curling ringlets and pinned back with silk organza flowers, she looked imperial as a princess. He laughed when he first saw her descend the stairs in all her glory, which only made Charlotte beam wider.

Now that they were at Somerset House, in an immense room crowded with city engineers, community tradesmen, gardeners, and a fair number of familiar faces from Kew, Chiswick, and the Chelsea Physic Garden, Will could only stand back and swell with pride as his wife dazzled them to stunned admiration the first minute, then charmed them to easy laughter the next.

No, he'd never find another like her. And he was letting her go to sail back to the land of his nightmares.

Wanting her to himself, he led her to a quiet corner. There was no privacy in it; the room followed them with their eyes. Charlotte would not go unnoticed.

"You haven't fooled me, you know," he said.

"I don't know what you mean." She straightened his necktie.

"You accepted this invitation for my comfort."

"I did not. I am an impassioned supporter of the London municipal cemeteries—"

"Municipal gardens," Will corrected.

"—and we are sure to have a lovely time. There is a mood of easy revelry. As a veteran of hundreds of such gatherings, I can sense such things in the first minutes."

"I've no doubt."

"And"—her eyes sparkled as she pulled the lapel of his coat—"*il est même possible que nous dansions avant la fin de la nuit…?*"

The playful tug brought her close to his chest. It wasn't time for their "good night," but he was desperate to kiss her. And God bless it, why did she always smell so good? "That's French, isn't it?"

She smiled. "It is."

"I don't speak French."

"No? But Jacob would tell you, any old wagon horse could understand that."

"I don't speak horse, either."

"I said, 'we may even dance before the night is through.'"

"Ah."

"Ah?"

For the first time in his life, he played coy and traced the seam of her glove with his finger. "Did I tell you how pretty you look tonight?"

"Are you avoiding my question?"

"Which one?"

"*Will!*"

A voice boomed from over Will's shoulder, and he stiffened with annoyance at the interruption. He and Charlotte turned to see Seth Mayhew grinning at them.

"I thought it was you," Seth said.

Will shook his hand. "Odd we didn't mention having the same plans for this evening."

"Do men never speak of matters besides work?" Charlotte asked. "You have been cloistered in that study together the past three days."

Seth winked at her. "The only time Will lets off work is to check the clock."

"The clock?"

"So he'll know when you're to enter with our tea."

Will frowned at the man, but Charlotte laughed. "Does he have me on a schedule for his sandwiches?"

"He's not starved for the sight of those sandwiches, Mrs. Repton."

"All right, all right," Will muttered. Was he that obvious?

Thankfully, a quintet began to play. Only when the assembly moved toward the walls did he realize the dancing was to begin.

Charlotte sidled closer. "The first dance is to be a waltz."

"Is it?" he murmured, feigning ignorance of her leading smile.

She sighed. "I do hope some gentleman asks me to dance."

Seth stepped forward with an eager clap of his hands and a waggle of his eyebrows. "Fear not, Mrs. Rep—"

Will's hand shot out to hold the man back. The bloody flirt. "Wait, I—" He scowled, realizing how possessive he looked. He stepped close and dropped his voice. "Charlotte, I thought we agreed I'd dance with you?"

Her eyes widened innocently. "I do not recall your being persuaded."

"Well, I…I might be persuaded if the right partner offered."

"Will I do?"

He made a play of examining her. "I suppose you're comely enough to draw attention from my feet."

"You will force my compliments saying such things. We both know you waltz exceptionally well."

"I know no such thing. Your memory is shockingly bad."

"It is far superior to yours, I fear."

He offered his arm. "I'm sorry your toes will soon learn the truth of it."

"You will not tread on my toes, sir."

With a smugly arched brow, he turned to Seth. "Excuse us."

"Save me the next, Mrs. Repton," Seth called.

"I think that unlikely, Seth." Will grinned at the

man. "Good thing you're a plant hunter, and accustomed to disappointment."

Will led Charlotte away from the laughing man. The music slowed, signaling the start of their waltz. He bowed and held out his hand; she curtsied and rose as if gravity had no hold on her, twirling into his arms.

The woman was a dancer. She danced walking and rising and gliding across rooms and leaning over his shoulder to see his work. Always on tiptoe, always orbiting him before he had a chance to turn. And yet, flat-footed as she always caught him, the moment she was in his arms, it was like he was dancing, too—breathless, exhilarated, reeling.

The music rose and he swept her round without a word. They danced without speaking, without looking from each other's eyes. Was she thinking of their first dance, too? Of how far they'd come? They kissed each other expertly now. They slept in each other's arms. He'd touched her like a lover once. Just the once. Was she tortured by the memory of that night, as well?

Enough.

He shook the thought away, stumbling a step or two. He had to stop wanting. Wanting to believe the dreams were done. Wanting to never see what he saw when he ran from the mission, chased by men who seemed more animal than human. Wanting his friends back. Wanting to find Aimee.

Wanting a new life in England. Wanting to stay. Wanting Charlotte.

But as the Chinese say, don't hunt moonlight in the water.

The pain in his leg stabbed, making his next turn clumsy and stiff.

Charlotte's hand squeezed his, a look of apology on her face. "Shall we stop?"

He hissed out a breath. Damn his leg. He nodded shortly and led her off the crowded floor. Her eyes were wide and watchful, and she kept hold of his hands. "Does it still hurt?"

"I'm fine, I'm sorry."

She searched his face, so he softened the pain from his countenance until the worry eased from her eyes. Evidently not caring they were in a crowded room, she placed a warm hand on his cheek and smiled at him like...*God help him*, like his mum did with his father, like Lucy did with Ben.

Like a wife.

He pulled her hand down and let it go with a slight squeeze of apology. But he didn't want to stop touching her, so he let himself touch the small of her back and lead her where Seth stood. Company was good at a moment like this. He knew better than to let himself feel too close to her.

The music ended and a group of ladies swooped in to claim Charlotte. Wives of the board. No doubt wanting to recruit her. Odds were good she might join; she belonged to a dozen boards already. They didn't spare a glance for him or Seth, and they stood dumbly watching the procession sashay away.

"Mrs. Repton's the belle of the ball, ain't she?" Seth said.

"That's usually the way of it."

"No wonder. A real lady from the ground up. How long you been married?"

"Coming on three weeks."

Seth frowned. "I thought you was newly wed. Won't it pain you to leave her?"

He shrugged, not meeting the man's eye. "That was the plan before we married."

Seth studied him. "Plans have a nasty habit of changing on a man though, don't they?"

Will crossed his arms to signal the end of the discussion and Seth sensibly changed the subject.

"In any case," Seth said, "thank you for getting me in to your lecture at the Geographical Society."

"I'm afraid there'll be little of educational value. All anyone wishes to speak of is the massacre. But I'm obligated—a condition of the grant they're giving me. The board's received too many requests for Chinese Will to ignore their members."

Seth shook his head. "One thing never made sense to me about Tibet."

"What's that?"

"The mission had been there for a time, hadn't it?"

"Since 1846."

"And it was attacked because the Tibetans wanted the foreigners gone, meaning the French Catholics."

"Right."

"So why'd they wait three years?"

"Some say China was overstepping in Tibet, opening to trade and forcing Tibet to follow suit. Some say it was the arrival of my crew, more foreigners and British to boot. I may never know."

"Sorry, I don't mean to—"

Will waved off the apology. "I ask myself all the time."

"Seems to me, men don't do such things to strangers." Seth paused. "Unless money's involved."

Money?

There was no money. The last batch of seedlings had been transported by ship and bullock train weeks before to India. He, Jack, and Cressey carried only a small stash of seeds and notes from the tea processing plants they'd scouted.

"Will Mrs. Repton be there?" Seth asked.

"She doesn't know of the lecture."

"You've not told her?"

"It's nothing a lady ought to hear. The Society doesn't admit women to their lectures, anyway."

"How did you keep her from learning of it?"

"The lecture was announced only to the Society's members."

Seth studied him. "But she knows all that happened...?"

Something curiously akin to guilt swept through him. "Not all."

"Will—"

"She knows nearly everything. Everything up to the last month in Tibet. She knows the names and stories of every one of my friends. She knows they're dead." The word felt unnatural in his mouth. "I just never told her...*how*."

Seth didn't appear to be dropping the subject, so Will asked, "The mail steamer is due in this week, isn't it?"

"It is. If I don't hear from George, it'll be eight months without word." Seth smiled tightly.

Will regretted asking. The man's smile didn't hide the worry underneath, and Will knew damn well the schedule for mail steamers. "The post is notoriously uncertain. You shouldn't worry."

"Been worried since the day George was born. I suppose that's an older brother's job."

There wasn't much Will could say. Eight months was a long time without a communication. Maybe too long. Cholera, dengue, bandits, drowning—George could have succumbed to any number of things.

And George's crew was the one he'd most hoped might respond to his pleas for help. They'd been in the southwest provinces of China immediately following the massacre. Seth knew the proximity, and had to be aware of Will's hope, but no one would wish their own family to attempt such a rescue so they didn't speak of it.

It was damn unlikely, in any case. Will hadn't been able to offer Lady Wynston's twenty-thousand-pound reward in those early letters. Only an angel or a madman would help him then.

Another dance came to an end with a swell of laughter and voices. Skirts spun and couples criss-crossed the floor. In the flurry of bodies he sought Charlotte, but she was not where she had been a moment ago.

She wasn't anywhere.

Irrational as it was, his muscles tightened, his senses sharpening to potential danger. Icy fear trickled down his back. It was a familiar reaction after Tibet. One he hoped he was leaving in the past.

The crowd was harmless. A hardworking middle class

intent on taking full advantage of the evening's gaiety and dancing. But as he scanned the crush of bodies, searching for that beautiful face, his unease grew.

And it wasn't just Charlotte's face he sought…but a viscount's as well.

"Excuse me, Seth. I need to find my wife."

"I received your letter and am acquainted with your feelings, Lord Spencer." Charlotte stared straight ahead, not daring to slow her stride in the too-empty corridor.

She had to remain calm, even though the sight of Hugh waiting outside the ladies' parlor had nearly given her an apoplexy.

It was obvious he had come for her. Viscount Spencer would not deign to keep company with civil servants or gardeners. From a distance, his suit appeared fine, but her eye was riveted to the top buttons of his shirt, overlooked and undone beneath his cravat. That small carelessness frightened her above all else.

Will was beyond the door. If she could only get there without angering Hugh.

"And I am not deserving of a reply?" Hugh followed, crowding her against the wall.

"Really, there is no need for this display."

Hugh gripped her arm, forcing her to stop. "You will listen to me."

Alarmed, she darted a glance at the two men who milled at the far end of the corridor. She could cry for help if—

"Everyone knows Repton is to sail," Hugh hissed.

"You make a fool of yourself, coming here—smiling at him, dancing with him."

"Release my arm." She pulled, but his grip tightened. Lifting her chin, she forced herself to meet his eye but her insides quaked.

His lips split in a horrible smile. "We will petition for abandonment once he sails. We will contrive some reason for an annulment." He grabbed her other shoulder. "You will not be reproached for returning to me."

"Return to you?"

"Your marriage has made a fool of me, but you can rectify the situation. You will tell my father the sort of man Repton is. How he persuaded you, ensnared you—"

"Spencer!"

Hugh flinched at the roar. Will charged toward them.

"Take your hands off her!" Will growled.

Despite the scene they caused, she breathed a sigh of relief. Will looked large and dangerous. And more furious than she'd ever seen him.

She pulled free of Hugh's slackening hold and moved to Will's side. "Please, let us leave."

But Will sidestepped her. "What the hell are you doing here, Spencer?"

Hugh smiled, arrogant as ever. "I wonder that myself. Is this the new society Charlotte is to keep? This drab middle class? Is this the best you can do?"

She narrowed her eyes at Hugh. "Oh, honestly!"

Will's eyes were cold and pale as a glacier. "If you care at all for Charlotte's reputation, you'll leave her alone."

"You caution *me* to have a care? I will be the sixth Earl of Harlowe—"

"She is my wife."

"And that means you aim to stay?"

"*She is my wife!*"

"Yes, your *wife*," Hugh sneered. "Shall we indulge the truth for a moment? You wanted her from the start. I saw how you looked at her."

"Shut your mouth," Will growled.

"I saw how you contrived to force this union, following us in the wood, all in service to your lust. You'll stay only as long as it takes to slake it."

"Enough, Hugh," she said.

To her shock, Hugh reached for her. "You mustn't get with child, Charlotte. Precautions can be taken—"

But the rest of his words were lost. With a roar, Will rammed Hugh into the wall.

Hugh grunted with the blow but stared defiantly at Will. "Will you defile her utterly, then? No man of honor will have her if she carries your babe—"

Will slammed him again. "Leave her alone!"

"We were nearly married. Do you honestly think you will keep us apart?"

"She'll never go back to you. *Stay away from her!*"

Charlotte's heart pounded in her throat. Will's white-knuckle fists appeared to tighten and twist beneath Hugh's chin and small, choked sounds gurgled from his throat. Hugh was turning blue. "Will, stop."

But Will didn't stop. "Stay away from her." The words rumbled from deep in his chest. "Touch her again and I swear…I'll skin you alive." He leaned close to deliver the rest, thinking she would not hear.

But she did hear. Every chilling word.

"*And it can be done, Spencer. I've seen it.*"

Hugh recoiled, his hands scrabbling frantically, but he couldn't break Will's grip.

"Will, please." She stepped closer, terrified by the sight of Hugh's sagging lids and his purple skin.

Hugh flailed helplessly, but lifted a defiant chin. "*Christ,* you…you *are* a savage. You're mad." His voice was hoarse, strangled. "Think…before you… threaten a peer."

"I'm thinking plenty," Will growled.

The men glared, nose to nose. She could not allow this. Hugh was right—he was a peer and untouchable. She grabbed Will's wrist and tried to pull him away, but it was like trying to pull a steamship. "Put him down."

He didn't listen, and when Hugh worked his lips into a smug smile, there was no time left. She swung in front of Will, hooked her arms about his neck, and surprised him into looking at her.

"*Damn it, Charlotte!*" But he shoved Hugh away instantly, his arms circling her protectively to move her back. "What are you doing?"

"You will not come to blows!" Her voice cracked and her body quaked against his.

His eyes darkened with annoyance and a blatant question: *why the hell not?*

She hissed her whisper into his ear. "He is a viscount." *And he will have you arrested and jailed and I could not bear it.*

His eyes narrowed at Hugh, then her, then his glare buckled with frustration. "Fine." He gritted the word between his teeth, grabbed her hand, and stormed down the hall, pulling her with him.

Even with his limping stride, she had to run to keep up. "Might we slow down?"

Will turned down an empty corridor.

"This is not the way to the party." Her words triggered a scowl. Perhaps it was best not to question his direction at the moment. But really, this was too unfair. He was not the only one upset. She was shaken herself. Will might have been hurt.

Though, to be honest, she was not feeling all that fragile anymore. This unexpected exercise was quickly reviving her.

Still, it was unkind to ignore her. Brooding silences were all well and good for the heroes in her novels, but she was of an opinion they should not be encouraged in reality. And Will was all too prone to brood.

"Thank goodness you came." Her words were breathless in her undignified trot. "I am speechless at Lord Spencer's behavior. He had the cheek to try to persuade me of how sorely I abused *him,* which is, of course, utterly absurd. Men can act so irrationally when their pride is pricked."

There. She said it. Will could go ahead and paint himself with the same brush.

Will stopped to try a closed door—locked. Then another, also locked, so he continued their march.

"Though I commend you for refraining from violence, especially as we know you could beat him handily." She pressed against the stitch in her side. "Still, I would not like it. I would find it impossible to suppress an anxiety for your safety. Who knows what tricks that man might play on you?"

Will tried another door, which opened, and

evidently satisfied by its dim confines, he dropped her hand—which felt a bit like a punishment—and stepped aside mutely till she entered.

The room was cluttered with bookshelves and cabinets, but that was all she noted before Will shut the door, extinguishing the light from the hall. From the windows, the lamplight of the Strand cast their amber glow.

Will rounded on her. "Did he hurt you?"

His voice was strained and instinctively she stepped closer. "Not at all."

Her dream husband would rush to hold her and murmur tender assurances in her ear. Leaning forward, she relaxed and waited to be caught up in his embrace.

And waited.

Will circled her, squinting to examine her and assess the truth of her denial. Appearing annoyed that she hadn't been battered, maimed, or murdered, he planted his feet wide and pointed a stern finger at her. "First of all, never place yourself between a man's fist and its target. Second, I don't give a damn that he's a viscount. And third, you're never to be alone with him again!"

Her mouth plopped open. "I was not alone with him." She rethought that. "Not on purpose. And why are you scolding me?"

"Because he's dangerous. He maneuvered you away from anyone who could help you."

"I was coming from the ladies' lounge. Besides"—she crossed her arms, and tried a lie—"I am not afraid of him."

His eyes narrowed, but before she could offer

further evidence of her blamelessness, hard arms banded around her and swept her into a dizzying turn. When she regained her bearings, her back was against the door and she couldn't move. His arms, legs, his entire body, imprisoned hers.

And cocooned in his strong hold…she melted. She was safe. And warm. And his lips were enticingly close.

Which made his next words hugely disappointing.

"Try to escape me."

She blinked. "Why?"

"Because you should be afraid." In the dark, the pupils of his blue eyes were wide, and a heated flush had crept onto his cheeks. The sight ignited something in her. He gave her a small shake. "Try, Charlotte."

"No. I don't want to."

His voice dropped to a growl. "So I could do whatever I want? Kiss you? Touch you? Lift your skirts right here and—"

"And what?" She was agreeable to any of those suggestions, actually.

He turned his head, swearing under his breath.

The poor man was truly worried. She should not tease him. He had already been denied a bout of fisticuffs and now she would not even oblige him with a quarrel.

"This is a fruitless exercise, you know," she said gently. She pulled her hand free to smooth a lock of hair at his temple and essayed a smile against his deepening frown. "Why would I want to escape you?"

He caught her fingers where they played in his hair and shut his eyes. Her heart sank in an all-too-familiar way. Will did not like her to tease or tread too close. She prepared to be put away from him.

But the hand at her waist cinched tight and the other cradled her head. And then she was pinned against the door with his kiss. He angled deep, deeper, demanding an impenetrable seal. Gruff sounds of satisfaction rumbled in Will's throat and she shuddered with pleasure to each one. She didn't try to lessen the force of his mouth, though his whiskers scraped the corners of her lips.

Please. Let this last. His kisses were always too brief.

A familiar, feminine ache blossomed at the core of her and unfurled its petals around her. The tingling demanded more, so much more, but her petticoats allowed no feeling. She strained closer. "My dress..."

He seemed to understand from the frustration in her voice. To her amazement, he scooped her bottom high so her hips rode his and latched his heated mouth to her neck. Her blood simmered where his lips met skin. It wasn't enough, it was never enough. Arms freed, she clung to his body. Pressed against him so relentlessly she could barely draw breath. Inside, though, she quaked with a violence.

Please...please let this last.

How did he do it? Other men were handsome and protective and strong. But Will was the man she needed, the man she craved. Every kiss, every touch and look, stirred her desire. Even after these weeks of quiet evenings, the friendly conversation, the meals shared, she never dreamed her passion would be this steadfast.

His heated mouth was everywhere, but she was too dazed to chase his lips. She could feel him, erect and strong, where she desired him most. Will's hand was beneath her skirt, beneath her crinoline, his fingers hot and strong where he gripped and squeezed her bottom.

Fused against him in the dark room, her senses narrowed to sound and feeling. The hard muscles of his back flexing beneath her arms. The groans and wet sounds of his mouth laving her skin. The leather soles of his boots scuffing the wood floors with every desperate press of his body for purchase. Her head spun with the erotic sounds until—

"There's no one in these rooms." A grumbling voice sounded in the hall. "We locked every door."

Her startled gasp was stifled by Will's hand. The warm palm was calloused and strong. And arousing. Never in her wildest fantasies…she shivered with desire and he gripped tighter.

"It's all right," Will whispered in her ear.

Oh yes. This was very all right. Trembling uncontrollably, she submitted to her lovely captivity.

A second man's voice came nearer. "Why should he care if some randy couple stole away for a bit o' fun?" Across the hall, a doorknob was tested, rattling but not turning. "See? All locked."

In a flash of movement, Will held the door handle still as the stranger in the hall gave it a jiggle.

"Come on, then," the second voice said. "Let's report to his bleedin' lordship that our curiosity, in respect to these two lovers, is satisfied. Bloody aristos. Think every man's at their beck and call."

The voices faded, leaving Will and Charlotte panting in the muffled quiet of the room.

Will's arms loosened and she sank against his hard shoulder. Bloody aristos, indeed. Hugh had sent those men and interrupted the most promising kiss Will had given her in weeks.

He eased away and her slippers touched ground. *No…no no no, please.* She clutched at his coat but he pulled away.

"What the hell am I doing?" Will muttered.

The self-contempt in his voice sobered her. Her eyes adjusted to the darkness. Will stood, feet planted wide, hands on his hips, chest laboring and an aggressive bulge straining the fall of his trousers. Desire flooded her anew at the sight.

Will stalked to the end of the room. "Spencer sent them."

There was no question. Besides the Lord Mayor, there were no titled men in attendance.

Will shook his head. "I knew Spencer would be jealous, but this…"

What could she say? Hugh was loathsome…but she had encouraged him for months. Was she a little responsible for his behavior now?

"Spencer means to have you back," he said.

"I suppose he does," she murmured, distracted by the irrationality of that.

He ground to a halt, weighing her with a baffled stare. "You *suppose*?"

Confused, it took her a moment to reply. "What? What more would you have me do?"

"I'd have you nowhere near that bastard!"

"And I would have you—" She blinked at the hot tears threatening to form. *Oh, bother it all!* She could never argue without crying.

"What?"

Her throat squeezed tight. No doubt exasperating Will further with her. "I should like to go home. You have quite spoiled the evening for me."

"*I have?*"

"Please call the carriage. I must make my excuses."

He spun from her with a low curse.

Uncertain what to do or say, she waited. Surely he would apologize, wouldn't he? A husband should not bully his wife as if she were wayward child. Or curse in front of her. Ben never spoke to Lucy like this.

Her heart hurt. And at the moment, she missed her sister terribly. Lucy would know what to do.

Will rubbed his temple, a habit of his when he was weary. "We don't have to leave, Charlotte. You've only danced once."

He even sounded weary. Because of her.

"I do not care to dance anymore," she said miserably.

"*Fine.*"

The growled word made her jump. He lunged at the door, flinging it wide and signaling her to precede him through it. "But don't think we're done discussing this."

Nineteen

THEY SURE AS HELL WEREN'T DONE DISCUSSING Spencer. Will drummed his fingers on the carriage, waiting as ever-graceful Charlotte slipped inside, her skirts slithering in behind her. She'd climbed in unassisted, ignoring his proffered hand.

With that betrayal he was tempted to slam the door and send her home alone. A hackney could deliver him to Spencer's house in a half hour—

From within the carriage, Charlotte drew the blind, pointedly avoiding his eye. God damn the man for starting all this.

A small crowd had followed them out of the assembly to bid them farewell and gape at his glamorous wife. Damn it all, there'd be no separate cab tonight.

He heaved himself into the seat opposite hers, the vehicle rocking with his weight. With a slap of the roof to signal the driver, he got on with the business of their so-called "discussion." Hardly the word for it, as it was one-sided. The woman chose *this* moment, in the entirety of their acquaintance, to hold her tongue.

"What did I do, Charlotte?" He angled his head, trying to catch her eye. "I only want you to be safe."

She twisted her head farther toward the window.

"You'll not go anywhere without my escort," he said. "Not until I figure out what to do with him."

Her bottom lip pouted, inconveniently diverting his attention to her pretty mouth.

"Charlotte?"

Silence.

Fine. He flopped back in his seat. In the close, swaying confines of the carriage, he let his knee jostle hers. "Aren't you going to say anything?"

"I have been to Somerset House many times—for art exhibits mostly—but never in those rooms. I thought them well-equipped for tonight's assembly. Though my dress shows to better advantage by candlelight."

He bit back a curse. "That's not what I meant and you know it."

She shifted so their legs didn't touch. "And you know I dislike to argue. You are my husband so you should not bait me."

"I'm trying to talk to you."

"You yelled at me."

"I wasn't—*damn it*, I was *worried* about you!"

"You are yelling again."

He dropped his head into his hands and nearly into her lap. Spencer wanted her, was certain she'd return to him. He sure as hell wouldn't let that happen. But how far would Spencer go?

But she was right. He had to learn to control his anger or they'd never get this problem sorted.

And damn him, his temper wasn't the only thing he

couldn't control. He'd been seconds away from freeing his cock and sliding into her lush, perfumed body right there against the wall. If those men hadn't come, he would have. It was getting harder to resist her.

But raising his voice was a mistake. The only other time he had, she'd cried. And Charlotte Baker wasn't meant to cry.

"I'm sorry I yelled." He worried he'd spoken too low to hear, but she faced him without delay.

"And I am sorry I caused you more worry."

The fatigue of her words drew his head up. Why had he yelled at her? He should have taken her away the instant he found her.

She reached for him and he jerked back in his seat. And damned if he knew why. It was either that or drag her into his lap and continue where they'd left off in that dark room. And it wouldn't be simple lust driving him. It had never been simple with her.

She looked hurt and he hurried to cover his reaction. "The, uh…the fact remains, Spencer will pursue you. And what he said of…"

"A baby?"

He frowned, not meeting her eye.

"His threats are inane," she said quietly. "A baby is impossible."

"I know but—"

"As appallingly as Hugh behaved, he has the right of it. Two months more and we separate. Besides…I did not marry you for your protection."

His heart was sinking fast. Why did she marry him, then? He was supposed to preserve her reputation. Wouldn't that mean keeping Spencer at a distance?

But wouldn't that also mean escorting her to dinners and dances? Tonight's assembly was the first she'd asked him to attend. And none of her social circle were there at all.

Was she ashamed of him? Was he so different?

He stared blindly out the window. A savage, Spencer called him.

He was a character from the papers, a carnival attraction. He *was* different. And once she was free of him, she'd seek the company of a gentleman.

But surely not a gentleman like Spencer? A man who could hurt her as he'd done? Or try to force her to his will? Or treat her as if she were beneath him?

Charlotte was unnervingly quiet. He didn't know the questions to ask or whether he was ready to hear what she'd say, so they rode the rest of the way in silence. She didn't look at him even as he handed her from the carriage. At least she let him this time.

She swept past him into the house to speak to Goodley. "Would you send Patty to me, please?"

The butler ducked his head. "Yes, miss."

She climbed the stairs and he followed with heavy steps. "Charlotte—"

"Patty is to come any moment."

"Then send her away. You don't understand what men like Spencer are capable of. I've seen men reduced to animals with little provocation—"

"Stop." She turned to face him. "I do not understand when you say things like that. Earlier you said it was possible to…to skin a man alive. That you had seen it."

She searched his eyes, but the pulse hammering in his throat was the only movement he allowed.

She stepped closer, her beautiful face creased with concern. "You say things sometimes that make me worry." Her hands wrung the fabric of her gown, her eyes monitoring and pleading. "Am I meant to believe you? You have never told me what happened at the end of your expedition—"

"Charlotte—"

"Or how you were injured—"

"There are some things a man doesn't share, even with a wife—"

"I know but—"

"And you," he held up his hands to stop her words, "you are not really my wife."

Her face crumpled and he heated with fury at himself.

A soft scratch sounded from the door and her maid peeked in. "Shall I come back in a few, then, Charlotte?"

Charlotte blinked. "Yes, later, Patty, please—"

But he couldn't take any more. He turned on his heel and escaped to his never-used bedroom.

Charlotte followed, but to her surprise, Will closed the door between their rooms.

Patty waited, her eyebrows raised at the tension in the room. "Is the honeymoon over, then, love?"

She dragged her attention back. "No, no. This is nothing."

"You best let your husband know that. He looked like Jacob when he's made to eat his peas."

Charlotte stood in the center of the room. Should

she follow him? Or did he need a moment alone? Away from her?

She sank onto her dressing table chair and Patty set to unbuttoning her gown. "What do you two have to quarrel about, anyway?"

What, indeed? She rested her head in her hand. In her heart, Will was her husband, but she was not his wife. If anything, she was his worry.

"Nothing, Patty. He will brood about the matter, as he does. And I will do as I do, and wait for him to realize he does not care at all."

"Don't talk nonsense." Patty prodded her to stand so she could remove her gown and loosen the back tie of her corset. She said nothing more, and Charlotte felt disapproval in the silence, but no disagreement.

Perhaps she was worried over nothing. Perhaps what had happened in China had resolved itself. Will had not had one of his nightmares. He seemed at peace. Even happy.

The door opened and Will cleared his throat to signal his return. He stood awkwardly there, his eyes on the rug. He did so whenever he caught her in any state of undress.

The sweet man…she was still fully covered in her chemise and petticoat.

"I thought we might have a bite of supper, Charlotte."

There. He had forgotten already. She could not pretend all was forgiven, though. A lady ought to have a little pride. "Did you? Please do so without me. I shall draw a bath. Our evening has chilled me quite."

She walked to her bath, leaving Patty to share a

look of sympathy with her husband. A terrible breach of loyalty, in her opinion.

One minute of steeping in the hot, rose-scented water of her bath was all she could bear. "Bother it all," she mumbled under her breath, rising from the water. She wanted to be with Will. Evidently, she had no pride where the man was concerned.

She hurried into her nightrail, but Will had gone. Downstairs for his supper, she supposed. Not bothering to ring for Patty, she sat near the fire, let her hair down, and started to hurriedly brush out the long ringlets.

With effort, she slowed her hand. How ridiculous she had become, so eager to be with him at all times. But wasn't everyone? At the assembly, they all had craned their necks and shuffled near. Will, humble dear that he was, was unaware of the excitement he had caused.

He was similarly oblivious to all the cards on the hall table left by the wives of men who wished to know him. Men rarely paid visits of ceremony, leaving their wives to attend to the matter during their calls. For every card Charlotte received, suddenly she received two from the lady's husband—one for her and one for Will. If he were to stay, he would surely win over the loftiest circles of the *ton*.

But what did it matter? Their marriage would be over long before next season.

How many invitations had she refused, wanting Will to herself? No entertainment compared to an evening at home with him and the conversations stretching from dinner to the study to the bed, where they lay talking side by side.

The only exception she had made was to accept tonight's invitation, because so many of Will's professional acquaintance were to attend. And she had dreamed they would dance.

And then Hugh appeared.

How quickly her dreams could crumble. For her marriage to a hero to be so fascinating a union that all of London would clamber for their presence at every assembly. For Lucy and Ben to walk into any ballroom and be welcomed with kindness. For Wally to have friends. *Real* friends. For the children to never hear a snide whisper behind their back.

Even her dream man…

No. Will was altogether more than she had dreamed: more challenging and aggravating and stubbornly male. More protective and honorable and inspiring. Altogether more wonderful than she had been capable of dreaming. The man surpassed even her formidable imagination.

Even now, she could imagine a marriage of love between them. They would quarrel and reconcile. They would grow and hurt and heal together. They would kiss good night and make love and fall asleep holding each other. She would have a child. She would be a mother.

She would be a wife loved by her husband.

And hadn't that dream crumbled, too?

The brush in her hand dropped heavily to her lap. No, this quarrel did not matter. Nothing of this marriage mattered.

She was only dreaming, after all.

"Charlotte?"

Will leaned against the door, still dressed in his trousers and shirt. "Oh." Embarrassed to be caught in her melancholy, she rose and moved to sit at her dressing table. "I did not hear you return."

"Are you done not speaking to me?"

She smiled. "Yes, I think so."

He pulled a chair near the dressing table and sat. "You're not angry with me."

It was not a question. He understood her moods—but something in Will distrusted her forgiveness, her willing resignation. Perhaps that was why he did not love her.

She hurried on, brightly as she could. "I did try, I promise you." He did not smile back. "Perhaps I am flawed. I do not take offense as deeply as others or as I should. I just cannot *stay* angry. It is as if there is a great balloon inside me and when sadness tries to pull me deeper and deeper under water, there is only so far I can sink before I feel a great pressure to rise again." She flushed in the silence between them. "I do not know how else to explain it."

"You explained it perfectly." His eyes did not waver from her, and a small grin curved his mouth. "And nothing about you is flawed."

At times like this, looking at him was difficult. The space between them filled with possibility. It so often did.

She could succumb to that strange pull in her breastbone when he was near and fly to his arms. Or she could laugh and braid her hair and remind herself all this was just a happy little dream.

Against every instinct in her body, she chose the latter.

The moment eased and Will leaned back in his

chair. "I don't often see your hair down. You look different. You look like a girl."

"I had hoped that was evident."

"I mean a simple country girl. Untouched. Innocent. Not the belle of the Municipal Gardens Ball." He caught a long tendril and studied it in the light.

"Did you have wine with your supper?" She added a teasing note to her voice she didn't feel.

"Why?"

"You are always more free with your words when you've had wine." She pulled the lock of hair from his hand. "And your touch."

He relaxed back in his chair. "Might have done a glass. My wife turned me out of our room."

"Oh dear. She sounds an ogre."

"I made her cross. I might have been a bit overzealous in warning her against someone."

Please...not Hugh again.

A long, steady look held between them. He was all brooding expectation but she would not argue. "A cup of tea sounds nice, doesn't it? I think I—"

He caught her hand before she could stand. "She didn't appreciate my advice, though it's meant to keep her from harm."

He *would* press the issue. "Perhaps she does not wish to be treated as a child."

"Perhaps she doesn't wish to accept what men are capable of." He pushed to his feet to pace the room. "What will you do when you're free, Charlotte? The man means to have you."

She winced at the word *free*. "For now, yes."

He stopped in his tracks. "*And?*"

"And it is a passing fancy. Hugh believes he wishes to reconcile *for now*. An eligible earl-in-waiting will not lack for female attention. Besides, it is no concern of yours."

Oh.

Oh no.

She might have gone too far with that.

Will blanched—then his brows snapped together. "I see," he said softly, and the effect was far more disquieting. He stalked into his bedchamber. A drawer slammed. The wardrobe door creaked in protest. Fabric whipped and snapped.

The violent sounds continued and she stood. Then sat. Then stood again.

She should apologize for her stupid words. Will *did* bear a sense of responsibility for her. It was unkind to suggest he did not.

Will stormed back, tugging the belt of his banyan tight. "Fine. Since what is between you and the viscount is no concern of mine, I'm going to bed. Kiss me good night."

His face was stony, his shoulders bunched, and his robe gaped, revealing a triangle of chest corded with muscle. And for the first time, she did not wish to participate in the evening ritual. He looked as capable of a gentle embrace as a boulder.

She rose slowly. "Of course I did not mean—"

Impatiently, he pulled her into his arms and she winced. "Will, do be careful. I'm sorry—"

Further words were silenced by his kiss. Immediately, she felt *him*…*it*…through her thin nightrail, free and unobstructed by his robe. *His male parts.* One long, rather large part in particular. A surprised mewl sounded in her throat.

The noise stirred him to lift his lips off hers and grumble. "What is it?"

"Your nightshirt? Where is it?"

He blinked and looked to his dressing room as if the lost nightshirt had cried out for him. His throat bobbed with a swallow. "I…uh. I'm not wearing it."

"Yes, I know."

"I was in a hurry," he said defensively. "I prefer not to wear the stupid thing anyway. Like some skittish virgin."

They stood like that a moment—he waiting for her to speak, and she disappointing him with a rare moment of speechlessness. She was stuck on that "virgin" insult, not that he had called *her* a virgin. She would not be a skittish one in any case.

Why was he not stepping away? Normally, when that part of him grew thick from their embrace, he set her back and put the room between them.

Sometimes several rooms, a flight of stairs, and a city block.

He wet his lips, and the dark, smoky wine she tasted on his tongue suffused the air. Had he drunk too much? Is that why he still held her? Why did he not close his robe?

More confusing yet, he subtly, almost experimentally, shifted his hips and—*oh, mercy*—wedged more closely between her thighs, nudging the core of her. She jolted, her eyelids fluttering as pleasure shot through her.

Oh my, he was so large and he was not even excited. Why that was so exciting to *her*, she didn't understand, but something primal in her understood to rejoice. And surrender. When he moved against her once more, she did.

A sigh escaped her lips and her head lolled back on her neck in silent submission. Warm hands caressed her backside, cupping her, molding her to him. His teeth scraped and teased the tendons of her neck, the lobe of her ear, the edge of her jaw, her lips.

He would stop soon. He always did. But for now… he was so exquisitely tender…

"Charlotte?" He nipped her bottom lip to get her attention. "Charlotte?"

She forced her heavy lids open and Will braced her neck so they were eye to eye. Surely he could see her heart, her soul. Surely, by now, he *must* know.

He leaned closer, their lips a sliver of breath apart. "You are my concern. Do you understand? You can't be with someone like him."

Why was he speaking? She pulled his head down to seal her mouth with his but—as he always did—he pulled back and her heart tore.

"Did you hear me?"

"Yes," she breathed. "I hear everything you say and there is not a word I will ever forget." She grasped his hair, not bothering to be gentle, desperate for him to believe her, to *hear her.*

His fingers on her neck kneaded deep and slow. Almost as if he was unaware of what he was doing. His lids were heavy with his desire, and his breathing labored. Fused against her, his manhood grew and hardened.

She gloried in it. *She* did this. His desire belonged to her and if she couldn't have his love, she would have this.

Tonight…tonight there might be a chance to persuade him…

"I want you to touch me, like you did that morning in the wood." She kissed his lips, stiff and sealed. "I want your body on mine." She kissed his chin. "I want to feel when you release on me because you want me, too. I know you do." She kissed his cheek, his brow, his temple, and his hands slid off her. "No, Will…don't let go."

"God…Charlotte…"

But she would not be put off. His arousal was warm on her thigh and somehow, he was still standing here.

She kissed his jaw, his neck, traveling lower to lick the scoop of flesh at the base of his throat. He seemed to like that attention. His groan vibrated beneath her lips. The planes of his chest were so hard, she skimmed her palms under his robes, pulling the halves apart to be closer.

But he stopped her hands, holding them against his taut waist at the point the muscles of his back began their flare to his shoulders.

She gasped for air, holding still. "Please don't push me away. Let me see you."

Will dipped his head and rested his lips on her shoulder. His heart pounded against her cheek and she could have stood like that forever.

"Curious Charlotte…have you seen a man before?"

She shook her head gently, not wanting to break contact, not for a second, with his skin. "I've seen anatomy books, and the Elgin and Phigalian marbles at the British Museum, and Japanese wood block prints but those were not representative so much as—"

"All right." He stroked her hair, pressing so her lips were silenced against his skin. "All right," he breathed. Without moving from her, Will untied his belt and the robe parted wide.

Acutely aware of his strength, his size, and the fragility of the moment, she kept her eyes on his neck, one of her favorite parts of his body. Not that she didn't adore every part of him…

Will shrugged off his robe and it slid to the floor. His breath was hot in her ear. "You can look at me."

How much had the man been drinking?

At his husky words, sensation shimmied down her neck to her toes. Laying her hands on the wall of his chest for support, she aimed her eyes downward and smiled in wonder at the lean, muscled torso, the carved ridge of his hips above his powerful thighs, the hard, segmented abdomen. And finally to the male appendage near her stomach, with the veined shaft and heavy sack beneath looking so soft and vulnerable.

"Oh…my," she breathed.

"Am I what you expected?"

She rested her head limply against his chest, feeling his heat to her toes. Her hands slid over the cobblestone of muscle but she didn't dare touch him lower. "Much of a muchness…"

His hands paused in their gentle stroking. "What's that?"

"I asked Wally if a man's male parts were the same and he said they were all much of a muchness. Which is no answer at all."

His hands stopped altogether. "You asked your brother this?"

"I was curious."

"Of course you were," he murmured. "Much of a muchness, is it?" He moved her hand and squeezed her around him. "I'm a little larger than most."

The shock of touching him *there* seized her breath, and she was afraid to do anything but rest her palm against him. Will covered her hand and used it to stroke himself from base to tip. Large as he was, her fingers could barely reach around him.

The slip and movement of skin fascinated her. She closed her eyes, imagining the pulsing flesh deep inside her. Helpless to the desire coursing through her, she pitched forward against him, her legs weakening.

Oh heavens, she was going to fall. No—she was going to swoon and swooning was so gauche.

Will saved her the indignity, lifting her and laying her on the bed. His naked body came atop her, and the room would not stop spinning. With a groan, he lifted off her and moved lower.

"No…Will?" She fumbled to hold his shoulders but he slid lower, pressing her flat on her back when she would sit up. "I want what you did before."

He pushed her nightgown up, parting her legs gently, and a soft, nibbling kiss behind her knee made her jerk, then tremble. "Oh…my…that's nice, but… before…" She was dizzy with the effort of speaking.

Another soft, nuzzling kiss. "I know, I promise. Relax, sweetheart."

Sweetheart. He'd never called her that before. He'd never called her any endearment. She smiled and closed her eyes, trying to relax as he wanted.

She'd been so patient—and patience was not one of

her virtues—waiting for when he might allow them the pleasure they'd given each other at the hermitage. Soon. Oh, soon—don't distract him. As soon as he was finished kissing her knees and thighs and her—oh, he was kissing her higher. That tickled, actually.

His head dipped under her nightrail and her eyes flew open. He would see her! "Will?"

His hand held her flat against the mattress. Yes, he was definitely seeing her. All of her. With nowhere else where her legs might go, he guided them over his shoulders. Fingers parted her and hot breath fanned her in the instant before he kissed her as intimately as she could be kissed.

Oh…this was naughty, this was—"*Oh my God!*"

His rough tongue lapped her again and again with slow, deliberate strokes. Teasing a pleasure that was almost pain from the junction of her legs, until he was gripping her bucking hips to lock her against his mouth. He sucked and swirled, his hard backside clenching and grinding into the mattress in an erotic rhythm.

She cried out, moaning like a wanton, but she couldn't stop and she couldn't look away from the large, powerful body working to bring her pleasure. The ache was building and building, her legs squeezed him tight, wanting more, wanting his hard flesh inside her, to fill her so there was no more room for this ache within her. "*Please…oh yes, please…*"

Will's hand squeezed her breast in what should have been pain but was only the most exquisite restraint. Strong as he was, gripped tight as she was, she couldn't move for lack of breath. Then his large finger penetrated her and she shattered. Her head arched back into the pillow, her body bucking off the mattress, until she went limp, paralyzed with bliss.

Her flesh shuddered, raw and quivering, and at last Will took mercy upon her, soothing her with his tongue and slipping his fingers from her gently.

Will pushed shakily up and lunged heavily to plant his mouth on Charlotte's. Their kiss was flavored by the essence of her sex and she shied from the taste on his tongue, but he wouldn't let her. He twined her soft hair through his fingers, holding her secure by the nape of her neck, and kissed her long and deep.

Christ, he was going to explode. His cock was granite, desperate for the wet sheath so tantalizingly close. But he'd not lose control.

None of this was for him.

He smiled and their kiss broke apart on her lips. "Was that all right? I've never done that before."

A choked, utterly unladylike sound burst from her lips. He chuckled and Charlotte clapped a hand over her lips and nodded fast.

Still chuckling, he kissed her, losing himself in the erotic taste of her, the heady perfume. Even before he knew the word for it, he'd dreamed of putting his mouth on a woman there. "You taste so good," he whispered.

"I need..."

"What do you need, sweetheart?"

"I need a moment to talk—*think*. I mean think."

He chuckled. "You mean talk, don't you?"

"What is that called? The...tasting?"

He whispered the word into her ear and she shuddered. She liked new words.

"Will…?" She smoothed his hair back from his brow, her eyes a little guarded.

He'd never gone that far before. No wonder she was confused.

"How much wine did you drink?" she asked.

"A half glass."

"Is that all?"

He nestled his cock along her slick folds, careful not to penetrate her. The rigidity of his flesh hurt, but it was a pain edged with rapture. Clamping her hips against his, he rocked slow and steady. "Come on, sweetheart. Come for me."

He moved faster, harder, and the grind of their bodies was making his vision blur and darken. Instantly, she seized with pleasure all over and his triumph crested with hers, but he held his own release at bay.

She went limp under him. God, he wanted to plunge into her, make her his. She was so luscious, so wet and ready. But he remembered his purpose…her words at the hermitage…

Only you…I would only feel this with you…

Only him. Not that bastard Spencer…or any bastard like Spencer.

His cock pulsed, jerking with denied release, but steeling himself, he positioned himself to start again.

But Charlotte's fingers slid around his length before he could. "What can I do? I want you to feel it, too."

He bit back the growl clawing at his throat. Her grip was so soft compared to his, so innocent—but he wouldn't come. He captured her wrists in one hand above her head so he could work unhindered.

Trying not to look at her and lose control, he positioned his erection against her. Damn, she felt like paradise, it would be paradise if he could. "Let me. We're so good together. I can make you come again."

"Will…wait."

He slid his cock on her, faster, harder. Her body tensed. Blue eyes, sultry, smoky, beckoned to him until, mercifully, they closed.

His Charlotte. His sweet Charlotte. Christ, she was almost there— "He can't make you come."

Her eyes blinked opened. He took her mouth, needing to feel it under his, but she slipped away, turning her cheek.

"Who, Will?"

Frustrated, he kissed behind her ear, her neck, but it wasn't working. She was stiffening beneath him.

"Will?" She touched his cheek. "What are you doing?"

"You know what I'm doing." He gripped her supple hips, tilting her to notch tighter against him. He checked her eyes, seeing the desire ebb and flow, slowing his rhythm but not stopping.

Her face changed, hardened. "Stop."

"Promise me you'll find a good man, a kind man."

Her eyes widened. "Promise you?" She shoved hard against his hips. "I said stop!"

Her palm slipped, shoving his cock, and pain sizzled into his loins. "*Argh! Dammit!*"

She pushed at his chest but he was too heavy, the throbbing agony in his body paralyzing him. "Charlotte—" he gasped.

"Do you think me a child?"

"No, I—"

"Get off me."

"Listen to me."

"Get off!"

He caught her head in his hands. "Listen! You don't know men, you don't know how cruel they can be."

She stared, her eyes glimmering. "I am beginning to." She pulled at his hands. "Go away. I don't want you in my bed."

"Yes, you do! *Damn it,* listen!" He grabbed her shoulders, forcing her still. "You want a man in your bed badly, and I'm telling you not any man will do. You make me kiss you every day and sleep with you every night. You feel desire and lust, but it's not enough."

Tears welled in her eyes. "I thought—"

"There are so many men who'll get pleasure from giving it to you as well as taking. Promise me you'll never wed a man like Spencer."

Tears stream down her red cheeks. "Promise you?" she whispered. "How dare you speak of another man? I am married to *you. Get off of me.*"

Desperate, he gripped harder. "I won't be here. He's dangerous, you can't trust—"

"Stop it!"

Her beautiful blue eyes filled with tears. Panic filled him. *Stop crying.* "Just…stop, Charlotte, please…"

"How could you? How could you make love to me to manipulate me? To persuade me from Hugh?"

The bastard's name from her lips unleashed a fresh anguish. "I wasn't making love to you—I was making you come!"

"Get off." She pushed, but he caught her wrists easily. "Get off!"

His hands tightened, pinning her. But her chin trembled and her eyes were wet. With a hissed curse, he pushed himself off her. "*Fine.*" He rolled off the bed and stalked to his bedchamber. "I only mean to protect you."

He slammed the door behind him. *Goddammit!* He looked back at the door to his bedroom, to Charlotte.

She didn't understand. He wouldn't apologize. *He wouldn't.* He was right about men. He wouldn't be here.

He sank on the edge of the bed, his body shuddering and painfully aroused—*damn it all.* He dropped his head in his hands. She was furious.

She was crying.

He rose and moved to the door, leaning his forehead against the cool wood. *Say something, Charlotte. Anything.*

But there was only silence.

Leave her alone. Let her sleep in peace.

The room was cold and dark, the fire dying. The servants never bothered to build a proper one. Why should they? No one slept here.

He dragged himself from the door and stared at the large bed, unused these five weeks.

Let the bloody dreams come then.

It was no less than he deserved.

Something woke her. Will's voice, muffled and agitated.

"No!"

The hoarse cry jolted her upright, her heart

lurching. *Will?* She launched to her feet and into his chamber. Thank God he'd not locked the door.

The fire was banked, red embers flickered, and sinister shadows leapt against the walls. Will was naked atop the blankets, his body flinching against an unseen tormentor. A sob burst from her. "Oh...God...Will?" She climbed onto the mattress, laying her hand on his shoulder. "Will? Wake—"

"*No!*"

An arm flew at her, the back of his wrist landed on her cheek. The blow knocked her teeth together. Pain rattled through her skull and her vision blackened at the edges, blinding her in the already dim room. The bed beneath her rocked.

Will had hit her.

Will's legs thrashed, agony contorted his sweat-streaked face. "Don't touch her!"

Dear God, what was he seeing?

"Will, wake up! It's me. WAKE UP!"

Her voice did not reach him. His fists were clenched and his arms taut with barely leashed strength. With a whispered prayer that he would not strike out, she threw her body on his and hugged his head against her chest.

"No!" A mighty contortion of his body lifted her off the mattress and nearly onto the floor. With a jolt, his eyes opened, wild and unseeing. "*Charlotte!*"

The scream reverberated against her chest. "I'm here," she whispered. *God—who had done this to him?*

Searching hands swept her body. "Charlotte?"

His heart...his heart would burst. "Wake up, Will."

"Charlotte?"

"Yes, dearest. Just a dream. You're safe."

Panting hard, he clung to her.

She stroked his hair, damp with sweat. *Dear God, how could she help him? What happened?* Tears choked her but she would let no sound escape. She kissed the corner of his eye, clenched shut, again and again until the skin eased.

His arms loosened, but when she moved to slide off him, he cinched tight and burrowed his face in her neck. "Don't go. Don't."

This was his nightmare? She hadn't understood when he'd warned her. She hadn't understood at all.

She reached for the blanket but Will's hold did not allow its retrieval. He seemed satisfied to use her for covering, so she relaxed her weight on him, the linen of her nightgown pasting to his clammy skin.

Her cheek touched the pillow and her breath was a hiss of pain. She tested her jaw gingerly, and an ache throbbed to the bone.

Will's head slackened on the pillow; sleep had claimed him. If there had been a trace of anger and sadness in her from their earlier argument, it evaporated at the sight of his face. Terror had etched deep lines there and his hair was dark with sweat in the chill room.

Cradling his head as close as she dared lest she wake him, she stared at the wall and recalled fragments of memory from those early months. Will's eyes, rimmed red with sleeplessness. His head, drooping with fatigue, over his books. His limp, his injury.

I'll skin you alive… And it can be done… I've seen it…

Charlotte hugged him tight and did not sleep the rest of the night.

Twenty

THIS WAS THE WRONG BED, THE WRONG ROOM. WHERE were his blankets? Grumbling, Will huddled closer to Charlotte. At least it was the right woman, though she usually slept in the bend of his arm and not with her back to him. He shifted closer—

Something was wrong. His eyes blinked open to add sensory confirmation to the knowledge he was naked. Oh…hell.

The memory of last night rushed back, bitter and shaming. Everything he'd said, everything he'd done. That's why he'd left their bed—she'd ordered him from it.

He stretched the sheet over his hips, the modesty idiotic considering the intimacies they'd shared.

Intimacies. When had it all become intimate? The taste of her was still on his tongue, but she was more his in a hundred other ways: teasing him about his habit of untucking the sheet before climbing into bed, forever asking to borrow the pencil he carried in his pocket, bringing him a cup of tea before he knew he wanted it.

He chased off the sleep-muddled thought and replaced it with cold truth. Charlotte wasn't his. So why the hell did he have to keep reminding himself of that?

He rubbed his eyes. Why was she in bed with him?

He reached for a blanket to cover her, but they were on the floor.

Like when he slept alone. Like when he dreamed of Tibet—

He'd dreamed last night. Dreamed of something worse than he'd ever dreamed before. So much worse because Charlotte was there.

He placed a kiss on her shoulder that lingered. Had he cried out? Had he scared her? Sweet Charlotte. She'd come to soothe him even when she'd been furious with him.

He rose and covered Charlotte with the blanket. Would she forgive him? Would she come to breakfast? He had no idea what she'd do.

He dressed and went to breakfast. Normally, he'd wait for Charlotte, but this was not a normal morning. And he needed a cup of coffee before he faced her.

The footmen looked at him strangely when he entered the dining room, though he greeted them normally. Uneasily, he focused on his breakfast. If he had to put a name to those looks, he might call them pitying.

The coffee was drunk and he was nearly done with his breakfast when Charlotte's steps sounded in the hall. He stood to greet her and froze. A black bruise marred her china skin across her cheek. He stumbled toward her. "Oh God…Charlotte?"

"It looks far worse than it feels, I assure you."

His fingers hovered over her skin. "What happened? Did you fall?"

Her head tilted a fraction. "You do not remember?"

His blood went cold. Dragging his gaze from her injury, he searched her eyes. "Remember what?"

"When I tried to wake you…? You were dreaming…?"

His stomach roiled and he reared back, his hands dropping to his side.

You were dreaming.

"I did this?" he asked. "I hit you?"

"Not intentionally." She tipped her head to smile into his eyes. "*I hope.* Though after our quarrel—"

"Christ, Charlotte! Don't laugh. Not of this. Has a doctor been sent for?"

"Goodness no. I have no need of a doctor. Cook will have any number of salves—"

He ran into the hall. "Jamie! Peter! Where the bloody—Goodley! Call the carriage, then send a footman—*Jamie*, send Jamie—into the study. And do we have ice? Bring ice and a towel."

Goodley hurried belowstairs. Will turned sharply toward the study and pain lanced his thigh from knee to hip. *Good—you bloody well hurt, you bastard.* Oh God, he had hit her. How could he hit her?

Charlotte followed him. "Don't fuss. A doctor is completely unnecessary."

He retrieved paper from the desk, and the pencil always in his coat pocket. Damn him. There was that boy…the one in his crew who'd knocked his head on an outcropping of rock and developed fits. Another fell, wrenched his neck, had vertigo for weeks.

The desk blurred and dipped, and he ran a shaking hand over his face, blinking to clear his vision. He began to scrawl his note, the first letters so illegible he flexed his hand and started again with control, his normally neat script wobbly.

Charlotte sighed and perched on the corner of the desk near his elbow. Her "staying-home" dress was gauzy and white and encroaching on his paper. He brushed the cotton aside and it floated back, threatening his inked message. He held the fabric back. "God, Charlotte! Where do you end?" He slammed a paperweight on the skirt.

"All right, call your physician. You will embarrass me quite, but if you must, you must. You *are* sensitive. I suppose it is not the worst trait..."

Will ignored the rest of her words—he had to focus—hastily rereading his note for clarity until Goodley and Jamie appeared. He grabbed the ice compress from Jamie and placed it in Charlotte's hand to hold against her cheek. She started to protest but he stared a warning, and she closed her lips, her bottom lip pushing into a pout.

He wheeled around. "Jamie, take the carriage to the address on this note. If Dr. Fellowes can't come, his partner, Henson, at the same address, should be available. If neither are in, go to the second address and return with Dr. Syndham. Go. *Now.* Don't return without a doctor."

Jamie and Goodley ducked their heads and exited.

His stomach plunged and the room spun, so he stood still. The world would steady. It always had—

"They have been my employees far longer than

yours," she said. "And not even a by-your-leave from me? You mustn't be uneasy with the staff—I explained to Patty what occurred and she explained to the rest." She jumped lightly from the desk.

"Don't move!" His heart plunged and he lurched toward her, pressing her into a chair. "Don't, Charlotte, please."

Thankfully, she obeyed, lowering with her usual grace. At least her balance seemed unaffected.

He took the ice from her and refolded the towel, holding it against her cheek himself. His eyes locked on the compress. How would he ever look at her?

Big blue eyes watched him balefully over the towel. "Now that your beloved plans are in motion, could we discuss what happened last night? I should like to have breakfast, too, and desire you to sit with me."

"I can't."

"Am I so hideous to look at?"

His stomach lurched, threatening to empty on the floor.

Christ... He closed his eyes to still the nausea but saw only the purple-black bloom marring her flawless skin. "God, Charlotte...I'm so sorry." He forced the words through his strangled throat.

She stood and took his arm. "Come, let's have our breakfast."

She needed to eat. And she was walking well. He steered her to the dining room, pressed her into a chair, and poured her a cup of tea that rattled in its saucer. "What will you have?"

"Will you sit?"

"You'll have eggs, won't you?"

"Will, I'm fine."

He piled a plate high, his fingers so stiff he nearly dropped the plate in front of her. He stood at the door, not looking at her, an ear cocked for the front door. It was too soon, it would be a quarter hour at least—

"Won't you tell me what you dreamed last night?"

Christ, no, he'd never do that. He fisted his hair in his hand. "I can't do this."

"Will?"

"Five weeks and it's back."

"What's back?" Charlotte stood and took a step toward him.

"Sit down, Charlotte!"

Her jaw dropped at his outburst.

"*Please*," he begged. "Sit until the doctor comes."

Her eyes were wide but she sat. "All right."

He slumped against the threshold of the door and tried not to think about the fact that his marriage had just ended.

Twenty-one

"What a fright I am, Patty." Charlotte touched her cheek gingerly as she studied herself in the dressing table mirror.

"The healing looks worse, love. Your skin'll be the most unholy color in a day or two."

But her thoughts ran rampant over Will. Why didn't he trust her with the truth? Did he think her too weak to bear it? If he told her, what could she do to help him?

Betsy, the new parlor maid, appeared at the door. "You've a caller, miss."

"A caller?" Charlotte held out her hand for the card. "Oh heavens, I cannot receive anyone." She stared an astonished moment at the name writ there: Hugh Spencer. "How dare he come here?"

Patty read the name over her shoulder and her lips thinned. "You send him right off. The coward likely waited for your husband to leave."

"Will is not in?" Charlotte asked.

"He went out after the doctors left."

"He didn't mention needing to go out," she

murmured. That was a relief, actually. If Will knew Hugh had come…

Charlotte stood and smoothed her skirt in a delaying tactic. The truth was, she *was* afraid of Hugh. To say to Will she wasn't had been a lie. But she would not live in fear.

"Fuss and bother…put him in the back parlor, please, Betsy. No tea, and do not offer to take his hat or stick. The man will not be here long. And please ask Jamie and Peter to stand at the ready."

Patty's look was full of disapproval.

"I must put an end to this nonsense sooner or later, Patty. And you'll be with me."

"I'd rather your big, strong husband were here."

"It is far better he is not. Come. We shall make quick work of it."

Bolstered by the sight of her large footmen flanking the door, Charlotte swept into the room as haughtily as she could. "I am astonished at this behavior. Do not imagine you will ever be received again."

Hugh's eyes bulged. "For God's sake! Did he do that?"

The outburst set her back—but she had no explanation for her contusion. "Don't be absurd." Feigning a calm she did not feel, she looked pointedly at her timepiece. "I haven't the slightest interest in hearing what you have to say, but I welcome the opportunity to tell you I never wish to see you again."

He stretched his neck as if his cravat were too tight. "I apologize for frightening you." His eyes narrowed. "But my…heart was broken, Charlotte. I was wild with grief. Never, *never* would I have compromised you. I merely wished—"

"To convince me of your ardor, as I recall."

"I love you."

A hard laugh burst from her. "So you say. I allow you were always gentlemanly to me, until you were not."

"If that man had not intruded—"

"That man is my husband and had he not intruded, your actions would have irreparably altered me."

"Do you not understand what I offer you?" His voice was almost gentle. "What I sacrifice in coming here? My father scorned my choice and now ridicules me for losing you." His eyes hardened. "How could you want *him*? I was to make you my countess."

Her fear spiked higher. My God, she had almost married this man. She pitched her words in low, measured tones so as not to upset him further. But there was nothing to say except, "I never loved you, Hugh."

"Is that so?" Hugh's face contorted with a bitter smile. "I imagine there's *love* enough with Repton. No doubt your heels are light for your *heroic* explorer, the lone survivor of a failed expedition—"

"What? What do you—?"

"Any tart might confuse lust with love."

Lone survivor—

"If I leave here today, Charlotte, I'll never return."

Her legs trembled, but she looked straight at him. "*Capital.*"

The fury in his eyes set her back a step, but he pivoted to the door and she moved with him—if only to keep the dangerous man in her sights.

"If that is how it is to be." He tugged his gloves tight. "I hope you find your husband as devoted a lover. Once he is tested."

Her blood chilled in her veins. "I do not take your meaning."

"No?" He smirked coldly. "Well, you never were terribly bright, were you?" He stalked out of the room, the front door slamming shut behind him seconds later.

The patrons of the Thorn and Crown Inn in Spitalfields were a sneering and surly lot, but Will barely heeded the company. No matter he was cheek to jowl with every pickpocket, footpad, and wagon hunter of the East End, the pub served its purpose. The ale was plentiful and no one cared that he was bloody *Chinese Will*, married to the incomparable Charlotte Baker.

He drained the last of his drink and signaled for another. The barman gave him a measuring look, but Will glared until the man's frown buckled and he refilled his tankard.

The ale wasn't working. The pictures from his nightmares were still there: Charlotte, lying on the dusty soil at the monastery, slit open like the others. Her blue eyes, open and unseeing, vivid against the red blood. The ground thirsty.

He took another numbing swig. Happy Charlotte, living with his darkness.

And he'd hit her.

With a hand that shook, he drained his glass.

The doctor said she would be fine, that she would be all right. And she would be. Once he was gone, she would be the incomparable Charlotte Baker again. He just needed a plan of extraction—and it was begun. His solicitor was preparing the annulment papers and tomorrow…

Tomorrow, they'd separate.

The room rolled over. He grabbed the table and waited for the walls to straighten.

On his fourth pint, Will determined that one, Spencer would never get near Charlotte again, and two, he'd recommit body and soul to his expedition. Three, he'd take an apartment post haste to keep far from his wife. Four, he'd never sleep in her bed again and they'd never talk in bed or laugh at their letters and—

He sniffled, wiping a bleary eye. And five, Wallace had to return to London to watch over his sister. Six, pay a call to that bastard Spencer—*aristocrat my arse*—and flatten his bloody nose into his bloody face and—he ought to be writing these down—and six, or was it seven? And *dammit*—Charlotte had borrowed his pencil again!

Stumbling from the pub into the empty street, he looked for his carriage until remembering he'd not come in one. "God's—balls!" He yelled into the sky. There'd be no jarvey offering rides this time of night.

Wait. He'd vowed not to sleep in that house another night. Or was it her bed? The house was fine. But tomorrow, *tomorrow*, he'd return to Richmond. There. A plan. A good plan. He'd make that list…

The streets were empty and the house was dark when he stumbled to the door. Of course it would be. His fumbling with the key was loud enough to draw one of the servants, because the door opened before his third attempt at the lock.

Damn. Not a servant.

"Where have you been?" Charlotte stood in her dressing gown, the flash of relief on her beautiful face quickly hardening to anger. "Have you any idea what time it is?"

"Hush, Charlotte. You'll wake your fancy neighbors."

Charlotte pulled a face and clapped a hand over her nose. "Oh, good heavens! What have you been drinking?"

Mustering every shred of dignity he might fake, he stepped into the house and headed for the back parlor where a comfortable rug awaited him. "Why aren't you in bed, Charlotte? You should be asleep."

"How, pray, was I to sleep imagining you bleeding out in an alley or floating in the Thames or with your head smashed on the cobblestones—"

"Why are your thoughts so violent?"

"—and without so much as a note to let me know your whereabouts?"

In the meager firelight of the parlor, he had to screw up his eyes to inspect her cheek. "Did you keep ice—?"

Charlotte batted his hand away. "Where were you?"

"The doctors said—"

The hand slap again. "They said it was a bruise. Where were you?"

He made for the decanter of whiskey in the cabinet. "Go to bed, Charlotte."

"I am *not* going to bed. I am making you a sandwich and weak tea and don't you dare touch another drop of drink!"

He turned to protest her ban of the whiskey and she was gone. She always moved too fast.

Empty-handed, he sank into the chair by the fire. He wasn't thirsty anyway. A wool blanket was slung on the arm of the chair. Had she been sitting here waiting for his return?

The thought made his stomach lurch with guilt. He didn't want her to see him this way, his brain sluggish and his tongue thick. A man wanted all his faculties with Charlotte.

He pitched forward in the chair and rested his forearms on his knees, the position unaccountably more comfortable. A white calling card lay singed in the ashes of the fire and he fished it near with the poker till he could read the name.

Spencer.

Fury and fear scrambled his brain, and he fought through the fog of drunkenness for lucidity. Didn't the maids sweep the fireplace every morning?

Charlotte returned with a tray.

"Spencer was here?" he croaked. Her eyes shuttered and her silence provided all the confirmation he needed. It made him want to retch. "*Was he?*"

Charlotte set the tray down and sat stiffly. "You cannot possibly imagine I received visitors looking as I do."

Will scowled, reminded of the injury he'd caused to his sweet wife.

"Here." She pressed a sandwich into his hand. "Try to eat something."

He threw the sandwich down and surged to his feet, setting the room spinning. "I told you not to be alone with him."

"We were not alone." Realizing the admission, she

pouted as if she'd been tricked. "Patty sat there by the fire, and Peter and Jamie were at the door."

His hands began to shake. Why? Why would he be here? Christ, he couldn't think—if only he could think. "Did you invite him?"

She looked at him, wide-eyed and wounded. Rising, she carefully covered his tea and sandwich with a napkin. "I will not talk to you in this state."

"Did you forgive him?"

Charlotte swanned out, climbing the stairs to bed, and he lurched to follow, his hard steps rattling the railing. "Answer me!"

"Why? You will not remember tomorrow."

In the bedroom, the door banged behind him.

"Do not slam the door," she said.

Why was the woman not talking? "You know what he did! And I have to sail three months and worry about you and go back where it happened—"

"Where what happened?"

"—and you let him visit in that damn parlor!"

"I suppose *you* are entitled to answers. I am left alone wondering why you stumble home an hour before sunrise. Or why you drink at all."

"Did he touch you?"

She spun around, her eyes wet. "Yes, he touched me. He kissed me, too, and he is vastly improved. I was so overwhelmed with passion, we made love right here in our bed. All his transgressions are forgiven and isn't that a relief? We may part, I will marry a peer, and you may transfer the upkeep of your lusting, empty-headed bride to another."

"Damn it, Charlotte!" He pivoted to leave and

collided hard with the bedpost. He nearly sank to the ground, but caught himself and collapsed heavily on the edge of the bed.

God damn Spencer.

And God damn him.

Oh no, no! Charlotte hurried to sit beside him. "Now look at you. You have hurt yourself."

Will folded over his knees, his head resting on his arms.

"Will?" Was he hurt? Had he not heard her or was he too inebriated to follow? Or was he being his usual silent self?

Blast him! She was afraid to comfort him. She couldn't bear his pushing her away tonight.

Her nerves had been stretched to snapping waiting for him to return. Afraid he never would. Afraid to think of what he'd endured, of what he was trying to forget. Even now, she was raw and jittery in the silence, so she did what she always did.

She talked.

"I know you would prefer to have it out with me but I will not argue. I cannot. No one in the family was ever any good at it. Lucy bursts into tears, Wally's face turns purple, and as for me, I resist the idea of anyone taking me seriously enough to take offense at the things I say or do. I am innocuous, you know, as I cannot bear a grudge longer than a quarter hour. I have tried and it is impossible.

"And I like you more than most, despite your grim moods and tonight's odors, so I worry. I do not know why you were gone so long or what is troubling you—though I have a few ideas—but I think it best you tell me. Not tonight, but soon. Tomorrow would be convenient. I have a dress fitting at ten and I thought to visit the fancy stationer for holiday cards, but otherwise I am not engaged."

"God, Charlotte," he groaned, plowing his fingers through his hair and fisting it into clumps. "You hurt my head."

She opened her mouth to reply but thought better of it. Will's torment did not begin or end with her, but she would not add to his troubles tonight. Besides, the man applied himself to one task at a time and the task at present appeared to be sleeping sitting upright.

"Come now," she said. "Let's get you undressed and in bed." She kneeled to remove his boots and stockings, his feet ice cold. His coat was undone and his necktie lost—likely to a lucky ragman in the street.

Sliding off his damp wool coat, she slid her hands over his hard shoulders. At work on the buttons of his waistcoat, Will grasped her wrists lightly in that peculiar way drunken men are riveted by simple acts of dexterity.

"Arms up, please," she said.

He heaved his head up to look at her and she wondered if he would continue growling at her, but he lifted his arms so she could pull the shirt over his head. The stale smell emanated from the fabric and she tossed it to a far corner. "There. You smell much better."

Yes…lovely shoulders. And chest. And stomach. He was so gorgeously muscled under his clothes. She rubbed his cold arms soothingly and with no little pride. A rare opportunity…touching her husband so freely.

Will was right. She was a shameless wanton where it concerned him.

"Lie down," she coaxed.

He blinked, tipping forward as if trying to focus on her face. "Did he hurt you?"

"No. Now lie down."

He complied without a word and she wished the man were half as obliging when sober.

She unbuttoned his trousers and, making fast work of it, pulled them off and covered his body quickly with the blanket. As tempted as she was to admire him naked, it would be unkind to ogle the man in his diminished state. "There," she whispered. "Now you're warm and cozy, you worrisome man."

"I'm sorry."

"I know. Go to sleep. If you are good tomorrow, I'll endeavor to argue with you." *And you will tell me everything.*

He caught her wrist. "One more night, Charlotte."

One?

Will pulled her closer. "I don't like sleep."

Too slow to stop the fracturing of her heart, she cupped his rough cheek, trying and failing to conjure even an ounce of irritation. No wonder she was rubbish at arguing if she couldn't sustain a most reasonable anger with the man. "Let go of my hand so I can get into bed."

But Will only transferred his hold from one hand to another, his eyelids sinking. Opening the blanket in a clumsy semblance of invitation, he pulled her until she was half lying, half falling beside him.

The cloud of whiskey and warm male enveloped her as he hugged her tight against him. How did he expect her to sleep so? She wrinkled her nose at the bouquet of cheap liquor emanating from the man. The sheets would have to be stripped tomorrow.

"Worrisome man…" she mumbled into his chest.

"…worry…wife…"

The sleepy words were breathed into her hair. She gave over to his crushing hold as he rolled onto his back, taking her with him, and proceeded to snore into her ear. This was not an aspect of marriage she had ever imagined.

Well. No man was perfect. Not even one assembled from her daydreams.

She strained to look at him, his face relaxing but not relaxed.

What had he been trying to forget?

And how was she going to help him?

Twenty-two

Nature never intended a man to wake like this. He cracked an eyelid and swiftly sealed it. Too bright. God, it was all so bright.

Why did he drink so much? His skull was pounding and his stomach churned in his throat. But damn him, he deserved all of it.

He stretched his arms left and right on the cool sheets, relieved not to feel Charlotte's there. "Good," he garbled. He didn't want anyone to see him in this state, let alone—

"You are awake," Charlotte answered from above him. And far too brightly.

Disoriented by the placement of her voice, he cracked open one eye. The pillow he believed his head rested on was her lap. Too fast, her china face dipped, her lips a blur of pink, her eyes bright blue orbs, and dizziness spun him.

Why are you here? was what he intended, but all he could manage to croak was, "Why?"

Her fingers stroked his head gently. "I knew you would not remember yesterday."

Yesterday. If only he could forget.

He squinted against the light to see her cheek. Worse today. Fighting nausea, he pushed himself to sitting and clutched his head in his hands. Ah, hell. He was naked. And stinking. And still a little drunk.

Will Repton. Famed explorer, celebrated plant collector, rancid bucket of sludge, and abuser of women.

"How are you feeling?" his angel wife asked.

"Like death."

Charlotte moved off the bed, the fabric of her nightrail rustling loud as thunder. "Take a little breakfast and you will be feeling yourself again."

Why wasn't she angry? Why didn't she hate him? Why didn't she ever behave the way she should?

Christ, all of this was wrong, all wrong. He didn't lose control. He didn't drink to oblivion. He'd never hurt a woman in his life.

Charlotte tilted her head, trying to see into his undoubtedly pasty, swollen face. Blessedly, her voice was low. "I shall call Michael to help you."

"No."

She pouted, looking from his dressing chamber to his polluted carcass on her pristine sheets. "I suppose I can assist you. I will have the bath made ready, in any case."

It was better she hate him. Better she be relieved to see the back of him. "Leave me alone."

"You are being very disagreeable this morning, Will, so I'll remind you it was not your wife pouring drink down your throat till you couldn't see a hole in a ladder."

"What wife?" he muttered.

She watched him a quiet moment. Had he managed to anger her at last?

Dropping his eyes, he swung his legs to the floor and dragged the sheet over his nakedness. Charlotte's stare weighed on his head like a mounting block, so he watched her toes curl into the rug. Even her feet were pretty. His were marred with scars, white and ragged like lightning. The memory of that piercing pain as vivid now as then. What perversion of fate had brought the two of them together?

"Will you drink a little water?"

"Don't nurse me."

"You should—"

"Go away, Charlotte." *Forgive me.* "I don't need you."

He didn't look, but the swish of fabric and the hurried padding of her feet told him she'd left.

He was glad of the nausea, the aches, the stabbing in his head, or he might have stood and caught her. He might have lifted his bleary eyes and seen the hurt in her sweet face and groveled in apology at her feet.

And she needed to hate him for what he planned next.

Charlotte successfully avoided her husband all day. Several times she had been tempted to corner the man and demand answers. What had happened in China? What did he dream of? Had Hugh spoken the truth? Was he the only survivor of his expedition? Is that why Will drank himself to obliteration last night?

But Will might not answer. Unlike most men of her acquaintance, he was immune to her usual tactics of persuasion. And she was not so patient to couch her words to best effect.

For now, she opted for solitude in her parlor to think. And in truth, to be soothed. He had been positively hateful this morning and her feelings were still tender. Or incensed, rather.

How remarkable. She had taken offense.

Yes. She was offended.

Thankfully, she would not have to see him until she was ready. Will never entered the ladies' parlor. Odd that, for it was the most wonderful room in the house, filled with her favorite things.

The most wonderful room…

The room where they first met.

Charlotte pushed to her feet and began to pace. She ought to write Lucy for her guidance. She could tell her if husbands often left without reporting where they were going, as Will had done. None of the servants had been apprised, either. The lack of consideration was not as troubling as his drinking, but she could not help but feel hurt.

But then, men were quite different from women in their freedoms. *She* could not simply sail out the door as he had done.

Yes, she would write to Lucy first—but carefully, so as not to alarm her sister. For if Lucy were alarmed, she would tell Ben, who would tell Wally, who would travel, purple-faced, all the way from Derbyshire to scold Will.

An hour later, engrossed in her writing, she was unaware Will had returned until he cleared his throat.

Slowly, she set down her pen. This did not bode

well—he had entered her parlor of his own accord. His face was ashen and his hair tousled, as if he'd not bothered to comb it after his bath and let the wind send it topsy-turvy.

His eyes settled on her letters. "May I speak with you?"

No. The thought rose immediately, instinctively. *No, not now.* "Did you have errands to run? I stayed in to complete my correspondence. I am shamefully overdue. Are you hungry? Shall I ring for something?" It was a ploy to delay with little hope of success. Will was efficient above all things.

"I had the annulment papers prepared." He rushed on as though she might speak. As if she could.

"There is no reason to prolong the marriage, Charlotte. It follows we'd know we didn't suit in three weeks rather than ten; incompatibility would be evident in as little as one."

...no reason...

She launched to her feet and made for the door.

"Where—Charlotte? Where are you going?"

"I...I have to tend to something upstairs. Shall we speak later?" She was nearly running for the stairs, all too aware Will followed.

"We should speak now."

Her heart constricted, a lightning bolt of pain that left her gasping. "Yes, you had the papers drawn."

"We can end this today—*wait.*"

She flew to their bedroom. He wanted to leave her. But he promised...he promised August...

He entered behind her. "Charlotte, please listen."

Terrified her face would betray her, she gazed out the window. Lucy's orchid house shone in the corner of the lawn, the glass reflecting a coral sky from the setting sun. Ben had built the hothouse for her before they were married and it was the most beautiful of all his creations.

Beautiful because he had built it for Lucy when he had no hope of her, when he thought she had tossed him aside. And *still* Ben built it because he did everything in his power to make Lucy happy.

Because he loved her.

The simple truth staggered her and she steadied herself with a hand on the wall. *Will did not love her.*

She knew that, she had always known that.

She turned and he flinched as if struck. "*Christ,*" he stammered, turning his back on her bruised face.

"Will?"

He didn't say anything, didn't look at her, and all at once she realized he might be leaving for another reason entirely. "It was an accident."

"The papers are downstairs."

"It was an accident."

He started for the door. "I won't hurt you again."

"But you are hurting me now," she cried. "You will hurt me far worse if take yourself away, before you even must. Why would you—?"

"*Because I have to.*"

He sounded so anguished that she started toward him, but he flung himself back, a staying hand raised against her approach. "Don't." A stubborn look hardened his face. "You'll be happy when I'm gone."

"That is not true! And you are being deliberately cruel to say so."

"You shouldn't be with me. I'm nothing like—"

"I know! I prefer you far more."

"You need a man suited to you, a man who'll stay and protect you, give you a family, provide for you. Marry one of—"

"*No!*" The word erupted, louder and angrier than she ever allowed herself to be.

She *could* argue. She could argue this.

The outburst stunned him to silence and she could have wept at the confusion in his face. After all this time, why did he not know?

"I will *never* marry again, Will."

She willed him to understand, to *finally* understand, but when his lips parted, no words came.

"Do I need to bloom some sort of flower from my ears?" She smiled sadly. "An explorer is meant to be observant, Will Repton. Can you not see when a woman is in love with you?"

He took her words like an arrow to the chest, piercing and inconceivable all at once.

Heat flooded her face, but she forced her smile to brighten. Briskly, she stepped back. "Honestly. I expected you to discern my feelings long ago. From the moment we met, but men can be frightfully thick about such matters."

His face was so stricken, she laughed weakly. "Yours is not the reaction a woman hopes for in revealing her love."

"Don't cry," he rasped.

Confused, she blinked. Only then did she feel the warm trail of a tear on her cheek. She *never* cried. She was happy, she was—

Will tugged her into his arms, rubbing her back in

hard, almost desperate strokes to soothe her. "Christ, Charlotte, don't."

His hands trembled. Sensitive Will. Of course they must separate. His nerves would never survive a lifetime of her. But while he was here, she burrowed close, reminded again how the man felt as if he'd been made to hold her. She touched the thick clips of his hair and inhaled the spicy heat of the oil of clove on his neck, wanting to draw the memory of his body deep, to never forget.

"No." He set her back and wiped a hand across his throat as if to erase her lips. "This is why this has to end. Right now."

If she were a foot taller, he would be forced to meet her eye. The man only needed to level his chin to stare over her head—a stance he affected all too often.

How hopeless this was. Still, how many times did she beg him to see her? To talk to her? And against every grim look and stubborn silence and harbored secret, all she could do was flitter and flutter and smile because she knew, *she knew*, she was a fool to love an explorer.

But her love was real. Even if it was a horrible idea.

She smiled a little at the absurdity. Really, what was the point of tears and drama? Her love was no surprise. At least not to her.

Will, however, looked as if he might collapse any moment under the weight of the revelation.

"I have no expectations. Just because I love you—"

"No." His stare faltered. "We're friends. We…we dine together, we kiss, we sleep side by side and"—he clenched his eyes—"I touch you in ways I shouldn't."

"You mustn't blame yourself—"

"You're doing that thing again—fanciful notions," he said roughly. "You can't possibly love a man who told you, from the first, *from the very beginning*, he was leaving." He landed on a new thought and his eyes cleared with something like relief. "My leaving is what's attracting you."

Out of respect, she considered this fresh bit of nonsense for four full seconds. "No."

He slumped against the wall, both hands clutching his head.

Poor Will. She had diverted him well and good from his plans and there was nothing he disliked more. But then, his plan was to annul their marriage today.

Her heart thumped painfully. And if he truly didn't wish to hurt her, could she hope? *Please...just till August.*

As if he could hear her prayer, his knees buckled and he swayed, catching himself on the wall to stay upright.

She braced his shoulder to better gauge whether he planned to keel over. "You are still unwell. Wouldn't you like Cook to make you a bowl of rice potage? Or a little clear pheasant soup?"

"I don't want this, I don't."

"A bit of broth, then?"

He huffed a strange, soundless laugh and hugged her tight. "God, Charlotte, what are you thinking? It's not as if you can wait for me."

She ought to make some noncommittal reply. Agree with him to ease his mind. But she was so tired of hiding her heart. Besides, a lie would change nothing. And neither would the truth.

"But I was always going to wait," she said quietly. "Wait for the mornings when the newspapers printed their stories of Chinese Will. And for your reports to be logged at the Geographical Society and your triumphant return to England. And then wait in some endless queue to see you lecture in some dreary room of the Linnean Society.

"And later, I will wait for Ben to invite you to dinner where you will nod politely at me." She closed her eyes and refused to be sad. "And then wait a little longer for the day you marry a new bride."

He was so still and she was glad not to see his eyes. She couldn't bear to see the responsibility there, the dismay.

"You see?" she whispered. "I was always going to wait, Will. You are not the only one with a plan."

His arms tightened, and if he hadn't been holding her so close, she wouldn't have heard his next words. "I'm leaving you."

The words sounded like a question. "I'm leaving you," he said again louder, but his voice was wretched.

"I know," she said gently, wanting only to comfort him now. "I know." She positioned her lips at his ear so there was no misunderstanding. "*But I was never leaving you.*"

Something seemed to break in him. His shoulders sagged and his head dropped onto her shoulder. "Charlotte..."

The whisper was full of regret, and of all the emotions she might have felt, relief washed over her. It was pointless but she was glad. He *would* miss her. Not with her depths, but a little.

After a while, he straightened to his full height, his lips at her temple. "You really love me, then?"

In answer, she hugged him tight. More words

would only upset him and he seemed to be coming to terms with the fact that the woman he married was inconveniently in love with him.

It was selfish, but she had to try. Could she persuade him to postpone the annulment a little longer? "Please. Not today."

He released a breath slowly. "All right, Charlotte."

Her breath caught with hope. "Truly?"

He set her back and took off his coat.

Excited, speechless, she bounced on her toes. But just once. Perhaps twice. She was a lady, after all, and a lady would keep her bounces to a minimum. "Thank you, Will! And you are not so unhappy here, are you? It is only a few weeks more and we will rub along and—"

She broke off when Will shrugged out of his waistcoat. She hadn't noticed him unbuttoning it. She glanced at the open door with the possessive thought a maid might see him in undress. It was a mere dart of her eyes, but Will's head swiveled to follow.

Strange how his senses were honed to the slightest movements and sounds. Yet he was astonished a woman who panted after him like a puppy was in love with him.

He strode to the door and shut it, turning the key in the lock. And then did the same to the door to his rooms—all the while tugging his shirt free of his trousers.

What was he doing? "Are you warm?"

"No." He flicked open the button at his neck.

"No?" she echoed softly, curious as to what he would do next. Strangely, she didn't know. Normally, she could puzzle him out—though she had no real objection to anything that involved Will removing his clothes.

His gaze traveled her body. "She loves me," he muttered.

She frowned at his unhappy words. Really, this was becoming a little insulting. Was it such a burden to be the object of her affection?

But he continued undressing and she could not attend to the question. Quickly, too quickly, shoes, socks, shirt, and trousers were all stripped and laid aside until he stood before her. Naked.

She stared, unable to breathe, unable to tear her gaze from him. He had been nude before for glimpses, peeks, but now…he stood, shoulders back and chin high, as if offering himself to her.

Her heart swelled. He would bare himself as she'd bared herself. He was never meant to be a true husband, yet how often did he oblige her? And always so adorably grave and purposeful when he did.

Shadows painted the corded muscle of his chest, his arms and legs, the hard plane of his abdomen drawn so taut above his manhood.

Her gaze followed the dusting of hair on his chest down the narrow trail on his abdomen and lower to nestle against his thick flesh. And something animal within her wanted to repeat that descent with her fingers, then her lips.

One powerful thigh was smooth where his bandages must have rubbed away the coarse hairs. Mottled patches on his calves matched those around his ankles. He'd explained they were merely leech scars. *Merely*…but she had read scores of them had attached to his legs in Burma and rendered him weak from loss of blood.

There was so much of his life he didn't share. Because he didn't share his pain.

He was so secretive and tormented and—oh goodness—naked and coming nearer.

She stood still, not wanting to miss a thing. The look he wore was pure Will, determined and focused. She made to step back to keep him in sight, but large hands pressed her close. Through the crisp cotton of her clothes, his skin was hot.

He was always hot. She used to worry he was feverish, but his embrace was familiar now. So familiar and so much theirs. His heat, his strength, his scent, the placement of his hands, the stubborn swirl of hair at his neckline, the curve of his ear, his kiss. He stroked her back idly and she imagined he could only be thinking the same of her.

She bit her lip, wanting to speak, desperate to know what exactly he had in mind, but afraid he would stop if she did.

His eyes roamed her face and softened with amusement at her mouth. He touched her chin. "Do you want to say something?"

Not a word, Charlotte. Don't even breathe, don't—
"Shall I take my dress off, too?"

The smile in his eyes was incinerated in a flare of desire. He gripped the nape of her neck and kissed her, and the instant their lips met, his hold became aggressive. A strong hand cupped her bottom, crushing her to him, and though she could feel nothing of his male parts through her skirts, her heart leapt at the suggestion.

No, the *intent*.

How wonderful he was! He was going to pleasure her like he did before, she knew it!

Wanting to touch him all over but not knowing where to start, she hugged his waist, her hands exploring the hard swell of his backside. But that light caress was cataclysmic. He stiffened and reared back, his gaze sharp and wary.

No…this embrace was not familiar at all.

This was different. Everything was different, even this passion. The same yearning and desire blazed between them, but Will was controlling the intensity with a new tenderness. A new *responsibility*.

Because she had confessed her love.

With a ragged breath, he cupped her cheek. "Right," he said huskily. "Right." He looked deep into her eyes. "Shall we take this dress off?"

She smiled in agreement but he didn't back away. He leaned closer.

"Shall we take everything off?" But his eyes asked her something quite different.

Her smile slipped. Belatedly, she nodded, too shocked to respond with anything more.

Oh goodness. They were going to make love. Like a real woman, a real wife.

With shaking fingers, she reached for her collar—but her dress buttoned in the back. "Oh, drat it!"

She blushed at her unmeasured reaction but Will simply moved behind her, the brush of his fingers on her back making it difficult to breathe.

The buttons popped free, her dress loosened, and the flounced muslin slipped over her crinoline. Will bent to take up the dress, as reverent as the finest lady's maid, and she watched, transfixed, as the rear view of a perfect male specimen walked her dress to her wardrobe.

He faced her, his head tilted to consider her in her underthings, and she was reminded to apply herself to the task at hand. Popping the button at her waist, the wire cage dropped to the floor in a chiming rattle. The sound stirred a smile from him and she was flooded with her aching love—overwhelming and hopeless as it was.

She loved him so. He was her most intimate friend and he was offering himself as a husband, a *true* husband.

The only one she would ever have.

She reached behind her to loosen her corset laces and his eyes followed the progress.

Enjoying his attention, she squeezed her breasts together and unhooked the front, flaunting her bosom—which she suspected he was partial to. He staggered a step closer, a sharp, interested light in his eye.

Her shamelessness rewarded, she reached under her chemise to loosen the ribbons of her drawers and they slipped to the rug. He wet his lips, his lids sank, and his penis, standing rigid from his body, did the oddest thing.

It twitched.

Fascinated, she slowed her undressing. The thick length of him bobbed and swayed when she stepped from her slippers and removed her stockings, leaving her in only her chemise. What would his male parts do when she was naked?

Without a moment's hesitation, without nervousness or shame, she drew the undergarment over her head. Her gaze was aimed at his male parts before the chemise drifted to the floor, but when she would have her curiosity assuaged, she could no longer see. Will's powerful body was before her and she was caught fast against him.

"Will!" His hands were rough and he was never rough. How thrilling! She was being *handled.*

"Have mercy, Charlotte."

Hard arms squeezed her too tight and his breath steamed her hair as if he were scenting her. It was animal, excited, and she could not escape.

Or very likely she could not—she had no inclination to try.

He dipped his head to whisper, "I've never seen anything like you, never anyone as beautiful as you."

And as she gloried in his wonderful words and he lowered his head to kiss her, his erection jerked between them.

He grimaced and she could laugh again. Which she did, but only briefly—and really only a snicker as Will was sensitive. She buried her face against his neck and held tight, but her shoulders shook with suppressed giggles.

He sighed and patted her back until her mirth subsided to a titter or two. "A nervous, less experienced man might find your amusement off-putting, you know."

"But not you."

His gaze drifted over her face fondly. "No, not me," he murmured.

He bent as if to kiss her, but instead lifted her off her feet and set her on the bed. She slid over and waited to see what he might do next. But patience was never one of her virtues. "What do I do? Should I do something?"

He climbed in next to her. "Do you want to lie down?"

She dropped to her back, sliding down the bed to better align their bodies, and reached to pull him atop her. Well, *invite* him atop her. She couldn't pull Will anywhere. "Now what?"

"Well." A smile tugged at his lips, but he settled his weight carefully on her so they were eye to eye. Such a change from the days when he barely met her gaze. "I'd like to kiss you a bit."

She nodded, unable to think of one normal thing to say when he gathered her close and brushed kisses down her throat. The open lips and flicker of tongue marked her, then left her tingling with heat from his slow, passing breath. Strong hands lifted her hips and he rocked gently against her sensitive folds to stoke her desire, coaxing a slick moisture from her.

A sigh of pure contentment floated from her throat. Of course he knew what she liked. The pace and pressure matched the last time he had pleasured her. But she would not think of that night or how badly it had ended. At this moment, she felt cherished and loved. The latter was illusion, but she could pretend. She had three weeks of practice already.

She circled her arms around his neck and savored his strong body, the rough thighs slid between her legs, the muscled hips dipped and rolled, retreated and surged, his hair flowed fluid and silky through her fingers.

"Ah…so sweet…Charlotte…" His low whispers fell like waves crashing the shore of her body, submerging her. There was no air to breathe. Broad shoulders rose and filled her vision and blocked the light. The salt scent of their skin swirled in the space between their bodies. His hard body was so strong, his weight drove her into the mattress, and she wanted to keep sinking under him.

But in the midst of all the feeling, even shuddering with pleasure and nearly blind with ecstasy, her thoughts floated to the surface. He was seducing her, enticing her, preparing her body to mate with his.

Yet this was Will…her friend…

And this felt so much like love…

She didn't want to think, to wonder, but she couldn't stop. And she didn't seem alone in her confusion.

"You love me?" Will slowed the pace of his hips.

"I do, I'm sorry," she whispered.

He kissed her, but when he raised his head, his eyes were clouded with some new worry and he stopped moving altogether. "This may hurt you. I don't know how, I've never—I mean, not with a…and it's been six years—"

She pulled his head down and kissed him to silence. Will had not been distracted by the intimacy of their lovemaking; he was distracted by the burden of her virginity. She wanted to either giggle or groan at the reemergence of the man's excessive caution, but she was a *little* afraid. Lucy had told her there was pain. And Will was large.

Or at least he said he was.

She giggled and he raised his head, his expression half fear, half hope. "Which male part is amusing you now?"

"The same one."

"Right, of course it is," he mumbled.

"You told me you were larger than most, remember?"

Will flushed, his eyes shy.

"You realize I have no way of knowing if you were boasting?"

He grinned but the amusement was faint in his eyes. She kissed him, trying to bring his attention back to ravishing her, but his mouth gentled and his weight was lifting off her.

She placed his hand on her breast—he seemed to like them well enough—and instantly he cupped her but still he hesitated. He wouldn't stop, would he? His erection still teased her and her blood simmered beneath her skin. Something had to happen soon. Honestly, how difficult could this be?

With a welcoming tilt of her hips, she took his heated flesh in hand and angled the tip approximately where she thought it belonged and eased down.

"Careful...Charlotte," he said through clenched teeth, but he didn't pull from her hold, even when she tried again.

"Oh no." She swept his tense face. "Will? How large are you?"

He winced and grumbled something that sounded like, "Let me, love."

Fingers brushed between her legs and she felt him again—but lower, the new pressure surprising and not at all pleasant. He was too broad to breach her. "Oh. That's"—*awful*—"odd."

His eyes swung to hers. "Odd? How odd?"

"This doesn't feel odd to you?"

The shake of his head was quick and jerky. "No,

sweetheart." He collapsed onto his elbows, his cheeks damp with sweat. Could this slow exploration be difficult for him, too?

He kissed her with bruising force before he seemed to master himself. "Will you let me in a little deeper, sweetheart? Can we see how odd that feels?"

He waited, his powerful body poised above hers. She was glad she couldn't see how he was meant to join with her, her imagination was alarming enough. She inhaled deep and nodded.

His answering smile was tight, his eyes dismayed and yet hungry. She gasped when he pressed, so he massaged her where they joined. The steady, circling pressure diverted the pain, but despite his efforts, a small, choked sound escaped her throat and Will stilled.

"Sorry," he whispered, his voice ragged with regret.

"No. This is fine." She smiled through gritted teeth. "This is quite…ah…*goodness*…momentous, really. A woman's rite of passage."

He didn't look at all convinced. "That's right, sweetheart." He tucked against her neck, so she clenched her eyes and braced.

"This reminds me," he said. "Did I ever show you my yak-bone pipe?"

Her grip eased on his biceps. "Your what?"

"My opium pipe from China? Made from yak bone?"

"I—? No, you've not shown me that."

He pushed up to look at her, his stiff penis propped rudely against her. "I thought I had."

"But you don't smoke."

"No, I don't smoke." He began small, soothing circles where she ached, his eyes holding hers. "Are you sure? It's about twelve inches? Bone? A little silver and turquoise?"

"I'm—oh, that's nice—I'm sure you didn't. What made you think of it?"

"It's carved with scenes of men and women." His lips caught her earlobe and tickled, his caressing fingers still drawing the heated moisture from the junction of her legs. "Erotic scenes."

"Like scrimshaw?"

"Is that what they call it?" At her quick nod, he continued. "One carving's a woman with three men and she's—right, that's why I didn't show you."

"Three?" Dimly, she felt another stretching push.

"Mm-hm."

"But how—"

A burning pinch distracted her and then Will released a massive sigh, his powerful body relaxing on top of her. "There, love, there," he grunted, dropping a kiss on her nose. "Your rite of passage."

"My…?" She reassessed their positions, feeling him deep inside her—"Oh."

"I'm sorry, sweetheart." But then he grinned and there was something distinctly wolflike about it.

She smiled back—but through clenched teeth because the man was enormous and lodged inside her and this still hurt. Was this normal? Was there more pain to come? What was he feeling? There was much to ask, starting with, "Do you really have that pipe?"

"Hmm?" The sound was low and guttered, rumbling against her neck as he nuzzled her.

But Will held still. And she held still and slowly,

slowly, he transformed and heated and filled her with the most extraordinary sensation. This completion was her husband, and he was joined with her as intimately as anyone could be.

Her vision blurred with tears and she hugged him as tight as she could. His taut stomach flexed against her, her heartbeat quickened, and pleasure spiked through her body.

"I love you," she whispered, helplessly, hopelessly, because he would not say it back.

She closed her eyes and his kiss brushed her cheek. She blinked her eyes dry and smiled at him. "What do we do now?"

His eyes smiled. "Wait a moment. Maybe we'll think of something."

He eased from her, her flesh clinging, and slid back in. This time, even seated fully as he was, the pain was fading…*had* faded. "Oh," she whispered. "That's nice."

He growled in agreement, his lids sinking, and did it again. And again. "All right?" The words were hoarse, delivered in a gasp of air.

"Yes." With every stroke, that lovely tension coiled, tighter and tighter, in the small of her back, between her thighs, suffusing her until she was sure he felt it too. "Oh, yes."

"Thank God," he groaned.

He stroked in her, rhythmic and shallow, bearing the weight of his body on his arms. But she wanted him hard and heavy and deep. She strained her hips high to meet his. "Please…more. Faster."

His jaw tensed. Locks of hair tumbled over his forehead. Powerful shoulders rolled over her, rising and falling, and all the while, his eyes locked on her and wouldn't let go. "I...Charlotte, I..."

But whatever he was going to say was lost. He plunged deeper but with control. Massive fists seized the pillow on either side of her head. His panting breath, the grunts like pain, washed the room with erotic sound. He slumped over her, and a hand trembling with restraint covered her breast and kneaded, surprising a cry of pleasure from her lips. At the sound, his mouth captured the other nipple and laved and suckled, greedy and possessing, demanding another moan from her lips.

Her dream man becoming her lover...no wonder she never imagined it, it was unimaginable.

He grunted her name again and again, the sounds barely human, so unlike his careful, controlled words. "I want—Charlotte...can't...slow."

He pushed up onto his arms and there was no air to breathe. Not against the relentless pace of his pistoning hips. The rhythm, the long, driving, deliberate thrusts, demanded her pleasure climb higher and higher to some blissful height until there was nowhere to go except to leap.

With a hoarse cry and a sinuous flex of his back, he held himself inside her. The deep thrust shattered her, shocked her into flight, and she was weightless and falling.

Awareness returned in a rush. Will's weight dropped on her and he held her hips immobile and plunged, over and over. His muscles quivered violently, restraining the power of his body even now. Hard grunts crowded the few words he delivered in her ear. "Ah...my God...Charlotte...so good..."

She understood. Oh goodness, she understood! She hugged him tight, too dazzled, too moved to do anything else, until he arched atop her, his body seizing to stillness, then collapsed on top of her.

Astonishing…it was astonishing. An adventure all her own. He *was* an explorer. Driving her to the end of the world and delivering her a new one.

His back was slick with sweat and his muscles had never been this slack or heavy, even in sleep. The beat of their hearts drummed in time as if they had summited some great mountaintop and were at last finding their rest together.

He was still inside her, warm and pulsing, and his body so heavy and slumberous that she let the perfection of the moment alone.

But just for a moment.

"Will?" Unable to see him, she tapped his shoulder. "Oh goodness. Will, are you listening?"

He stirred but before he looked at her, he wiped his eyes. He looked confused again.

"I—" Her throat tightened and she felt…she felt…

Later. She'd know what she felt later. "Thank you," she whispered. "I'll not forget one moment, not one second and—"

He lurched upward, interrupting her with a hard kiss that subdued her like nothing and no one had ever done, and when he raised his head a long while later, it was the intense look in his eyes keeping her silent. "I can't promise, but I'll try to come back. Every day I'll try."

His words darkened the room. Her heart was already raw with emotion. Why did he have to bring this up now? The voyage could kill him. Or a fall, a fever. Anything at all and he was so precious.

"Of course you will," she blurted. "You are strong and healthy and you will return a hero. And then you will have the longest, most wonderful life and fall in love and have a wife and family. You shouldn't even *think* such things. *Honestly*." To even *suggest* dying. "As few words as you speak, Will Repton, you might parcel out the more sensible ones."

He searched her eyes, looking more his usual self—perplexed. His usual countenance with her, anyway. He cupped her cheek and a small smile curled his lips. "God...I don't want to leave you."

The wonderment on his face pinched her heart, and then she had to smile. "Oh. Those words are all right. That's the nicest thing you've ever said to me."

He blinked. "That can't be true."

"But it is."

"I'm sure it's not. I just asked you to be my wife."

Her smile collapsed and for several seconds, her brain did not function at all. "You did? When?"

"Didn't I?" He was looking panicked again. "I thought I—I mean, I meant to. We made love, Charlotte. For God's sake, I'm still inside—"

"Will?" She waited for his eyes to focus on hers. "Only the sensible words...please? I don't understand. Would you really? Would you really ask me?"

He wet his lips and parted them. But no words came. His gaze drifted to her bruised cheek and stalled there.

She tipped her head so he was looking into her eyes. "Would you?"

He lowered his head to kiss her, his lips light, barely

grazing hers, but warm and soothing and familiar. Her heart strengthened. Of course familiar. He was her husband, he always had been, and she had recognized him from the first.

He raised his head to look at her, his eyes brilliant and steady. "Marry me. Be my wife." He rested his forehead on hers. "And…and wait for me."

Joy, wild and boundless, crashed through her. She wrapped her arms around his hard neck and cinched tight—which was likely not pleasant for him but she could not help it. "Yes! Oh, yes! I will." She pushed him a little so she could look into his face. "*That* was the nicest thing you've ever said to me."

Will shook his head. "You're happy again, aren't you?"

Tears spilled onto her cheeks, but she laughed. "Yes."

"Thank God." He kissed her cheeks, her eyes, her laughing mouth. And in one of the lovelier kisses he'd ever given her, he kissed her heart and rested his forehead on her breast.

He was so still, he could almost be praying.

"My wife," he whispered under his breath. "God forgive me."

The rain drumming the window grew louder. A midnight storm. The raindrops beaded the glass and merged and raced to the sill. Deeper, the glass mirrored the glow of the fire in the hearth and deeper still, the pale reflection of Will and a sleeping Charlotte in bed.

How long had it been since they'd become man and wife? Six hours? Seven?

Seven hours since learning Charlotte loved him.

He pulled the blanket high to cover her, and the perfume of peonies wafted between them, blended with the more elemental scent of her skin, his sweat, their couplings. He settled his arm on her waist, careful not to wake her after their strenuous night.

Once should have been enough. But he'd loved her twice more, and each time came harder and longer than the last. And damn him, he was hard again.

Enough. He rolled away, his body tight with some nameless annoyance.

He thought he'd understood the pleasure to be had in a woman's body. He thought he'd been satisfied with the encounters he'd had. Yet what he felt with her, what she made him feel, how deep it went…

He hadn't understood a thing.

He arched his back, feeling the little-used muscles that ached from the restraint of loving her as gently as he could. He'd never been more aware how large and heavy he must be atop her. She was so delicate. Every touch of her hands and slender limbs wrapping to hold him, trying to somehow guide and contain him, reminded him how delicate.

And yet Charlotte—being Charlotte—opened herself to him with all the reckless trust she'd always granted him. Each time, she strained for him to love her with more force. But her body was precious, adored, *known*. Making love could only be tender—eyes locked, lips hovering, words whispered.

Charlotte rolled toward him, cuddling him in her usual position. He held her and tried to ignore how sweet the familiar weight was.

No. He'd not hurt her. Not ever. This happy, innocent woman wouldn't worry over him any more than she already did. There was no reason to tell her of the massacre, the return to Tibet…

What if he gave back the money? If he went only to find the child? He could return in a year.

Return to Charlotte.

He could crew on a tea clipper. The passage was harder, the bunks so short he'd be folded in half, and the waves pounding the hull ensured no man slept. Let alone a man plagued with nightmares. What did that matter if he couldn't sleep without her anyway?

He could find a ship on a route via Australia. Those ships always lost men secretly emigrating there. He was lame but he was strong, and they'd need men to finish the route to India. Where he would jump ship himself.

But if he gave all the money back, would he have enough to find Aimee?

Exhausted, he closed his eyes. He wouldn't sleep. Not tonight.

He pressed his head back into the pillow, confused by the rubbery smile on his lips. *Damn me, she loves me.* She said she'd wait, she said she loved him—*damn it*, why didn't he say it back? Hell, he probably loved her, didn't he? If he had a heart left to love with. And if he left her with child—

The bed seemed to tilt and his heart plunged to his guts as if he were teetering on the edge of a cliff.

A child. How could he be a father, a husband? There was a voyage to make to a hostile country. A voyage he wasn't sure he'd survive. What had he done?

More importantly, what had he done to Charlotte now that she was his wife?

"The herbs are potent, my lord. I must caution again the importance of the dosage."

Hugh Swift, Viscount Spencer, next Earl of Harlowe, fixed the apothecary with a stare. The old man's warnings were beginning to rankle. All Hugh required was the glass vial gleaming atop the counter between them.

"In truth," the elderly man continued, "I strongly advise against your administering the tincture yourself, my lord. Could I not be present to—?"

"That is impossible, sir."

The apothecary's hand stole an inch closer to the vial. "If I may be so bold, could you not reason with the lady? The bleeding will undoubtedly distress her, the pain—"

"My mistress is quite willful, I'm afraid." His lips thinned with a fresh anger at Charlotte and Repton. Never had he imagined being troubled with this unsavory business. He swept the vial into his waistcoat pocket. "I told them I would not condone a child and I am a man of my word."

"There is my point. Surely she will understand a gentleman of your circumstances cannot suffer a bastard—"

"Your caution is noted, sir."

The gray-haired man diverted his gaze. So be it. He had no use for the man's approval. Not when his own father had laughed. A cuckold, he'd called him. How else had Repton blighted his good name? If he would steal his bride, let his seed rot inside her.

"At the least, take this." The apothecary handed him a tiny spoon.

"It looks like it was made for a doll."

"I assure you it is no toy, my lord. No more than a spoonful is needed for the abortifacient to do its work. Any more and her muscles may relax to an extreme degree, her heart—"

"Capital." Hugh slipped the spoon into his pocket with the vial. He would pass along that instruction to the girl he had successfully installed at Charlotte's house. Though he wondered if the chit understood fractions—no, she worked somewhat about a kitchen. Surely she'd know measurements. "I am in your debt, sir, for delivering me of this complication."

The apothecary said nothing as Hugh slid the coins onto the counter. For this particular transaction, there would be no name on any account. The physic's expression was still troubled. A pang of conscience, perhaps. "What sort of plants are these, anyway?"

"Mugwort has long been in use. The other is a stalklike herb, my lord. With pale violet blossoms."

"Indeed?"

"In the language of flowers, it has a most apt meaning," the apothecary said.

The viscount paused at the door to tug on his gloves. "And what would that be?"

"Malevolence, my lord. Lobelia is the flower of malevolence."

Twenty-three

"But once you reach Hong Kong, how will you get to Guangi?" Charlotte studied the map before her on the table in Ben's study.

Will stood behind her, resting his chin on her shoulder. He pointed to an area of the map, marked with a series of triangles and waving lines. "The mules will pull the wagons northwest through Huangpu. The crew follows and makes camp here."

Charlotte leaned back against the solid wall of Will's body. The past month living as man and wife had been the happiest of her life—and the most worrying. Now that she had persuaded Will to share his planning with her, she couldn't stop imagining the treacherous paths up the mountainsides, the drenching rains, the cold winds and muddy ground denying Will rest and comfort.

"It's an easy enough trek," he said in her silence.

She wasn't fooled. It would be a brutal passage. Knowing *had* to be better. At least this way she would know approximately where he was as the weeks progressed.

The weeks. The years.

And if she were with child as she suspected—

"I was thinking," she started slowly, "if the post office in Hong Kong will hold my letter only two months, I ought to send a letter every month, oughtn't I? And I have heard rumor there may be two mail steamers a month soon, even an overland route, delivering our letters with more speed."

Will said nothing.

"That is good news," she said. "Don't you think?"

"I'll write as often as I can—"

"Every fortnight."

"Yes, every fortnight," Will said, a small smile in his voice. "Even if they are all bundled and sent in the same post."

The map was large, covering the table. Will's neat lettering marking the twisting rivers, villages, mountains. But that meandering line, the breadth of a hair, was an endless river and those green Vs were impenetrable jungles.

"Charlotte…you understand not every letter you write will reach me?"

"Yes."

"And every letter I write to you—"

"Yes," she blurted before her lungs choked off the words. There was a growing pain in her chest like her heart turning inside out because she *did* know. He could fall ill or shipwreck or lose his way. And he might die somewhere and she might never, ever learn exactly how.

She knew that—she *did*.

Will nuzzled the sensitive hollow behind her ear. "Turn around and kiss me, sweetheart."

She turned her head to smile at him, but he watched her mouth. It had been two days since he'd really looked at her, yet he'd barely let her sleep, as often as he wanted to make love. And again, his hands were growing possessive.

He angled for her mouth but she dodged his lips and curled her hands under his, twining their fingers together. "After your time in Zhaoqing, you must return to deliver the plants to the river docks in…Zhenhai?"

"Hmm?"

"Will…it's two in the afternoon."

"Is it?" he murmured. "You've never confined me to a schedule. Or to one room, or position, or climax. In fact, you've grown accustomed to multiple—"

"You're teasing me."

His smile stretched across her cheek. "I'm not teasing, sweetheart."

But he had accused her of lust before. And normally she *was* the one to deepen their kisses and lure him to bed. But then…she was the one in love.

His arms slid lower.

"Are you avoiding my question?" she asked.

He sighed, planting his chin on her shoulder in surrender. "Which one, sweetheart?"

"The docks in Zhenhai. How many days will you spend there? Will you have time to restore yourself?"

He swirled a finger beneath her breast. "You mean here by the Chenwan Bay?"

The tickling sent tremors down her back, and lower, that she did her best to ignore. "Yes."

"We'll need a week to restock supplies and see the cases off to England." His finger traveled down her stomach. "Then we make camp in Xinxing." Lower to her hip. "Then to Yunfu." His fingers walked to between her breasts. "Then south to Luoding."

"You moved north."

"So I did. The terrain here is magnificent."

She pulled at his hands cupping her breasts but he continued to knead her gently, his erection prodding her through her skirts.

"Come upstairs, sweetheart," he crooned. "I need you."

She slipped from his heated hold and put space between them. Presumptuous as ever when it came to her accord, he followed, loosening his necktie en route. Pivoting to the door, he turned the lock.

"I am in earnest. I want to know," she said, allowing her frustration to color her words.

"I know you are, sweetheart."

"Then why lock the door?"

"I don't want us to be interrupted." He moved to the curtains and tugged the heavy silk from the tiebacks to close off the view to the street. "Now, where did we leave off?" he murmured, his eyes fixed on her body.

Her traitorous body tightened in anticipation but as he neared, his eyes bright, her heart raced as if stalked. A lightning-fast hand caught her wrist and he slid behind her, maneuvering her to face the table. Gripping the edge on either side of her arms, he pressed against her bottom.

She wanted this—*she did*. She loved him and he made her *feel* loved.

Even if he never said the words.

She turned and wrapped her arms about his neck, forcing him to kiss her. And he let her. But only for a moment.

To her surprise, Will spun her around and pressed her over the table. Hot breath steamed her neck as he aligned their hips, his weight pinning her to the table. Warm hands lifted the back of her skirt and his fingers found the seam of her pantalets and moved the fabric aside.

"Will? What are you doing?"

The blunt tip of him stroked her, parting her from back to front, teasing her relentlessly, liquefying her where she wanted him most, till she dropped onto her elbows, limp with desire.

"Will?" she breathed. "I—"

"Say you want me," he murmured in her ear.

She moaned softly at the command. There were no words she could utter. Not with the shallow strokes he teased her with, the small movement tormenting her until she was arching back against him, desperate for release.

"Not till you say it," he crooned, his long, thick fingers delving between her legs to circle the sensitive bud.

She reached for him but he caught her arms and stretched them over her head. Dazed, the dusting of gold hair on his strong wrists riveted her. Involuntarily, her body tightened around him and he groaned. He clamped down, aggressive and dominating, until she was denied all movement under his body. "Will...please..."

He trapped both her wrists in one hand and swept her hair back to rub his cheek against hers and nibble her lips. His breath steamed the table surface beneath them. "I like when you talk." His body shuddered. "*Ah, Christ,* tell me what you want."

Want…she wanted—

"Tell me how good this feels," he whispered. "Tell me—"

"I love you."

The hand in her hair seized in a tight grip and she cried out. Instantly his fingers released, but a growl tore from his throat and he pushed into her hard. Only when he was fully seated did he thread his arms beneath her so she wouldn't be crushed flat on the table.

The deep claiming shocked her, paralyzed her. Their joining had never been like this. He pistoned into her, faster and faster, until the friction of their bodies heated and she was mindless with pleasure, moaning with each return. The growls vibrating from his chest coursed through her and she kept her eyes open to remind herself this was her husband mounting her like an animal. She could see his whiskered jaw from the corner of her eye, the thick, gold hair bobbing as he surged forward.

Powerful hands gripped her hips and lifted her bottom to grind against him and she cried out, her body bucking in ecstasy. But he ratcheted tight, plunging again and again until he collapsed on her, holding himself deep within her, his shaft jerking and spilling its seed. "Ah God…God." He lowered her to the table, resting on her until he mastered himself, and dazed by the frenzied taking, she lay still.

Panting hard, Will pulled his heavy flesh from her and lifted her to stand on unsteady legs. His face was flushed and his eyes wide open, but he was quick to embrace her before she could study him.

His heartbeat thundered against her cheek until he stepped back to put himself back in his pants and fumble at his trouser buttons. She threaded her arms tentatively about his neck, but his eyes shied from hers. Will swept a light kiss on her lips and released her.

And she stood where he left her.

What was happening? They knew every inch of each other's bodies, and yet he was so distant. Was this marriage? Did you trade one intimacy for another?

I don't want this.

The revelation startled her like a slamming door.

She didn't want this. She didn't want a marriage without love. She didn't want a husband who could leave his family a week, let alone the entirety of an expedition. This was not enough. It would never be enough. How had she ever imagined…?

Yet she *had* imagined.

Cold panic crept over her skin. There was so little time left. It was the end of July. Somehow, her life had become hostage to the calendar. Her courses were late twelve days. Seventeen days and she would be late again. Twelve days after that…Will would sail.

What had she done?

The silence was terrible. Will combed his fingers through his hair, but she could make no attempt to appear normal.

With an intense air, Will wiped the surface of the table with his palm, but returned to slide an arm about her waist. His need to touch her was apparently too strong an urge to resist today.

"Would you go for a walk with me?"

She blinked at the abrupt question. "A walk? There is to be rain."

Will scowled at the closed curtains. "Is there anywhere you wish to go? You wanted a hat for your yellow gown."

She smiled more from dismay than amusement at the strange offer. "You would dislike shopping with me. *Everyone* dislikes shopping with me."

His eyes swept the maps and she could have sworn she saw a flare of anger. But it was gone when he turned back. At last, *at last*, he looked into her eyes. But there was a plea in their depths. "I'm not inclined to work today."

She didn't know what to say and yet Will's eyes beseeched her to speak. Now was the moment to ask him to stay, to never leave her.

But this was the one test she feared Will would fail.

He lifted her hand, kissed her palm. And didn't let go.

"You seem…distracted. Is there something wrong?"

He was quiet a moment, then shook his head. "No, sweetheart, don't worry."

Her heart sank, feeling again the wall he kept between them. "Is there something you wish to do?"

He shrugged, and twined a curl of her hair around his finger. "I don't know. Anything with you is fine."

Her heart buckled. Oh no. No, there was no falling out of love with Will Repton. "My only plan for the afternoon was to tend to Lucy's flowers in the orchid house."

"I might be of some use there." He tugged her

close and pressed her head into his shoulder. "I'm sorry," he whispered. "I was too rough."

She opened her mouth to protest but he spoke before she could.

"I'll not be able to dine with you. I have that appointment this evening."

"With Mr. Mayhew?"

"Hmm? Right."

Doubt flickered through her mind. Was he really going to visit Mr. Mayhew this evening?

But if not, what was he doing?

Twenty-four

THE LECTURE THEATER AT THE ROYAL INSTITUTION WAS filled to capacity. Every seat on the semicircular risers was occupied from the front of the room to the back wall where men and women stood three bodies deep.

Will waited for his introduction, his papers rolled in a fist. Too many women were in the audience. The transfer of his lecture from the modest Geographical Society office on Waterloo Place to the larger-capacity Royal Institution on Albermarle had been necessary to accommodate the number—and as the RI had no restrictions against women, dozens had come.

Charlotte couldn't have learned of it…there wouldn't have been time. Still, he couldn't shake the niggling sense she was somehow near.

He scanned the crowd but the excited audience stood in the aisles, blocking his view.

No, Charlotte was safe at home, believing he was meeting with Seth.

What a bloody horrible husband he was. There'd always been a deficit of truth in their relationship, and here was another withholding.

And yet Charlotte withheld nothing. Even when he'd taken her this afternoon.

He gripped his temples, fighting the shame flooding him. He could have hurt her. Had he? He'd never been rough before. Preparing for today's lecture had weakened him somehow, left him vulnerable to his dark memories. And sweet Charlotte had sensed the change in him, moving quietly around him, laying gentle touches on his arm. And when they made love—*Christ,* when they made love, he'd taken her with a desperation that sought her light, her happy spirit. Her love.

But this afternoon, he'd gone too far.

Damn it all, let's get on with it. Will marched to the lectern and waved off the RI fellow meant to introduce him. The crowd hushed and he swept them with an unseeing eye. They had no interest in the collection work of his crew. They sought to satisfy bloodier urges.

"Good evening. I am William Repton." Will breathed deep but kept his gaze lowered. "In the winter of 1843, I, along with a crew of four others, was jointly commissioned by the East India Company to procure tea plants for propagation in our nation's plantations in India..."

And for the next half hour, he spoke of the collection work, the travel into the border provinces of Western China, the difficulties in dealing with the various bureaucracies. Then the time came to address what the audience had come for.

"The last portion of this evening's address"—his throat tightened—"concerns the native aggression of a band of Tibetan marauders against the foreign presence comprised of my British crew and the French mission of Father Marcel Bourianne on December twenty-fourth, 1849.

"Antiforeign sentiment was not unknown to us. The Catholic mission had long abandoned efforts of religious conversion. They focused their efforts instead on an exchange of cultural information and goodwill between the French and Tibetans.

"My crew had taken the Qamdo Pass on our journey to Bhutan, but we were intercepted by local authorities who did not honor our passports and demanded we break our travel at the mission until a ruling could be made as to whether we could proceed. At the time of the incident, we had spent eight days with the French missionaries. On the ninth day, I trekked several miles uphill, alone, to take a survey of the land. The daylight had faded, so I returned to camp at the mission."

The drought...then the blood...

He saw it all again. The body splayed in the dirt, drenching the thirsty ground with his blood. That body was Owen Cressman of Nottingham. Cressey. His best friend.

An arm stretched from the door, motionless. Jack. And inside the mission...

Dead. All dead...

"I discovered—" *a slaughter.* He cleared his throat roughly. "I discovered..."

The audience shifted in their seats, waiting.

He closed his eyes. And knew he couldn't do this.

He couldn't speak of how the bandits must have

descended from the ridge and overtaken his friends, overtaken them all. Couldn't speak of seeing Père Bourianne staked to the ground, not yet dead but disemboweled.

He couldn't speak of the drought and how the ground was arid, *thirsty*, and there was nothing to muffle the sound of his steps so they heard him and chased him. Of how he saw Emile dead in the brush. How he ran and lost his footing and fell, breaking the bones in his leg. And how the fall had saved his life because he'd fallen so far. Of how he bled—and Christ, the thirst—until the shepherd found him.

How he was transported, near dead with fever and infection, to Xiaduxiang, where no one claimed him, but he was carried onto a Dutch supply ship anyway and sent down the Yangtze and transferred to the HMS *Jupiter*. And returned home.

No. He wouldn't speak of that.

Will folded his papers.

"I suppose it's the experience of every human being to feel pain, to see cruelty. To ask, again and again, why things happen. And to regret."

He raised his head. "My wife told me I would be looked to as a messenger." He took a deep breath, and then he could almost smile. "And she loved reading about the places I traveled, and the good people I met. So tonight I will not speak of the massacre. That is not a message I will ever give."

The audience didn't applaud or raise their hands. A sort of dull confusion settled over them and they avoided his eyes, avoided each other's eyes. Slowly, and in silence, they began to rise to their feet and make for the doors.

To his left, a pale oval face did not look away. And he nearly dropped to his knees.

Charlotte.

He pushed from the lectern, seeing only her bloodless face. Hurtling up the aisle, he pulled her from her seat and nearly carried her to the hall. "Charlotte? Sweetheart? Christ, why are you here?"

She blinked and her face crumpled. Clinging to him, she breathed jagged, hitching breaths into his neck.

"Charlotte?" He tried to look into her face but she hid. Ignoring the gaping people all about them, he tried to shelter her from their stares. *Goddammit…not like this.* "It's all right. I'm so sorry. I should have told you, you should have known."

She trembled but stood on her own two feet. And she was bracing him right back. "I love you."

Damn it, why did she have to say that now?

And why was it all he needed to hear?

The vise on his chest eased. Thank God for her. Somehow she understood. Of course she did. The woman could think circles around him and leave him in knots.

"I never wanted you to know of the killing," he said gruffly.

Her small fist thumped his back. "Well, *obviously*." Her scold squeaked, but she raised her chin, her beautiful face streaked with tears. "You will not hide the truth anymore. Not now that I know." A spasm of emotion flashed across her face, but she steadied her chin. "You will share every stupid, trifling observation, even if it is only to say you dislike the anchovy toast or my hatpin is hideous or you feel logy, because if you sit silent and brooding as you are wont to do, I will imagine you suffering unspeakable torments and I will not endure that."

He nodded obediently. He even followed most of that. "I will, I promise."

"Good." She sniffed. "That is my seventh requirement."

On this wretched day, at this horrible hour, only Charlotte could make him smile. "We're far beyond seven, sweetheart."

She shrugged and wiped her nose, her voice muffled beneath her handkerchief. "Well, I lost count."

Her face was a mix of worry and love, but when she lifted her gaze to his, a stone lodged in the pit of his stomach.

She wouldn't ask…please, God, don't let her ask…

He shook his head even before she spoke. "Please, you don't understand—there's a…"

He trailed off when she slid his hand to her warm belly.

"Mrs. Repton?" The loud male voice broke the spell of their intimate circle. Seth hurried toward them from the lecture hall. "Are you all right?"

Charlotte pulled out of his arms. "Yes, Mr. Mayhew. Thank you."

Seth's face was a shifting mask of stony anger and fear. "I'm sorry to be interrupting."

His deep voice rumbled strangely. As if with fear.

Seth pulled a square of yellowed paper from his pocket. "I got a letter from George. And in it was a letter for you, Will. George assumed I'd know how to reach you."

Will's heart lodged in his throat. He eyed the paper in Seth's fist, the inked words smeared nearly illegible.

"George went into Tibet." Seth's voice rasped, urgent and bitter, like a hand reaching out to choke the nearest man it could find.

Will ripped his gaze from the letter and found Seth's glare trained on him. "I'm sorry. I never thought George would—"

"Bombay's where they're headed next, the letter says." A muscle flexed in Seth's jaw. "You heard the baby cry. It was in your report. She was alive when you ran."

His heart pounded, but he met Seth's steely glare.

"You might've saved her. But you ran." Seth crammed the letter into Will's hand. "Read it."

And without another word, Seth stormed off.

Twenty-five

Dear Mr. Repton:

In regards to your Inquiry…British expeditionary crew led by R. Milford, of which I serve in the capacity of botanical illustrator: we are advised… possible survival of an infant…Bourianne family of the Mission Estrangeres, of which you were acquainted before their demise…

…colleague recently returned from the village of Langxiang…rumor of a foreign (white) orphan of a like age and gender…will attempt a crossing of the Tibet border and ascertain if there is any truth to this information. If we are fortunate to meet with such a happy outcome…endeavor by all means to secure the child…

If we are successful, I shall be obliged…enlist those living relations…the necessary arrangements for the reception of the child…return to England.

…further communication at my earliest opportunity.

Yours faithfully, G. Mayhew
11 May, 1850

With a hand that shook, Charlotte raised the carriage blind higher to make use of the lamplight and read the fragile letter again, patching together the meaning of the smeared words. In the dim interior, Will sat across from her, his skin pale and his eyes so empty he might have been a waxwork. The carriage outside the Royal Institution was at a standstill due to the traffic, but he hardly seemed to notice. He'd not said a word since reading the letter.

Charlotte lowered the letter into her lap. "I don't understand. An infant?"

The tremors in her body deepened. Already shaken by all Will had endured and the horrible, confusing things Mr. Mayhew had said, the truth rolled over her and crushed her into her seat.

Will's nightmare wasn't over.

She understood so much now. Even more than Will's lecture had made her understand. His nightmares, his guardedness. His need to return.

In that instant, her dream he would stay, her dream of some clean, fresh beginning crumbled. And she could barely ask the question… "There were children there?"

Will moved to sit beside her, taking her hand and lacing their fingers together. "Two."

She gripped his hand. "Tell me."

And for the first time, he did. He told her everything omitted from the lecture, as if lashed by the memories. Every detail until his back hunched and his face burrowed into her lap and his fists nearly rent the seam of her skirt in two. "I found everyone but her. I ran to her cot, but it was empty and…I heard them coming, heckling, and I was screaming for her, for anyone, but they were dead—and damn me to hell, I ran. I ran away—"

He ran…

Oh God…

"Charlotte, I couldn't find her. I ran—"

"*I'm glad.*" She said the words loud and defiant because he wouldn't. "I'm glad you ran and stayed alive." Bending low, she held him with all her strength. She hated them for hurting him, for making him so afraid that day, for hurting him still.

She waited, stroking his golden hair, not wanting to ask but knowing he needed her to. "What is the baby's name?"

"Aimee. I…I heard her cry. I'd fallen and broken my leg. I heard her cry and I couldn't get to her. She was alive somewhere. When I ran, she was alive—"

Pain tore through her heart and she buckled in two over him, clamping a hand over her lips before she cried out.

Alive.

Aimee was the reason Will was never going to stay. And the reason she had to let him go, even knowing now how dangerous the search would be.

And yet, all this time…she'd harbored the smallest flicker of hope he might stay.

Oh God…God, she *was* prone to fanciful notions.

She took a deep breath. "You want to find her." It was not a question.

Will straightened from her lap and wiped his face. He cleared his throat roughly but stared straight ahead. A muscle worked in his jaw. "I'm sorry, Charlotte. I'm sorry I didn't save her then. I…should have, somehow. I should have done *something*—" His head dropped. "She may live."

Her heart ached, and somehow there was not a doubt in her mind. "She does live."

A sound of relief burst from his lips and he caught her face in his hands and kissed her. He kissed her long and hard as if to thank her. And when his fingers threaded through her hair and caressed her neck, he kissed her as if to tell her he cherished her.

His kisses softened and broke, and traveled across her cheek to her ear, until his forehead rested on hers and he just held her. And her own relief strengthened her.

Wherever Will had been the last few days, he had come back to her.

With a gentle squeeze, he released her and reached across the carriage to slide the letter into his coat pocket. "Langxian village is over two hundred miles from the mission."

She nodded numbly. "That is not so far, is it?"

He lifted their entwined hands and kissed the back of hers. "To move anyplace in that country requires strength, sometimes violence, and money—to cross the borders, to pay for information." He shook his head wearily. "George wouldn't have anything like that."

Her fear multiplied, but she would not say anything. He had to go back. For Aimee.

Just for Aimee…

She rounded on him. "Will? Without investors, you do not need to collect."

"No, but—"

"How soon could you return? If you go only to

find her?" The carriage was slowing—they had arrived home—but she would have Will's answer first.

"I don't… I never planned—"

"But you know. I know you know. How long?"

"A year. Maybe less."

A year. She was nearly ill—no, she *was* ill with fear. Or excitement. An increasingly familiar nausea scaled her throat and she gripped the edge of the velvet cushion beneath her. The carriage door opened and with a hurried "just a moment" she pulled it shut, to the coachman's grunt of confusion.

She grabbed Will's lapel, needing him to be very, very clear. "One year?"

"I won't take your money."

"*Our* money." She leveled her gaze with his and spoke as seriously as she was able with her roiling stomach. "You have all you need. You require two thousand. We have ten times that. So much more, actually. That does not even count the annual income our trust brings."

"Charlotte—"

"*Honestly*, you and your secrets. We have all you need for bribes and we will finance an army to protect you. Find her, Will. And come back to me as fast as you can."

"Charlotte—"

"This is no time to indulge your perverse desire to argue." She threw open the carriage door, but not before sending a smile back to her husband. And yes… still her hero. "We have to make a new plan."

Twenty-six

"Married?" Ben towered over her and Will on the settee. The spacious front parlor seemed to shrink from his intimidating brawn. At six foot three with a frame that had never lost the plowman's muscle of his youth, an irate Ben Paxton would give anyone pause.

Not her, of course. Her brother-in-law was the gentlest man in the world, and this misdirected show of temper would soon be swept aside. After all, the family had come up in the week before Will's sail *because* of their love for him. Despite Ben and Wally's glowers, they would be overjoyed once a full understanding of the situation was comprehended.

"What do you mean, *married*?" Ben growled.

Well. Very likely they would, later.

"Exactly that." Charlotte smiled in turn at her beloved family, all seated with varying degrees of shock and anger etched on their faces. "Our marriage was the reason I have not been forthcoming about the progress of the annulment petition. We delayed our news until we could tell you in person."

Speech-depriving news, it seemed.

At least John and Liz Repton, who had come to Sunday supper as they always did, appeared cautiously pleased.

Ben swiveled his head, pinning Will with a glare. "And how did this happen, Repton? We agreed on an annulment."

Will squeezed her hand. "I remember."

"You gave us your word, Will!"

"I never should have allowed them to sleep in the same bed," Wally muttered, pacing the length of the room.

Liz Repton raised a tentative hand. "I had the most wonderful thought. Charlotte could live with us in Richmond."

"Oh!" she gasped, tears pricking her eyes. "Oh—like a *real* daughter!" She beamed at John and Liz, and they at her, and they all basked in their mutual affection.

Which Wally and Ben grudgingly allowed. For one second.

Ben rounded on Will. "So is the expedition canceled?"

"Whose idea was this?" asked Wally.

"Oh, honestly," she mumbled in protest.

"When did this happen?" Ben piled on.

And then the interrogation continued, seemingly without a pause for breath from either of her brothers. *Have you made any arrangements for her? Are you taking precautions? What is your plan if there's a child? What becomes of her if you die? Do you even suit each other? Why didn't you tell us this was a possibility from the start?*

"So you are in love?"

Lucy's lone question silenced the room. Charlotte's heart stilled in her breast. Will had never said so. But she was so very sure he did, *that he must.*

So she could not explain the quaking at her core waiting for him to speak.

"*My goodness*," she blurted, smiling woodenly. "This is not at all the reaction I expected."

Her family seemed to deflate in unison and Lucy hurried to sit beside her. "Oh, dearest, you know we wish you happy. But you'll not see Will for years."

"Not years. *One* year..."

She pulled her hand from Will's to lay it upon her stomach as if she might shelter the little stranger within. Now that she was certain there was a baby...

If only she could tell them. But she wouldn't until Will sailed.

Betsy, the new maid, entered with the tray and all fell silent while she set up the service, oddly placing the cups before each of them. Was the girl unaccustomed to service?

"Thank you, Betsy," Lucy murmured.

The maid curtsied clumsily in her haste to leave the room.

The silence lingered past her departure, so Charlotte poured herself a cup. "This is not Mrs. Allen's usual blend." The brew was bitter, and while the taste did not appeal, the cup was something to occupy her hands.

With a reassuring squeeze to her shoulder, Will rose and faced her family. "I realize I do not deserve your sister, but I care about Charlotte a great deal."

"Everyone *cares* for her, Will," Wally snapped. "That is not our objection."

"Then what is?"

"If you loved her, you couldn't leave."

"*Enough!*" Her cup rattled in the saucer as she dropped it on the table and fled the room.

It was enough. No one would rejoice a one-sided love. And once news of the baby was known, they would not rejoice the life growing inside her.

The truth had been baldly spoken for all to hear. If Will loved her, he would never, ever leave.

But she loved him. And she would never make him choose between the baby he had lost and the one he would meet when he returned.

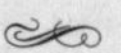

"You afraid the boy will break?"

Will grimaced at his father, who stood holding Ben and Lucy's tiny babe toward him. "I can't. I've never held a baby."

The Repton men had fled to the nursery after the announcement, allowing Charlotte's family the freedom to curse him at will. He ought to invite Seth to join them. The man still blamed him for putting George in danger and had yet to answer any of Will's requests to see him.

As for Charlotte, she had taken refuge in the ladies' parlor. His inability to simply say, "I love her"—the three words her family wanted to hear—would take time to forgive.

But it appeared his father had just succeeded in making the nursery the most uncomfortable room in the house.

"Try, Son. It's the easiest thing in the world."

"What if I drop him?" Will angled his head to examine the placement of arms, legs, neck, and oddly large head of Edward Paxton, roused from a peaceful slumber. "Shouldn't he be a bit more…?"

"What?"

"Substantial?"

His father turned the baby about to inspect his sleepy face, bouncing him higher to coo at him. "He's just a wee thing yet. He's quite sound for a three-month-old. Come now, don't be an old woman." He pushed the baby forward and Will had no choice but to grasp the infant. Immediately, Edward began to writhe and fuss.

"See? Already he wishes to be away from me."

"That's because you got him dangling in the air like a sack of manure." His father pressed the baby toward his chest till its head rested upon his shoulder. "There's the way…you got it."

The baby quieted, soft and warm and smelling like sweet milk. Will didn't dare breathe too deep, or move at all, watching his father's eyes for assurance. "Like this? Is this right?"

"Perfect, Son. Look at how content the boy is."

And he was. Will smiled at the achievement. "He's heavy, isn't he? Dense." He dipped slowly, testing the baby's weight. "I wasn't expecting that."

"I remember how frightened I was, first holding you."

"How long before you were easy with me?"

"What makes you think I'm easy with you now?" His father's eyes crinkled with mirth. And a little sadness.

Will smiled back, distracted by a memory of the missionary's wife. He never saw Madame Bourianne without Aimee in her arms. The sight had tugged at his insides every time. He'd never seen a baby that small, her little back round as a fern shoot, her eyes usually closed in sleep.

"But you'll not have to worry over that yet. Will you?" his father asked.

The question drew Will's attention back. "Hmm?"

"A baby?"

"A baby? No, I...no." Charlotte hadn't gained weight; she was as slender as ever.

His father's face fell and Will felt a corresponding pang of disappointment he didn't want to examine.

"But, wouldn't a woman...it's just, Charlotte hasn't refused me once. And I thought she might be...*inconvenienced*? Or perhaps I'm not understanding the matter correctly." He watched his father carefully. "Or at all."

"You mean her courses?" his father said far too loudly. "Your mother—"

"God, please don't talk about Mum—"

"—never let me touch her during her delicate times each month." His father tilted his head, watching him. "You know that's not the case when a woman is with child, don't you?"

Automatically, he nodded. "So that...just stops, does it?"

His father lowered his brows, a rare look of disapproval. "You best talk to Charlotte and make sure, Son. If she's expecting, you need to know." He grinned. "And then you need to tell your mother so she can die a happy woman."

"I will." The words came out shaky and he cleared his throat. "Right. We've probably been carrying on through her courses and I'd not noticed."

"That's not how it works, Son."

Will's eyes shot to his father's, his heart juddering with terror. Or was it something else? There was a lot he didn't understand, it seemed. He took a shaky breath. "I never planned this. Somehow I lost control of everything."

His father took the baby from him. "You've not been out of control a day in your life. You just don't like what's happened."

"What's happened?"

"You fell in love."

Did he dare to say the words? "What if I didn't?"

His father consulted the baby with a mournful look, then put him back in his cot. "What do you want, Will? You'll not bring back those who died, or punish the ones who killed them. That little baby…well, you can't really believe she's alive."

Will's jaw tightened. "She could be."

"What happened over there wasn't in your control. No one controls the human heart. The heart will hate what it hates, and love what it loves.

"You think if you trek through that undiscovered country, you'll grind those nightmares under your boot and life will start, but it won't. It's the past. You look ahead to another adventure, and there's none like letting yourself love someone completely, the way I love your mother and the way I love you."

Will shook his head until he could find his voice. "I don't love her."

"Courage, Son."

"I don't."

"It takes courage to love people when you can't control when they'll be taken from you."

"I can't love her! I leave in eight days." He frowned at that stupidity. "I just don't want to worry over her."

"Oh no, no, I imagine not. Too late now, though, isn't it?" His father smiled sadly. "The day you were born was the most wonderful and horrible day of my life. How could I protect you when you started to walk? When you went off to school? When you sailed across an ocean?

"They told us you were dead of fever, *twice.* We didn't hear from you for months, and one day, we received a telegram to collect your body on the East India quay. *Your body*, Will. And they carried you off that ship looking about as broken as a man can look when still breathing." He paused, his eyes glassy with emotion. "*That's* fear. Your mother and I have fear every day, but we don't stop loving you.

"You'll not escape it. Not by sailing across an ocean, so you may as well stay here." His eyes strayed to the window. Charlotte was walking on the lawn. "She's your adventure now, Son."

His father didn't understand. He couldn't love Charlotte because…

Because if something ever happened to her, it would break him.

The setting sun cast long shadows behind Charlotte, her walk slow and meandering on the lawn. His eyes latched on her hands, cupped lightly on her flat stomach. Lately that stance had become a habit…

Was it possible?

You best talk to Charlotte and make sure, Son.

Was it possible?

Charlotte stilled, as if hearing a distant sound.

Then crumpled to the ground.

Twenty-seven

"Will, let her go."

Someone was talking, small hands pulled at his arm. Charlotte wouldn't wake. She was so pale and she wouldn't wake— "*What's wrong with her!*" he yelled.

"Will?"

Lucy's face swam into focus and he forced himself to listen. "Will? We have to loosen her dress. You have to let her go. She needs air."

Air, she needs air. He released her but refused to move from the bed. Lucy was here, and Patty. And Ben and Wallace, his parents. All here, in their bedroom. The women worked furiously, unhooking buttons, tugging at laces.

Christ, she was pale. His head swiveled, seeking his father. "Where's the doctor? Why isn't he here?"

"He's coming, Son, he's coming as fast as he can."

They opened Charlotte's blouse, her corset, and when they maneuvered her skirts down her crinoline...seven pairs of eyes arrowed to the vicinity of Charlotte's legs.

And the blood.

The air rushed from his body. *No. Please God.*

"Will?"

He twisted back but it was too late. Charlotte saw. And her wail cracked his heart.

"No, no, Charlotte." He grabbed her, trying to stop this, trying to make her not see.

"Is he all right?" Her eyes locked on his. "Is the baby all right?"

The baby.

Feeling drained from his body, his arms braced on the mattress barely held him upright.

Charlotte turned from him and gripped her sister's hand. "Lucy?" Her voice broke. "Tell me."

"No, please." But he couldn't make his voice heard.

Lucy scrambled onto the bed. "You're with child?"

"I…yes."

"All right, dearest, all right," Lucy said. "The doctor is coming. Bleeding is…not always uncommon, not early on, and it's…it's not that much."

Charlotte stared as if her life depended on every word falling from Lucy's lips.

But Will could no longer hear. The memories roared back…the blood-soaked ground, the bodies, the flesh smeared with…with the blood. Christ, the smell of it, he could smell it—

No! He heaved in air. Charlotte was alive. Her face was pale and tears streamed down her cheek but she was alive. She needed him here.

And he would be here.

Oh God…he would. He would—he couldn't leave her—

"Do you feel any pain?" Lucy asked.

Charlotte shook her head.

"That's good," Lucy said. "That's good. Let's relax, for the baby."

Charlotte clenched her eyes. He reached for her but she angled from him. He touched her arm, her hand, laced his fingers through hers, but she didn't look at him. "Charlotte? I'm here."

She wrenched her hand from his.

What was happening? What had he done? "Sweetheart?"

Her face crumpled. "Go away."

"Charlotte?"

She covered her ears and screamed, "*Go away!*"

He stared, unable to move. Charlotte was shaking, her body curling into a defensive ball.

No. Not Charlotte. He'd not leave Charlotte, not ever. He launched himself against her back and wrapped his arm around her. "Please, love, don't." But she wailed louder.

Hard hands grabbed him with a strength he could barely resist. Ben's hands. "Will, come away."

"*Leave us alone!*" he growled.

The grip tightened and pulled him off the bed. His legs unfolded and dropped under him, his feet meeting the floor with a slap. Ben shook him and Will turned to snarl at the man who would dare separate him from his wife.

"She's upset, Will. *Listen.*" Ben's eyes were wide and worried. "Listen to her."

Charlotte was sobbing, her body shaking as she crawled to bury her head on her sister's lap. Pain stabbed him in the chest, doubling him in half. He pulled out of Ben's grip and staggered to the hall.

His father followed and stood beside him. "Courage, Son."

Will collapsed against the wall and covered his mouth with his hand, but it was his father's hand on his shoulder that kept him from screaming.

Will wasn't sure how much time had passed since Dr. Simmons entered the bedroom, but it felt like hours by the time the man reappeared in the hall. "What is it?" he demanded. "Is she hurt? What happened?"

Dr. Simmons motioned him further down the hall, presumably to not be overheard by Charlotte, and Will's fear spiked higher.

"It appears to have been some sort of spontaneous contraction."

He staggered against the wall. "Is the baby…?"

"It is far too early to hear a heartbeat—"

"But can't you—"

"She is young and healthy and I have seen women bleed a small measure and bring forth perfectly sound babies. I'll know more in a week's time. If she bleeds again, that would be concerning, but she tells me she felt no pain in her womb, which is encouraging. And, to be honest, a bit puzzling."

Will could barely follow the man's words but he forced himself to listen. "Why?"

"You'll forgive me…I normally only see this sort of response in the girls in the rookeries."

"See what?"

"The sudden insensibility, the overstimulation of the nerves. I am not suggesting such a thing with your wife—but in cases where girls wish for their menses to return, to avoid pregnancy, they use a mash of parsley, rapunzel, or pennyroyal. Would Mrs. Repton have... *handled* any of these herbs?"

"I don't know, I don't think so."

"There are other herbs that are dangerous, brewed in a tincture or a tea."

"She drinks tea all day but—"

This is not Mrs. Allen's usual blend.

Not the usual blend...

He ran down the stairs, calling into the kitchen. "Bring Mrs. Allen here. *Now.*"

The doctor followed, not speaking as Will paced the entryway. Mrs. Allen appeared, her face drawn and concerned. "Is Mrs. Repton doing better?"

"What was in the tea you served today?"

Her eyes grew round. "The tea? Oh lord, did I do this to our sweet girl? It was tea, is all."

"What was in it?"

"The usual tea. The same we've been drinking." She wrung her hands in her skirt. "Betsy will bring it. Jamie, where's Betsy?"

The footman stared blankly back. "But she's gone, Mrs. Allen."

"What do you mean, 'gone'?"

"Didn't you send her off? She said she was going back to her last post, said it was grander than here—"

"Where?" Will interrupted.

Jamie's earnest face creased with concentration, he gripped a handful of hair as if to pull the name forward. "A Lord something-or-other, she said. Harland, maybe?"

Will's blood ran cold. "Harlowe?"

You mustn't get with child…

No man of honor will have her if she carries your babe…

"The Earl of Harlowe?" he asked again.

Jamie's eyes met his. "That's the one. He's to be the next Earl of Harlowe, Betsy said."

"That would be the viscount, then, wouldn't it?" Mrs. Allen said. "Betsy's gone to…"

But her words trailed off as Will raced out the door.

"Who the devil is making that commotion?" Viscount Spencer swept off his valet's offer of his coat. Someone was pounding on his front door.

Buttoning his waistcoat along the way, he headed to the stairs. Barrows opened the front door. Repton stood in the shadow of his portico, his coat unbuttoned and his arms cocked at his sides.

Repton spied him over the butler's shoulder and pushed Barrows aside. "Spencer!"

With a roar of fury, Repton lunged up the stairs, muscled thighs pumping and shoulders rolling. Hands like claws pushed off the railing, the steps, propelling him upwards. He was halfway to Hugh before two footmen dragged him to his knees.

His heart stumbling in his chest, Hugh gripped the banister, eyeing the still-struggling Repton on the stairs. "What the hell are you doing? How dare—"

"I know what you did to the tea!" Repton yelled, his teeth bared.

"I… Throw him out! He's mad."

"You did this! If she loses the baby, I'll kill you."

"Barrows! I will not suffer this man in my home."

A third footman scrambled to grapple with Repton, slowing—but not stopping—his advance.

Repton broke their hold and lurched toward him. "I'll kill you!"

"Grab him!"

The footmen slammed him from behind, forcing his cheek to the tread of the step, but still the man struggled.

"You'll regret this!" His words were strangled beneath the weight of the three men.

When a fourth entered the fray, Hugh squared his shoulders. "Get out or meet a Blue Devil on the street."

Repton strained against the arms binding him but he was losing ground. Forced back, forced out, until Barrows managed to close the front door, leaving the footmen out on the pavement with him.

A wave of dizziness buckled his knees. His heart pounded. It would for several minutes more. He did not recover from excitements as other men did.

If she loses the baby…

If.

Pounding rattled the doors. Repton had broken free. He eyed the massive walnut doors shuddering in their frame. "Don't let him in." Not that Barrows appeared to have any inclination of doing any such thing.

Slowly, mindful of further strain, he returned to his rooms and locked the door.

So Betsy had guessed correctly. Charlotte was with child.

He had to be rid of that stupid maid. Not only had she lost all nerve and come running to his door, she'd brought the poison back with her. The vial was in his dressing room with what was left of the powder.

No wonder Repton knew. Did Charlotte taste something in the tea? If the apothecary gave him something discernible…

He fished the glass vial from the back of his chest of drawers, swept the inside with his finger, and moved it to his lips. A flash of uncertainty stilled his hand as he stared at the powder. It was an insignificant amount. And he was male, twice her size.

He closed his lips around his finger. Bitter. And woody. But it would have been diluted in tea, not as he'd taken it.

"Goddamned incompetence." He marched to the fire and cast the vial into it. Idiotic girl. He'd send the baggage to his house in Wales, far from here.

God damn them all. *Christ*, what possessed him to go so far? What if Repton told his father? The earl would believe *Repton*. Over his own son.

A strange fluttering in his chest slowed his step. His skin was…it was freezing, it was—

"Jenson?" His valet was never far. He marched toward the bellpull and tugged it hard. But that small effort left him panting. Something was wrong. "Jenson!"

What had the apothecary said? About relaxing muscles? About the heart? He said something…

A pain like lightning cracked his chest. He sank to his knees on the thick rug.

An apt name…malevolence…

"Jenson!"

Christ, his heart…his heart was going to burst…

He heard the rattle of the door, a voice calling.

And then nothing ever again.

Twenty-eight

WILL BOUNDED UP THE STAIRS TO HIS AND Charlotte's bedroom, his muscles still quaking with unfulfilled vengeance. Spencer would pay. And soon.

But Charlotte needed him now.

Wallace and Jacob stood in the hall. Alerted to his presence, Wallace squared his shoulders and moved to block the bedroom door.

"Where did you go, Uncle Will?" Jacob asked, his small face full of blame.

He couldn't have Jacob angry with him too. Not now. The little boy held his body stiff and resentful, but Will hugged him anyway. "I'm sorry, Jacob. I needed to see someone about your Aunt Charlotte, but I came back as soon as I could."

Little arms hugged his neck and a nearly crippling surge of love for the child swept over him. Like Charlotte, Jacob forgave quickly.

"She's sick, so I'm being quiet."

With a last tight squeeze, Will set him down. "You're a good boy." He straightened to face Wallace.

The man had a white-knuckle grip on the door handle and his legs were planted wide.

"She is not ready to see you, Will."

"Let me pass."

Wallace swallowed, a flash of futility weakening his expression. They both knew if Will wanted in, Wallace couldn't stop him. "Allow her a little time."

"She's my wife—"

The door opened. Lucy stepped from the room, her face drawn. "It's all right. Will, you can go in."

Ignoring the troubling look of compassion on Lucy's face, he swept past her into the room, closing the door behind him.

Charlotte was sitting up. Her hair had been let down and the gloss of those curling, dark tresses almost disguised the fact that her skin was too pale, her expression too lost. And in the same sweep of his eye, he noted the too-firm set of her chin, the fingers fidgeting with the extra blanket at her waist, the tracks of dried tears on her cheeks, the fresh nightgown she wore. Charlotte wasn't wearing her wedding rings—

Christ. He clenched his fist, the nails biting into his palm. He wasn't cataloging some specimen—this was Charlotte. And her hair tickled his nose when they slept, and she was always depriving him of his pencil, and she smelled like peonies in the sun, and she was a talented sleeper and a terrible artist, and she couldn't let five minutes pass without smiling at him.

His Charlotte. And he hadn't protected her.

"Will you sit?" she asked quietly.

He lurched forward, his feet leaden. The bedside

chair was in his way and he dragged it aside to climb on the bed—but Charlotte jerked up her blanket.

"No—would you…would you not?" she said.

His hand still gripped the chair, and it was only this tactile prod that made him comprehend. She didn't want him in their bed.

He pulled the chair close and sat. "How are you feeling?"

"I am not in pain."

He searched her eyes. "You didn't tell me."

Her fingers tightened on the blanket. "I thought… not to burden you—"

"Burden me?" He grabbed her hand. It was cold and limp, and it was a shock when she slipped it away.

"Ignorance would have been better. And you are sensitive, Will, though you are loath to confess it. Would the news of another child be welcome to you?"

"I don't know." He regretted the truth but he wouldn't be false with her. *I wasn't prepared.*

Her lips quirked in a small, sad smile. "The day we met, you said I see only what I wish to see. Do you remember?"

The fear in his gut grew heavier. But damn it, when had it *not* been heavy? He'd picked it up in Tibet, carried it back to England, found there was more to bear in caring for a woman. He knew its weight.

He couldn't put it down.

"I remember," he said quietly. "I was wrong."

"But you weren't wrong. I wish I had understood then how right you were. None of this would have happened."

"Charlotte—"

"You rejected me and I sought your friendship. You growled at me and I kissed you. You warned me not to touch and I gloried in our lust." She paused. "I married you when there was no need."

"That's not—"

"And you do not love me, Will," she said, slow and clear. "Yet I dared to have a baby."

The fear that bowed his back crushed him. "That's not—no, listen—"

"My love was not supposed to hurt anyone, but look what has happened. God is punishing my selfishness. But he is offering me a chance at redemption, as well." Her eyes slid from his. "We cannot be married anymore," she whispered, as if the words stunned her as well.

"What are you doing?" He wanted his voice to command an answer, but he sounded desperate, afraid.

"If I am to be a mother, I cannot dream the world my child lives in. Not as I dreamed our marriage."

He grabbed her shoulders, but she looked through him. "Listen to me. This child is mine, *you* are mine, we are married because *you were right*. You saw the truth, all of it, under every cover, under every stupid thing I said and did. You saw what was between us."

"No, Will. I saw *more*."

His hands gripped tight, wanting her to stop her talking, stop her saying good-bye. The ground dropped from under him, the room whirled, and he didn't know where he would land… "Charlotte—"

"If the baby survives—"

…his fate in the hands of a woman who never did what was expected…

"—I will thank you every day for him—"

"*I love you.*" He flung the words because they were his last hope.

Charlotte. The love of his life. The greatest adventure of his life…

A horrible look of compassion dawned in her eyes. She didn't believe him.

She was letting him fall.

"That is the second-nicest thing you have ever said to me," she said, smiling sadly.

"Charlotte—"

"Thank you for the days we were married, every one of them. We need to end this as we had planned. Just as you planned to find what you lost in Tibet and I planned to live without you."

He shook his head, his hands dropped, lifeless, to the bed. "You love me."

"Perhaps." Her eyes clouded and her beautiful face stilled, as faraway as a porcelain doll's. "Perhaps you were only the man of my dreams."

Twenty-nine

"Christ, what did you do to your wife?" Seth Mayhew said by way of greeting as he stood on the threshold of Will's parents' door in Richmond.

Will froze with his hand on the knob. "You saw her?"

"Just come from the house, looking for you. I'd never seen her so down in her pretty mouth." Seth peered behind Will into his parents' kitchen, the table strewn with letters, maps, and papers. He stepped past him and took a seat.

Will followed, failing to close the door. The thought that Seth was the last person he expected to see was obliterated by news of Charlotte. "How was she?"

Seth nudged an empty chair in Will's direction in a crude invitation to sit. "I just said she looked all weepy." He crossed his arms and eyed him. "And you've got the same look about you. It was damned awkward then and worse now, so stop it."

His heart was good and shattered—and Seth wasn't helping a damn bit—but Will sat. "I'd hoped to see you before I set sail Monday." He met Seth's eye. "I never wanted George to search for Aimee."

"I know it." Seth sighed. "And I shouldn't have said what I did. I know you couldn't find that baby."

Will's heart tore deeper. "I'll do everything I can to see they both get back safe. I'll start in Bombay, I know a man there. Then move east—"

"Here's what I propose, Will." Seth turned the map on the table to face him. "You give me your funds… and *I* find George and Aimee."

"Seth—"

"I don't have the blunt to go myself. But I can't stay here, not knowing what happened."

Sadness weighed Will down like an anchor. He knew that feeling well, and the moment he left England, he'd feel it double with Charlotte. But she didn't need him to stay.

And she didn't want him to.

Will shoved his chair back from the table, tired of sitting. "You don't speak any of the languages. You don't know the culture—"

He shrugged, studying the map. "There's Englishmen enough in India. And I'm adaptive."

Adaptive… Will scrubbed a hand over his face. "I've spent months preparing. You don't—"

"Didn't speak Portuguese when I landed in Recife, either." Seth dropped the map lightly on the table. "We're explorers, Will. There's no *preparing*, no *protecting*. Hell…you know that better than anyone. And George is the only soul left belonging to me."

Will stared. Christ, if Seth went…no. He shook his head. "You can't—"

"You won't find her," Seth said plain. "I know you

won't. You won't even survive the first week outside of Bombay."

Will froze in anger. And doubt. "Why would you say that to me?"

"Because this ain't your adventure no more." Seth angled over the table to lance him with his sea-green stare. "I'm going to get my family, Will." He grinned. "Go get yours."

Thirty

THE CLOCK BEGAN ITS ELEVEN CHIMES AND Charlotte locked her eyes on her drawing pad. The pencil gripped in her hand hadn't made a mark on the paper. Another scene drew itself in her mind instead: the Blackwall Frigate in the East India quay, its three masts towering into the sky, the sails ruffling in the wind. Will, heavy with the silver ingots and coins sewn into his clothes, taking leave of a tearful John and Liz on the dock and climbing the steep gangplank onto the deck.

She tried to erase the scene. She did not want to imagine Will as he must look now. His hair ruffled by the ocean wind, his eyes squinting against the sun glinting off the Channel, girding against the next hundred days at sea.

She did not want to imagine him. But he was there every time she closed her eyes.

The last chime tolled in her ears, reverberating long and mournful. Eleven o'clock. The ship would have cast off. Her fist opened, the pencil that was glued to her palm dropped to the paper.

She covered her face. *Please keep Will safe,* she prayed as she prayed every day. *Let him find the Bouriannes' baby safe. Let our baby be safe.*

Dear God…how was she to endure this? A year not knowing if he lived?

She wiped her eyes and sat up. One week and there had been no more bleeding. On the day of Hugh's funeral, fittingly, every trace of pain had vanished and her color had returned. Doctor Simmons said there was hope if she rested and stayed calm.

She would be calm. She would be anything he told her to be.

The doorbell sounded and she jumped, until she remembered it could not be him. Not today.

The past six days, Will had called every day, leaving a bouquet of white blossoms, but she had refused to see him. She could not. It had been too hard to send him away the first time.

In the hall, Goodley's steps sounded. The front door opened. And then…

"Will she see me today, Mr. Goodley?"

Will?

The shock of his voice made her rise on unsteady legs. Had she imagined it?

But Goodley answered. And then the door opened and she stared at the butler with alarm.

"No," she said before Goodley could speak. "He cannot—"

But there he stood beyond the parlor door, a bouquet of white peonies in his hand, looking so dear she could have wept. And she very likely would, later. "Are you really here?"

A smile spread across his face and he inhaled long and deep, his eyes coursing over her. "I've missed you."

She gaped at him, then the butler. Surely she was dreaming this. She was dreaming and she had to stay calm. "What day is it, Mr. Goodley?"

He grinned, his chest puffing up. "I am sure it is Monday, the twenty-sixth of August, Miss Charlotte." With a duck of his head, Goodley closed the parlor door, leaving the two of them alone.

Will watched her hands, which she held crossed over her stomach, and he smiled wider. He lifted his gaze. "How are you, Charlotte?"

She wrapped her arms about her waist, knowing what he was truly asking, but years of etiquette lessons propelled the words from her lips. "I am well, thank you." She lowered her arms. "I am well," she said more pointedly. "Ben has been sending word, I believe?"

"Twice a day. I understand Doctor Simmons is very hopeful—"

"Why are you here? Are you unwell? Is John or Liz unwell? Did you have to postpone? Is the ship not sailing? Have you booked passage on another? Have you received word of Aimee?"

He looked at the flowers in his hand, then swung them forward at her. "These are for you."

She blinked at the flowers. "What is the matter with you?"

He appeared to consider this. "Fewer things now, actually."

"Are you avoiding my question?"

"Which one, sweetheart?"

"Any one."

He took a step closer. "I would like to sit."

"Sit? All right, but that is not a question I asked."

Her legs shaking, she sat on the settee and, though there were a dozen other seats far more spacious, Will sat beside her, just as he had done the day they met.

She shifted to the end of the settee, but he followed, crowding her, and stretched a muscled arm across the back to lean close. Could he mean to kiss her? She ought to rebuke him if she could manage it—but then he rested his head on his hand. The way he used to hold his head up when he was fatigued.

Her heart tightened with concern. "Are you sleeping?"

"Not as well as when you were sleeping all over me." He smiled. "But the nightmares are gone, Charlotte. All this week, I was alone, I didn't have you, and the nightmares didn't come back."

There was something different about him. The guarded look in his eyes had disappeared. The skin about his mouth and nose was no longer strained. He looked...*peaceful*. Tears welled in her eyes. "I'm glad."

"But I *am* dreaming. Dreams of us. I dreamed of our baby. And he looked like me." He threw his hand up weakly. "And he was dressed in a sailor suit."

He wiped his face, and when he looked at her, his eyes were wet.

"I believe the Bourianne baby is alive." He swallowed, a tear coursed down his cheek. "I need to. And I need to believe someone good and kind is taking care of her and I need to believe she forgives me for being too late to find her that day. I need to believe they all forgive me and I think they finally do, because

I…I dreamed of them, too. My friends. And in the dream, they were all alive and happy.

"They don't want me to sail. They don't want me to save them anymore," he said. "I think they want me to save myself."

She nodded, gasping in a breath she forgot to take, too relieved for him, too overcome to speak.

"I still don't know why I was spared and they weren't. I don't think I ever will. But I thank God for my life." His eyes met hers, unashamed of the tears that spilled free. "I thank God because you are in it. I love you. You know that. Please know that."

And suddenly she did. In the unwavering hold of his gaze, the warmth of his hand, and above all, the feeling—horrible as it was—that Will had fought his way to her from some place further than the other side of the world and deep as the darkest hell in his mind.

The tears in her eyes spilled over and she flung her arms about his neck, laughing and crying in relief.

They held each other a long time, until her tears dried and Will sat back to brush a stray hair from her cheek. "I was wondering…all this week actually, if you might love me, too? Or if you were still mistaking me for the man of your dreams."

Her heart cramped in her chest. Why had she said that? "Will, I did not—"

He pressed a finger to her lips. "I just wondered if your dream man argued daily with his valet over who has the right to shave his own face?"

She hesitated, uncertain what he was asking. "He is not overfond of quarrelling, no."

"And if he locks himself in the study so he can

spend a half hour hefting *The Atlas of British Flora* over his head because his wife is partial to his shoulders?"

She shook her head, a smile growing on her lips. "No, I...I don't believe he exerts himself in quite that way."

"And if he counts toad in the hole among his favorite foods?"

"Now you are just being absurd."

He leaned close, his eyes latched to hers and his lips a breath away. "Then I can't possibly be the man of your dreams, sweetheart. So maybe there's a chance you love me, too?"

Her heart was beating hard, and her body flooded with so much love that for one of the few times in her life, she could not speak the words to tell him how completely, how ecstatically, she loved him.

So she kissed him and showed him, and very likely she would smother him with a thousand words of love.

Yes, very likely she would.

Later.

Epilogue

April 1851

"That's good, sweetheart." And Will meant it. Charlotte's drawing was improving with the help of her new drawing teacher. He could discern a human form, too small to be an adult. Their son, John, then. A safe enough guess. He was her favorite subject.

This was how they often spent their leisure time in their new home in Richmond. Though there was little of that for him the past month. The published collection of his travels, even without the salacious recounting of Tibet, had sold so well, the book was in its fourth printing and was being translated for sale on the Continent. With the popularity of the book, there were speaking engagements to prepare for and assemblies to attend with his dazzling wife now that she was delivered of their baby.

Fortunately, Lucy, Ben, and Wallace were often invited to the same events so there were friends for him to speak with. And nothing made Charlotte happier than to have her family with her in Society.

And nothing made him happier than spending a

quiet afternoon planning his next expedition. This time to Cumbria in the north. With his family.

"Good, is it?" She held up her drawing. "Then tell me what it is."

"Not a *what*, a *who*. Obviously, it's our son sleeping in a wheelbarrow."

Her smile fell and she looked at her drawing, a puzzled look on her face.

"I mean, a…sled?"

She looked at him as though there was something very wrong with him. "That is a crib."

"Right, a crib." He grinned.

"Why would he be in a wheelbarrow?"

Will squinted at the picture, but Charlotte pulled it away. "*Honestly*. Your son is lying two feet from us *in his crib* and—"

He kissed her to silence, trying not to laugh.

"Mr. Repton?" their butler called from the door.

Stifling a sigh, he lifted his head. "Yes, Mr. Simms?"

"You have visitors, sir. A Miss Georgiana Mayhew."

The laughter rumbling in his chest died and he stared, unable to understand what the man had said. "George is dead."

Charlotte's delphinium blue eyes swung to his, wide with surprise.

He didn't know why he blurted that, but all these months, all these long months, there'd not been any news of George. Seth hadn't given up hope for Aimee—but he'd written…

Seth believed his sister was dead.

The butler inclined his head and spoke slowly. "The young *lady* is a Georgiana Mayhew—"

"Yes," he said, the word barely breathed, barely audible. Will sank next to Charlotte, only dimly feeling her arm around him.

"Please put Miss Mayhew in the front parlor," Charlotte said, and the butler dipped his head and left.

"Will?" Charlotte squeezed his hand. "George is *alive.* She made it back."

Alive…how…?

Charlotte tightened her arm about him. "Shall we see her together?"

He wiped his face with a hand that quaked. John slept in his crib, his blond hair looking so soft on his pallet. His little boy. The sight propelled him to standing.

"I'll call the nurse to sit with John," Charlotte said.

He nodded. He never left his son alone, asleep or awake. Charlotte understood his need to keep him near and never shamed him for his weakness, never questioned his wish to have John's cot in their bedroom. He was still such a little thing, as small as…as small as Aimee had been.

Charlotte released his hand to pull the bell. Will started to pace. "Why would she come here?"

"She will tell you what she learned in Tibet."

"Right, right." He held out a hand to Charlotte and she took it, standing beside him. Always beside him. He'd come to depend so much on her.

He was his father's son, after all.

John's nurse arrived and he could delay no longer.

The door to the parlor was ajar and Will hesitated before entering. Charlotte laced her fingers through his and, impulsively, he lifted her hand and pressed a kiss into the palm.

He could bear this. He could bear anything.

They stepped into the room.

He'd never met the intrepid, wholly remarkable Georgiana Mayhew, but he couldn't tear his eyes from the child in her arms.

"Oh…God," he whispered, before he staggered forward. *Please…please…*

Georgiana turned the child to face him, and when the little girl's wide blue eyes found his, she lifted her arms and squealed happily.

It was almost as if she remembered him.

About the Author

Susanne Lord lives beside a beautiful pond surrounded by hawthorn trees and wildflowers. When it's quiet and no one is about, she can pretend she is taking her exercise on the grounds of an ancient family estate. When it's not, she's reminded her family is not of the landed gentry, the pond is in the middle of Chicago, and the only adventure in her day comes in the form of emails marked "urgent" at her advertising job. She is an active member of Chicago North RWA. When not working, writing, attending theater, or reading, she travels to England, where she enjoys getting lost in the woods.

Wicked Little Secrets

by Susanna Ives

It's not easy being good...

Vivacious Vivienne Taylor has finally won her family's approval by getting engaged to the wealthy and upright John Vandergrift. But when threatened by a vicious blackmail scheme, it is to her childhood friend that Vivienne turns: the deliciously wicked Viscount Dashiell.

When being wicked is so much more exciting...

Lord Dashiell promised himself long ago that his friendship with Vivienne would be the one relationship with a woman that he wouldn't ruin. He agrees to help her just to keep the little hothead safe, but soon finds that Vivienne has grown up to be very, very dangerous to all of Dash's best intentions.

"With *Wicked Little Secrets*' intriguing plot, quirky characters, witty escapades, and heartfelt dialogue, Ives has created a read that's as thought-provoking as it is romantic." —*RT Book Reviews*, 4 1/2 Stars

"If you love historical romances, this book is a must!" —*Long and Short Reviews*

Wicked, My Love

by Susanna Ives

A smooth-talking rogue and a dowdy financial genius

Handsome, silver-tongued politician Lord Randall doesn't get along with his bank partner, the financially brilliant but hopelessly frumpish Isabella St. Vincent. Ever since she was his childhood nemesis, he's tried—and failed—to get the better of her.

Make a perfectly wicked combination

When both Randall's political career and their mutual bank interests are threatened by scandal, he has to admit he needs Isabella's help. They set off on a madcap scheme to set matters right. With her wits and his charm, what could possibly go wrong? Only a volatile mutual attraction that's catching them completely off guard...

Praise for Susanna Ives:

"A fresh voice that reminded me of Julia Quinn's characters." —Eloisa James, *New York Times* bestselling author

For more Susanna Ives, visit:

www.sourcebooks.com

A Talent for Trickery

by Alissa Johnson

The lady is a thief

Years ago, Owen Renderwell earned acclaim—and a title—for the dashing rescue of a kidnapped duchess. But only a select few knew that Scotland Yard's most famous detective was working alongside London's most infamous thief…and his criminally brilliant daughter, Charlotte Walker.

Lottie was like no other woman in Victorian England. She challenged him. She dazzled him. She questioned everything he believed and everything he was, and he has never wanted anyone more. And then he lost her.

Now a private detective on the trail of a murderer, Owen has stormed back into Lottie's life. She knows that no matter what they may pretend, he will always be a man of the law and she a criminal. Yet whenever he's near, Owen has a way of making things complicated…and making her long for a future that can never be theirs.